WATER MARK

Visit us at www.boldstrokesbooks.com

Acclaim for J.M. Redmann's Micky Knight Series

Death of a Dying Man

"Set with wrenching reality against the backdrop of a city whose soul has been ravaged by Hurricane Katrina, Redmann's...*Death of a Dying Man*...is a riveting and emotionally complex novel—weaving together a dying man's poignant last wish, the pain of a crumbling lesbian romance, and (of course) a murder—is a virtuoso literary whodunit."
—Richard Labonte, *Q Syndicate*

"Mickey Knight is back and how! J.M. Redmann is one of the top mystery writers today, bar none."—Greg Herren, author of the Scott Bradley mystery series

The Intersection of Law and Desire

Lambda Literary Award Winner

San Francisco Chronicle Editor's Choice for the year

Profiled on *Fresh Air*, hosted by Terry Gross, and selected for book reviewer Maureen Corrigan's recommended holiday book list.

"Superbly crafted, multi-layered...One of the most hard-boiled and complex female detectives in print today."—*San Francisco Chronicle* (An Editor's Choice selection for 1995)

"Fine, hard-boiled tale-telling."—*Washington Post Book World*

"An edge-of-the-seat, action-packed New Orleans adventure... Micky Knight is a fast-moving, fearless, fascinating character...*The Intersection of Law and Desire* will win Redmann lots more fans." —*New Orleans Times-Picayune*

"Crackling with tension...an uncommonly rich book...Redmann has the making of a landmark series."—*Kirkus Review*

"Perceptive, sensitive prose; in-depth characterization; and pensive, wry wit add up to a memorable and compelling read."—*Library Journal*

"Powerful and page turning...A rip-roaring read, as randy as it is reflective...Micky Knight is a to-die-for creation...a Cajun firebrand with the proverbial quick wit, fast tongue, and heavy heart."—*Lambda Book Report*

Lost Daughters

"Few writers understand the human heart as well as J.M. Redmann. *Lost Daughters* manages the rare trick of being a mystery packed with surprises as well as a moving exploration of the pain of loss between parents and children. Don't start reading *Lost Daughters* at bedtime unless you plan to be up all night."—Val McDermid, Gold Dagger–winning author of *The Mermaids Singing*

"A sophisticated, funny, plot-driven, character-laden murder mystery set in New Orleans…as tightly plotted a page-turner as they come… One of the pleasures of *Lost Daughters* is its highly accurate portrayal of the real work of private detection—a standout accomplishment in the usually sloppily conjectured world of thriller-killer fiction. Redmann has a firm grasp of both the techniques and the emotions of real-life cases—in this instance, why people decide to search for their relatives, why people don't, what they fear finding and losing…and Knight is a competent, tightly wound, sardonic, passionate detective with a keen eye for detail and a spine made of steel."—*San Francisco Chronicle*

"Redmann's Mickey Knight series just gets better…For finely delineated characters, unerring timing, and page-turning action, Redmann deserves the widest possible audience."—*Booklist*, starred review

"…tastefully sexy…"—*USA Today*

"Like fine wine, J.M. Redmann's private eye has developed interesting depths and nuances with age…Redmann continues to write some of the fastest-moving action scenes in the business…In *Lost Daughters*, Redmann has found a winning combination of action and emotion that should attract new fans—both gay and straight—in droves."—*New Orleans Times-Picayune*

"An admirable, tough PI with an eye for detail and the courage, finally, to confront her own fear. Recommended."—*Library Journal*

"The best mysteries are character-driven and still have great moments of atmosphere and a tightly wound plot. J.M. Redmann succeeds on all three counts in this story of a smart lesbian private eye who unravels the fascinating evidence in a string of bizarre cases, involving missing children, grisly mutilations, and a runaway teen driven from her own home because she is gay."—*Outsmart*

By the Author

Death by the Riverside

Deaths of Jocasta

The Intersection of Law and Desire

Lost Daughters

Death of a Dying Man

Water Mark

WATER MARK

by

J.M. Redmann

2010

WATER MARK

ISBN 10: 1-60282-179-8
ISBN 13: 978-1-60282-179-8

This Trade Paperback Original Is Published By
Bold Strokes Books, Inc.
P.O. Box 249
Valley Falls, NY 12185

First Edition: September 2010

Credits
Editor: Shelley Thrasher
Production Design: Stacia Seaman
Cover Design by Sheri (graphicartist2020@hotmail.com)

Acknowledgments

No book gets written without support, or at least the kindness of strangers. The events that have forever marked New Orleans, Katrina and the levees failing, have been hard to relive. I want to thank my friends who live here who have put up with me asking things like, "Do you remember when the stoplights started working again?" Beth and Cherry, of course. Marie, Yvonne, Candy, and Barb. I also need to thank Professor Gillian Rodger for allowing me to use her research into nineteenth-century theater and the women who made their living there. I need to thank the day job coworkers, especially my staff, for having to deal with a woman who has two careers and not enough time for either of them—Noel, Enrique, Doreen, Lisa, Pam, Jeannette, Seema, Deanne, Josh, Mark, Narquis, Ked, Allison, Brian, Mary Ellen, and Pegah, everyone at the CAN office and the Tulane office. I also need to thank Computer Mark for rescuing my wayward machine when it decided to melt down in the middle of writing this.

Needless to say, Greg Herren for gym torture and writing discussions as he attempts to distract me from noticing that he did indeed increase the weights. Also, Paul Willis; both he and Greg have been great friends through the years.

Shelley Thrasher was a thorough and not too brutal editor, especially helpful with my amazing ability to use the same word five times in one paragraph. I need to thank everyone at Bold Strokes: Connie, Cindy, Stacia, Lee, and especially Rad for their support and encouragement. Like most things, publishing books takes a lot more work than one might think. I also want to thank all the grand writers at BSB; it's a great gang to be a part of.

The most important people to thank are the ones that for the most part I don't know—the people who read my books, who make it worthwhile for me to put the words on the page because someone out there wants to read those words.

Dedication

To GMR.

Thanks, dear, I'm so glad you thought the books "didn't suck." Isn't it Cosmo time yet?

CHAPTER ONE

The approaching twilight offered only dense shadows. I regretted my hasty decision. It had seemed reasonable in my office, a still-golden sun slanting through the windows, power restored, the lights on.

But this area was dark—no lights, ghost houses with empty blank windows, no streetlights, no cars save for overturned, muddy wrecks. This used to be a nice, middle-class neighborhood of tidy houses, cars washed once a week, people who knew their neighbors. Then Katrina came, the levees failed, and water washed away everything, leaving wrecked houses, wrecked cars, and wrecked lives. Two houses down, a body had been found. I knew the scribbled signs of the rescuers well enough to know what they meant. They had left a similar sign on my house, only with zero instead of one. In the dark gloaming, with no light other than the circle of my flashlight, this area felt haunted. People had died here, died horrible, needless deaths, and the land bore the scars.

The house in front of me was the pale gray of white in encroaching darkness, cut in half by a dark water line. Five minutes, I told myself. Look around for five minutes; get some ideas of what I have to do, then come back in broad daylight.

The flashlight was almost too strong, the brightness of its beam turning what was left beyond the light even more hidden and dark. Like most of us who had come back, I had taken preparedness to an almost obsessive level. Two flashlights and spare batteries in the trunk of my car, and one in the glove compartment. The one in my hand was a foot-long Maglite. I was counting on its bright beam to keep away the ghosts and its heavy metal weight to deal with miscreants remaining on this side of the divide.

I carefully picked my way across the lawn, still littered with debris from the flood. It was colder now, November sliding into December, but too many snakes had been washed from the swamps for me to step easily over fallen tree limbs. A ripped sofa cushion, if it hadn't started out as a muddy brown, it was now. A bent child's bicycle wheel, no bike attached. The moldering body of a dead cat. I quickly covered it with the sofa cushion, partly as the only makeshift grave marking available, partly so I wouldn't risk stepping on it as I returned this way. I didn't want to offend even a cat ghost.

The stairs had little debris on them, probably knocked away by whoever had searched this house. The screen door was hanging, barely held in place by one screw in one hinge, but the wooden door behind it was closed. Either the searchers had shut it, or they had entered through a window. It was hard to tell if any of the windows were passable. Better to look for glass shards in the strong sunlight.

In the five minutes I had given myself, the last glimmer of the sun had fled; everything was turning into a coalescing gray and would be black in another ten minutes.

Come back tomorrow, I told myself, this can wait. A damp, chill wind rattled the dying leaves. Even the sturdy evergreens, the oaks, the pines hadn't survived being bathed for weeks in the toxic waters.

I turned to go.

A car door slammed. An unmarked van had pulled up at the corner. With my beam of light, I was easily visible. These desolate neighborhoods had been plagued by all-too-human ghouls, stealing everything they could strip from the empty houses, from copper wire to upstairs carpet.

Leave, just leave now, I told myself. You don't bother them, maybe they won't bother you.

I swiftly turned from the watermarked house and scrambled across the yard, barely managing to avoid stepping on the hasty grave of the cat.

Just as I got to my car, I heard a high-pitched, girlish giggle. Looking again at the van, I watched as it disgorged a group of teenagers, all wearing matching lime-green T-shirts.

"Okay," said a voice that sounded like an older adult's. "I'm sorry you got in so late, but I wanted you to at least have a first look at where we'll be working tomorrow."

I slowed my stride, making a last-minute course change for my trunk instead of my car door so—in the off chance that anyone was looking—it wouldn't seem like a group of teenage volunteers here to gut a house had scared me off. Between the van dome light, their flashlights, and the last fading glimmer of the day, they looked about as threatening as a stuffed pink poodle, so well-scrubbed and apple-cheeked that they were probably from a small town in Minnesota and this well-supervised and escorted trip was their first ever to a big city.

As if proving my point, one of the girlish voices said, "Let's pray before we begin." They pulled together in a huddle of holding hands, or at least touching shoulders for the more shy—or agnostic—ones. Her high-pitched voice began, "Oh, Lord, guide our steps, protect us from harm, lead us not into temptation..."

It was easy to tune out her nasal voice—a blessing even. I opened my trunk and rummaged as if looking for something important before I picked up the small crowbar right in front of me. More out of respect for the ghosts of the neighborhood than the praying Midwesterners, I softly closed my trunk.

As I walked back to the porch steps, the skittering of clawed feet made me whip my flashlight in that direction, and its beam caught the snakelike tail of either a large mouse or a small rat. I can deal with mammals. The presence of rats meant the absence of snakes, all in all a bargain I'd take.

The rodent was headed in the direction of the corn-fed huddle— "keep us strong in spirit, healthy in body—" but I was guessing that Divine Will and rat instinct would keep them apart.

Just see what's up with the door, I told myself as I mounted the steps. If it opens easily, take a quick look inside. If it doesn't, then bring a bigger crowbar tomorrow. Juggling the flashlight and the crowbar, I managed to get the blade into the crack before thinking that maybe I should just try the door and see if it opened. Odds were heavily against that, but if the wood was cypress it might have survived the soaking and not be warped beyond use.

"Amen" finally sounded.

Followed by a high-pierced shriek. "Oh, my God. It moved! Something moved out there!"

It seemed that Mr. Rat was a religious kind of rodent and had wanted to join the prayer circle.

Another voice, picking up the panic said, "It could be an alligator!"

The adult voice said, a bit shakily to be truly calming, "It's okay. I don't think alligators attack groups."

Damn Yankees. I turned from the door to face them and called, "There are no alligators here. That's a mouse or a rat. It's probably more scared of you than you are of it." The last wasn't likely to be true, but someone needed to keep them from seeing ten-foot-long alligators with bloodred fangs.

"What the hel-leck?" the adult voice shouted.

"There's someone else here!" high-pitched, nasal said.

Corn-fed Midwesterners in a desolate, devastated area of New Orleans, who were too busy praying to notice my car and a flashlight the size of a Super Trouper followspot.

"I'm checking on a house for someone," I said. "There are no alligators in this neighborhood. It's too cold and too far from water."

"It's a woman," one of the boys said. That seemed all it took to make me "safe" in their minds.

"Can't help it, was born that way," I mumbled as I turned back to the door.

The adult's voice said, "Let's go in the house, but be careful. We'll take a quick look around, then back to someplace warm with food." A few cheers and giggles followed, and a mass of flashlight-lit lime shirts headed for the house at the corner.

The door on my house didn't budge, even the knob wouldn't turn. After trying for a full minute, I again shimmied the crowbar into the door.

Just as I started to put pressure on the bar, a loud shriek stopped me. Lime shirts were vomiting from the house, helter-skelter, tripping over themselves in their panic to get out.

"Oh, Mr. Rat, you're being very bad," I murmured to myself. Then hoped that was all it was. I'd feel real bad if I was wrong about the alligators.

Two people vaulted off the porch, taking a third and part of the railing with them.

Amidst the incoherent screams and yells, all I could make out was, "It's horrible, horrible!" repeated over and over, and "My leg! Damn, my leg!"

I hastened back to my car, threw the crowbar in, and grabbed my cell phone, keeping the flashlight.

When I got to them, someone in the van was shouting, "Let's get out of here! Where are the keys?"

Two of the porch jumpers were still on the lawn, including the one moaning about his leg. I made them my first priority.

One was a boy holding his ankle. He had misjudged his jump. The other was the one adult with the group. A quick look told me his leg was broken, with some of the bone showing.

The rest of the group had retreated to the alligator-proof van.

I knelt by the man. "What's your name?" I asked him.

"Bob," he managed to gasp.

First and last would have been nice, but I settled for what I could get. "Bob, you'll be okay, but your leg is broken."

"No shi-oot," he said through gritted teeth.

"No shoot," I echoed. I dialed 911 on my cell phone. No signal. No shit. I glowered at it. Of course there was no signal. To get a signal in my unflooded neighborhood, I had to go outside and face west. How could I hope for a signal here? "Damn," I muttered. "Do you have the keys to the van?" I asked Bob.

"What? Why do you need them?"

"To send someone for help."

"Every kid here has a cell phone," he said.

"Welcome to New Orleans," I said. "There's no signal here."

He nodded with his head to his left front pocket and I fished a set of keys out of it.

As I approached the van, the high-pitched, nasal voice demanded, "Who are you?"

I pulled out my PI license, flashed it just long enough for the kids to get the hint that I was someone somehow official, without giving them a chance to really see it. I wasn't counting on private eye impressing them much.

"Who can drive? Legally?" They all looked far too young, but two of them put their hands up, a boy and Ms. Nasal. "No cell signal here, so I need someone to drive to where there's a phone."

"I'll do it," Ms. Nasal said. "Someone should stay here with Coach." She nodded decisively at the other driver.

The other legal driver had to argue. "I was sitting up front. I have a better idea of where we are."

I decided for them. "Both of you go. I'll stay here." After all, I wasn't scared of either real rats or improbable alligators. "Get to a phone as quickly as you can, call 911, and send an ambulance to this address. Do you know where you are? Do you know where you need to go?"

Mr. Driver and Ms. Nasal exchanged a look as if asking if the other had the answer.

I quickly gave them directions to where I knew they would find phones.

One girl jumped out. "I'll stay," she said, then added, "It's just a dead body. It can't really hurt us."

The van started, drowning out the question I was about to ask.

CHAPTER TWO

As the van disappeared, I headed back to my car. My questions about the dead could wait while I took care of the living.

Preparedness, of course, required a big first-aid kit in the trunk. With a glance at the gas gauge, I started my car, drove the short distance to the corner house, and parked at enough of an angle that the headlights swept near where the two hurt men were.

Bob was moaning slightly, though he was still aware enough not to curse in front of the kids. But I was worried about him. He had to be bleeding, and even my obsessive first-aid kit wasn't much use for a broken leg. The best I could do was to try to keep him comfortable and out of shock until help arrived.

It had been warm enough to not really need a jacket during the day, but the humidity of New Orleans can quickly put a chill dampness into the air. I got a mat from my car, had Bob lie on that, then covered him with the space-blanket thing from the first-aid kit. The boy, Nathan, seemed to have only a sprain. I wrapped his ankle with an Ace bandage and loosened his boot so it would be easy to get off as the ankle swelled. With help from Nathalie, the girl, I moved them so that they were sitting next to Bob—on the side away from his broken leg. They sat back to back, so all three could help warm each other.

That was as much as I could do.

"What made you all run from the house?" I asked.

"Carmen said she saw a dead body, she started running, so we all started running," Nathan told me.

"Did any of you actually see a body?" I asked.

Both kids shook their head no and Bob grunted something that sounded half no/yes.

I looked at the house. The marking of the searchers, clearly spray painted next to the door, indicated that no body was in this house. Admittedly some of the searches were hurried, some incomplete because of debris or unsafe structures. But something seemed off about these kids finding a body in less than a minute that trained rescue workers hadn't noticed.

I stood up. "Let me see what's in there."

"Be careful," Nathalie called after me as I started up the stairs.

I might find a months-old decaying body, but I was worried that it was an owner—or even a thief—who had been hurt while checking out the house. The kids hadn't been inside long enough to test for a pulse.

I hesitated at the door, swinging my flashlight across the porch. I didn't want anything, even innocent rats, to creep up on me in this dismal darkness.

Nothing moved. I opened the door and went in.

The heavy smell of mold hit me. I swung my flashlight across walls blooming with gray, green, and black patterns. The floor was a grayish cracked pattern of dried mud. I suspected that even the bright light of the sun would show only shades of gray in this house. That was all the water left behind.

The house was ranch style, probably built sometime in the forties or fifties, with an open floor plan. The door opened to a foyer that opened to the living room, the living room leading into a kitchen and dining room. I guessed that by the furniture the flood had heaped in haphazard piles.

I retraced the quick arc of my flashlight with a slow one. Same gray-green mold and mud. The dried muck crunched softly as I stepped into the room. I could easily follow the footmarks of the kids. The entrance area was well trampled, with several paths coming into the house. One ended abruptly after a few feet, two had traveled a little farther before ending. One led around an overturned sofa. I carefully followed, pausing every few seconds to probe the room with my flashlight.

"Anyone here?" I called. Only the rustling wind answered.

The sofa sprawled upside down, almost cutting the room in half. It had been light green in another lifetime, but now the mold seemed to mock its delicate pale mint, as if nature couldn't be cosseted with such a delicate hue.

I slowly edged around it and my flashlight caught what had terrified the children. Save for the staring eyes, he could have just been asleep. I looked at him for a moment. One thing was clear; this body hadn't been here since Katrina came though. Maybe a day, most likely a few hours, but this wasn't a body that was several months old. Beyond the fetid smell of the mold, I could smell no other decay. Not that I intended to look closely, but there was no insect damage.

Oddly, he was dressed in a dark pin-striped three-piece suit, the tie perfectly knotted. He seemed very young, little beard visible on his face.

Could this be a joke, I wondered. Or a perfect mannequin that the vagaries of the water somehow washed here?

I knelt down to feel for a pulse, to feel if the skin was plastic.

The flesh was cool, all too human. I could detect no pulse. The face seemed almost serene save for the staring eyes. Something in them was haunted.

In the harsh beam of my flashlight, I noticed faint lines at the corner of the eyes. Maybe he wasn't such a young boy. I gently ran a finger along the lapel of the suit. No, not a boy at all.

I stood up and backed away from the body. I couldn't do anything else, except perhaps mess up a crime scene even more.

How had a woman, dressed as a man, been killed and ended up in this deserted location? But it wasn't my problem to solve.

I turned from her and went back outside.

Chapter Three

Instead of rejoining the small group immediately, I hurried to the corner to see if I could flag down any help. Nothing, not a gleam other than my flashlight and the beams of my car. The only sound, save for my breathing and the hushed murmurs from the group, was the shush of the wind. I stood there a few minutes, willing our rescuers to come. But, at least in this case, my will was weak and no friendly ambulance lights appeared.

I didn't want to be here. What should have been a quick jaunt was turning into a marathon—with me, two kids, one injured-and-out-of-it adult, and a dead body.

As I returned to the group, Nathalie asked, "Did you find the—?"

Nathan chimed in. "Carmen probably made it up to get us out of there. She's smart that way. She's too refined to want to hang around this place at night."

"Or even in the day," Nathalie muttered.

I looked at my trio of companions. Nathan was a gangly, dark-haired boy, his bones aching for adulthood and leaving the rest of his body stretched behind. His face still had traces of baby fat, but his legs gave "skinny" new meaning. It was hard to tell if he would fill out or turn into someone whose only hope at athletics would be as a distance runner. He was already too tall for a jockey. He wore glasses that my generation would have described as nerdy, thick black squares. Maybe they were cool now. His hair was almost black, straight, brushing his eyebrows, just needing a haircut, not yet at rebellion stage, unless his parents were beyond strict. He wore fairly neat chinos, too new and nice for this neighborhood. The lime T-shirt was over a long-sleeved shirt, his wrists jutting out of the cuff as if his clothes couldn't keep up with his adolescent body.

At a quick glance, he and the girl Nathalie didn't look alike. She was much shorter, with the first hints of a body that would make boys (probably some girls) follow her down the hallway. Already her breasts had a fullness that many grown women would envy (or pay for). Her hair was much lighter, longer and well kept. It had clearly been cut just before this trip, with the ends neat and straight, even as disheveled as it was at the moment. But the light streaks in his hair matched hers, and something in the bone structure of their faces, the brows and eyes and their chins, matched almost point for point. Both had heartbreaker brown eyes, intense and brooding pools. In contrast to his outfit, she wore old jeans with a waffle-weave long-sleeved shirt under the required T-shirt, a size too big—just what one should wear to gut a house. But it seemed that the biggest difference between them was attitude. I'd bet that neither of them were the most popular kids, more the faceless middle. It seemed to matter to him but not to her, as if it gave her greater latitude to be who she was.

Admittedly, a man with a broken leg might not be putting his best side forward, but Coach Bob seemed to be one of those men you could pass on the street and ten minutes later swear that the street was empty. His sparse hair was a sandy color that blended into his flesh. Even cut short on his balding head, it was thin and stringy. If his face ever held the sharpness of youth, it had long faded into rounded corners, cheeks that sagged into a soft chin. He wasn't handsome; perhaps his wife called him cute, but nothing stood out, his eyes small and some light brown-gray color. He was probably the kind of guy everyone called nice because the only way he could be noticed was to shovel your driveway or hold your mail. His dress was just as nondescript, also a new pair of chinos, now ruined by blood and mud. An off-white button-down shirt was covered by a twill jacket, its cuffs starting to pull, and the beige of the jacket was just a shade off from the beige of the pants.

"So who are you and how did you end up down here?" I addressed the whole group, but looked more at Nathan. I was guessing that he was the older, so I would give him that much deference.

"Came here to volunteer," he said. Verbal skills didn't seem his strong point. Or maybe his ankle hurt and he wasn't up to talking.

Nathalie gave him a moment, then stepped in. "We're from the

Greater Pillar of Jesus Church, just outside of Sheboygan. Wisconsin. We all go to church school together and the elders decided that they wanted to help out, so they volunteered us. We were supposed to get in around three, but the plane was late, so we didn't get in 'til five. Coach and Carmen decided that we'd swing by here on the way to where we're staying. And…well, here we are."

Ah, Wisconsin, I was almost ashamed to be off by one state, and from New Orleans, Wisconsin and Minnesota weren't that different— snow, cold, didn't know how to spice food. It was as challenging as bobbing for apples with both hands. Nathalie did seem to have the verbal skills her brother lacked. I decided to check my hunch on that one as well.

"You brother and sister?" I asked her, with a nod at Nathan.

"That obvious?" He snorted.

"No, I'm just observant," I replied. Adolescence was hard enough. I'd spare him being easily linked to a younger sister.

"Twins," she interjected.

Two out of three. Their height difference had made me assume that she was younger. "Fraternal? Or a sex change?"

Oops, over the line. I needed to remember that I might be in New Orleans, but was right now on a little piece of the rural Midwest.

"Yeah, Nate used to be a girl," Nathalie shot back.

Nathan gave her a look as if he couldn't believe that came out of his sister's mouth. She gave him a saucy grin as if to say, "I'm away from home."

Cutting into this tender sibling banter, Coach Bob coughed and said, "Just our dumb luck to get a house with some poor soul still here from the storm."

The cops would be questioning these kids, so I saw no reason to withhold that this wasn't a storm victim. I started to say so, but instead asked, "Did you get a glimpse of the body?"

"Enough of one. Carmen froze for a moment. I knew something wasn't right, got a look over her shoulder before everyone started running out."

I wondered if Coach Bob really thought what he had seen was a body that could have been dead for three months or if he was just pretending to putatively protect the kids.

I've always thought that the truth was a better protection. They would find out the truth—the Internet makes it even easier these days— better to find it out and not also find out that they'd been lied to. "I doubt that body's been here since August twenty-ninth."

"Yeah? You an expert on these things?" Bob argued. "What else could it be but a storm victim?"

He was probably in pain, and I would give him a pass on a stupid argument, but using "it" to refer to the dead woman annoyed me.

"I'm a licensed private investigator, so I've seen a few dead bodies. Plus my partner is a doctor, and she's seen plenty of dead bodies and has a habit of talking about her work." The pronouns alone should guarantee that I didn't get invited to any reunions with this group. Which is what I intended to accomplish. Looks were exchanged that seemed to say that the dreaded alligator had just been promoted to better company than a lesbian who knew too much about dead bodies. I decided to limit my pronoun damage and not mention that the dead person was also a she. Nathan and Nathalie were young; their seeming nonchalance (hers anyway, he was in pain) was likely to be a defense against the chaos of death intruding into their lives. "I don't mean to argue, but I doubt that body has been there very long. The police will probably question your group."

"I'd like to hear that from the police," Bob said, his voice hostile, whether from my disagreeing with his forensic experience or that pesky pronoun problem, I couldn't tell. Not that it mattered. In another twenty minutes (I hoped) I would never see these people again. "Damn, my leg hurts," he said, and turned his head away, removing himself from the conversation.

"What's taking Carmen so long?" Nathan said.

"She has to do her nails before she calls for help," Nathalie muttered.

"Who is Carmen?" I asked.

Nathan answered quickly, as if making sure that Nathalie didn't get a chance. "She graduated last year from a sister school in Michigan and is working for the church as a youth leader."

"They thought her example would be good for us," Nathalie added. She was just sardonic enough that you couldn't quite catch her on it. Her brother seemed not to.

"So she's one of the leaders here?" I asked. Despite her nasal, whiny voice she seemed older than the others, more sophisticated, although that was only relative—sophisticated wasn't a word that described this bunch. She was pretty in a conventional way, brown hair in a ponytail that she worked, flipping and playing with it even in the brief moments I'd observed her. She was medium height and too obviously wearing a bra that made the most of her better-than-average assets. Between that and a little too much makeup, it seemed as if she was trying too hard. She had eschewed the lime-green shirts for a girly pink.

"Yeah," Nathan said. "Her and Coach."

"How many of you?"

Between Nathan and Nathalie, I found out that there were twelve of them, aged fifteen to the elderly Carmen at eighteen, save for Coach Bob, the real adult. They were supposed to be here a week. I also got the impression that Nathan had a crush on Carmen and that Nathalie thought she was a stuck-up, pious phony. Nothing said, but I had little to do but read between the lines.

My twenty minutes had just passed when I heard the faint wail of a siren in the distance. Better be ours, I told myself as I got up and trotted to the corner, the better to wave them down and get this over with.

It was odd how comforting those two circles of approaching lights felt. It seemed that I had been marooned on an island of darkness with three un-chosen people. For a moment, I thought it would turn into a surreal dream and the lights would pass me—or turn out to be the eyes of a monster alligator. You're getting spooked by this neighborhood, I admonished myself. Just because you're in the middle of a desolate, destroyed place with two injured people, one teenage girl, and a dead body is no reason to get nervous.

The lights slowed as they approached, a comfortingly real ambulance taking shape behind their penumbra.

Two guys jumped out. I pointed to Coach Bob and Nathan and said, "Badly broken leg and probably sprained ankle."

They spoke little and worked quickly. In a bare few minutes Coach Bob was on a gurney and rolled into the back of the truck. Then Nathan. They shut the back door and were walking around to the front, without a backward glance at Nathalie and me.

"Hey," I called. "She's got to go with them."

The one going for the driver's side kept walking; the passenger-side one looked back at me. "Can't, no room." The expression on my face prompted him to add, "Can't. ERs are crazy. We'll have to go to

West Jeff to get a bed." With that he got in and shut the door. It had barely snicked closed when the ambulance pulled away.

The waters had destroyed most of the hospitals, and their emergency rooms, in Orleans Parish. West Jeff was on the other side of the river, west because it was on the Westbank and Jeff for Jefferson Parish, the suburbs of New Orleans. Much as I wasn't thrilled about Nathalie tagging along with me, that was better than stranding her out there. If she had to depend on the kindness of Carmen—and her knowledge of the city—to get to where she needed to go, it would be a long night.

I gave her a look. "Okay, where do I need to take you?"

She looked back at me. "Uh…I'm not sure."

"I live here, I can probably figure out whatever address you have."

"Umm…I don't have an address. We weren't supposed to get separated."

"You have no idea where you're staying?"

"No, we came right here from the airport, so I didn't even get a glimpse."

"Name of a church, a group, who invited you? Anything?"

She slowly shook her head.

I glanced at my watch. It was past eight. Not likely to be anyone at her church in Wisconsin. "Would your parents know?"

She looked alarmed. First day in New Orleans and already in trouble. So much for the great grownup adventure.

Nathalie looked down. "They won't hear it."

"Hearing impaired? But they have to answer the phone somehow."

"It's in the barn. Father says it's only for business, so it might as well be where the business is being done. He won't be in the barn this late and he won't hear it." She said the last bit in a rush, as if to get the words and her odd parents out and over with.

I stared at her for a long moment. Could this night get any weirder? I immediately smacked that thought down, reminding myself not to tempt fate. The alligators might appear. No butch points were lost as Nathalie was staring at the ground, her face caught between fear at being in this desolate place with a stranger and shame that she had to reveal to that stranger the peculiar behavior of her family.

I decided for both of us. "Let's get out of here. Some places in this city have phones and light and food." I headed for my car and Nathalie slowly followed, probably too accustomed to obeying adults to even question getting into a car with an avowed lesbian stranger.

Maybe Carmen had been mature and smart enough to call the cops as well, but it didn't seem like sure money to me. And I didn't intend to wait around to see what the odds were. If they did show up there I couldn't tell them much other than presumably what Carmen and the others would say. I'd go back to my place, with its phones and lights, and let them know about the dead woman.

CHAPTER FOUR

I t never ends, does it?" Nathalie asked quietly.

"There will be lights soon," I answered, somehow knowing she was referring to the block after block after block of dark houses, no streetlights, a dirty gray landscape illuminated only by the beams from my car. We had been in the Gentilly section of town, near the lake. The waters had stretched from there nearly to the French Quarter. It was close to two miles of desolate houses, an eerie journey even in the day.

"Where are we going?" she asked.

I had been debating that since I'd U-turned away from the haunted house. Cordelia hadn't returned yet; she'd been doing some work in Boston where she was staying with one of her sisters. She had called two days ago to tell me that she'd be here this weekend. I hadn't answered the phone, just let her leave a message. That message didn't tell me whether she was coming back to stay or if this was a brief visit to grab a few things or someplace in between. I had been a jerk and not picked up the phone, instead listening to her voice as she talked to my brand-new answering machine. I could have asked any of those questions and the score of other queries I had.

But if I'd done that I wouldn't make it to the semi-finals for asshole passive-aggressive contest. And I was clearly aiming to take home a trophy.

However, that little muddle in my life was a few days away. At the moment, I had a hayseed kid from the boonies in my car and had to decide what to do with her.

The choices were limited. She had a place to stay but neither of us had a clue as to where that might be, nor did there seem any way to contact anyone to return their wayward child tonight. The second choice was my office, sort of living space. The third choice was complicated.

Cordelia and I lived in a house in the Tremé area of the city. The water had reached our block, but only a few feet, and our house, an old Creole cottage built in the days when houses were raised, had not flooded. But on the Friday before Katrina, when the forecasts still called for it to hit Florida, I had surprised her at her office in the arms of another woman. Did I still live there? I didn't know. If Katrina hadn't hit and the levees failed, we would have worked it out by now—one way or another.

But the storm came and one miniscule part of its destruction was to tear our lives apart as well. Cordelia had been trapped in Charity Hospital, left with no food, no water, sweltering heat, and unable to do much for those left sick and dying. As angry as I was with her, that had not been the time to do anything other than let her recover from her ordeal. I was offered a place to stay in San Francisco; Cordelia had opted to go stay with one of her sisters in Boston.

Even though I had evacuated in time, that didn't mean I was okay. The shipyard out on the bayous where I had grown up was gone, utterly gone. Only a clearing piled high with debris and one post to the gate from the road were left. My childhood home had survived Betsy and Camille and other hurricanes, but this one had taken it. My office hadn't flooded, but had been vandalized. What they hadn't stolen they'd destroyed—computers smashed across the floor, file cabinets overturned with the contents spewed everywhere, and the final insult, a big pile of excrement in the center of my desk. The one saving grace was that they hadn't been thorough, so the side rooms, the tiny kitchen, and my old bedroom had only been tossed for valuables.

My anger at Cordelia ebbed and flowed, and at one high point, I vowed that I'd live in my office. I'd attacked it in a frenzy of cleaning, swathed in gloves and dust masks to keep the stench out, until the light faded or I was exhausted. Those days took their toll until one afternoon, with the sweat gumming up the mask, my arms aching, it seemed hopeless. I'd torn off the mask and gloves, all my clothes, poured a liberal shot of Scotch into a plastic cup, and stepped into the shower, sipping the alcohol between scrubbing myself. I threw on clean clothes, grabbed a few things, and spent the rest of the night at the house in Tremé getting drunk and feeling sorry for myself.

I didn't even bother going back to my office for several days; everything just felt overwhelming. The house contained the memories of all the time Cordelia and I had been together, and I swung between wanting her back and being angry at what she'd done. When I had the energy to be honest with myself, I admitted that I didn't really know what she'd done—only the brief moment that I'd seen. Was it a single moment of temptation yielded to, five minutes of indiscretion, and if I hadn't walked in on them, she would have pulled away, said "No, I can't do this?" And nothing would have changed. Or had they already pledged love, made promises? And everything had already changed.

I'd finally pulled myself together, drunk a lot of water, eaten a decent breakfast, taken as much aspirin as I could, and gone back to the work of cleaning my office. It was rote, a few hours every day, and admittedly a good portion of those hours spent flipping through office catalogues, taking forever to make decisions like should the new file cabinets be gray or black? I told myself I only needed to get it livable by the time Cordelia returned to the city.

So at this juncture, it was mostly clean, or at least I no longer imagined I could smell the lingering stench of human shit. I had dragged everything that needed to be thrown out down the stairs and replaced a few things. Still no couch or table, but a few chairs, the black file cabinets, and an inflatable mattress. I'd even trolled the junk/antique stores uptown until I finally found a replacement for my desk. I paid more than I should have, but I wanted an old wooden one, like the one I had. I even stayed there most of the time. But it was getting cold and Bywater, where my office was, still lacked gas service. The building and water were heated by gas. I made it through exactly one cold shower on a cold day before moving back to the house, where the gas had been restored, so hot water and cooking were possible. Cordelia wasn't here so she wouldn't know where I was staying, and my anger had ebbed enough that I couldn't see any point in being cold when she didn't even know it.

I stopped at a desolate intersection, the only evidence of recent human activity a stop sign atop an aluminum tripod replacing the destroyed stoplight. I glanced over at my unwanted charge. Clearly tired, but her eyes were wide open, as if she didn't dare close them. Her world had changed, I realized. Last night at this time she had been on an isolated farm in Wisconsin. Now she was in a stranger's car in a city with more destruction than she probably could have imagined. Her brother was hurt, she was cut off from him and the group she was supposed to stick close together with, and she had been left with a choice of either staying in a dark, desolate neighborhood or going with a complete stranger, one she had no guarantee would be kind.

"I live fairly close to the French Quarter. There will be lights and people there," I told her, trying to be as reassuring as I could.

"Okay, thanks," she mumbled.

Go to the house, I told myself. There really was no other choice. But I didn't want to let this unknown kid into my life, to let her see the home I'd made with Cordelia, to pretend that everything was okay when it was so far from okay. It's just one night, I told myself. She's tired, probably capable only of eating something and falling into bed. You can get rid of her in the morning.

The decision was made; I turned at City Park onto Esplanade Avenue. Finally I saw a few cars, mine no longer the only headlights. Esplanade ran from City Park to the river, through some of the older sections of the city.

"Is this the first time you've been to New Orleans?" Having decided where to take her, I felt able to concentrate on driving and talking at the same time. Only a bare handful of stoplights worked. Some intersections had hastily erected stop signs; others relied on there being so few drivers. The flooding had opened up craters of potholes, and everything from glass to nails littered the roads. In the less than a month that I'd been back, I'd already had to have two tires repaired.

"First time I've been anywhere," she answered slowly. "Well, Milwaukee once, but I was five at the time and only remember seeing some tall buildings."

"I'm guessing that you don't have a cell phone," I said.

"No, Nathan and I got one to share. He's the boy, so he gets to keep it."

"You're the same age, but he gets it?"

"Yeah. And I'm better at keeping track of stuff. But…" Her voice faded, as if actually saying what was obvious, that it was unfair, would be too traitorous.

"But the cell phone is in his pocket and you're the one who needs it now."

"Yeah. Nothing seems to be going right," she said tiredly.

"Look at the benefits," I said. Off in the distance was the red of a working stoplight. Claiborne and Esplanade, I was guessing. With everything changed, trees downed, houses darkened, at times it was hard to get my bearings, even on streets I'd traveled my whole life. "You get to meet me and you get an unescorted tour of the city. You've probably crammed more adventure into the last twenty-four hours than you've had…all year." I almost said "your entire life" but that was patronizing. Milking cows could have thrills that I was unaware of.

As if to prove that not everything was going wrong, the stoplight changed to green just as we approached and I glided through the intersection. A boat was still parked next to the pumps at one of the gas stations at this crossroads, as if it had floated up, hoping to pump some fuel. Stacks of debris and a couple of discarded refrigerators were littering the median. Traffic, still not heavy, was regular, a welcome change from the deserted darkness we'd left behind.

I turned off Esplanade onto Marais.

"Where are we going?" she suddenly asked.

"My house. Not sure where else to take you." I turned onto Barracks Street. One more block and we'd be home. Or at least a house I could use for the night.

"You're taking me to your house?"

"That's the plan. Unless you can figure out where the rest of your group is staying."

"Oh." She was silent for a moment, but the fidgeting told me that something was going on. "Look, back there, you seemed to say, well, you said something about that you're, like homo—gay, and I just want you to know I'm not into that."

Ah, so that was the problem. She was worried that she was being kidnapped for the lesbian orgy. I was annoyed enough at this whole situation that I almost played it out. But I'd feel bad if she bolted from my car, especially as it was still going.

However, I wasn't kind enough to not be patronizing. "You what? Fifteen? I hope you're not into anything sexual yet. Even cows."

"Cows? That's gross."

"Exactly." I pulled up to the curb. "This is my house. You can come inside and we can make some phone calls, see if we can figure out where you need to go. If we can't do that tonight, then you can bunk in the spare bedroom. Alone. And we'll figure it out tomorrow. Or," I pointed down the road, "the French Quarter is two blocks that way. You can head there and find someone else to help you. However, don't expect to find too many church ladies wandering in among the bars. Your choice." Not that I actually intended to let her toddle off into the French Quarter by herself. Fifteen-and-been-to-Milwaukee-once wasn't much protection against what those streets held.

"I'm sorry," she mumbled. "I just…you hear stories. I didn't mean to imply…anything."

"Like me being a child molester?"

"I'm not a child…and no, I just thought you might think I'd be into things that I'm not into and I didn't want you trying something that I wasn't going to do and I wanted to make that clear."

I opened the door and got out. This is just want I needed. Clearly I was saddled with such a baby dyke that she didn't even have a clue she was a dyke. Nathalie's tone was mostly relief, but had an undertone of disappointment. Fifteen, budding hormones, no place for them to go on that conservative farm—cows were indeed gross—and suddenly she's in the big, bad city, alone with another woman, one who made it clear that she slept with other women. For a moment, I wished Cordelia was already back. She'd be so much better at handling this situation than I was. Plus it wouldn't hurt to have a chaperone.

Nathalie will be gone tomorrow.

I missed terribly being touched—sex, yes, but also a quick hug, a kiss good-bye and hello, all the daily moments of feeling the warmth of another person closely in my life. I'd been alone here for the last month and before that staying at the place of a friend of a friend in San Francisco. More time by myself than I'd had in the past ten years. It felt like a breach to bring a strange young girl into my alone place.

A loneliness I hadn't chosen, I reminded myself.

However, none of these longings made a fifteen-year-old, even a cute fifteen-year-old, the slightest bit tempting. Instead I fervently wished I knew someone to palm her off on and out of my life. However, everything was so disrupted and broken here, people gone or people back, but the buildings, businesses, and agencies gone.

My keys were in the lock and Nathalie was following me inside.

"Sorry to disappoint you, kiddo—no sex, no lesbian orgies. The highlight of the rest of the evening might be to see if cable TV has been restored."

I flipped on lights.

"I'm not a kid," she protested again.

I thought about telling her that yes, she was. Certainly to me she was. I started to say all those things I hated to hear when I was that young. I didn't. I merely said, "No, you're not a kid, but you're not an adult yet either. We need to get you back with your group. Right now, how about some food? I'll call the hospital and see if we can locate your brother—with his cell phone—and we'll take it from there."

That seemed to mollify her; she followed me into the kitchen. I opened the refrigerator to see what I could scrounge up. Its gleaming, brand-new bright white shelves mocked me. I hadn't even made it out to the 'burbs to replace the basics like mustard and ketchup, let alone real food. To be fair, this new refrigerator had arrived less than a week ago. The old one was still out on the curb, with enough duct tape sealing it that zombies couldn't get out. I had opened it once, just long enough to see the putrid piles of decayed food and the bugs feasting on its rottenness, before closing and sealing it forever. Food had been haphazard since I'd gotten back. More peanut butter and Scotch than I'd care to admit, especially that on occasion I'd combined the two.

"Welcome to New Orleans." I sighed. Turning to Nathalie I asked, "Do you eat pizza?"

She did and a place in the Quarter on the corner of Decatur and Governor Nichols was open. I called and placed an order. My to-do list for tomorrow was complete—get this kid back to where she belonged and make a serious grocery run. I looked in my wallet, then added, go to the bank. I had enough cash to cover the pizza, but that was about it. A number of places could not take credit cards as they could no longer connect to post the transactions.

Everything takes so much more time and effort, I thought as I led Nathalie back out to my car. The open grocery stores were far uptown or out in the suburbs. A forgotten loaf of bread was a half-hour drive—one way. And because so few had re-opened, the lines were long. Cash machines and banks were just as iffy. Just getting a tire aired up had been an ordeal. Few gas stations were open, and I had gone to over five and finally out of New Orleans proper to find a working air pump.

The Quarter hadn't been flooded and was one of the first places to have power, water, and gas restored. The businesses, bars, restaurants able to reopen were beyond busy. Menus were limited. I double-parked down the block; cars were flocking to this oasis.

She probably drives a tractor, I thought as I left Nathalie in my running car, although I hoped she wouldn't need to take a spin around the block. The wait was long because they were short-staffed, but my car was still where I illegally parked it. Nathalie's tractor skills were not tested.

"That smells good," she said, with the pizza balanced on her lap.

"Hope so, it'll be breakfast as well," I replied as I maneuvered around a Humvee, probably as intent on pizza as we were.

"Pizza for breakfast? Is that okay?"

"It is in hurricane zones." I didn't want to encourage bad eating habits in the young and unspoiled.

"We don't eat much pizza. Father says it's bad for us." She added softly, "That it's foreign food."

"Pizza? Guess that's true. It's such an American staple that we forget its Italian roots." Nathalie was rebelling—in a quiet, Midwestern way—putting her family's values up to scrutiny, one she suspected they couldn't withstand. I kept my answer carefully neutral. From the few things she'd said, her family was close to the zealot-nutcase boundary line. But I couldn't do much for her in our brief, unwanted overnight stay. I had too much shit going on in my own life to get involved. I'd found my way; Nathalie would find hers. Or not.

We were again at my house, Nathalie leading the way in with our food.

Dinner was a brief affair. Paper plates with pizza slapped on them. I thought about asking questions, at least ones focused on finding how to get her back where she belonged. But I was too tired for what she might reveal. I liked this kid and I didn't want to like her, or even know her any more. If she was indeed destined to be gay, hers would be a hard path. My heart had enough breaks in it; I couldn't risk even a small tear on her behalf.

Once we finished eating, I got up and put clean sheets (well, they'd been clean in August and no one had slept on them since) on the futon in the spare bedroom. She joined me to help.

"Are you tired?" I asked. "We can see if the cable is back and if we can get more than two fuzzy TV stations. Or just crash for the night. I'm going to make phone calls, see if the hospital has any news of your brother."

"We're not allowed to watch TV, so maybe I'll wait and see if you can find Nathan and then go to bed."

The woman who answered the phone at West Jeff was clearly frazzled, but managed to be polite and as helpful as she could. However, she couldn't find a Nathan Hummle listed as being admitted, but she would ask around. My guess was that he probably got a quick look and was handed an Ace bandage and sent to rejoin his group. Too few ERs were open for them to handle the wounded who could walk away. I left both my home and cell numbers, hoping that if he did call, one of them might work. My next two phone calls, one to Joanne Ranson, a cop, and Danny Clayton, an assistant district attorney, netted me only their voice mail. "There is nothing going on in this city," I muttered. "Where can they be?"

Not home—or willing to call back—before eleven. Or they were in places where cell towers weren't working—which on a bad day could be just about anywhere. Nathalie was gamely trying to stay awake, but it had been a long day for her, and even on a good day this was past her bedtime.

"They'll call in the morning," I reassured her. "Let's go to bed."

CHAPTER FIVE

The phone didn't wake me, it didn't ring at all. I got up a little after eight, still tired, but I had the immediate problem of a lost child—teenager—to deal with. The door to the spare room was shut, so I let her be while I took what I planned to be a quick shower. It was record-setting quick as there was no hot water. During the flooding, water had soaked into the gas lines so about once a week or so, a slug of water would hiccup long enough for the pilots to go out. I managed to get them re-lit just before Nathalie emerged. She was dressed, but her clothes looked slept in, as if she wasn't about to be anything less than perfectly modest in a stranger's home. Even sleeping in a room she could lock.

It was pizza for breakfast; I was kind enough to heat it in the microwave for her. I figured that cold pizza was probably too radical for someone who rarely ate pizza at all, let alone for breakfast.

Staring at the non-ringing phone (I'd already picked it up twice to make sure the dial tone was still there) I resolved, I'm a PI, I can trace down a cell phone. Then I stepped in what I was beginning to think of as the Katrina swamp—what had been normal and easy no longer was. I hadn't done PI work in the last few months; the last time I'd logged onto my computer with all its bookmarked and paid-in-full, whiz-bang data-access sites had been August 26, 2005. I didn't have a computer here and the one at my office had been delivered two weeks ago and was still in its shipping boxes. I had no cases, no clients, and no Internet access, so saw little reason to unpack it. I had a crappy little laptop that I plugged into the modem in Cordelia's office when I wanted to check my e-mail. I mostly didn't want to check my e-mail because it was mostly people asking me how I was doing, and I couldn't write back saying that I was doing fine because I wasn't, and I couldn't write back saying everything was insane and I felt like I was falling off the edge of the world, because I couldn't deal with explaining things or people wanting to help via e-mail sympathy that I didn't have time or energy to respond to.

Get a grip, I thought. I can hook up the laptop, reconnect to a few skip-trace sites, and get Nathan's cell-phone number. Except that the little purple notebook I kept all my logins and passwords in was at my office.

"Fuck," I muttered.

Nathalie looked like the devil had entered the room. Then she tried to put on an adult sophisticated expression like the cows used the word all the time.

"Sorry," I said. I almost added that I don't deal well with dead bodies and live kids, but I had rocked her world enough for one morning. "On August twenty-eighth, it would have taken me a few clicks on a computer keyboard to get Nathan's cell number. We connect to him and then to your group and everything is groovy." I explained about the work computer (leaving out the many "fucks" that would have accompanied any other telling of this story) and how easy it would have been to solve this puzzle under normal circumstances, but post-Katrina New Orleans wasn't even close to our usual abnormal.

I didn't suggest calling the phone in her father's barn and Nathalie didn't mention it either. We'd come to an unspoken agreement that it was best that her parents have as few details as possible about Nathalie's little adventure in New Orleans. I also discarded calling 911—assuming that the 911 system was up and functioning. Someone in authority should take a look at the body, but bodies were still being recovered from the storm, possibly hundreds still decaying in what was left of their flooded homes. One more didn't feel like an urgent situation. Besides, Carmen should have called, and I had phoned the only law-enforcement people I knew.

I stared at Nathalie for a long minute. Pizza, even hot pizza, is not good brain food. Then something closer to desperation than inspiration hit. I scrolled through the contacts on my cell phone and hit in a number.

"Chanse, Micky Knight. I need a favor." It is galling to ask another

PI to do something in any other situation I could easily do. "Cell number, Nathan Hummle, from?" I gave Nathalie a questioning look.

"Washer Farm, Wisconsin. Got the phone in Sheboygan."

I repeated that to Chanse. He lived in the Garden District, had gotten back a few weeks before I did. I was hoping he had his computer hooked back up. He didn't even ask why I needed him to look up something this simple, just told me to wait a minute.

After about a minute and thirty seconds, he was back on the phone and gave me the number.

Problem Nathalie solved. I dialed the number. The phone rang. And rang. And went to voice mail. Maybe he's not answering because he doesn't recognize the number. I left a message, a brief one just giving my name, that Nathalie had ended up with me, and would he please call, instead of saying that his innocent sibling was about to be auctioned off to the highest lesbian bondage bidder unless he answered the phone within three minutes.

"He's not real good about remembering to charge it," Nathalie said. "I usually have to remind him."

I was good. I didn't say the "fuck" that I really, really wanted to. Another inspiration/desperation thought hit. "That house you were at last night? Your group is supposed to gut it? Any chance they're there today?"

"I...don't know. That was the plan, but with Coach messed up and Carmen..."

"Carmen what?" Nathalie clearly didn't like Carmen and I was curious as to why.

"Carmen won't do much without him. If there's not some older guy for her to suck up to and show off for, she's not real motivated."

"I have to go back out there anyway, so why don't we do that? If your group is there, great. If not...we move on to plans X, Y, and Z."

I left messages again for both Danny and Joanne. This time I gave the address, a very brief description, including that the house had a very recently dead body in it.

And with that, Nathalie got to continue her great adventure.

CHAPTER SIX

The day was perfect, a beautiful blue sky, no rain or even any clouds. Since Katrina, it had rarely rained, as if New Orleans had more than its share of water and nature was trying to right the balance. The clarity of the day seemed to mock the destruction on the ground, miles of empty houses, the broken windows like staring eyes. Color was muted, the houses all turned to shades of mud gray, many with watermarks above doors or just below the eaves.

Nathalie was quiet until we passed a church, its pews hanging out broken windows, the lines of mud and water covering the stained glass. "Did God do this?" she asked. "Punish the city for being…sinful?"

I had my opinion, but only said, "What do you think?"

"That's what they told us, that we had to help to overcome the sins that took this city and threaten our nation."

She hadn't answered my query, her quiet rebellion questioning what they told her.

"A hundred years ago, Louisiana had a lot more coastline. Then men dredged the channels, built canals in the marsh, laid pipeline for the oil industry. A lot of the marsh is gone and the open water much closer. Even so, the levees should have held, but they didn't. A lot of human mistake in here. Maybe God was counting on us to be that dumb and incompetent. What do you think?"

"I don't know. It seems a lot of sinners got punished. Or that's what they said."

"A lot of old people, disabled people were drowned. The ones who couldn't get away or for whom the cost of leaving was so high they took their chances with the storm. God punished a lot of old, sick, poor people. I'm not sure I want to believe in that God." I had tried to be neutral, but I couldn't. It probably wouldn't make Nathalie's life easier to know others questioned the beliefs of her kin, but my silence wouldn't save her.

"I don't know, I just don't know," she said softly, then turned her face to the window, as if she had rebelled far enough to scare herself.

The clarity of the sunshine didn't dispel the ghosts; the houses held too many for them to be confined only to darkness. But at least I can see them more clearly, I thought as I again parked in front of the same place I'd been last night.

The first piece of bad news was that no one else was there. It was late enough in the day that any self-respecting, God-fearing church group should have been here hours ago, yet too early for them to leave for lunch.

The second piece of bad news was a cop car pulling in right behind my car.

The third piece of bad news was that the cops didn't get out and a bright white van pulled up behind them, with an official logo on the side that had something to do with public health. The three people in the van got out, so masked and gloved I couldn't tell if they were male or female.

"Oh, this is so not good," I muttered to myself. Nathalie and I were standing halfway across the lawn, feeling positively naked with only clothes on.

"Who are you?" one of the masked people asked. Still no clue to sex as the voice was either a high-pitched male or low-pitched female.

"Who and what are you?" I answered. We stared at each other for a moment, a stalemate of questions.

A distinctly male voice growled, "We ask the questions here."

I took a few steps to them, placing myself between Nathalie and these strangers. I didn't immediately answer as my immediate answer would have been, "That doesn't mean we answer the questions here," but these people were too official for me to drag my underage ward into a pissing contest.

The third masked person spoke. "Dick, don't live up to your name. This isn't cops and robbers."

Female, I decided, not so much by the voice but that she was calling the boys on their behavior in a way men wouldn't do. Plus de-escalating the situation.

She continued. "I'm Elizabeth Ward, an epi person from CDC. A body was reported out here, one that seems to have died recently, and we're here to investigate."

The thought ran through my head that I'd just walked into a science-fiction movie. One step at a time. "Epi?"

"Epidemiology. We study diseases and epidemics."

"You think the woman in there died from some need-to-be-spacesuit-protected disease?" I asked.

"Probably not, but better to be overcautious than not."

Dick, being a dick, said, "How the fuck do you know about the body?" The threat of some pestilential disease kept him a safe distance from us.

"Hey, kids here," I said with a nod at Nathalie.

"Kids today have heard everything," he muttered.

I resisted the urge to clamp my hands over Nathalie's innocent ears. Her New Orleans adventure was getting more surreal by the second. Taking a cue from Elizabeth Ward, I explained. "I'm a private detective. I was hired to retrieve some things from this house. When I got here last night, a church group was just arriving to take a look at that house." I pointed each house out respectively. "They went in and came rushing out again, saying that they'd seen a body. Worried that it might be someone hurt, I went in to look. I stayed long enough to check for a pulse, then left."

"So, who's the kid?" the still-androgynous space suit asked.

"And why are you here now?" Dick added.

"She's part of the church group. It was somewhat chaotic last night. The group leader broke his leg pretty badly in the frenzy of running from the house. He was the only adult. No cell service here, so the others had to leave to call for help. She stayed, but then couldn't go with the ambulance, so I took in a stray.

"We're back," I continued, "hoping that her group might be here. And I needed to finish what I was hired to do."

"You touched the body?" Elizabeth asked me.

"Briefly. Only for the pulse."

"Let's check her out," she said, starting for the house.

Dick didn't move. "Did she look diseased? Sick, stuff like that?"

"Other than being dead, she looked fine." I don't think he got my sarcasm.

Androgyne wavered and finally opted to follow Elizabeth.

"Stay here," Elizabeth said as she passed us.

I waited until they were in the house, or almost—Dick made it to the door and decided that was his station—before I said to Nathalie, "If they don't quarantine us, this much government firepower can get you back where you belong."

The cops didn't get out of their car. Maybe they were tired and were taking the opportunity to rest and not petrified of an unseeable microbe. I tried chatting with Nathalie, inane stuff like how to milk a cow, but our voices made Dick stare in our direction as if speech might draw the germs out, and Nathalie answered in one or two words. She was clearly worried—and I couldn't blame her.

I gave myself a reassuring pep talk. I lived with a doctor for over ten years, she's been exposed to multiple diseases, which means that I have. We're both hale and hearty. I had a tetanus shot a few weeks ago, was just barely old enough to have been vaccinated against smallpox, didn't have any open wounds, had been drinking only bottled water and bordering on OCD with the hand washing. I did a quick run-through of the diseases the scare-you TV anchors had mentioned as possible after the storm. Typhoid, cholera, *E. coli*, dysentery. They weren't likely transmitted by just touching someone.

It was about half an hour before they emerged from the house.

Elizabeth Ward stopped when she got to us; the other two continued to their van.

"If you only briefly checked for a pulse, how did you know she was a she?" She asked as if she knew the real answer, that I was queer and more accustomed to gender fuck than most people. The mask and goggles made it impossible to know if the almost-flirting I thought I heard in her voice was indeed the case.

"I'm an astute observer."

"What'd you observe?"

"No trace of beard, but laugh lines at the eyes. No Adam's apple, small hands. And her shape wasn't..." I searched for the word to indicate that something about her body shape was feminine.

"Wasn't butch enough?" Elizabeth Ward supplied for me.

"Bingo," I said, wondering if she'd get my double meaning. We were talking in code—the dance of "I'm gay. I think you are, are you?" I was answering her question, but also saying that she was correct in her read on me.

Then we both seemed to remember where we were.

"Can I get a tube of blood from you and your friend?" she asked.

Nathalie looked alarmed.

I quickly said, "From me, yeah, but Nathalie was only in the house a few seconds. She didn't even see the woman."

Elizabeth pulled her mask down around her neck and pushed her goggles up. I guessed her to be in her early fifties, with one of those faces most people would consider about ten years younger. Not many lines, only at her eyes and from the nose to the mouth, but those were marked and even in sleep would be there. The tendrils of hair escaping from her hood were steel gray with just a few strands of brown in them. Her eyes were hazel, intelligent and observing. She was medium height, maybe five-six or seven, but her posture was perfect and that made her seem taller, or more commanding. "Diseases leave their marks, and nothing on that poor woman indicates she's infected with anything. But this is an unprecedented situation, so my orders and my instinct are to err on the side of caution. There is nothing this flood can throw at us that modern medicine can't treat—if it's caught in time."

"Makes sense," I admitted. "Are you okay with giving a sample of blood?" I asked Nathalie. I wondered if she could legally consent or if we should be calling her parents on their barn phone? Somehow I suspected that was not something either of us wanted to attempt.

"I...don't know. I've never been stuck with a needle before," she stammered.

"You don't have to," Elizabeth told her. "We'll draw...?" she looked at me.

"Micky."

"We'll do Micky first and you can see how it's done. Then you can decide whether to join the fun."

Nathalie didn't seem to mind seeing me stuck as part of her great New Orleans adventure, especially as she had the option to avoid it. We followed Elizabeth to the van, where she opened the back. Her two compatriots hung back. This was clearly her area and they were content to help only if directly asked.

"Micky, sit on my bumper," she told me, indicating that I should sit in the open back of the van. She busied herself gathering what she'd need for the blood draw.

"Best offer I've had all day," I said, quietly enough to be directed only at her. "Dr. Ward? Or Elizabeth?"

"Liz. Seems like a bad day if your best offer is getting stuck in the arm." She smiled as she said it. Bingo, that settled that we were both lesbians. We'd probably never see each other again, but for a brief respite I didn't have to have the always slightly defensive posture of wondering if someone would tell a homophobic joke, or call someone faggot and I'd have to be silent or say something, and neither was a good choice.

She swabbed my arm with an alcohol patch, gave it a moment to dry, then gently inserted a needle.

"Not bad," I commented. I felt a slight sting, done like she kept in mind that she was poking an actual person, not a depersonalized vein, with something sharp.

"You'd never know I haven't done this to a live person in about ten years," she bantered.

I'm not squeamish about giving blood; indeed I've even allowed myself to be coerced into being a pincushion for budding trainees at Cordelia's clinic. As freakish as this whole scene was, it also had a tinge of normalcy. The mild flirting and banter, the efficient competence with which Liz handled the situation, all felt more normal than anything in the last day. Weeks even. And maybe it was a relief to have someone else in charge. I didn't have to make any decisions here.

She loosened the tourniquet, letting the blood fill a tube. Her motions were quick and sure. If she indeed hadn't done this in ten years, then she'd done it a lot before then, enough to have no hesitation now.

"Did you survive?" she asked me as she took the needle from my arm.

"Seems so, if I'm walking and talking. Otherwise I've turned into a swamp zombie."

"Swamp zombies have moss growing on their arms."

"I guess I survived then."

"Enough to talk your friend into it?" she asked.

"Hey, Nathalie," I said. "Are you up for this? It's pretty easy."

Nathalie looked a little pale, but nodded.

"Sit here," Liz told her, perching Nathalie on the van's bumper.

"You'll feel a little sting, but it should be brief. Most people do better if they don't look at what I'm doing."

"Okay," Nathalie said, scrunching her eyes closed.

"Just talk to me," I said to her, taking her free hand in mine. She clutched it tightly. I wasn't sure if it was fear or her inner baby dyke roaring out at the chance to hold a woman's hand. She didn't say much, but I chatted about what foods she should try, extolling the wonders of a perfectly cooked oyster po-boy.

Liz quickly drew her blood, being both professional and gentle, as if feeling that she might influence Nathalie's lifelong relationship with the medical profession with how she got this one tube of blood.

The oyster po-boys must have done it. Nathalie blinked her eyes open as Liz put a Band-Aid on her arm, looking like she couldn't believe that was all. "You done?" she said, looking at the beige strip on her arm.

"All done."

"That wasn't bad," she said, as if triumphing over a great adversary.

"Try not to worry," Liz assured us. "So far there have been no signs of outbreaks of disease, and it's not likely this is the first one. I'd bet money that you'll both be fine. This is just extra caution."

"Better too much caution than not enough," I agreed.

"I need contact info."

"You want my phone number?" I asked.

"Exactly." She had a great smile.

I wrote it down for her. I also wrote down the number I had for Nathan's cell phone, with a quick explanation of the circumstances.

"I'll be very discreet when I call you," Liz assured Nathalie. I was interested to note that she didn't promise me discretion. "Time to get back to the lab," she said as she put away her supplies and closed the van door.

"Hey," I said. "If you hear anything about…her—and you can let me know, I'd appreciate it."

Liz and I looked at each other for a moment, the mild flirting gone. A young woman had died. "I'll do what I can," she told me.

Dick took the hint, stubbing out his cigarette. It was an odd sight, him in high-tech public-health gear smoking a low-tech and not very public-health cancer stick.

I tapped on the cop-car window, and the driver cracked it long enough to ignore my request that they help a long-lost kid find her way home and to tell me that their duty was to escort the doctors.

Liz waved as she got in the van. The cops pulled in front of them to lead the way and then Nathalie and I were alone again.

"Lunchtime," I said, and we headed to my car.

Nathalie was quiet as we rode back to my place. I was glad she wasn't one of those people who feel every moment of silence must be filled. It's bad enough with adults, who might have at least lived enough of a life to occasionally say something interesting. But the "one precious child" weaned on years of eager adult attention who insisted on babbling even if it was about going to the mall solidified my support for birth control. Nathalie looked out the window as if needing to see the vacant houses, waterlines, and debris from thousands of lives, knowing that it would mark her for life.

I had my own thoughts to occupy me. It's not my problem, I told myself, but I couldn't help thinking about the woman still left in the house. She wasn't old and she hadn't been killed by the storm. The likely explanation was that this was her house and she was there checking on it and something happened—a blood clot, an aneurism, any of the maladies that befell the young, but that didn't explain why she was dressed in drag. A woman doesn't put on a man's suit to clean mold out of her house. Who was she and why was she there?

I was already making a list, I realized. What women did male drag? Had any of them returned post-Katrina? Was this woman connected to them? Who could I talk to who might answer those questions?

It's not your problem. You have enough problems, including the immediate one of young Nathalie. And Cordelia. And your career. Your life.

The young woman still haunted me. Too many ghosts.

Chapter Seven

We were at my house again. With one slice of cold pizza in the refrigerator. There was peanut butter, but no bread. There was one box of crackers, but they were garlic flavored, which didn't seem like a tasty combination.

Inspiration/desperation again hit.

"Chanse, I need another favor," I said as he answered his phone. "What's Carmen's name," I asked Nathalie. "Carmen Gecklebacher," I repeated to Chanse. "Cell-phone number, probably Wisconsin." It took him a minute.

You're slipping, Micky, I told myself as I dialed her number. I could have done this yesterday.

"Look, I told you I'll meet you later. I can't talk right now" was how Carmen answered the phone.

"What?" I asked, deliberately mumbling, curious enough—or enough of an asshole—to see if she would continue.

Her voice was a harsh whisper. "I'm with Coach in the hospital. I don't want him to know about you, okay? If I spend enough time with him, he won't be suspicious when I need to get away."

I was willing to bet that she hadn't been smart enough to cover her mouth with her hand, depending on whispering to make sure no one overheard. I was also willing to bet that she was young enough to not be aware that harsh whispers carried very well and everyone in the vicinity had probably heard her. Maybe Coach was on enough pain meds that he would think he was dreaming.

I switched to my professional, don't-mess-with-me voice.

"Carmen Gecklebacher? This is Michele Knight. We met under unfortunate circumstances last night. I need to know—"

"What the hell?" She demanded, "Who is this? How did you get this number?"

Ms. Gecklebacher was pissing me off. I suspected that Nathalie's estimation of her was much more accurate than her brother's. She was game playing and obviously not overly concerned with the kids she was supposed to be looking after.

"I'm in investigations and law enforcement." That was stretching it, but not far enough to break. "It took me about thirty seconds to get your phone number. I need to know where your group is housed, because last night Nathalie Hummle got separated from them and we need to get her back where she belongs." Giving her no time to take umbrage, I said, "Give me the address."

"I'm at the hospital," she said.

"So you have no clue as to where the group is staying?" I packed as much stupid-young-kid-who-is-clueless contempt into my voice as I could.

"I don't really know the address." The petulance came through the line clearly.

"I can either take Nathalie to the hospital and leave her with you, or you can give me enough information to find where the group is staying."

That focused her. "It was somewhere off Williams Boulevard." She seemed to think that was enough.

It took literally about twenty questions for me to get enough directions and descriptions, such as "We passed a pink building that sold daiquiris," for me to feel I would be able to return Nathalie to her group.

"Thanks, Carmen," I said, not meaning it at all. "Oh, and you're way too young to be screwing Coach, let alone screwing him and screwing around on him." I hung up on her surprised yelp.

Nathalie had been listening to my phone conversation. "Carmen's not going to be happy," but she said it in a way that let me know Carmen's happiness was not her top priority.

"She doesn't know me, and if she sits and thinks about it for a few minutes, she'll know that I can't know that much about her."

"But it's true," Nathalie said. "She gives Coach blow jobs in his office in the church rec area." She blushed when she said "blow jobs."

"How do you know?" Carmen was certainly a suck-up to those she thought could benefit her, but that didn't mean that actual sex was happening. Coach would be an idiot if he took her up on it.

Nathalie's blush spread across her face and down her neck. "My mom had baked an apple cobbler that I took to youth group. I was supposed to get the pan, but forgot, so I went back for it…"

"And you saw them."

"Well…I saw her disappear on her knees behind his desk and he got this weird look on his face and started breathing funny…" Her face was bright red and she was staring at the floor.

"Enough details. I don't think either you or I want to know more than that."

"And Enid came back with me and she saw it too and I think she told some others."

"Coach is an idiot. Carmen is too, but she's also young and stupid. They were bound to get caught. If it hadn't been you and Enid, it would have been someone else." Nathalie seemed guilty, knowing something she shouldn't and being part of having that secret spread around.

This was a mess. I briefly considered just keeping Nathalie until it was time for her to get back on a plane. Coach and Carmen didn't sound adult enough to care for this group. Coach might have been adequate except for occasionally thinking with his dick, but he was out of commission and that left Carmen, who clearly was only worried about getting away with sneaking around. However, someone had to be the host, and presumably some adults were involved there. Plus my own life was enough of a mess. Cordelia was supposed to be back in a few days, and the last thing we'd need for our meeting was a teenaged house guest.

"Time to take you back where you belong. We'll stop and get an oyster po-boy on the way."

CHAPTER EIGHT

Nathalie was back with her group. At least she was well-fed before I left her for the wolves. An older woman had been there, but it took her about five minutes to understand that Nathalie was part of the group staying with her church, then another five minutes to think of what to do with her, and when I left she was still debating whom to call first. Nathan was there, limping slightly, and maybe he would offer some stability. I gave her my phone number, secretly hoping she wouldn't call because she was fifteen, and only time, and a lot of it, would get her to where she needed to go.

I took advantage of being far out in the suburbs to make a major grocery run and found myself standing in the aisle looking at my mustard choices, wondering if I should get a couple of jars, one for the house in Tremé and one for my office. I wasn't sure where I'd end up. I was determined not to have Cordelia come home to a bare refrigerator since her credit card had paid for the replacement. The least I could do was stock it, even if it was no longer really mine and I didn't live there anymore. You can't stand here forever staring at the mustard. Buy two of things that will keep and parcel them between the two places.

It's your goddamned fault that I'm stuck out here, I thought. How can mustard make me so furious? Oh, yeah, my supposed forever partner got tired me of me, dumped my ass right before Katrina blew into town, and now I was here alone having to deal with everything from human shit left in my office to the long drive to civilization to get basics like mustard. I started to turn and walk out, fuck it, just fuck it all. I can't take the long lines, the stupid people who don't live here, all the swirling media commentary of people saying that New Orleans got what it deserved. Why did we live in a swamp?

It wasn't a fucking swamp three hundred years ago when the Bienville boys planted a French flag here. Cut a canal through the marsh to dig for oil, then another and another until the marsh that used to protect us is a sieve.

I was halfway down the aisle before reality sank in. If I didn't get it now, I'd just have to come back out here. Just fucking do it. I got the spicy hot mustard that I like. Cordelia could get her own fucking mustard if it wasn't good enough for her. Then I grabbed our usual brand as well. I'd take the hot mustard to my office.

She was returning this weekend. Friday? Saturday? Sunday? I didn't know. Was she flying or driving?

Call her back and ask, I told myself, as I put two bags of flour in the cart.

But I wouldn't. I'd divide myself between the two locations, unload groceries twice, clean twice, not think about anything once. Or if I did think, it'd be about how a woman, dressed as a man, died.

Cordelia had left me and if she wanted me back she'd have to work for it. She'd have to come to me, coax me back into her life and her home. It was her responsibility, not mine.

If she wanted me back. I didn't ask myself if I wanted her back or if I just wanted the chance to reject her. Nor did I ask myself what if she didn't want me back.

Did I need cooking oil or not? Olive oil? Canola oil? Two bottles of each? Cordelia can cook, but I'd done most of it. She often worked late, so it made sense for me to do the cooking and leave the cleanup for her.

All the decisions about my life confronted me in the bottles of olive oil. My pride said get two, but my bank account wasn't as big as my pride.

I'm standing in a grocery store and I can't make a fucking decision about olive oil. There were too many decisions, so I made none, just stared at the yellow-gold liquid until someone bumped me with a cart. Like all the grocery stores that were open, this one was busy.

Get what you need, be nice and get a few things to tide Cordelia over until…until the next day or the day after.

I put back most of the doubles, save for a few things that I'd keep at my office in any case—water, bread, peanut butter, and some cold cuts. Enough to either get me through a few days or provide lunch for a week.

Standing in line, I felt defeated. If grocery shopping was too hard, how would I handle the rest of my life? The detective business wasn't exactly booming. Cordelia and I had co-mingled our finances years ago—after I'd finally trusted her enough to not need total control of at least some money. She wouldn't begrudge me using some, in fact during one of our brief phone conversations had said, "Take what you need."

I cut out of line, made a run by the liquor aisle, got what I needed—two bottles of decent Scotch. Those would go back to the office with me.

Again, in line, I felt calmer. I couldn't solve the problems today—or tomorrow, but I could make them disappear for a little while. Knowing that I could get away from my problems made it easier to think about them. The tasks of today fell into line—go home and to my office and unpack this stuff. Then go back out to those cursed houses and finish the one job that had come my way since Katrina.

It wasn't much of one. Mrs. Louellen Frist was too old to ever come back to New Orleans. The attic of her flooded house contained keepsakes and mementos of days that held happy memories. She'd hired me to retrieve whatever I could find and ship it to her in Dallas.

She'd probably know who lived in the house next door to hers. Maybe even how to contact them. And ask why a body might end up in their house.

I glanced at my watch. It was almost three. The line was moving slowly. Going back to the house would have to wait until tomorrow. But I could do a French Quarter bar crawl, see if any drag kings were missing. Or if anyone knew about cross-dressing women. Yeah, and I might have to buy a few drinks to fit in. I wasn't fooling myself; I just wasn't sure if the alcohol was a piece of my falling apart or helping me hold it together.

CHAPTER NINE

The groceries were stowed; I had survived my trip out to the suburbs. Nathalie hadn't called, so I seemed safe from having to worry about her.

I looked at the stocked refrigerator: the skim milk Cordelia preferred; several of her favorite kinds of teas (decidedly not herbal, she appreciated her caffeine); apples and pears (she'd been trying to eat more fruit in her diet); some goat cheese and a good cheddar—apples and cheese being one of her favorite snacks.

Did you get anything for yourself, I wondered as I surveyed the shelves. Oh, yeah, Scotch and chocolate. Everything else was hers. Or ours. We used the same mustard brand, ate the same bread, cereals.

I closed the door. I had food. It was too much effort to pick a whole new brand of mustard and bread.

I headed down to my office to stow the Scotch, chocolate, also some bread, mustard, and sliced turkey. This would have been usual before the storm; I was being a little more obsessive about it now that I couldn't run out to a store a few blocks away.

As I was driving, I realized there was a message in the food. I had choices. I could have left Cordelia a barren refrigerator or just a few generic necessities, or got stuff that only I like and would eat, like anchovies. That would have been a message, a brand-new refrigerator that she paid for stocked full of cans of anchovies. Why had I been kind, picked up things she liked, when I was still so angry at her? Maybe I wanted to prove that I was a nice person even if she was a cheating, lying bitch. Or to make her feel even more guilty.

Or to let her know that it might take some work, but I was leaving the door open.

I parked in front of my office building. Or maybe some inchoate jumbled version of all three and a few more I wasn't aware of.

I carried the groceries up the three flights of stairs to my office.

Before I'd met Cordelia it had been both office and home, with one big area in the center that was the office proper. Off to one side was a kitchen and bath and to the other side two smaller rooms. Once a bedroom and a darkroom, those had been converted, one to storage and one filled with filing cabinets. I had gone through everything in storage, ruthlessly weeding out anything that I didn't absolutely need, so that room was now mostly empty, filled with an inflatable mattress.

My home away from the home that was no longer really my home? It seemed that my goal of the last few weeks was to go to bed so tired—and a little drunk—that it didn't matter where I slept, on the inflatable mattress or the bed I'd slept in for years. It mostly worked, but in the morning when I woke up nothing had changed. My life was still in limbo—career, relationship, where to live, nothing settled or set.

I unloaded my groceries. I still had a full bottle of Scotch here. Three vessels of amber liquid reassured me that I could get through the next few days. I didn't like that I needed that kind of reassurance. What happened to the Micky Knight who managed life without a bottle and could plan days, even years ahead? "She's gone with the wind and the water," I said out loud. I'd taken to talking to myself just to fill the silence.

One of the tenants on the first floor was in and out, but even before Katrina, I'd seen him only on occasion. I wasn't even sure what he did. He seemed one of those characters who might have been interesting somewhere else, but this was New Orleans and we knew how to do characters better than just about any other city. I suspected he wanted to be an artist, but whatever talent he had had gone up in a cloud of marijuana smoke so he paid the rent and bought the pot by painting portraits for drunken tourists on a sidewalk in the French Quarter. Slightly seedy artists in this city were outnumbered only by Mardi Gras beads. Every time we passed coming in or out of the building, he looked at me like he'd never seen me before. Katrina had done nothing to change that.

As far as I could tell the tenants on the second floor hadn't returned.

Or hadn't survived.

My floor, the third, was too empty. The other half had been used by Sara Clavish, an older woman who had started out doing cookbooks, then discovered the Internet and had reinvented herself as a Web sleuth. I had hired her to do a lot of the tedious Internet crawling required in modern-day detecting. She had been caught in the flood in the lower parishes. They still hadn't found her body.

The ghosts were everywhere, even dry land held its share.

I started to open one of the bottles of Scotch, but decided against it. If I started drinking before I went to the bars, then I couldn't even pretend that I was trying to do something useful—find the identity of one more body among the already-too-many dead. I wasn't sure I could ask the right questions sober; I knew I couldn't if I was impaired. And the bottle would be here when I came back. I returned it to its cupboard and put the glass back as well. Another little game, like I wouldn't just take them back out when I returned later tonight.

Almost desperate to have motion and something to do, even if it was probably pointless, I headed down the stairs. For all the burden she was, Nathalie had also been a welcome distraction—someone to pull me away from my solitary obsessions.

I could use the dead woman the same way if I had to.

I started outside the Quarter in the Marigny, but these bars were local and had only a few people in them. Everyone knew someone who was missing: a friend, an acquaintance, some second cousin that they hadn't heard from since the storm. How do you find a missing person in a city of missing people?

After the third bar, I realized that I didn't know enough about the woman to even ask questions that might help me. But I couldn't face going back to that empty house.

Not enough people had come back from Katrina to make parking in the French Quarter the challenge it had been previously. Probably the straight, tourist part nearer to Canal was horrendous, but I was in the quieter residential end, what was considered the gay end of the Quarter. The gay bars were some of the first businesses to re-open after the storm.

The hypnotic music, the swirling lights, people—people I didn't know and didn't have to worry about—helped keep the ghosts away. Most of the bar patrons were men; the few women mainly seemed from out of town, probably straight and probably in the gay bars to dance without being pawed. I stopped asking questions, just got a beer, stood off to the side and watched the parade. Out-of-town gawkers, here for the first time, their do-gooder hearts pasted on their sleeves and their lack of sophistication on their faces; the jaded locals searching for what they needed—sex, drugs, booze—to ease the ragged holes where houses, friends, family, a job, a life used to be.

By the fourth beer I only vaguely remembered that I was supposed to be asking questions, supposed to be doing anything other than being another local seeking what I needed to get through to the morning.

The flash on the video screen was brief, so quick I might have hallucinated it. A snippet from some show somewhere. Men dressed as women and women dressed as men. One of them looked like her. I tried to push my way to the bartender to ask if he knew anything about it, but the demand for alcohol was great and by the time he finally turned to where I had wormed my way to the bar, it was too late. I asked my question anyway. "That drag-king show that was just on the screen, what do you know about it?" He looked at me blankly, as if the question made no sense. "Scotch on the rocks," I said, a language he understood. I forgot that I had planned to stick to beer. When he brought me my drink, I asked again about the drag king on the video, but even a five-dollar tip got only a shrug of the shoulders.

Had I even seen it, I wondered as I stumbled out of the bar. Or had I seen what I wanted to see, some tenuous justification for my going from bar to bar?

Go home, go to sleep. Nothing will change between now and the morning. I was sober enough to know that I was too drunk to drive, so left my car where it was and walked back to the house in Tremé. It was close to the Quarter and an easy walk, compared to almost a mile back to my office. That was one of the reasons we had bought the house, just on the other side of Rampart Street from the French Quarter, an easy shot to Charity and Tulane Hospital for Cordelia.

I breathed in the cool fall air, a welcome change to the smoky bar atmosphere.

Tomorrow morning, you pull it together, I reproached myself. The beer and Scotch hadn't made any of the decisions I needed to make, hadn't changed what had happened in the last three months.

Cordelia had cheated on me and in retaliation I had cheated on her. Or just succumbed to the need to be held and touched. Dr. Lauren Calder had come to New Orleans to do research, including at Cordelia's clinic. Her partner, the journalist Shannon Wild, and I had ended up together, because she was here, had little to do, and her investigative skills seemed like a perfect fit for working with me. It had been more their idea than mine.

Katrina changed everything. I had walked in on Cordelia and Lauren Calder in an embrace that was more than friendly, stormed out, then stumbled over Shannon back at my office. She was humiliated, I was angry, so we left together for the old shipyard I owned out in the bayous. I drank more than I should have, didn't notice the hammering of windows being boarded up, had left my cell phone in the car, so we came close to being caught by the storm, managing to leave late Sunday morning with landfall less than a day away. In our traveling together, we ended up sleeping together. We had used the word "love," but love didn't feel possible to me or I just couldn't make the leap to start my life anew with a new person in a new place. She lived in New York; I stayed in San Francisco. I called it fate that I ended up on the other side of the country—a friend of a friend was in Thailand for three months and willing to let someone use his apartment. I pretended it wasn't a choice, but I could have gone east, stayed with my mother, found other options closer to home. Or closer to Shannon. She called and e-mailed, was still calling and e-mailing, but I had come back here with an inchoate need to settle what was left of my life here before I could think of moving on.

I stumbled over a crack in the sidewalk. The problem was I was neither moving on nor returning, instead caught in some agonized limbo. In the morning I wanted to stay here, rebuild my life as I helped rebuild New Orleans, but by the afternoon, I was ready to leave and never look back. And the next day swung again. I kept asking myself what I wanted, but kept circling around to the same answer—I wanted what I couldn't have, to return to that day in August, find Cordelia alone in her office, go home with her, watch the news and be together through the storm and together in whatever we decided to do beyond that.

Few cars were out, a Humvee caught up with me. "Where you going?" one of them asked.

Damn, curfew. I'd forgotten that we had to be off the streets or risk being arrested.

"Home, just two blocks up." I tried to sound as sober as I could.

"We'll make sure you get there," the voice said. They slowed to my pace, seeming neither friendly nor hostile. Either way it was a good deed for them, get a resident home safe or prevent a robbery.

I pulled out my keys as I approached my house, jangling them as a signal that I was home and they could continue their patrol.

"You be safe, now," the voice, a strange accent from someplace far away, said.

"You, too," I said as I slipped inside.

CHAPTER TEN

I woke to a vague dawn, far too few hours of sleep, the late fall sun clear and cold. I snuggled under the covers wanting to go back to sleep, a few more hours of no decisions, no wondering what to do with my life. But my brain and my body were too restless.

Finally giving in to reality, I went to the kitchen and put the coffee on. Half a cup was enough to get me into the shower. After another cup of coffee, and something vaguely resembling breakfast, I felt awake and aware enough to think. My first chore was to clean up, do the dishes, make the bed. Cordelia wouldn't be here for a few days, but I needed to have everything ready, as if being clean and neat proved something.

It was time to do the one job I'd gotten since Katrina. Mrs. Frist needed her memories; she didn't have much left anymore.

The area seemed less haunted in the day, the bright sun, brilliant blue sky seeming to say that nature could renew itself, so could we.

A bright ribbon of yellow crime-scene tape marked the house where the body had been. That was the only sign that anything had changed from when I was here yesterday. I hoped she had been taken. I would assume that she had, as I didn't intend to check. No one else was about. Maybe they had come and been efficient and left, leaving only the yellow tape.

I turned from that house and crossed the yard of the one next door, the one I had been hired to search.

The quiet made me realize how much background noise we humans add—the hums of air conditioners or clothes dryers, the purr of cars, muted voices from TV or radio. All were silent now. Even being out in the woods wasn't like this, no wind in the trees or chirp of birds. Nothing, dead silence.

Just do your job, Micky, I told myself. If you think about what was lost, imagine all the people in all these houses, you might never stop crying. Or drinking.

I jimmied the crowbar into the door jamb and gently pulled on it, increasing the leverage until most of my body weight was leaning into it. Just when I was about to think I wouldn't get in this way, the door gave slightly, the quiet broken by the creaking splintering of the lock coming out of the frame.

I'd asked Mrs. Frist how careful she wanted me to be.

"Nothing is left, only for those mementos in the attic. It's already destroyed. If you have to, just break it a different way."

I had a right to be here, but I still felt like an intruder. This was someone else's life. I made no attempt to hide what I was doing, although there was no one around that I could see.

The door slowly yielded to the pressure. It opened about six inches then stopped. It was probably caught against debris, furniture glued in place by the drying mud. I gave it a hard shove with my shoulder and it moved about an inch. I started to see if I could wedge myself in sideways, but a glance at my just-three-months-old sneakers suggested that I do the sensible thing.

I went back to my car, dug out the old, already muddied sneakers, and put them on; took off my half-decent jean jacket and pulled a ratty T-shirt over my not-quite-as-ratty T-shirt. Then I got latex gloves, a painter's face mask, and safety glasses. I also grabbed my Maglite— even with the sunlight, it could be dark in the house. For a moment I thought about my gun, but chose instead one of those multi-function tools. The gun would make me feel safer, but blasting mice with 9mm was overkill and beyond, and I might actually need a screwdriver or a wrench.

I was back at the door. Another hard shove, another inch. Time to see if I could get through. Using the flashlight, I tried to get a look at what was in there. I could see little in the opening—a thick layer of cracked mud, dishes, and the contents of a sewing kit embedded in it. Little color was visible except the blacks and greens of mold and mud.

No alligators, no writhing mass of water moccasins.

No dead bodies.

I put one foot through the door, trying to find secure footing in the uneven layer of sludge. Then I followed with my hips—if they could get through the rest of me should fit. I heard the soft crunch of crumbling muck as my weight shifted. I hesitated for a moment, not wanting to exchange the sunlight for the dim interior, then one arm, a shoulder, my head—the sunlight was gone—and I was through the door.

It had caught against a massive overturned couch, which in turn had one of its armrests jammed against a table that was pressing into a wall. Diffused light came through the shuttered windows, which had held, but not stopped the water. The shafts of light were almost smoky with dust and mold spores. I put the mask over my face and the safety glasses on.

Slowly I scanned the room with the flashlight. People's lives had been washed into a haphazard jumble. The furniture all overturned, an end table half-impaled into a recliner, CDs and video tapes spewed across the floor. A TV staring up at the ceiling.

I only needed to look for alligators—or protruding nails, snakes, broken glass, anything that might harm me. I didn't need to look at everything that had been destroyed.

I crossed the living room as quickly as I safely could. The increasing stench told me that I was heading to the kitchen. The refrigerator was on its side, a black sludge leaking out of it. The stairs to the attic were off behind the pantry.

Keeping far away from the noxious ooze sliming the floor, I edged around the pantry to the back entryway, a small area where the back door, kitchen, and attic stairs met. It was even darker here, only a small window above the back door. A tangled pile of boots and sandals littered the floor.

I jumped back a foot when I saw a snake, but it didn't move and a minute in the beam of my flashlight showed that it was dead, beginning to mummify in the mud.

The door to the attic had been ripped off its hinges and listed open. New splintering indicated that rescuers had probably pried it open. The good news was that they had kicked most of the debris to the side so a narrow path was cleared up the stairs. A quick glance at the back door showed that was how they entered the house.

There was no light in the stairs save my flashlight and a wan diffusion from below. I inched up, scanning each stair carefully before putting my weight on it. These houses were full of hazards from mud that cracked through to slippery goo to creatures that could bite and sting to unstable walls and ceilings ready to fall in with a breeze.

The stairs creaked softly underfoot. As I reached the top I could clearly see the watermark, a harsh black line, with several faded ones below it. The highest one was where the water had reached, the lower ones left as the flood ebbed away. This was a one-story house and everything in the one story was destroyed. Mrs. Frist was right; I could do no more damage than had already been done.

The trapdoor into the attic had been flung open, probably also the searchers. I held at the top of the stairs, my head below the door, listening, trying to make sure nothing would be up there to meet me. Only the unnatural silence of this destroyed neighborhood greeted me.

I took another step, then another, head and shoulders into the attic. I swung the flashlight around once quickly, then more slowly. Nothing moved; the slow arc of the light revealed what one would expect to find in an attic save for the mold slowly reaching up the walls.

Boxes were piled on boxes, a dress form for a long-ago young figure, some old chairs, all covered in dust. The water hadn't reached here. Even so the damage was creeping in, mold starting to grow on the walls, a close cloying smell of decay, everything from the putrid refrigerator to the rot in the walls. Being careful where I put my weight, I left the stairs behind. The air up here was dense with dust and reek.

Mrs. Frist has described what she wanted me to find, a small chest. "I called it my treasure chest, although it was treasure only to me." It was a faded navy blue, bound with worn leather straps, something handed down from mother to daughter to daughter. She wasn't sure what it had originally been used for—her grandmother had joked that it held the whalebone for the corsets—but her mother had used it for keepsakes, old photos, birth certificates, family Bibles, the kind of box that was more about memories than value.

The floating dust turned everything a muted russet, the soft colors second place to the harsh smells of decay. I slowly searched with my light, pointing its bright beam into the dim corners. The air was starting to feel too impenetrable to breathe, the mask on my face increasing my claustrophobia.

I needed to find that box and get out of here. I took a step and the boards creaked. I had to slow myself and not let my panic goad me into falling through rotten wood. I took another cautious step, peering behind a stack of cardboard boxes. Only more beige boxes were there. I took another cautious step to see what was behind those boxes. A stack of old magazines. A glance at the cover of the top one told me this was the porn collection, albeit nothing that would qualify today. The blouse was low-cut, the breasts thrust out, but only a come-hither smile hinted at more.

I turned around. These pinup mags were probably in the part of the attic where any of the women were least likely to go.

Indicating that I was right, the other side of the attic held an old sewing machine and the dress form. Gender segregation in storage.

But cardboard didn't seem to have a gender as boxes were piled on this side as well. Behind the boxes perched two cribs piled on top of one another, one a dusty white, the other dark wood.

I suddenly tensed, then realized I was hearing a car in the street. That normal sound now seemed so out of place. I could feel the sweat dripping in my mask, salt at my lips. I took another careful step, an awkward dance with the dress form to see behind it. Back in the far corner, under a stack of books, was a dark shape.

I swung my flashlight around the rest of the attic. No, the dark shape was the most likely to be a small, faded navy chest. The way to it was blocked by a bent aluminum Christmas tree, still tinseled with strings of lights wrapped around it. It'll never be in anyone's holiday memories again, I told myself as I shoved it out of the way. It probably hadn't been used for years, from the dust on it and the shedding of faded silver as I moved it.

I had to move a few more boxes, the first two lightweight and marked as containing the ornaments for the tree. But the boxes under them were heavy, weighty with paper. Or rocks. I tore off my mask, unable to bear its confining presence on my face. For a moment, the sudden cool felt good, but then I was hit with what the mask had been keeping out, the dust and odor. It now smelled like the rancid ooze from the refrigerator was just underfoot. I took a deep breath, coughed at the dust, wiped my face with my sleeve, and put the mask back on.

A few more boxes and I got close enough to the dark shape to have a better look at it. It was as described, a tattered navy canvas, with leather used to join the pieces. I quickly uncovered it, heaving the books aside, leaving some of them as they toppled over. It was the chest, now I just had to get it out of here. I gave it a good tug and it pulled halfway out of the corner it was wedged in by other boxes. It was heavy, weighted with papers collected over lifetimes. I pulled it another few inches, then glanced behind me to the trapdoor to the staircase. It wouldn't be easy to clear enough of a path to drag it. Bending awkwardly, I managed to get one hand under the bottom and, with a grunt, I hefted it, barely able to lift it. Balancing care and haste, I stumbled around the tree and boxes. I put it down halfway across the attic, balancing it on one of the full boxes, to catch my breath. I again had to resist the urge to pull off the mask. Five feet and you're there. I again squatted to avoid strain on my back and lifted the box. Several more lurching steps got me to the stairway.

Again a few rasping breaths, then I went down the stairs a few steps. I grabbed the two near corners of the chest and began to drag it down the stairs.

We did an awkward dance, me blindly stepping backward down the stairs and pulling the chest one step at a time. It was slow going, the leather binding catching over and over, and each time I had to gently wrangle it down another step. In the confined stairway, it was hard to get a good angle on the chest; I had to tug from the front, couldn't really get a grip on the back. Halfway down the stairs, I had to take a break; my thighs and forearms were starting to tremble, and my hands so sweaty that what little grip I had was slippery.

Just as I was wiping my hands on my pants, I heard a loud crash at the back door.

Two male voices rumbled obscenities.

The chest was half-balanced resting against my knee and blocking my way up. If I tried to run down the stairs not only would I run straight into the intruders, but I'd risk having the chest barreling down behind me, and it was heavy enough to do damage.

I uselessly pulled out the one-of-everything tool, now wishing I'd brought my gun instead, and slowly turned around, so I could at least be facing them. If you're going to get shot and killed, you might as well see it coming.

Another crash as the broken door was thrown out of the way. The tramp of heavy boots in the entryway. The light changed as shadows crossed it.

Suddenly two men were silhouetted in the dusty light at the foot of the stairs.

I said very softly, but it was a roar in the silence, "You gentlemen looking for something?"

They spun toward me and then one of them let out a shriek that was the high-pitched vibrato of someone usually billed as "girl number 2" in C-grade horror movies just as she was about to get slashed.

The shrieker remained a deer in headlights only long enough for his lower-pitched partner to knock him to the floor next to the dead snake, before he almost levitated back up and vanished out the door.

"You could have stayed and helped me with this," I muttered, turning back to the trunk.

I began yanking it down the stairs with a vengeance. This time I was lucky, thieves who were as spooked by the silence and the desolation as I was. And who didn't have guns that they fired wildly into their fear.

My back ached, I had bloodied one of my fingers, and my arms were exhausted, but I was finally at the foot of the stairs. And just had to get the trunk out of the house and into my car. The path through the living room and to the front door was a debris-strewn obstacle course. I looked out the back door and into the yard. It would be farther, but it wasn't a mess of wreckage cosseted by walls.

Alternating pushing and pulling, and constantly cursing, I managed to get the chest around the back of the house, across the front lawn, and to the trunk of my car. I had to flop in the front seat, drink an entire bottle of water, and not move for ten minutes before I was able to laboriously get one end of the chest on the bumper and slowly lever it over the lip of the trunk and safely into my car.

The lid barely closed. Mrs. Frist was getting a bargain. I had agreed to do this for two hundred dollars, far below my going rate for things that were usually as taxing as sitting in a car and watching people do nothing or staring at a computer screen. I had called it heavy lifting if I had to go to another parish and look at court records. Next time add an actual heavy-lifting charge, I told myself.

If there was a next time. Did a destroyed New Orleans, with less than half the population, even need or care whether one private dick stayed or left?

It was barely past noon and I already felt like the day should be over.

Or at least late enough that I could again do a bar crawl in a putative search for who a woman dressed as a man might be.

It had seemed easy during my brief conversation with Mrs. Frist. Find the chest, send it to her. I could feel the weight in my car as it hit a pothole. New Orleans streets were never the most road-worthy of surfaces, but the weeks of stewing in the flood waters had created craters that could eat an entire tire. I slowed down. A broken axle or even a flat tire wouldn't improve my mood or make the tasks ahead of me any easier.

The chest was big and heavy enough that I couldn't just slap an address on it and leave it at the post office. Even if I could send it, the weight alone would cost more than my fee.

The first option that came to mind was what I was beginning to call the "oh, fuck it all" option—it can't be done, no way, no how, welcome to New Orleans where nothing works anymore anyway.

I had to drive halfway across town to get mail, and even that was only first class and even then mostly late enough that the bills were past due before I got them. Forget magazines or packages. Most of the post offices had been destroyed, and even if they hadn't there were few people to staff them. Only a few stations were open. Mailing anything was an iffy proposition.

So I could just tell Mrs. Frist, sorry, can't do it, if someone happens to drive by with a truck, they can pick up the chest. Or if I happened to be evacuating by Dallas next hurricane season, I'd drop it off.

Then I reminded myself that the sun was still shining and I didn't have much else to do with my time except obsess about Cordelia's arrival, so I might as well work on another solution.

Drag the chest up the stairs to my office. No, that could wait until tomorrow. My arms and back weren't up for that without a good solid twenty-four hours of rest. I'd call Mrs. Frist, ask her if it was okay if I opened the chest and divided the contents into manageable shipping piles. Once I got her okay—I was assuming she'd be okay with it, as this was about the only viable option unless some friend with a truck was here and soon returning to Dallas—then I'd take a long, leisurely drive out to the suburbs of civilization to get shipping supplies. The long was required, nothing that would suit my purpose was in short driving distance, and the leisurely was to rest my tired body while maintaining the illusion that I was actually accomplishing something useful.

I could also ask Mrs. Frist if she knew who lived in the house next door. And who might have died there.

Chapter Eleven

One benefit of my indecisive grocery run was that I could slap together a sandwich at my office and call it lunch. As I hastily gobbled it down, I realized that I was ravenous. Probably not just from the morning's hard labor, but a deficit from derelict eating from the past few months. With the routines of my life stripped away, the mundane details had become unmoored—cooking, meal times, going to the grocery store.

Before Katrina, Cordelia and I usually had dinner at six or seven, depending on when she got home. I cooked more often than not, as I had greater latitude in my schedule. It was easy for me to do a quick run by the grocery store on my way home and start the meal prep. Often I'd make enough for another lunch or dinner. She pitched in with cleaning up and, on weekends, would putter in the kitchen trying out some new recipe. I tended to throw things together, making it up as I went along, which meant that I stuck more with what I was familiar with. Cordelia liked to experiment; sometimes it was scrumptious and sometimes we ended up eating out.

But those routines were gone. In the meantime, I'd done little to replace them with anything like a regular meal schedule. If I noticed I was hungry, I'd grab whatever was handy, anything from a candy bar at a gas station to an MRE—Meals Ready to Eat, the military packets designed for eighteen-year-olds out in the middle of nowhere fighting bad guys—mega salt and calories. Various aid organizations had been handing out food. If you were lucky, you'd stumble across some locals brewing up a big pot of red beans and rice. Or you'd have volunteers from Indiana cooking up what they were calling jambalaya, and you knew it'd taste like the only spices they'd ever encountered were salt and pepper and those had to be used sparingly so it turned into a big pot of soggy rice with a few unidentifiable things thrown in. But it was food, and bad food versus no food made bad food a winner.

I'd spent the last month waking up without a clue what I'd eat that day.

I stopped at a desolate stop sign, no one else was around. For a moment I stared at the bright sunshine filtering through a surviving tree. I'd stopped making decisions, except when I had to. The friend of a friend who'd let me stay at his apartment in San Francisco was coming back, so I had to leave. That's why I came back.

Now that I'm in New Orleans, I can't decide whether to go or stay, but I'm doing nothing to head in either direction. Except not leaving. I'd been here just over a month and hadn't decided about anything except to get up in the morning and deal with whatever needed to be dealt with to get through the day until I could go to bed.

I had lingered at the stop sign long enough. I needed to at least finish this case.

Make decisions, I told myself as I passed the long blocks of ghost houses. Nothing is written in stone. I can always unmake any decision, but having some direction and activity to my life had to be better than remaining in this stagnant limbo.

Alex, in one of our phone conversations, had been untactful enough to outright suggest that I was depressed. I, of course, had denied it. My house hadn't flooded; I had no right to be anything but gleefully joyous.

She and Joanne had eight feet of water in their home and, more tragically, Alex was almost two months pregnant when Katrina hit and had miscarried. It was the second time and I didn't know if they'd try again.

So, of course I wasn't depressed. I just couldn't make a decision other than which piece of bread to slap the peanut butter on and whether I wanted grape or strawberry on the other slice. I hadn't even bothered to set up the computer in my office, had only taken the one not-very-well-paying case because Mrs. Frist had called out of the blue (her grandson was a bartender at the Pub, knew my cousin Torbin and he passed my name along), and didn't know how I'd pay next month's bills.

Danny and Elly, Joanne and Alex, and Torbin and Andy had all called, wanted to get together, but I somehow couldn't find time in my busy schedule of peanut-butter decisions to get back to them or actually set up a time to meet them.

It seemed an impossibly long trip to go uptown to get mail or groceries, let alone cross the Orleans Parish line into the unflooded world on the other side of the 17th Street Canal. So the things I needed, like a new surge protector for my new computer at the office, remained unbought. And until I bought that I couldn't set up the computer, and if I couldn't set up the computer, then I couldn't do any work. And if I couldn't do any work, then I needed to distract myself contemplating strawberry or grape to go with the peanut butter. Wait, I hated grape jelly. Why was that even a possibility? Oh, yeah, I'd bought it at some mini-mart because it seemed a more nutritious foodstuff than marshmallows.

I'd started drinking again.

No, I'm not depressed. Not at all.

Finally a working stoplight. It was a new one. It hadn't worked yesterday. As small as it was—and as minor as it would have been anywhere else, a stoplight was out and it was fixed—this tiny sign of progress cheered me. The world could be restored. One stoplight at a time.

As I drove back to my office, I started a mental to-do list. Nothing too radical—the first thing on it was eat lunch. But today it would be something vaguely decent, a turkey sandwich, an apple, whatever was in my office that best hit the nutrition mark.

Then call Mrs. Frist. Get her mementos back to her. Try and find out who the dead woman was. She didn't deserve to be lost in the chaos of post-Katrina.

Call my friends. Make actual this date, this place, plans to get together with them.

Admit that I'm falling apart and can't do this alone.

I'd have to see about that one.

Decide what I wanted from Cordelia.

I'd also have to see about that one.

I pulled up in front of my office.

As I climbed the stairs, I glanced at my cell phone. Someone had called. I didn't recognize the number or the area code.

Then I realized the number was vaguely familiar. I quickly scrolled through previous calls.

Nathalie. It could have been Nathan, since the cell phone was technically in his possession, but I was willing to bet that after he'd left it uncharged when it really needed to be charged that she was now the controlling interest.

I unlocked my door.

I didn't want to call her back. Saving a kid whom I couldn't really save wasn't on my to-do list.

Maybe just knowing that there are gay people out there and that we live okay lives would be enough to get her through what would probably be a few years of hell. If she figured out she was gay, life on the farm would be a nightmare—repression, lies, pretending she was someone she wasn't. Hard enough for an adult, let alone a girl barely beyond pigtails. The only thing worse would be admitting who she was. As a child, she had no rights; her parents could send her to anti-queer camp, therapy that would teach her to hate herself—or everyone around her. Or both.

I tossed the phone on my desk. I'd call her back. Later. Maybe tomorrow.

Yes, I'd prepped my larder with turkey slices, whole-wheat bread, apples, and even some yogurt (key-lime flavored—I'd call that dessert).

Lunch beckoned. Then the to-do list. Maybe after that I'd call Nathalie.

After eating, I looked up Mrs. Frist's number.

Four rings, then someone answered, a high-pitched kid's voice. When I asked for Mrs. Frist she responded with a wary, "Who's calling?" I gave my name and then the kid asked, "What're you calling for?"

I wondered what had happened to the family that they had to be so cautious—and what kind of lesson was the child who answered the phone this way learning?

"I'm calling her back," I said.

The child sighed, dropped the phone with a clunk, and then I heard only a TV on in the background for several minutes.

Then someone picked up the phone. "What do you want my mama for?" an adult voice asked.

"I'm not a bill collector," I immediately reassured her. "Mrs. Frist hired me to retrieve something from the attic in her house. I wanted to give her a report."

"You tell me what you need to tell her."

"I'm sorry, I can't do that. Is there a time that would be convenient for her to come to the phone?"

I got another dropped phone and the background TV. Mrs. Frist was probably staying with relatives in Dallas, a daughter, I'd guess. Even the most loving families can be worn by the sudden imposition of mothers, sisters, husbands, their kids, even dogs for a stay that started in disaster and had no foreseeable end. I wondered how many people were in that household and what the unseen, unnumbered cost was.

Finally the phone was picked up, then a breathy, "Hello?"

"Mrs. Frist?" It sounded like her, but tired, worn.

"Yes."

"This is Michele Knight. I found the chest in your attic."

"It's okay?"

"It's okay. The water didn't touch it."

She didn't say anything. The only noise was the background TV and quiet crying.

I gave her a moment before continuing. "The only problem is that it's pretty heavy. It might weigh too much to ship, period, and even if were possible, it'd be expensive."

Again silence on her end. I could almost feel the tumult of emotions—these precious memories, now close, but another obstacle to keep her from them. "Would it be okay for me to sort through it and make smaller bundles that could be shipped? If I can do that, especially if we don't have to ship the chest itself, then I can probably have everything to you in a week."

Another moment of silence. I heard her blow her nose away from the phone, then she came on the line. "That would be wonderful. I don't need the chest. It's probably about ready to fall to pieces anyway. I just want the photos and papers. There are a lot of people I'll never see again in person, but I still want to have their pictures and memories with me."

I had made an old woman happy. Her voice was stronger now, some of the worn tiredness gone.

"Don't mail anything until the end of this coming week," she said.

"They found me a place and we're moving in over the weekend. I'll be out of my children's hair and can find a proper place for things then. The address…oh, I don't even know what the address is. I'll have to get it to you."

By the end of next week, I could easily have everything sorted and ready to mail.

"Do you know who lived next door? In the corner house?" I asked.

"Why? Something happen over there?" She said it like she suspected that something had happened, that it was the kind of house where things were always happening.

"Were you close to them?" I didn't want to just blurt out that a dead person had been found there.

"Close in the neighborly way, gave them tomatoes from my garden, watched the place if they were away, an occasional beer over the fence. It was Jordy and Mae. Jordy's been gone about ten years now. Mae was holding on, but her pressure was bad and she had trouble with the sugar and her kids in and out. But there were too many of them for me to keep track of."

"How many kids did they have?" How many was too many to keep track of when you lived right beside them, I wondered.

"Five of their kids. But Mae had a no-count brother, so his were in and out as well. Then their friends. Sometimes it seemed there were friends of friends of friends. I'd see ten people in the backyard that I'd never seen before.

"Nothing worked out for them. Jordy was always saying that their luck would change, but they were cursed and it never did."

"Cursed?" A strong word from this woman.

"Every plan and hope they had went a different direction. Jordy had a good job for about ten years, then did his back in and couldn't work. Their oldest son got himself killed on a motorcycle. Their daughter Latisha Mae got hooked up with a bad boyfriend, drugs, that kind of stuff. Don't think she used, but he used her to hide stuff and she got busted. Another son went off to the Iraq war—the first one—and came back with a wheelchair and a drug problem. He went in and out of jail until he finally overdosed. The youngest son just made bad choices in women. He kept bringing home white women with teased blond hair, the kind that just set Mae's teeth on edge. I could tell she was barely being polite. He finally ended up with someone fifteen years older than him and already four kids. Mae wasn't too fond of them visiting, said she was glad Jordy passed before it happened. Their other daughter Alma was okay, the smartest one, went to college, then worked on her Ph.D. She was all right, but broke Mae's heart because she liked women better than men."

"That's a lot to happen to one family."

"Why are you asking?"

From her litany, I decided that Mrs. Frist knew them as neighbors; it might upset her to find out that one of them had died, but it wouldn't be a cruel shock. "A church group was there to gut the house while I was about to go into your house, and they found a dead person in there."

"Doesn't surprise me. So many people in and out. I'll bet some of the young ones thought they were tougher than the storm."

"They panicked—the church group, so I went in the house to see what was going on. I was worried it might be someone hurt."

"You saw whoever it was?"

"Yeah. The storm didn't kill her. Whoever she was, she hadn't been there long."

"A woman? You expect men to be foolish and go into a wrecked house, but not a woman. Sad, just another sad bit to this whole thing."

I left a silence, hoping she might fill it.

"Can't be Mae, saw her just the other week. She's up here with her sister, all staying at her niece's place. She's not doing well, probably going to a home. Niece said she's been off her meds since the storm."

"This woman seemed fairly young, dressed in a tailored suit."

"Maybe could be Alma, but she was more a jeans and sweatshirt kind of girl. Naw, she's too smart to go and get herself killed in an old house."

"Do you have any idea how to contact her?"

"No, can't say I do."

"What about Mae?"

"One of those chance things, we ran into each other at the Red Cross place. I gave her my number. She couldn't remember her niece's. If she calls I'll pass it on to you."

She couldn't tell me much more. Maybe when I talked to her later in the week to get her new address, she'd remember something else. I didn't want to push too hard, make it sound like I wanted something I shouldn't want. It was just someone dead to keep me distracted from my life.

As I put down the phone, I glanced at the calendar. Thursday. Tomorrow was Friday. Was that the weekend? Cordelia had said the weekend, but that could be anytime from Friday to Sunday.

I stared at my phone. Call Alex? Joanne? Danny and Elly? It was the middle of the day, they were all busy working.

I glanced at the bottle of Scotch on top of the filing cabinet.

Later.

I made a list of things that I needed and had been avoiding getting. Like the surge protector. What else did I need to get a computer up and going? Mouse pad, wrist guard, compact discs, printer paper. I made a whole list of office supplies. Oh, and an actual desk chair. On a run out to one of the big-box office stores I'd looked at furniture, but couldn't bear to buy one of those cheap plasterboard desks, so I'd just said "fuck it" (very softly, I was out in the 'burbs after all) and left. Then I'd hit the junk stores, found one I liked, but the antique store I'd finally bought a real wooden desk at had nothing resembling a comfortable office chair in my price range. It's tedious, and expensive, to replace all those things you've accumulated over the years.

Just keep moving. I added shipping supplies to the list.

At least most of this is tax-deductible, I told myself as I headed down the stairs.

I again confirmed my suspicion that the suburbs and I don't get along. I swear I have some learning disability that makes me lose all geographic sense when I'm out amidst the chain stores. They all seem alike, all bright yellows and reds, and once I'm out there I'm never sure if the Max Office Store Depot is just beyond the Sprawl-mart or by the Burger Thing.

After some aimless driving and a couple of U-turns I found a place that would provide most of the items on my shopping list.

Of course the minute I walked in, I felt like I had a purple Q branded on my forehead. I was a woman of a certain age, still wearing blue jeans and a T-shirt and shoes not just sensible, but scruffy in the bargain. All the other women in the place had on makeup and hair that seemed such a uniform shade of blond that they could all be auditioning for a revival of the girl singing groups. Only the fifteen-year-old boys wore clothes similar to mine.

But my money seemed to be green enough for them.

When I got back to my office, I had to spend the rest of the afternoon setting up my computer, connecting the printer and actually printing things, connecting to the Internet—so hard, a wire into the phone jack—finding the perfect place to store my new office supplies, including trying out several different locations and putting together the new desk chair and trying as many different seating positions as possible.

It was almost six by the time I was done.

Probably not a good time to call people, since they were likely to be eating or getting ready to eat. I'd call tomorrow.

In the meantime, I knew exactly which slice of bread required peanut butter. And the grape jelly had to go, strawberry preserves only from now on. Disaster be damned, I refused to besmirch my palate with something that came only in jars with cartoon dinosaurs on them. I actually one-upped my dining habits and threw a frozen pizza in the newly bought toaster oven. It seemed a proper christening.

Then I sat at my desk, eating a slightly burned pizza, and wondered what the fuck to do next.

I got up and started to cross the room to get the bottle of Scotch but stopped halfway there.

Going through the contents of Mrs. Frist's chest would be more useful than creating the perfect conditions for one hell of a hangover. I had dismissed that task earlier because I didn't want to drag the chest up the three flights of stairs to my office. And it was too close to Cordelia's arrival for me to take it to the house we shared. Maybe shared? Were about to not share?

But it just occurred to me that I didn't need to bring up the whole thing. I could open it in my trunk, grab a handful, and easily carry it back here.

I turned away from the beckoning siren of the Scotch and hurried downstairs.

The crowbar was still in the trunk of my car, so if the chest was locked that would be my key. While Mrs. Frist had seemed to not care about the chest, I didn't want to damage it more than I had to.

The lid wiggled a little as if whatever was holding it didn't want to put up much of a struggle. I gently tried to lift it, but it moved only half an inch. I tried to find the locking mechanism, hoping it had been built in the innocent era before the advent of credit cards and their lock-picking potential.

The light was waning, a bare remnant of the sunset. But this time I was on my street, familiar ground, with sporadic lights on. And a cell phone that worked if I pointed it west.

Oddly, I couldn't find a lock, almost as if the chest was held closed by secrets inside that didn't want to come out.

The dark is spooking you, I admonished myself.

In the daylight, I could be gentle; in the dark, it was time for the crowbar. However, as gentle a crowbar as I could manage. I shimmied it under the lip of the lid, then slowly put pressure on it. For a moment, nothing happened. Then with a groaning sigh, the ancient hinges of the chest let go. Putting the crowbar down, I lifted the cover. It had been held in place by an odd little spring lock, its catch concealed in the leather binding.

The chest held piles of yellowed paper, old cigar boxes of what I guessed would be photographs. I grabbed a decent armload, closed it and then my car trunk, and headed upstairs to my office.

With the retreating light, the chill was advancing.

I'd plow through this stack for about an hour until I got too cold, then return to the house.

What if Cordelia's weekend included Thursday?

No, she was too practical to extend the weekend that far. For her, weekend was probably Saturday or Sunday.

I could safely spend another night in the house with the reconnected gas and its attendant heat. Maybe Entergy would have the gas restored out here in the next day or two and I wouldn't have to choose between my comfort and my pride.

I headed back upstairs into the light, if not the heat.

First I spread several paper towels over my desk, then placed the stack on them. That would keep anything that fell out from being lost on the desk. Plus if a spider crawled out, it was easier to smash it on disposable paper towels than a desk that would require cleaning.

I poured two fingers of Scotch into a glass, no ice; it was cold enough that I didn't need any. I'd slowly sip it as I sorted through the papers.

On top were report cards, the paper trail of kids going to school. Under the report cards was more evidence of children growing up, crayon pictures that only a parent could love. Baptism reports mixed with vaccination records and school pictures. All the things a mother would want from the days when her children were young and she was the strongest person in the world. I was trying to come up with reasonable piles that didn't sunder events like separating first grade into two shipments.

My fingers were getting cold turning the pages. The Scotch warmed only my throat.

Just a bit more, then you go somewhere warm. I put the papers down and picked up an old cigar box. It contained pictures. Few were labeled, although some I could guess. One of them seemed to include the neighbors and I thought I could pick out Jordy and Mae and their kids, including the boyish Alma. It was really her that gave it away. No one would notice if they knew her day by day growing up, change incremental, but once I saw her picture, my lesbo-gaydar went off.

Or maybe I was completely wrong and this was a Frist cousin, now happily married with three kids. It is so easy to see what we want to see.

My phone rang.

It was a Wisconsin number.

Damn. Missing the first call had been legit. Deliberately ducking out on a scared fifteen-year-old felt too cowardly, even for me.

That didn't mean I needed to be perfectly nice. I answered the phone with, "Hey, honey, I had missed you so damn much. These shit phones, I tried calling earlier but it kept dropping the call. When are we going to get together?"

After a moment of silence, a hesitant voice said, "I'm trying to reach Micky Knight. Is she there?"

Poor Nathalie.

"Hey, sorry, I thought you were someone else. My girlfriend and I have been trying to have an actual conversation with each other for half the day, but our cell phones haven't cooperated." My lie would explain why I hadn't called her back—and it might give her the notion that I led a busy life and my time was limited.

Still timid—or blindsided by the hint of sexuality in my fake reply, she stammered, "This…uh…is Micky Knight, right?"

"Right. It's Knight." I almost added the rest of them—in sight of the bright light in the night, etc. One evening Cordelia and I had gone through every word that could rhyme with our last names. Mine obviously had a lot more possibilities than hers. In the days and weeks afterward, we'd occasionally pop up with another one until it became an in-joke between us. Silly. Endearing. And not something I wanted to think about at all, especially right now.

I continued. "This is Nathalie? What's up? Having indigestion from the too-spicy food? Need some more pizza?"

"Uh…no. The food here is weird, though. What are grits?"

"Lumpy white stuff."

"They don't taste like anything."

"Don't give up on them until you've tried shrimp cheese grits. Done right."

"But that's not what I'm calling about. Grits are okay with enough butter and salt."

She used salt. There was hope for her. Maybe I could sneak some cayenne into her grits next time and really corrupt her.

"I'm calling because something weird is going on," she said.

"Something weirder than coming down to a city destroyed by the worst engineering failure in America history, finding a dead body, and spending the night with a pinko socialist dyke?"

"Uh…yeah. Isn't a dike something like a levee?" she asked, full-earnest Midwestern mode at full throttle.

"D-Y-K-E," I spelled for her. "Slang word for a woman who is interested in other women. That way," I added for clarity.

"Oh." A moment of silence. "You already told me that. Is there a reason you need to tell me again?"

That caught me off guard. Two reasons came to mind—I lived in a pretty liberal, gay world and words like "dyke" were part of my everyday conversation. Or I wanted to scare her off by emphasizing that she was talking to someone who wasn't socially acceptable in her world. Then I decided, fuck analysis. "Context. I was trying to understand what you would think of as weird in this context."

"Okay. Well, I guess 'weird' isn't the best word. Maybe worrisome." She added softly, almost an apology, "I didn't know anyone else to call. The folks back home would tell me I'm crazy or don't know what I'm talking about. Or that I'm trying to get Carmen in trouble. You're the only person I know who might be able to give me useful advice."

"Weird" was the word for it if a Midwestern virgin needed the advice of a Big Easy dyke.

"Tell me what's going on."

"Coach Bob is still in the hospital, so Carmen is trying to be the group leader. But one of the people at the church we're staying at, Mrs. Herbert, is watching out for us, so she really is the one telling us what to do, like organizing going to the house—we're at a different one—and getting us food. So Carmen tries to boss us in other things, little things like who gets to go to the corner store for ice cream, that sort of stuff."

She paused for breath, and I interjected, "Okay, that doesn't sound too weird so far. Petty is all too depressingly normal."

"I'm getting to the weird part. So yesterday after work, Carmen told Nathan to take this package to someone who would meet him out by the Dumpster near the little store we go to. I went along with him—he's so love-struck with Carmen, he'll do anything for her. Well, dufus brother of mine, he drops the package—it was pretty heavy—and some white powder comes out. When we get to the store, the guy he's meeting gets nasty first when he sees me along, so I did a dumb, bored sister act. Then he gets really upset when he sees the tear in the package. Asks us about fifty questions about it, like Nathan could be smart enough to do it on purpose. He finally asked Nathan what this stuff was, and Nathan said Carmen said it was special hypoallergenic laundry detergent. Then the guy laughs a sort of nasty laugh, says that's exactly what it is and that Nathan should be more careful in the future because if any dirt gets in the special hypoallergenic detergent it could ruin it.

"As we were walking back, Nathan blabbed about not getting why someone should be so upset over laundry detergent, even if it was special. That's what Carmen told him it was and he's so sure Carmen wouldn't lie to him."

"What do you think?"

"If Carmen is doing a favor for a friend and getting some fancy detergent to him, why didn't she just take the package herself? And what laundry detergent comes wrapped in plain brown paper?"

"I have to admit that laundry detergent is a little unlikely. Your friend Carmen—"

"Carmen's not my friend."

"I know that," I said gently. "I was being sarcastic. She's no kind of friend. It sounds like she's using Nathan as a mule—a go-between for a drug deal."

"You really think so? I mean, sometimes I go to friends' homes and see stuff like this on TV, but…"

"But never thought it could happen to you. I don't know for sure." I hedged, not wanting to scare the crap out of her. "However, it sounds like something you want to avoid."

"How do I get Nathan to avoid it? He'll do anything she asks."

"Let me think," I told her. I really did need to think this through. Unless it actually was special hypoallergenic laundry detergent, this was a mess. Carmen was old enough to think she was an adult and young enough to think that nothing would ever happen to her, and those two were a dangerous combination, especially in a budding young sociopath like she seemed to be. Nathan and Nathalie were pawns in her game. "I'm still thinking," I said as time passed.

We could just call the cops. But that still might snare Nathan in the mix. It wasn't likely that the Jefferson Parish sheriffs would believe that Nathan was as gosh-darn wide-eyed innocent as he truly was, especially as Carmen would probably be more than happy to pin it on whomever she could. In the scheme of things—post-Katrina New Orleans scheme, that is—a small-time drug deal was hardly worth bothering with. They were still searching houses for bodies.

I finally admitted, "I need time to figure this out."

"Okay. What should I do?"

"Only touch laundry detergent that advertises on TV."

"I try to avoid doing anything Carmen asks me to. What about Nathan?"

How could I tell this innocent girl that at times people fall and you can't catch them? No matter what Nathalie did, Nathan might go along with Carmen, might get caught up in the dangerous games she was playing and go down with her, even instead of her.

"Try and keep him busy, volunteer the both of you for any time-consuming task that comes your way. If he's doing something it's harder for her to ask him to do something else." It wasn't great advice. Maybe there wasn't any great advice available.

"Okay. I'll try. He won't like that."

I started to say that he'd like it better than going to jail, but that seemed too stark for her. "No, he won't like it, but in ten years he'll thank you. Call me tomorrow. Maybe around this time?"

She agreed and we hung up.

Maybe Carmen really believed that her God would protect her. A few prayers and she could get away with dealing drugs. Bibles and bling. Or maybe she was as cynical as any con-man preacher. No, I was willing to bet that she was clueless as to how naïve she really was, that the boyfriend she was cheating on Coach Bob with was using her just the way she used Nathan—except he was getting sex as well. Carmen wasn't that far off the farm for her to play this game. She was blinded by the big city, its neon lights and her hubris. I didn't care if she flew too close to the sun, but I didn't want her taking Nathan, and therefore Nathalie, with her.

I blew on my fingers; they had gotten cold holding the phone. It was time to go home, or at least someplace warm. And to think about Nathalie, a woman who might be named Alma…and what I would do when Cordelia arrived.

CHAPTER TWELVE

I quickly turned up the heat when I got home, then put a kettle on for tea. I'm not a big tea drinker, but it was a night for something warm. I didn't even take off my jacket. There was only a new moon in the sky, and its wan light did little to dispel the darkness that seemed to make the night even colder.

I added some rum to the tea—I was in for the night—all the better to warm me. Sipping it slowly, I considered what I needed to do. First off was Nathalie. As much as I didn't want to be involved with her, I couldn't just walk away. She was right; she didn't have anyone to turn to. The people in her background would think she was hallucinating if she accused one of the church "elders," albeit a young, foolish one, of being involved with drugs. Jaded as I was, I had no problem believing it.

No immediate solution came to mind. Next I thought about the dead woman. Somebody was missing her right now. Maybe her girlfriend, her lover was sitting alone just as I was, staring at a blank wall and hoping she'd come in the door any minute—or that she'd at least know what had happened to her, could stop watching the door and hoping.

In the next few days, Cordelia would walk through the door. I didn't know what I wanted. Harder still, I didn't know what she wanted. It was useless to want something I couldn't have. If she didn't want to salvage our relationship, it seemed pointless for me to think about wanting it. I left it there.

Move back to Nathalie. The woman was dead and nothing would

change that, but Nathalie had a big problem that was likely to blow up on her.

I picked up the phone and stared at it. Call Joanne, call Danny. Those were obvious steps in the Nathalie problem. Joanne was a cop, Danny an assistant DA; they could give me a clue as to what Nathan was facing and how best to get him out of it. But I was reluctant to break my isolation—to be asked questions I didn't have the answer to. To see the disappointment if they knew I was thrashing around in the swamp and not doing much to get out.

As if not giving me a choice, the phone rang in my hand. I glanced at the caller ID. Joanne. Giving myself no more time to think, I punched the connect button.

"Hey," she said. "Sorry to be so long in getting back to you—call went right to voice mail and then didn't send a notification I had a new message, so I just got it. What's up?"

"Can you arrest someone out in Kenner?" I asked.

"No. Well, yes, but I'd have to turn him over to the cops out there. It'd be complicated. Is that what you called about?"

"No, I called about a dead body, but now I have a live Midwestern kid possibly involved in a drug deal out in Kenner."

After a moment of silence Joanne said in a tone just cheery enough to be sarcastic, "My, it's been a while since we caught up, hasn't it?"

I explained about the dead body; I explained about Nathalie.

"Damn," Joanne said quietly when I finished. "We were hoping that all the criminals would stay in Houston and Atlanta. Guess they're making their way back."

"What do I do about Nathalie—and Nathan? I doubt that milking cows would prepare them for jail down here."

"Can you have your friend call us the next time they're about to deliver 'special laundry detergent'?"

"I think so."

"I'll get Hutch. We haven't been doing much other than enforcing curfew and helping search destroyed houses. We're due a change of scenery."

"What do you have in mind?"

"A conversation in which we suggest that he desist from using nice Midwesterners when there are enough common criminals—and more arriving every day—who will do just as well."

"Nathalie is supposed to call me tomorrow. I'll set it up with her then." To avoid Joanne asking any questions I couldn't answer, I asked, "What about the body? I talked to a neighbor and she might be someone named Alma Groome."

Joanne sighed, then said, "I don't have to tell you the morgue here was destroyed. They're carting the bodies up to a makeshift one near St. Gabrielle. I probably also don't have to tell you that with hundreds of bodies yet to be identified, one more won't get attention anytime soon. It could be weeks—or longer—before we even know how she died and who she is."

"She was dressed in drag and I think I saw her in a snippet of a video of a drag performance."

"Where did you see the video? Maybe we can get a copy?"

I hesitated. If I said I didn't remember, she'd know I was lying—and assume that I was drinking. If I told the truth, she'd assume that I was in the bar drinking. With no way to win, I went with the truth. "I think it was at the Pub."

Joanne was silent.

This is why I fucking didn't want to talk to my friends. They were holding it together somehow; I wasn't and I didn't need their disapproval and judgment.

"You were out in the bars?"

"I was checking out drag-king acts."

"Drinking?"

I was silent. Then defiant. "Yeah, why the fuck not?"

I heard Joanne take a deep breath, then she said, "Look, you get another month or two of falling apart. Okay? Then we're going to sit down and have a long talk."

That was it? I'd been preparing for fire and brimstone, secular style. Then I had to ask, "How the hell are you holding it together?"

"I was here. I didn't have to worry about anyone," she answered quietly. "I knew our house was flooded. I could move on while the rest of you had no idea of whether to hope or despair."

"Joanne, you went through hell staying here in the city."

"But I knew Alex had left and she would be okay—while she could do nothing but worry about me." Then she added, "And I don't know that I'm okay, I still wake up and it takes a moment to realize what bed I'm in and where. We're safe, even the cats are back with us." With their house flooded, Alex had ended up in Houston until about two weeks ago. Joanne, with the NOPD, had floated around to wherever a place to stay was, from a converted cruise ship docked on the Mississippi to a hotel out near the airport to a friend's house on the Westbank. Danny and Elly lived in a double shotgun house; their tenant wasn't returning, so Joanne and Alex had taken the apartment on the other side of the house.

She continued. "And...sometimes you wonder how you'll do when things are hard, when you're really tested. Will you fall apart? Hesitate? Freeze? I found out. Doubt I'll win any hero awards, but I stopped the bad guys when it was needed, didn't hesitate to wade into water that I had to swim through to help someone. I don't have to wonder anymore."

"I don't have a right to fall apart," I said.

"According to whom?"

"Me, I guess."

"Not a good authority on the subject. Call me tomorrow, set up the thing out in Kenner. And, Micky, drink enough to get through to high ground, not enough to drown yourself."

Then Joanne was gone. I felt both comforted and ashamed after talking to her. Comfort from hearing her voice, knowing that she was my friend even if I wasn't perfect. And ashamed because I wasn't the hero she had been.

It was time to go back to the bars and see if I could see a fleeting face in a video again.

CHAPTER THIRTEEN

But the bars had only the same desperate and bored people in them, some of the faces changed, but their needs the same. The only thing I found that I was looking for was enough Scotch to blur the edges and give me enough of a buzz that I easily stumbled into bed and fell asleep.

In the morning, after aspirin and a full bottle of water to flush out what I'd taken in, I started cleaning the house. It was Friday; Cordelia might be here sometime this afternoon or evening. I intended to make sure there was nothing like an unwashed dish or dusty floor to distract her from her guilt. Or maybe I just wanted to be a nice person on the way out the door. Or maybe there was so much chaos in every step of every day—no stoplights, no mail delivery—that I couldn't bear any more? Why the hell couldn't I figure this out?

The booze sleep had been deep and short, waking me early enough that I was done cleaning by about noon. I didn't want to hang around the house. The one thing I had figured out that I wanted was to not be here when Cordelia arrived.

I had found out a lot of things about Mrs. Frist and her family from the box in the attic. Maybe the house where the dead woman was held similar secrets. Could you break in and enter a house that the storm had already broken and destroyed? I wouldn't steal anything—except maybe family secrets not meant for outsiders. I could use the same excuse I had for Mrs. Frist's house—could even act like I'd gotten the address wrong if it came to that.

I packed up everything. Even though it was cold and the gas to Bywater still hadn't been restored, I wasn't planning to stay here again.

Then I headed out to that deserted neighborhood, hoping the bright sunshine would keep the spirits away.

But the sunlight couldn't hide the despair of the empty blocks. I drove past other areas that were beginning to show signs of life—a work truck, someone in gloves and dust mask visible through the broken windows. But no signs of movement and hope were here. Maybe, like Mrs. Frist, this was a neighborhood of older people, too old, disabled, poor to have a hope of recreating what they had had.

I parked in front of the house on the corner, mine the only car about, save for the watermarked wrecks. No sound of cars in the distance even.

The church group, then the cops, and maybe the same burglars I had surprised had all saved me the need for a crowbar and breaking down the door. Someone had been kind enough to prop the destroyed door closed to give the house the veneer of security. I gently pushed it aside, sweeping the inside with the beam of my flashlight. A vestige of yellow crime tape fluttered in the wind, but most of it was gone. The entryway mud showed overlapping footprints, multiple people in and out here.

I slowly made my way in, the bright sunlight muted in the interior. The chaos of the water was clear—a heavy couch that would have taken several men to lift thrown against a wall, other furniture tumbled and tossed about. Cards, CDs, a doll, all embedded in the mud.

I looked at the place where the woman had lain. She had been on top of the layer of muck, not clutched in it, another indication that she wasn't killed by the storm. I carefully looked around the room and could see no signs of a struggle—the dried mud would have easily shown the marks of a scuffle, heavy steps, someone pushed. The footsteps leading in were a trample and maybe the fight had been short and the tell-tale marks were lost in the crisscross of boot imprints. Odd as it sounds, it seemed the chaos of the room was from the storm, not her death. The dust and mold seemed undisturbed, no grabbing hand streaking the mold on the couch or etching in the dust that covered everything. I used my flashlight to closely examine the entryway. The mark I found was buried under the other footprints, but could be from someone being dragged in, heels scuffing the floor from a dead weight hauled in and hidden behind a pile of furniture.

I crossed the room to the back wall, again carefully playing my flashlight over the floor and surfaces. There were two footmarks where someone would have stood if he—or she—had dragged the body to where it was found. One set of footprints came to almost where I was, but then stopped and turned around—coming in, they indicated the person was walking. Going away, heavier indentations that were farther apart, as if the person was running. Were they disturbed? Looking for something? Or just spooked by a random noise?

If she hadn't been killed here, why was she brought here? To be recognized by the neighbors? Assuming that this was the daughter of the next-door neighbors. Or to be hidden in a destroyed city overrun with dead bodies? Would a couple of weeks of decay make it hard to tell her from the corpses left by the storm?

My journey here had only given me more questions. It was time to look for answers.

I wanted to find something that could tell me who the dead woman was. Did she belong to this house, this land, or had she been left to die a stranger in a strange place?

People's lives leave paper trails. I had to see if Katrina had left enough for me to find. Nothing on this level would have survived. From the outside, the house looked like it had an upstairs. Little light entered the center hallway, but my flashlight found the stairway. I carefully swept the beam along the stairs. One set of footprints went up and the same came back down. They seemed to be old, deeply imprinted in the mud as if made when it was still soft. The sole impression was from a practical boot, something a rescue worker might wear. I was wearing my ratty old sneakers.

I paused to listen before mounting the stairs. Someone had died here and perhaps the reason she died was somewhere in this house. I carefully climbed the stairs, matching my footsteps to those of the rescuer, so it would be unclear that another person had been up these steps. Even if this house had nothing to do with the murdered woman, I was breaking and entering.

The muck and debris ended just below the top step. The mold had found its way beyond the waterline; the walls were covered with the familiar random patterns of green and gray.

The first room was a bathroom, unchanged since August, towels still hanging on hooks near the tub. It would have been normal if I could believe the mold was just a pattern on the towels and wall.

But I wasn't here to check what shampoo they had been using. I turned away from the bathroom.

What was I really here for? I had no business, other than coincidence and curiosity, to investigate this woman's death. The best reason was some inchoate desire to fix something that had been broken by the storm, give her relatives the stark mercy of knowing what had become of her. The other reasons were to avoid my own life, my own problems, to use someone else's tragedy as a crutch to get through my days.

I caught a glimpse of myself in a hallway mirror. For a moment, my face appeared as haunted as any of the ghosts I imagined here, eyes a pool of need and fear. Then I banished that image, which was a reflection of the distorted light, spider lines of mold on the glass. It was just the same face I'd seen every day—a little older, more gray in the hair than I remembered. It was still mostly black, a mess of curls that needed a haircut, another daunting task in post-Katrina New Orleans. I was tall enough that the top of my head disappeared into the mirror frame. I'd lost weight, my cheekbones and eye sockets verging on emaciated. No, that was the light and the dark circles from lack of sleep. My figure had always been on the boyish, even skinny side. Eyes brown, no, almost black now as if they contained too much sorrow to allow color anymore. Olive skin that the light made appear sallow. For a moment the face went from familiar to someone I didn't know. Was it me or a gaunt, haunted stranger?

It ends here, I vowed, turning from the mirror. I'd play out this folly, search the house, likely find nothing, then I'd leave this woman where she properly belonged, with those whose dispassionate job it was to track the lost souls of the storm.

I passed the mirror without looking at it again. The two rooms at the back of the house were bedrooms. One was used, the bed hastily made, a glass of water, face cream, an alarm clock all next to the bed as if someone would come back and sleep here again this evening. I quickly glanced through the closet, but could see only clothes. The second bedroom seemed to be set up as a guest bedroom, the bed neatly made, devoid of anything that seemed to expect someone to come home to this room. Its closet held spare pillows and blankets, some heavy coats for the few cold days that came every winter.

I went back into the hall, again passing the mirror without looking at it. The first room at the front end of the hall was a sewing or craft room. It had several work tables covered with projects ranging from finger paints for the youngest generation to a half-finished hand-embroidered piece that took obvious skill and patience. But as I looked closer, I could see the mold weaving its way into the piece. A few more months and it would be entombed in gray and green. I started to pick it up, to save something from the slow destruction of decay that was following the swift destruction of the water. Then I stopped—what would I do with it? So much was lost, could one little piece matter?

The last room in the front was an office, cluttered with bookshelves, a desk piled with paper. Oddly, there was no computer. Perhaps they didn't use one, or had a laptop that had been taken on the evacuation. If I was going to find anything, it would be here.

I quickly glanced through what was on top of the desk. The usual, a stack of just-paid bills and one of bills to be paid. A pile of junk mail to be sorted through. A stack of cooking magazines with scraps of paper sticking out, marking recipes to try. Underneath the magazines was last year's tax return. Then the year before under that. Under that was a thick manila envelope that I assumed would be more tax returns. But across it was scrawled "Alma's shows." It contained a stack of programs, newspaper clippings, and photos. All of them about a tall, handsome woman in men's clothes. "A historically accurate representation of women of the 19th century who made their living on the stage dressed as men," one of the blurbs read. As I looked at the pictures, I realized that she was dressed in male clothes more appropriate for the 1880s. I stuffed the contents back into the envelope. I could look at them later, but they might tell me who this woman was and why she was dressed as a man.

Wedged between the desk and the window was a file cabinet. I started to search for a key, then remembered to try the easy route first. It wasn't locked, like everything else in the house, expecting the occupants to return soon. The top file contained stacks of neatly rubber-banded bills and about ten years' worth of old tax returns. I guess the Groomes didn't mess with the IRS. The second drawer, as if echoing the desk, held older copies of cooking magazines and cookbooks.

The third drawer held dusty sports trophies and ribbons, the cheap plastic coming apart from the wood, perhaps too many memories to throw away, but too tattered to proudly display.

The bottom drawer was crammed full of even more cooking magazines, yellowed bills, the leftovers stuffed down here. I flipped through them, more yellow paper and dust and spider tendrils of the mold that would take over soon. I started to close the drawer, then spotted a file folder in the back, the newness of some of its papers a contrast to the yellow of everything else in the drawer. In a very neat handwriting, obviously different from the person who wrote on the other envelope, were the words Historical Research. I pulled out the file.

It held a number of property records, some of the copies of deeds decades old. In back were two sheets of typed paper, a narrative of sorts. I read, "History holds secrets. Should have had money, but for an illegal marriage, and our great-great-grandmother kept from her inheritance."

A car door slammed.

I broke off from reading to look out on the street. A large dark SUV had just pulled up in front of the house. Two men, one in a black trench coat, a black baseball cap, and dark sunglasses, and the other in a hooded sweatshirt and mirrored glasses, got out.

The broken windows—and their seeming assurance that no one was around so they spoke in normal tones—let me hear what they were saying.

"Fucking amateurs. Didn't do one fucking thing you were supposed to do," the taller one growled.

"We got it dumped here," his shorter companion said in a tone that he might have used to defend taking the garbage out on the wrong night. "It was dark and late and somethin' was moving out there."

"Yeah, and you left her the one place you weren't supposed to leave her. And didn't get the shit you were supposed to get. Now I gotta fucking clean up after."

Silly me, I had been worried about the owner or some authority finding me doing a little breaking and entering. I had not considered that the killers would come back to the scene of the crime in a coincidence of incredibly bad timing.

"You get spooked by a friggin' raccoon," the taller one continued. "Then that goddamned church group finds the fucking body. So they bail. Ya think the john works in this place? I came here so quick I didn't even have time to pee afore I got off the plane."

"You can piss here all you want. Can't fuck it up worse."

They were coming up the steps to the front door. I had a minute or two to find some way to avoid them. Lifting my sweatshirt, I stuffed the file folder and envelope into the waistband of my pants then pulled the shirt back over them. The best plan I could come up with was to wait for them to enter the house, then jump out, hope I landed without breaking anything, and run like hell for my car. They both had beer bellies; maybe they weren't in the best of shape.

"You stay out here and keep a watch," the taller one said.

My best plan wasn't looking so good.

Plan B. The attic? A glance out in the hallway revealed that the attic door was in the ceiling. I'd need a ladder to get to it. I ran as quietly as I could to the bedrooms in back. Maybe I could drop down from those windows. Cement patio below them. Then I saw a drainpipe within reach.

I heard the front door being pushed aside and used the noise to cover opening the window. The explosive wind had partly shattered it, half of it gone, so the other half was loose enough in the frame for me to shimmy out. I grabbed the drainpipe, using it to steady myself until I was standing on the window sill.

I heard footsteps on the stairs.

While I wouldn't put money on their IQ being in the rocket-science range, they probably weren't stupid enough to miss the feet on the window sill and the body attached.

I could reach the roof with my hand, but I wasn't twenty anymore and it would take some luck and energy to heave myself up there—especially given the major time crunch.

I heard a "What's this shit" from inside and something crashing around.

Now or never. I pushed off as hard as I could with my legs, thrust one hand over the lip of the roof, used that hand and the one on the drainpipe to haul myself up. It wasn't elegant, but I somehow managed to get a foot to the top of the window, and that saved me from an inglorious fall.

I was suspended in air, the edge of my foot on the brick framing the top of the window. One hand grasped over the edge of the roof, the other still clutching the drainpipe. My muscles were already starting to scream, just holding myself in this awkward position.

The only way not to fall—and it was pretty iffy—was to lever my body up onto the roof. If I was going down, it might as well be by trying to go up.

I didn't even bother with a count of three—I didn't think I could hold myself much beyond two anyway. I let go of the drainpipe and threw the other hand onto the roof, pushing off with both legs at the same time. I had to give up the bare inch of safety, the window ledge that had been holding me.

The effort got me partly on the roof, my shoulders and chest over the edge, but my hips and legs dangling in the air. There was little to hold on to, save for loose shingles, and gravity was not on my side. I was starting to slip back down.

Suddenly, accounting looked like a good career move. Assuming I survived this.

I scrabbled with my feet, trying to get a little more of my weight onto the roof. They skittered uselessly against the slick brick of the house. Then I managed a bare toehold against one of the metal straps that held the drainpipe in place. In a second bit of luck, I found a hole in the damaged roof and grasped its edge with my fingers. Those two slight holds were enough for me to hoist the rest of my weight over the edge and to safety.

The patron saint—or sinner, I wasn't particular at this point—of wayward detectives was watching out for me.

Sort of.

"What the hell was that noise?" someone shouted from inside the house.

Admittedly sound control hadn't been at the top of my agenda.

"Probably a rat, they're all over the place," the other voice answered.

"Take a fucking look out back. I hate rats. Shoot if you see a skinny tail."

I didn't have a skinny tail, but shoot might apply to a person on top of the house who wasn't supposed to be there. That would be me. I heard the stomp of feet as one of them crossed to the back of the house.

Being as quiet as I could—and hoping their noise would mask mine—I crawled to the peak of the roof.

The back door slammed open.

I rolled over the apex just in time to see the top of someone's head out in the backyard. I ducked below the apex of the roofline, hoping that if I couldn't see him he couldn't see me.

"Bunch of tree limbs down out here. Probably one of 'em finally fell," he called to his fellow thug.

On this side of the roof, I was easily visible from the street, unless by some unprecedented streak of luck they never looked above their navels.

"I can see how we got spooked," called the thug in the backyard. "It's a fucking mess out here. Could be hundreds of bodies all ready to turn into zombies."

"Ain't no fucking zombies. Now get back in here and help me find the stuff."

"Okay, but let's make this quick. Not a good place to hang around."

"If you'd help, it'd be quicker. I just spent four hours on a plane, haven't slept a wink since you fucked it up, could barely eat. All I want is to take care of things and get someplace warm with booze and easy girls."

"Don't like it," his friend muttered as he went back in. "Feels like someone is watching."

Listening, more like it. The sun had gone behind a cloud and my sky perch was getting chilly.

I again crossed the peak of the roof, betting they'd have to go out the front door but might not be in back again.

This is not what a private detective usually does. Most of my time is spent reading boring papers, doing Internet searches, talking to people on the phone—basically sitting in a comfortable armchair. I was trying to think of another time when I'd been forced to perch on the top of a house. Nope, this was it, the first. Another new experience I could cross off my list of things I never wanted to be familiar with.

Bangs and crashes were coming from inside the house. From the sound of it, they were determined to finish what Katrina had started.

After a particularly loud crash, I heard a matching loud curse. "I can't fucking find it. It was supposed to be a folder in a file drawer, but everything is fucked up about this. Let's just burn this place down. That should fucking get rid of it."

If they hadn't already overused the word, I'd be tempted to throw in a few "fucks" of my own. I was perfectly content to have only climbing on a roof the extent of my skyline adventures. Roof of a burning house was way out of line.

I wondered if I could imitate a police siren well enough to scare them off? Long shot, especially as the sound would be coming from over their head, not a common direction for a car to arrive.

"Gimme your lighter," the top thug demanded.

"Uh…don't got one. Gave up smoking a couple of months ago," his partner sheepishly admitted.

"How the fuck I'm gonna burn the house down without nothing to start a fire?"

"There's got to be a little store around here. We can buy something."

"The fucking area is a wreck, there ain't no 7-Eleven around here. Even if something opened up, we gonna go in there, buy a light, some gasoline, and hope nobody notices two strange men buying that shit and a house catching fire?"

"We can buy it out somewhere else."

"You wanna work for me, you fucking better start smoking again."

"Okay, okay. So what're we going to do?"

"I'm fucking thinking."

And I was fucking freezing. A steady wind was blowing and doing a good job of sucking every bit of body heat out of me. I was spread-eagle across the roof, which had a pitch steep enough that any other position was precarious, plus I hadn't planned on hanging out motionless outside for—I glanced at my watch—going on half an hour now. New Orleans doesn't turn into the frozen tundra during the winter, but I've had many a northern friend unpleasantly surprised by how chilly forty-five degrees is in a city with high humidity.

If they burned the house down, at least I'd be warm.

"You see if you can find anything in the car. May be some matches there. I'm going out back to take a leak."

At least I wasn't wearing the red shirt I'd almost put on this morning. Instead I had on faded black jeans, a gray sweatshirt over a black T-shirt, and a charcoal jean jacket over that. This game of "dodge roof" was getting to be no fun. I decided to stay on the back side of the roof, aligning my body as much as I could with the top ridge, so maybe I'd look like a pile of debris. I was hoping Mr. Leak would be paying more attention to what was on the ground that might jump up and bite him on his exposed part.

Both the front door and the back slammed at the same time. I wanted to get a look at these men, but it was hard to see them without making it easier for them to see me. I chanced a peek over the top at the one I was thinking of as Mr. Stooge as he headed for the car.

He had pulled his sweatshirt hood back and had light greasy hair—hard to tell if it was light brown or blond covered by dirt—that would have reached his shoulders if he wasn't so stoop-shouldered. Even with a jacket, it looked like the heaviest thing he lifted was a beer can. His chest was slight, and the bulge of a stomach below it indicated that it had seen much couch sitting and imbibing of beverages. I couldn't get a good look at his face; he was turned away from me.

From behind me I heard a stream of something liquid and a contented "Ahhh." Clearly needed, as the leak sounded more like a waterfall.

I slowly and carefully turned my head, keeping all but my eyes hidden in the crook of my arm. Mr. Leak was also turned away from me, which, while not good for getting a decent look at him, did improve my chances of not being seen.

He had the bulk Mr. Stooge was lacking, a big man all around. He probably worked out and then used that to justify the six-pack and pizza with all the toppings afterward. His stomach was broad but so were his shoulders. His hair was dark; what I could see of it under the cap was combed straight back and held with something that kept it from moving even with a gust of wind that threatened to roll me off the roof. He was much better dressed than his companion; the trench coat looked like an expensive one or he had been lucky enough get one to fit him perfectly from off the rack.

"Hey, what the hell is that?" Mr. Stooge yelled from the front.

I had a hand over the top of the roof, needing it to steady me.

"What the fuck?" Mr. Leak yelled from in back, still streaming.

"I found a silver dollar," he shouted back. "Pretty damn lucky."

You and me both.

"I gotta get the fuck out of here," Mr. Leak muttered as he zipped up.

He turned around and I got a good look at him. Big, ugly head, bulbous nose, heavy, sloping forehead, with eyebrows that were a dark line dividing his face in half, a mouth that was too wide and rubbery, leaving his cheeks with little room between his lips and his ears.

Unfortunately, he got a good look at me, too.

"What the fuck? Hey, hey, what are you doing up there?"

My brain stopped working. The only reply it came up with was to claim that I was working on my winter tan. Not helpful. One was in front of me, one in back. Fire or frying pan? You choose.

"What's goin' on?" Mr. Stooge called from the front.

"Someone's on the roof!"

"What the...? There's a dead body on the roof! We were walking under a dead person?" Mr. Stooge shouted back. His zombie panic was returning.

It worked for opossums. I didn't move.

"Hey, hey, you alive?" Mr. Leak shouted.

"We got to get out of here," Mr. Stooge yelled back.

I didn't stir a fraction of an inch, not even an eye blink.

"It ain't moving," Mr. Leak observed.

"'Cause it's dead!" Mr. Stooge shouted back. "I'm getting out of here."

"Hey, asshole, don't you leave me, you fuckwad." Mr. Leak thundered back into the house. I could feel the tramp of his feet vibrating up to the roof as he stomped back to the front.

Mr. Stooge started the car.

"Goddamn it, I said don't you dare leave me, you shit-for-brains," Mr. Leak yelled at him.

I didn't dare even turn my head to watch them. Playing dead has its drawbacks.

A car door slammed, then a car took off with a roar and screech of tires. I lifted my head enough to see them careen around the corner.

Once Mr. Leak got Mr. Stooge calmed down, they'd be back. Mr. Leak was smart enough to know he had to make sure I was really dead—and if I wasn't already, to make sure I transitioned to that state. I had maybe five minutes.

Forget pretty or easy, just hope that nothing is so badly broken that I couldn't get to my car and out of here. I half-shimmied and rolled down the roof, aiming for the corner where the drainpipe was. Maybe I could slide down it, at least break my fall. At the corner of the roof, I scrabbled to slow myself and not just flop over the edge. Using some of the momentum, I slid my legs off the lip. They dangled in the air for a moment, then found the drainpipe. I cupped it with my feet. I didn't give myself time to think, because if I thought about it I wouldn't like how much coming off this roof would probably hurt and that might slow me down.

Grasping the drainpipe as much as I could with two shoed feet, I kept one hand on the roof and grabbed blindly with the other one for the pipe. Gravity was pulling me down; I just had to control how quickly it accomplished that. Or attempt to.

My feet and one hand had the pipe, the other hand followed. And I was going down. Like a scared rat, abandoning ship, I clawed desperately at an impossible hold. For about five feet, I had some grasp of the pipe, braking with my feet, steadying myself with my hands. Then I was falling, managing only to push myself to fall into the grass and not onto the concrete.

I came down on my side, rolling over twice.

Don't even think about it, just get up and run, I told myself. I could see blood on a skinned wrist, and my heaving chest hurt with each intake of breath. But I shoved myself up, a few paces on hands and knees, then using a tree, I pulled myself upright. A few hobbling steps, then a shambling run.

I cut across the next backyard; a tree through the fence gave enough of an opening to shove through. Across that yard, then wiggling through another damaged fence. A nail added to the blood on my wrist. Maybe I'd need another tetanus shot just to be sure. This let me out on the street where my car was parked. It was half a block down.

Keep moving, I told myself as I stumbled over a fallen tree limb.

In the distance, I heard the sound of a car engine.

It wasn't a sprint, but it was as near to one as my painful body could manage. I had to get to my car.

A quarter of a block more. The approaching car engine was closer.

Did I really have to park this far away? My breathing was heavy, making it hard to hear anything beyond the rasping in my ears. I shoved my hand in my pants pocket, my cold fingers fumbling with the keys.

Don't drop them, I thought as they snagged on a loose thread.

I stumbled the last few feet, falling against my car, careening off the rear fender to the driver's door just as my finger finally found the open door button on the key ring. The click of the lock was astonishingly welcome.

I threw myself into the car, then shoved the key into the ignition without even getting the door shut.

I heard the sound of two car doors slamming.

Then someone shouted, "What the fuck? It's gone. The body is gone!"

"A zombie?" probably Mr. Stooge answered.

"No, you shit-fuck idiot. That was a live person!"

I turned the key, threw the car into first, and was already into second gear by the time I managed to close my door.

I blew through the stop sign at the end of the street—there were no other cars around—then the next one. Then I took a screeching left turn, then a right, then another left. Two blocks down I turned again. With this random zigzag pattern, I finally made my way to Elysian Fields, a large enough street to have other cars. I sped past several, then calmed myself enough to blend in with the other traffic.

Instead of heading home, I took the entrance to I-610, heading west, past the merge with I-10 and on out almost to the airport, only exiting at Williams, the next-to-last exit before leaving the city. I doubled back, using the much slower Veterans Highway, with its stoplights and crowded length of everything that could possibly be for sale, from cars to books to burgers. I was so obsessively checking my rearview mirror I had to brake sharply as the traffic in front of me slowed.

As I neared the Orleans Parish line, I pulled into a Burger Thing. I took my time getting out of my car, carefully observing those around me. Partly to look around, partly because I had bruises on my bruises and I was stiff and it was hard to move. Nothing suspicious, no broad-shouldered or stoop-shouldered men about. I pretended to have a hard time deciding on the shake and fries I finally settled on.

A good tail takes patience and cunning. I'd bet those two didn't possess great amounts of either, but I wasn't willing to bet my life on it. I planned to be as slow and methodical as I could before getting anywhere close to where I lived, where they could find me.

What did I know? I hadn't gotten a really good look at either of them, only a brief glance at their car, but no license plate or anything identifying. The conversation I had heard was suspicious certainly, but what could I prove? At best it would be my word against theirs. I wasn't the property owner; in fact, I had been breaking and entering. I could argue that I was doing it for the right reasons, but what were my reasons really? I was putatively pursuing justice for some unknown woman because my own life was so messed up that I'd do anything not to think about it.

I paid for my fries and shake and meandered back to my car.

Why do grease, calories, and salt taste so good?

I looked at what I'd stolen, beside me on the passenger seat. The folder was rumpled and bent from being tucked inside my jacket during my sojourn on the roof. Would it tell me who this woman was? Would it tell me why she died? And even if it did, was there anything I could do about it?

CHAPTER FOURTEEN

Being a good citizen—and not wanting a car that smelled like grease—I got out of my car and threw away the paper wrappings of my afternoon snack. Given that potatoes were as close as I'd been to a vegetable in the last few days, I could almost call it a healthy snack, but everything being relative can only go so far. I used the extra napkins I had snagged to clean up the blood on my wrist, the dirt on my knees. Then I raided the first-aid kit in the glove box and downed three aspirin to help dull the pain and tamp down the inflammation.

My cell phone rang. I was still on the side of the flood wall that hadn't failed, so things worked somewhat better out here. Many of the cell towers had still been blown down, but the buildings and people hadn't been flooded and that made a big difference.

It was a Wisconsin number. Nathalie.

I hesitated for a moment. I'd already had enough adventure for the day. Then guilt kicked in and I answered.

She immediately launched in. "Got to be quick. We're washing dogs and I said I had to go to the bathroom. She talked him into doing it again. Right after we get finished."

Washing dogs? Whatever. "Stall as long as you can. Give me directions to the store. I'll see what I can do." That was all I could promise.

"It's rescue dogs. They need to have oil and stuff washed off them. I volunteered me and Nathan. We have about five more dogs to do," she explained. I guess washing dogs was something that needed to be explained.

She gave me directions to the store—"We meet out back by the

Dumpster"—and said she'd try to stall for at least an hour before they were free to do Carmen's errand.

Not letting my aching body make any decisions, I punched in Joanne's number. The fates were obviously on Nathalie's side as Joanne answered instead of the call going to voice mail. I explained the situation.

"So, we have an hour to go until we play with the drug boys out in Kenner?" she summed up.

"It looks that way. Unless you think it's too risky." My hurt wrist did seem to have an opinion about this.

"Leave the Midwesterners to the drug dealers?"

"I suppose not." I told my wrist—and the rest of my painful places—to shut up.

We agreed to meet in the parking lot of a megastore out in the area, then go in Joanne's car.

So there was nothing to do but drive back out to Kenner. If anyone was tailing me, this would confuse the hell out of them.

I parked at the far end of the lot, the part no decent red-blooded shopper would touch as it was too far to walk toting their precious goods. I had only enough time to take a final slurp from my shake and throw it into a trash can before Joanne arrived. Hutch wasn't with her.

"Where's the big guy?" I asked as I got in her car. Hutch was Joanne's usual partner and about the size of a Saints linebacker, big enough to make most crooks think twice about arguing.

"He couldn't make it." Her terse reply hid more than it revealed.

"He doesn't like me anymore?" The Hutch I knew would have jumped at rescuing naïve teenagers.

Joanne started the car, then said softly, "I didn't think it would be a good idea to bring him along." Hutch had lived near the lake; one partial wall of his house was all that had been left. I'd only seen him once since the storm, at a get-together at Danny's house. He was chugging a big mug of beer when I arrived and his maudlin welcome told me it was one of many. He'd draped himself over me, a long welcome hug, partly needed for him to rebalance himself enough to let go. I'd blown it off as the alcohol and the emotion of reconnecting to someone he'd known before Katrina. One more piece of the familiar returned in the midst of so much that had changed.

"What's going on," I asked as she pulled out of the parking lot.

"Some days he's okay and some days…not so okay."

"How not okay?"

"Blowing up at the little things. Because he can't blow up at the big things. Shaking his fist at the sky won't bring his house back. Drinking a lot. More than I've even seen him. Millie stayed in Houston. She's working there, so that's an extra strain."

He and Millie had lived together forever. They'd never gotten around to getting married, but it was hard to imagine them apart.

"Why didn't you want him here today?" I asked.

"The anger. I was worried he'd be too eager to knock some heads together. Which is something I really want to avoid."

For her to say it worried me. In the past, Hutch had relied on his size to keep things cool—the occasions he fought were rare and unavoidable. Joanne was also smart enough to know that, as much as we wanted an equal world, crooks can be amazingly gender normative and having a big guy with us would have been a major help in dealing with these thugs. For Joanne to leave him behind, she had to be seriously worried.

We're all falling apart.

Joanne pulled into the convenience store. I didn't see either Nathan or Nathalie.

We sat in the car for a minute, then Joanne said, "Go in and get a beer."

"You're encouraging me to drink?"

"Not to drink. Get a bottle. It'll make things seem more mellow than they are. Plus you can use it as a weapon."

"Let's hope it doesn't come to that," I said as I got out.

Only the clerk and one other customer were in the store. I used the shoplifting mirror to keep an eye on the parking lot as I perused my beverage choices. I couldn't see Joanne but could see where Nathalie and Nathan should be coming from.

While I was pondering Piss Light or Piss Regular, I noticed another customer arriving. Central casting had sent a thug wannabe. He looked younger than he was, skinny and slight, trying to be taller with the hood of his sweatshirt pulled over his head. He wore clone thug wear, the black hooded sweatshirt, jeans slung low, and a white T-shirt just peeking out. But his clothes were too new, jeans bought to look distressed, the sweatshirt still a dark black. The tags could have been clipped off the clothes this morning. Cheap mirrored sunglasses completed his look.

His skin was pasty, a scraggly brush of beard trying to grow, but unless he'd shaved an hour ago, it'd be a long time before he'd sprout a real beard. I could see the beginning of lines at the corners of his eyes, putting him in at least his mid-twenties if he was a heavy smoker. Oddly, he had the same sloping shoulders of my earlier thug encounter, almost as if he and Mr. Stooge could be cousins. Or maybe thugs just didn't go in for good posture.

His age interested me. Either he had entered this gig late or he wasn't very good at it. By their mid-twenties, most dealers had worked their way up from the street corner. Or not survived.

I quickly decided on Piss Regular; I wasn't going to drink it and it was cheaper. I paid and left just as he approached the counter with his Piss Lite.

Don't let appearances fool you; even crooks worried about calories can be dangerous.

I sauntered back to the car, going to the driver's side to look like I was talking to Joanne.

Thug Lite took his time buying his beer before he exited the store. He was trying too hard to look casual. No wonder he needed to screw with naïve Midwesterners. They were the only people that could make him look sophisticated and experienced.

I noticed movement at a far street corner, too far to be sure of faces, but a garish green and gold sweatshirt on the taller one suggested Green Bay Packers and that suggested Wisconsin. It's Saints or die down here, so these weren't locals.

I kneeled down, as if to be at Joanne's level, but it also put the car between me and Nathan and Nathalie. He would recognize me and I didn't want that to happen until we'd done what we came here to do.

"They've just rounded the corner," I narrated to Joanne. As they got closer, I was proved right. Nathan in the football sweatshirt and Nathalie in a gray one that didn't seem to need to announce allegiance to anything. Nathan was carrying a package wrapped in brown paper, which he shifted from arm to arm as if it was heavy or awkward to carry.

Thug Lite saw them, too, and started a far-too-conspicuously casual amble toward the back of the store where the Dumpster was.

Joanne didn't say anything, just rolled her eyes. Thug Lite seemed pretty sure that two middle-aged beer-drinking women weren't a worry.

"They're rounding the corner to the parking lot." I continued my drug deal play-by-play.

Nathalie glanced around. I suspected she was looking for me, but I was hidden behind the car and Joanne. Nathan was only focusing in the direction he was going, to the back corner of the building where the Dumpster was.

Two people meeting by a convenience-store Dumpster, one with mirrored sunglasses and one carrying something wrapped in brown paper. Who'd ever guess this was a drug deal?

"They're almost at the Dumpster," I told Joanne.

"Time to close this amateur show down," she replied. She switched from feigning boredom at what I'd been telling her to being a woman of action. She barely gave me time to get out of the way before sliding out of the car in one quick motion. The Dumpster was about ten yards away from us; she covered the distance quickly. I trailed behind.

Joanne stopped just short of the surprised trio. She put her hands on her hips, brushing back her jacket to reveal her gun and badge. "What the hell do you idiots think you're doing?" she demanded.

"Wha…what are you talking about?" Thug Lite stammered out.

"Little Bo Peep could figure out what's going on here. Are you really so fucking stupid to think I'd sit in my car and not notice?" Giving them no time to answer, she grabbed the package out of Nathan's hands, then quickly tossed it to me, keeping her hand far too near her gun for Thug Lite to try anything. "See what's in that," she told me, not bothering to look away from them.

I started to tear the paper.

"Hey, hey." Thug Lite came to life. "You can't mess with that. It's private property."

"Yours?" Joanne growled.

"Uh…well, maybe." He went back to his stammering.

"It's yours if we don't open it, but theirs if we do open it and it turns out to be cocaine or heroin?" Joanne queried, knowing the answer.

Nathan finally chimed in. "It's laundry detergent."

"Are you really stupid enough to think I'll believe that?" Joanne shot at him.

I knew she was playing bad cop, but Nathan didn't.

"It is. It really is laundry detergent," he said in an incredibly earnest Midwestern voice. "It's special hypoallergenic that Mr. Smith here needs."

"And that Mr. Smith can't buy in a grocery store, but has to procure behind a Dumpster. Right." To me she said, "You got it open yet?"

I had ceased tearing open the package to watch the show. I went back to work.

"You're going to be embarrassed when you find out it really is laundry detergent," Nathan said. "Carmen wouldn't lie to me." With that, he crossed his arms for extra emphasis. Of course, the woman he loved wouldn't lie to him.

I ripped open a corner. White power spilled out. Thug Lite, aka Mr. Smith, let out a small groan as it fell to the ground.

I caught a little bit of it on my finger and smelled it. Nope, nothing soapy about this. I dusted most of it off my fingertip, then touched it with my tongue. Alcohol has been my drug of choice, but I've done cocaine a few times. Enough to recognize it.

"Coke," I told Joanne.

"You're wrong," Nathan retorted, still not believing that that woman he loved—well, had a major schoolboy crush on—would lie to him.

"What do you think, Mr. Smith?" Joanne said to Thug Lite. "We can run it into the station, do a proper lab test. Of course, if I have to go to all that trouble, I'll book all of you if it is indeed cocaine." She paused to let that sink in. "But I'm off duty and not in the mood to fill out piles of paperwork. We can just dump your 'hypoallergenic' shit out, let a few pigeons get buzzed on it and you promise to never show your face around here again, and we can all call it a day."

"Ah, shit, man," he muttered.

"You can't do this. Take it in and test it, that'll prove we're right," Nathan said.

Mr. Smith Thug Lite for some reason didn't back Nathan up. "I got places I got to go. It'd be too much of a hassle to run through this."

"This isn't right," Nathan protested.

"If it's detergent, I can't arrest you," Joanne said.

"Naw, naw, I don't got the time." Thug Lite shrugged.

"I'll go," Nathan said.

"Nathan," I said. "This is cocaine. It's not laundry detergent. Maybe Carmen was fooled, too. Or maybe she used you. But unless you want to stay here for another five years or so, depending on parole, let this one go."

"She's right," Nathalie chimed in. "We need to get out of this. Without an arrest record."

He looked from her to me to Joanne to Thug Lite, then to the ground. He just shook his head, but didn't protest again.

Thug Lite gave the bundle in my hand one last regretful look and then scurried away. He clearly wanted distance between himself and a woman with a badge.

"Dump it back there in the drainage ditch," Joanne told me. New Orleans and suburbs—bless its waterlogged location—is riddled with canals and ditches. One was conveniently behind the store.

When I got to the edge of the ditch, I tore open the rest of the package, letting the white powder pour into the water. "Gonna be some coked-out gators here tonight," I muttered to myself as the powder drifted on the sluggish canal.

As I rejoined the group, Nathan continued his protest. "But Carmen wouldn't lie to me." Joanne had been giving them the don't-trust-people-with-special-laundry-detergents lecture.

Nathalie started to say something then stopped, as if knowing that if she criticized Carmen, Nathan would defend her more.

Joanne gave me a look as if to say, "Your turn now, I've been the bad cop for you."

"Nathan," I scrambled for what to say to him that might break the lust bubble, "maybe she was fooled as well. But if so, all of you are giving new meaning to wide-eyed and naïve. And even if Carmen thought it was laundry detergent, why did she send you to fetch and carry for her?"

"She has other things to do," Nathan said in her defense.

"So important she couldn't take a fifteen-minute walk?" I noted. "Maybe she didn't know it was drugs, but I'll bet money I can't afford to lose that she had some inkling it wasn't special hypoallergenic laundry detergent. You're just blindly besotted enough with her to do whatever she wants, and what she wanted was to make sure she didn't have her hands on this in case something went wrong."

"Micky is right," Joanne said. "You both got very lucky this time.

It really doesn't matter what your friend knew—you both ended up in a dangerous situation. If the threat of being arrested isn't enough to make you keep your noses squeaky clean, consider this. There are a lot of desperate drug dealers in the area. A number of them lost all their dope in the flood and FEMA won't cover their losses. They're out the money, and their suppliers are out the money. Many lost their usual territory and they're horning in on other locations. Desperate people and guns aren't a good combination. You're risking getting shot and killed."

Nathalie had enough sense to look pale at Joanne's words.

"But we're from Wisconsin," Nathan said, as if enough dairy cows should be a protective shield. "It's not possible that we're here less than a week and involved in a drug deal. That only happens on TV."

"It happens on TV because it happens in real life," I pointed out. "Only real life doesn't have a scriptwriter to make sure innocent Wisconsinites don't get killed."

He turned to Nathalie. "You told them, didn't you? You messed it all up. What am I going to tell Carmen?" He was upset and taking it out on her.

"She didn't tell us." I lied, jumping in before Nathalie had a chance be the nice Midwestern girl she was. "Joanne and I are working on something else out here—and in one incredible piece of luck we stumbled over what was going on here. Lucky for you."

"I don't believe that."

It was a pretty obvious lie, but he had fallen for cocaine as laundry detergent, so I figured my odds were good.

Suddenly I was tired of his immature churlishness. "Believe what you want," I said tersely. "Believe that it was fairy dust in that package and believe that Miss Carmen is Glenda the Good Witch. The reality is that you're a naïve idiot who was duped into being a mule for drug runners. You're damn lucky it was me and Joanne and not the local cops, and more than damn lucky it wasn't some rival gang getting rid of the competition."

"What am I going to I tell Carmen? She'll be mad at me."

The experts are right; boys mature more slowly than girls. Nathan was living in his self-absorbed world. He had the raging hormones, but no brain power to keep them in perspective.

"Tell Carmen you won't let her use you anymore," I suggested.

"I was doing her a favor. She wasn't using me," he replied hotly.

"Tell Carmen you won't do anything that might get you arrested or killed. Even as a favor."

Even my amended suggestion didn't get to him. "Why should I trust you over her? She's part of our church. Who are you? Some deviant locals? Just because my stupid sister thinks she likes you doesn't mean I should. How do I know you're not the rival drug lords you're claiming to warn me about?"

I told myself that I needed to be more mature and rational than he was. Really I did. But the part of me that was getting more pissed by the second at this idiot boy and what I suspected was a healthy dose of sexism—his sister is stupid, we're just women—took over.

"You can tell he's been home-schooled—he has the IQ of the cows he tends," I said to Joanne, but with every intent that he would hear. Then to him, I said, "A rival drug dealer would not dump thousands of dollars of cocaine into the water. And I guess it just can't get through that cow-dung-encrusted head of yours that you just got your butt saved big-time. You're not arrested, you're not dead. Your sister, who you dragged into this, isn't dead either. No, the only thing that can rattle around in your head is whether or not the woman who is contemptuously using you will be upset."

"She's my friend! And I'm not stupid. You're the stupid ones here." He crossed his arms and glared at me.

My outburst made me feel better, but it obviously wasn't the best method for ripping the blinders from Nathan's eyes.

"She's right, Nathan," Nathalie ventured. "We could have been in big trouble, hurt or arrested."

He turned on her. "Shut up!"

I wanted to take Nathalie by the hand and lead her away, to rescue her from her ignorant brother and rigid family. But that wasn't possible. She was a minor and I was a stranger in her life.

"Nathalie," I said. "Next time he wants to be an idiot, let him go. If he can't learn, you can't risk the consequences." That was all I could do. "Let's get out of here," I said to Joanne. I wanted to grab him by the collar and shake some sense into him. But that wouldn't work. It would take months and probably years for him to understand how Carmen was using him, and maybe his ego was so small and his defenses so high that he'd always think she liked him and he did favors for her.

I turned from them and headed back to the car.

Nathan taunted us as Joanne followed me. "I want your badge number."

It seemed that she was as tired of him as I was. I heard her stop and turn to him. "You want my badge number? I'll give it to you. When I give it to the Kenner police as they arrest you for felony possession of cocaine."

"Let's go," Nathalie urged him.

Maybe he had enough sense to not continue the fight, or maybe he used her request as an excuse to get out of a fight he couldn't win.

We walked stiffly back to the car, obstinately not looking back at them.

"Well, that worked out well," Joanne muttered as she opened her door.

I kept silent until I was seated. "You really think so?" I asked, obnoxiously jolly. "I think it sucked just about as much as it could suck."

In an annoyingly calm voice, she said, "Can't call it a happy ending. But I don't know what we could have said that would have made the boy see the light. He's lost in love."

"And we're just two old ladies trying to take the joy out of life." Then I muttered, "Sexist pig."

"Certainly a boy who hasn't been given many lessons in respecting women."

"His sister is stuck in that family."

Joanne started the car. As she pulled out of the parking lot she said, "It's better now than when we were growing up. We survived."

"Some of us did. Some of us didn't."

I was upset and angry. Angry at the world that held so few places for young girls like Nathalie. And angry at myself for having done so little to make it better for her and perhaps making it worse.

"Don't make it harder than it is," Joanne said as she merged into the traffic on Veteran's. "We did what we set out to do, get them out of being used as drug gofers. No one got hurt or arrested. Including us. Maybe once things cool down, some sense will creep in. Even if he remains clueless, his sister—"

"Nathalie, she has a name."

"Nathalie may decide she's not her brother's keeper. She's going to have to learn one of life's hard lessons one day—that you can't stop people from making mistakes and wrong choices. No matter how much you care for them." Joanne pointedly glanced at me, as much as the insane traffic allowed.

I looked down at my hands. They were empty. Only a cut from my earlier adventure on the roof justified my scrutiny.

Finally I said it. "You think I'm fucking up?"

Joanne was quiet, then replied. "It's not easy to cope with everything that's happened, but alcohol and isolation don't seem like the best answers."

"Well, this is turning out to be a really fucking cheery day."

"What do you want me to do? Just ignore what's in plain sight?"

"What the hell?" I exploded. "This is all my fault? My girlfriend cheats on me after years of preaching monogamy? A fucking hurricane rams into levees anchored in slippery clay and our city goes under? Why did you 'ignore in plain sight' that Cordelia was running around on me? Why is she still the saint and I'm the bad guy?"

Joanne turned into the mega parking lot where we'd left my car. "I'm not saying anyone is a saint. Or a sinner. You're both falling apart and you need each other."

"She didn't fucking need me," I spat back.

"She does now."

"Yeah? Maybe I don't need her anymore." Maybe I didn't need my heart ripped in half again.

"Micky, she was wrong, okay? But she spent a week in Charity Hospital in hellish conditions. Can't you at least love her enough to help her through this?"

We were at my car. Joanne put her hand on my arm, as if to keep me long enough to get an answer.

I didn't have one. "I don't know. I'm not sure I can help myself, let alone anyone else."

We sat in silence. She finally took her hand off my arm, as if acknowledging that, for the moment, I had no better answer.

As I started to reach for the door she said very quietly, "Alex is... is not doing well. I'm worried about her."

"What's going on?" Alex had evacuated, first staying with an uncle in Baton Rouge, but he was to the right of Attila the Hun, so it wasn't a happy family reunion, especially given that she was pregnant. Miscarrying only made it worse as her Red Stick branch of the family was so rabidly anti-choice they berated her for letting the stress of Katrina affect her pregnancy. As soon as she was well enough to travel I picked her up and we ended up spending a week or two together out in San Francisco. We had managed to distract ourselves, away from the ruins of the city, but she'd left to go to Houston, to be closer to Joanne. Joanne, like Cordelia, had stayed during Katrina.

I had lingered in San Francisco, spinning through what I should do with my life—return? Start again elsewhere? Not deciding finally became a decision. I came back here because I had nowhere else to go. Alex and I kept in contact, although not with the frequency we had right after Katrina. I had to admit that I hadn't spoken or e-mailed her in over a week. Before that she and Cordelia had been close, friends since high school, and usually when we got together, Joanne and I talked shop, and she and Cordelia went their own way. That had changed with the flood and levee failures. Alex and I had gotten out, watched our city destroyed on TV. Joanne and Cordelia had remained, and those searing experiences had bonded us in different ways.

Joanne answered slowly, as if searching for words that wouldn't open wounds, "She seems…lost. Doesn't talk much."

"That's not like Alex."

"No, it's not. It's hard to get her to do anything, she seems listless. She's pretty much given up looking for work." Alex had worked for the city promoting culture and tourism, but her job had vanished in the first round of budget cuts. Half the population meant half the taxes.

"You think she's depressed?" I asked. Takes one to know one.

"I talked to her about going to a therapist."

"She say no?"

"She said she'd think about it. But there aren't many therapists left. And we're struggling to pay COBRA to keep her insured as it is. Even if we could find someone good, I'm not sure where the money would come from."

"What can I do?"

"Don't become another casualty."

"Can we stay with something within reason?"

Joanne managed a wan smile. "Catch yourself before you fall too far. Is that too much to ask?" Then, as if it was, she said, "Call Alex. See if you can get her out of the house and moving forward. Or just moving. Phone me every once in a while so I know you're still here."

"Keep in mind that cell service is still crap. If I'm not pointing west with the wind from the right direction, I can't get a signal."

"Just do it, okay?"

"Okay. I'll call Alex this evening," I promised.

I swung out of the car. Finally. Joanne was right and I didn't want to hear it.

I gave her a quick wave as I got in my car, letting her pull out and away before I started it. You need to get your shit together, I told myself. But that was the last thing I wanted to do. I wanted to howl at the moon and at FEMA and all the bureaucrats who let the levees rot. I wanted someone to take care of me, hold me while I fell apart, someone to make decisions for me since I didn't seem able to make them for myself. Someone to just listen while I talked about cleaning up human shit from a desk that I'd worked at for over a decade, or about there being only a few pilings left of the home where I'd grown up in the bayous.

I wanted Cordelia back. No, I wanted the Cordelia she had been before the storm, before she betrayed me. Did that woman exist anymore? Had she ever? Maybe it was time to find someone who would hold me.

Maybe falling apart together was better than falling apart alone. You take the mornings and I'll take the afternoons. We can flip coins for who gets to be strong and who yowls at the moon on weekends.

In the meantime I had to get myself out of the suburbs and back to civilization.

Maybe you just made a decision, I thought, as I pulled out of the parking lot.

I'd been too numb to realize how lonely I was. I could try to work things out with Cordelia. Or I could try dating in a city that had turned into some bizarre version of the Wild Wild West—nothing worked and everyone was crazy.

Traffic proved the "crazy" assertion right. I was beginning to hate on sight any car with a Texas license plate. A swarm of workers had invaded the area. Even the fast-food places were offering $500 bonuses for staff—if they stayed long enough. So now every other car was someone from somewhere else who didn't have a clue as to where they were going and seemed to think that the best way to get there was either to speed heedlessly or stop in the middle of the street to wait for the street signs to be re-posted.

"They haven't been up for the last ten years. Why do you think they're going to reappear in the next ten minutes," I yelled at a big car with a Tennessee license plate who was stopping uncertainly at every corner down Esplanade. "Pull the fuck over," I muttered at the next corner, where he stopped for a full minute before deciding that wasn't the corner he wanted. Okay, maybe thirty seconds, but long enough for one of the cars behind me to honk.

At the next corner, I honked. Why do they allow people with an IQ too low to think to pull over instead of holding up ten cars to get a driver's license? Of course, I was assuming this person had a license.

I screeched around a corner to get away from this idiot.

You're letting the small things get to you. Well, people driving big hunks of metal that could kill you might not be so small, but I did have the sense to realize that it didn't take much to push me to anger or tears.

I made a bargain with myself; I got one more evening of falling apart. I wasn't throwing away all the liquor. Tomorrow I would become a sane, sober citizen dedicated to rebuilding New Orleans. One more night of Scotch and chocolate and not thinking about all the decisions I had to make, things I needed to do.

What I'd say to Cordelia when I saw her. This was Friday night; she might be here. No, probably not. Weekends had rarely started for her on Friday evenings. It felt like I should know when she arrived, a sixth sense that would warn me if she was close.

But just to be sure I scanned the cars on our block.

Nope, nothing resembling her vehicle.

Maybe she flew, I thought as I parked. But evening was approaching and no lights were on at the house. I can be warm another night, I decided as I climbed the stairs. And drink Scotch and eat chocolate without anyone around to judge.

I headed straight for the kitchen. And the bar.

Today I'd broken into a house, almost been caught at it by two possible murderers, and still had enough scrapes and bruises from my inelegant jump off the roof that no matter how drunk I got tonight, tomorrow I'd know it really happened; and gone out to the suburbs to save a young girl from evil drug dealers only to discover that white knighting isn't all it's cracked up to be.

I deserved a drink, right? Rationalization is my friend, I thought as I scanned the bottles.

Vodka. A shot of good vodka would warm me up and probably go better with chocolate. I poured a generous measure into a glass. Took a sip. Then a bigger sip. Fuck this, I downed it. I started to lick the rim to get the last burning drop.

Someone was watching me.

Cordelia was standing at the far end of the kitchen. Watching me.

This was not the grand reunion I'd started to hope for. I'd have called it a disaster except that Katrina had shown us what a real disaster was.

I couldn't think of one goddamned thing to say.

Neither could she. We just stared at each other.

"You could have warned me," I finally yelled, slamming down the shot glass. Then I couldn't think of anything to do except leave.

Hastily. Running out of the house and to my car.

"Fuck, fuck, fuck, goddamn fuck," I chanted as I drove away.

CHAPTER FIFTEEN

I'd told Joanne that I'd call Alex, but that didn't seem possible. I was back at my cold office, bundled in two sweaters and a scarf. I'd picked up the phone at least ten times to call Cordelia, even managed to punch in several numbers a few times. But I couldn't get beyond that.

She hadn't called me. Of course, that could just be the lousy cell reception.

Or maybe she didn't want me in her life. Or even if she had been considering getting back together, seeing me drinking had decided her against it. She might have decided that the Wild West dating might be a better option. Or had another girlfriend.

I put the phone down and picked up the Scotch I'd poured myself. One more night of falling apart; I'd deal with it in the morning. Or the afternoon, whenever I rolled out of bed.

Whatever. I downed a good finger's worth of the amber liquid.

But even the booze wasn't blurring my rough edges. I got up and paced around my apartment.

How could I have been so stupid?

Why didn't I just walk into her arms and tell her I needed her?

Because she didn't seem to need me anymore.

I took another drink.

I needed to think about something else. Anything. This hurt too much.

Then I remembered the papers I'd gotten from the house. They were where I'd left them, shoved under the seat of my car.

Taking only long enough to throw a jacket over my sweaters, I rushed downstairs to retrieve them.

The night air was cold, the wet chill from a city carved and surrounded by water. I quickly gathered the papers from under my seat and headed back up the stairs. My apartment was barely warmer, so I just left my jacket on as I sat behind my new desk. I had tried to clean the old one; it had so many memories, but the smell remained, perhaps only in my memory, but even that was too strong. In a fit of anger and despair, I'd shoved it down the stairs, letting it drop to the landing, watching it crack as it hit. Another heave, another few steps, another break. By the time it crashed at the bottom, it was more a pile of wood than a desk. A stinking pile of wood.

I took another sip of the Scotch, then began to sort through the papers.

At first it seemed a blur of badly copied microfilm, a jumble of ancient papers, marriage licenses, property deeds. Why would anyone kill for something that happened over a hundred years ago, I wondered as I made out the writing on a death certificate from 1905. I squinted at the smudged letters. Died of yellow fever.

I turned on my computer and did a quick Internet search. The last yellow-fever epidemic in America was in 1905 in New Orleans. Only a few years earlier they had finally discovered that mosquitoes carried the disease and that controlling mosquitoes could prevent the disease. But then, as now, myth and disbelief persisted, long enough to allow another epidemic five years later.

Someone had painstakingly combed through archives to amass these disparate documents. Why? What was so important in them? I grabbed a legal pad and started making a timeline, with the earliest date and the event on the date first.

As I slowly and laboriously constructed the timeline, a story started to emerge.

Josiah Benoit was born in 1872, as attested to by a faded copy of a page from a family Bible with his birth listed. No parents were named, but the space was cramped.

He was married in 1890 to Maria-Josephina Despaux. The marriage license had an X for his signature, although she wrote her name in a shaky scrawl. Clipped to this was census data from 1890. He was listed as white; she was black. At that time it was illegal for people of different races to marry, so someone was passing. Either Maria-Josephina was claiming to be white or Josiah that he was not.

Theirs was a fertile marriage with children born in 1890—perhaps the reason for the marriage—in 1891, 1892, 1894, and 1895.

There was another marriage license for Josiah Benoit. In 1902 he married Mary Gallier, whose census data listed her as white. Perhaps Josiah had crossed the color line.

It was Maria-Josephina who died of yellow fever in 1905—three years after Josiah had married again.

In 1898, Josiah had acquired property on Perdido Street. He added an adjacent lot in 1899 and another in 1900. The third one clearly stated it was payment for a gambling debt and, given that no sums were mentioned for the first two, it seemed possible that Josiah was a lucky man. Or a clever one with fast hands.

Perdido is now in what's known as the CBD or Central Business District, a swath of tall, modern buildings where most of the commerce, oil, gas—and city hall—politics is as commercial as anything else in New Orleans—are located. But a hundred years ago? I had some vague memory of it being named for Perdition for a reason, that it was a rough area of bars and gambling dens frequented by the human flotsam and jetsam of the river trade.

This time the Internet was less helpful, with only brief histories of the CBD. Other than brief mentions of river rats—the human kind—it gave little information about what the area might have been like over a hundred years ago.

I sat up and rubbed my eyes. The ice in my Scotch had melted. I had been at this for a while. It was too chilly for ice to quickly melt.

I still didn't have the answer to my main question—what was in these papers that might get someone killed after a century had passed?

Love or money. Those were the usual reasons. If Josiah Benoit had remarried without a divorce—hard to get back then—he was a bigamist and his second marriage might not be valid.

What happened to the property on Perdido Street?

I looked again at the deeds. The lots weren't adjacent, but fairly close. Perhaps the owner had gambled away bits and pieces of the land—a common occurrence here. Josiah picked up the ones he could, maybe someone else won some other parts of it.

Josiah had obtained the property while married to Maria-

Josephina. That didn't mean she had any right to them—somehow I doubted that property laws back then recognized women as equal. But they had children, and Louisiana makes it hard to disinherit them.

I got up and stretched, then rummaged around in my desk drawer to find a magnifying glass. It was hard enough to read these copies and I could use a little extra help. Besides, isn't a magnifying glass one of the prime tools of a private eye?

Josiah's second wife, Mary Gallier, also had children. From these records, three of them.

I again rubbed my eyes and this time took a sip of the watered-down Scotch. Then I glanced at my watch. I had been at this for over three hours and had made it through about half of the pile of paper.

I looked at my silent phone. Cordelia hadn't called.

Maybe she had. Maybe she didn't get through. Or maybe she did what I did, started to dial over and over again, then got scared. It was too late to call now. Even if I could find the courage and the words.

I looked back at the pile of papers and started reading the next one.

Another hour of scanning the papers told me that Mary Gallier's children had inherited the property. Her grandchildren had sold the land in 1955. For a lot of money.

Maria-Josephina's children had been orphaned with her death. Two were sent to a home for wayward children. One had died in the First World War. One died at the age of five. The others were lost to history.

Using two pieces of paper, I made family trees for both lines of descendants. Whoever did the research had been thorough. She or he had searched out birth certificates, marriage licenses, death notices, and even census information.

Maria-Josephina had six children, including a pair of twins, before she died. She was only thirty-one when the fever took her. The two children sent to the orphanage were both girls. One, Eunice, married, and it seemed that the other, Eleanor, did not. Her death certificate gave her name as Eleanor Benoit, her birth name. The other woman matched her mother in fertility, giving birth to four children in as many years. She had married Alphonse Johnson, who died in the flu epidemic of 1918, leaving her to raise the children.

Mary Gallier's children had a better life. Josiah Benoit died in 1932, she made it to 1949. Her three children, two girls and one boy, were born in 1903, 1905, and 1908. None of them were lost in time. All had marriage licenses, and their death certificates indicated they made it to a respectable old age.

I started skipping through the papers, beginning to feel like I was creating a list of "begats."

Maria-Josephina's line led to Alma Groome, the woman left in the abandoned house.

Mary Gallier's great-great-granddaughter was Brooke Overhill. Oh, yes, they had done well from Josiah Benoit's gambling. The Overhills weren't people you read much about in the paper; they were too upper-class for that. Occasional appearances at charity events. I went to my old friend the Internet to see if my memory was correct. Yep, a few mentions of a charity work and a fairly long obituary for the patriarch of the family, Jameson Overhill, who had married Jessica Stern, Mary Gallier's descendant. Brooke, their granddaughter, was the one who broke the family mold. She was a singer, on the upswing of a promising career. She had started out as part of a folkie duet, with a high-school friend named Lynn, and they had performed as Brooke-Lynn. I'd even seen them a few times as they did their act in clubs around here—including some of the gay bars. Although it had been the boy bars, so no indication that they were more than friends who were cool about gays, or at least the men. The Lynn part had disappeared and Brooke had reemerged as a singer on the cusp of jazz and pop. She recorded as Brooke O. Her first album had been nominated for a Grammy. Her second one had just come out.

I glanced at my watch. It was past two in the morning and exhaustion hit me. The day had been too much, one that in many ways I wished I could take back.

As I was getting ready for bed, I couldn't stop the questions running through my head. I wasn't a lawyer, and probably most lawyers couldn't answer whether Alma Groome and her family had any claim to the proceeds for the sale of the Perdido properties. Just because a record of a divorce wasn't in this stack of paper didn't mean one hadn't taken place. Would the laws of the time have any validity now? The Overhills were pinkish, blond people. Most likely their forebears were also on the white side of the color line. Josiah Benoit had looked like a white man to marry Mary Gallier. That meant that under the repugnant laws of the time, either his marriage to Maria-Josephina or Mary wasn't legal.

I got into bed. It might be enough for a lawsuit to get some compensation, but given how well-heeled—and lawyered up—the Overhills were, could that in any way justify murder? Do rich people really kill over a few hundred thousand?

I turned out the light. I'd never know, since I'd never be that rich.

CHAPTER SIXTEEN

The phone woke me and I hastily glanced at the clock before answering it. Nine thirty, more than late enough for respectable people to be up. Too bad I wasn't one of those respectable people.

I didn't recognize the number. Throwing caution to the wind, I answered it. Maybe I was hoping it would be Cordelia, with a new Boston cell phone. But it wasn't her voice.

I guess some of the disappointment came through in my hello.

"Hey, that's not usually how I'm greeted with good news," a vaguely familiar tone said. Then added, "Did I wake you?"

"No," I quickly lied. "Was doing dishes." That sounded like a nice respectable thing to do at nine thirty in the morning.

"This is Liz," my caller said. "The vampire who took your blood?"

"Careful, we have real vampires in this city. You could get yourself into trouble by claiming to be one."

"Thanks for the warning. The good news is that your blood tests showed no signs of any scary illnesses. Perfect for vampires."

"Good to know. However, I'd appreciate if you didn't spread that around. I sometimes like to go out at night, and having vampires coming after me could make that hard."

"Don't want to waste you on the vampires."

It sounded like flirting and I didn't know how to respond.

She filled the silence. "I've been trying to get in touch with your young friend. I've called her cell number a couple of times. Of course, I've been discreet, so maybe she's getting the message but doesn't know who it is or why I'd call. I was wondering if you'd talked to her lately or have a better idea of how to contact her."

"Her test came out okay? Oh, I guess you can't tell me that."

"Nope, I can't. I would appreciate if you could help me get in touch with her."

"I'll try my best. I have her cell number and some idea of where she's staying."

"Give her a call and see if you can get her to phone me. Otherwise, I might have to hit you up for directions to where she's staying."

"Okay, I can do that." I hoped she'd say more. Her voice and words were neutral, but I wondered if this was just protocol to give results no matter what? Or was there some reason Liz needed talk to Nathalie?

"Can I change the subject?"

"Can I stop you?"

"Perhaps slow me down," she bantered.

I liked Liz. I wished I was meeting her when my life wasn't so messed up.

"You're a local, right? I'm in search of navigation help."

"You can't turn left on Tulane Avenue, and yes, the streets do change names without warning or reason."

"Helpful in the long run, but I have to get from the hotel I'm staying at to some swanky uptown house."

"Rampart to Loyola, to Simon Bolivar, to LaSalle, to Freret. Although the tourists usually just take St. Charles and get stuck in all the other tourist traffic."

"Okay," she said slowly. "If I had a clue as to what streets those were it might be helpful. I've been here four days. Want to go with me and give directions?"

"Are you asking me out?" I blurted. "I'm sorry, it's just...uh, just that. Oh, hell." I finally quit trying to compensate for my stupid question.

"Just a friend," she said easily. "I'm a stranger here, my work colleagues want to go to the girly bars in the French Quarter, and I chanced onto this invite. Thought it would be nice to have company."

"Um...sure." It wasn't like my social calendar was booked.

"Cool," she said, like she actually meant it. "It's a networking party, mostly liberal, progressive types, from what I can gather. I ran into an old med school friend—totally unexpected. Then he ran into the friend throwing this party and I was included in the invitation. Seemed a much nicer way to spend the evening than sitting alone in my hotel room."

We sorted out where, when, and who was driving, then I was back to staring at the ceiling, the phone in my hand, wondering what I was doing.

Taking a shower seemed a reasonable excuse to get out of bed. Then I remembered, no gas, no hot water. But I had bruises and scrapes from yesterday and I wanted to be clean. Time to do it the old-fashioned way. I warmed up enough water to manage a passably tepid bath. After something resembling breakfast as an excuse to drink massive amounts of caffeine, I tried calling Nathalie. All I got was voice mail. I didn't leave a message.

She was supposed to be out doing good, I reminded myself, not a typical teenager hanging around chatting on the phone.

She'll be okay, I told myself. Then amended it to, even if she's not, what could I do to save her?

I had told Joanne I'd call Alex, so that was next on my list of things I didn't want to fuck up. But I got her voice mail, too. Maybe none of the cell phones in the area worked anymore. Maybe an alligator knocked down the one functioning tower.

After I poured another large cup of coffee, I put on an extra sweater and returned to the pile of papers.

I had questions that needed answers, the main one being why would anyone kill for what was in these papers? Was there anything to indicate that the children, the multiple generations of them, had a legal right to the proceeds of the property? And even if so, was it limited to the value at the time they were deprived of it or was it worth some portion of what it was sold for? Even if it was likely that money would have to change hands, why kill one of the descendants? Wouldn't every child from Maria-Josephina be entitled to something?

Josiah Benoit had left his second family fairly well-off, with a house near the Garden District and a bank account that paid for a lavish funeral, bequests to multiple friends, and nice sums for his children in addition to the property. Not enough to live off, but enough to get through college or launched on a career.

I then did some basic research on Jessica Stern, the descendant who had brought the property into the family. She was still hale and hearty, born in 1926. It was her husband who had sold the Perdido Street properties and moved the family from merely very well-off to major mojo moneybags. As befitted a woman of her generation, I found her birth announcement, her Mardi Gras debut write-up, her marriage notice, and several articles about various charities she was involved with. Of course she had taken her husband's name, Overhill. She had three children, seemingly a family tradition. The oldest son, John, was being groomed to take over the business, or more likely was doing most of it by this point. He was born in 1945. He had two sisters, Janice and Laura, who seemed to have disappeared into proper Southern womanhood. John married Marilyn Jordan, and they had three children: Jared, born in 1969, Harold in '74, and Brooke in '79. Jared had joined his father in the company, the next heir-apparent. I could find little on the second child, Harold, only a picture of him at the Special Olympics, hinting that he probably suffered some physical or mental disability. Brooke was the youngest of the three.

She didn't follow in her mother's tradition; her name was all over the papers, everything from mentions of her early concerts to the latest updates. Her birth date of 1979 meant that she was ten years younger than her oldest brother and now twenty-six. I glanced at the Internet list of her life.

The words blurred.

What are you doing, I asked myself. This was an old wound, money stolen a century ago, love lost to bones now dust. Maybe it had something to do with the dead woman; maybe it didn't. I had no reason to investigate it.

It became so easy, just sitting here peering into a life that had nothing to do with me, deciding nothing. Until time decided for me. Not picking up the phone. Or getting in the car and driving to see her. Just let the time pass. I didn't risk anything if I simply let time wash me away. Like a flood.

Pick up the phone and call her. Ask to talk.

What if she only wants to end it, the practical sorting out of our entwined lives?

If that's true, then finding out won't change anything. I'll just know.

I picked up the phone.

Started to dial.

Put it down.

I needed a few more hours of hope. I couldn't bear to know just yet.

I got up, splashed water on my face, then looked out the window. It was a bright, cold day.

The bitter truth was that Cordelia had moved on and left me behind. She was pragmatic and practical. If she wanted to know if there was a chance we'd get back together she would have tried to do so by now.

So why hadn't she just told me it was over? Why leave it hanging?

Because why would she want to deal with my anger? Why not just avoid what would turn out to be a nasty, ugly fight? She was sensible. What would that accomplish, except have us say words we'd both regret forever. In truth, words that I'd say and regret. I'd swing, but at times, my fury felt overwhelming as if every day, long line, lost neighborhood, crying friend made it worse.

I stared at the glinting sunshine, cold and clear, as if a metaphor for my life. If she didn't ask, she didn't want me back. Cold and clear.

Maybe all I could manage was to hold on to the few remaining tendrils of love for her to not make this any harder than it needed to be.

The wind whipped a paper bag across the road.

What would that be for? Maybe we could be friends someday? I couldn't see that, didn't think it possible there would be a day when I could easily meet her at a party, be polite and friendly when she introduced me to the new woman she was making a life with.

I choked back a sob of anger and pain.

I could be kind, but what would it get me other than leaving enough anger to eat at part of every day? Fifty years probably wasn't enough to get rid of it. She'd once asked for fifty years with me. I'd said fifty years wasn't enough. Damn her.

Again, I looked at a decision I couldn't make. Did I want one last cathartic blast of anger or did I want to prove I really had loved her, well enough to gently let go?

As I had told myself so many times in the last few weeks, you don't need to decide right now. It can hold a while. Actually seeing her was a shock—and it left me no longer able to grasp some inchoate future in

which we somehow found our way back to each other. She could have
said something, called me back. But she had been silent, only staring. I
needed a day or two to adjust to what I now knew was real.

I turned from the bright day and headed back to my desk. I needed
to think about someone else's life.

What if Alma Groome was the only person who knew about
this tangled family tree? It would be impossible—or certainly very
noticeable—to kill off every family member who had a claim, but what
if they didn't know? Kill Alma, destroy the evidence, and nothing has
to change. Josiah Benoit's second family gets to keep it all.

I'd found out a lot about the rich side of the family, but what about
the poor side? Who was Alma Groome?

I clicked off Brooke Overhill's long list of notices, annoyed at
how easy it seemed for her.

The Internet didn't easily reveal who Alma Groome was. No list
of pages and pages with her name on them. Nothing came up on the
quick-and-easy searches. But people leave a paper trail, although not
always a paper trail that has made it to the Internet.

After about an hour of searching using various forms of her name
and getting nothing more than I already knew, I switched from her name
to searching for the few other things I knew about her—that she was
from New Orleans and seemed to have done male drag at one time.

Nothing, nothing, nothing. And something.

An article titled "Your Grandmaw Did Drag," from a gay paper
in Tennessee.

Alma Groome always felt drawn to the stage. She
never knew why until doing research into her family. A
great-great-grandmother of hers performed in vaudeville
theatre, appearing as a first-wave, so to speak, drag king. In
her current performance Alma is trying to recreate the act
her historical forebearer put on. Alma will be doing a pre-
performance talk, including a slide show to discuss drag-
king performances through the ages.

The article then listed the time and place for the performances,
about two years ago.

Investigations are often an uncovering of one detail at a time that leads to another and then another until a story emerges. From this small article, I was able to expand my search, adding the details about her history.

Time passed and an outline slowly emerged. Alma Groome performed what she called a cross-dressing act, based on what she could find in the historical records about her great-great-aunt, Octavia Alma Despaux. Her name Alma was handed down as Great-aunt Octavia used the wages she earned to support her extended family, especially her sister Maria-Josephina, whose husband abandoned her and her children.

Alma performed mostly at festivals and at universities interested in the historical aspects of her work. I was able to find one academic article that filled in most of the historical details about Octavia Alma Despaux. She never married, worked in the precursor to vaudeville, variety theater. Had started out in the Atlanta area, but in the circuits for black people. She had resurfaced in New Orleans, performing in an amateur contest, this time on the more lucrative side of the race line. She had been good enough to be a headliner for about a decade, then disappeared in a cloud of scandal, running off with her dresser—a woman—to Europe. Money still occasionally arrived for the family, so presumably she had reinvented herself over there. The article ended with a quote from Alma: "I like to think that they lived happily ever after, Octavia and her dresser, a woman whose name I have yet to find. Performing, traveling through Europe, wine and cheese after the show, putting enough aside to retire quietly in the south of France. As history has revealed no other ending, I'm free to conjure up a good one for her. I hope wherever she is, she's looking down on my performance. Perhaps whispering a few directions, but mostly approving."

It had taken me about five hours to get this much. I had learned little more about the present-day Alma Groome. She had probably stumbled over the family history while researching her great-great-aunt. But what had she done with it that had gotten her killed? Maybe she had tried something not so legal as a court challenge. Blackmail? What if the Overhills didn't like the idea that their racial lineage wasn't as white as the proverbial driven snow? Could anyone be so racist today that they would kill to keep secret that one of their ancestors was a light-skinned black man?

In some ways I hadn't learned much more than I already knew.

Alma Groome was murdered and it might have had something to do with the history she had uncovered. I didn't know her very well, but the woman who did careful historical research to recreate a bygone era didn't seem a likely blackmailer.

Maybe it was time to go back to the Overhills. Which one of them would be the most likely killer?

I again redirected my Internet search to the moneyed side of the family. Don't forget the women, I told myself, but pay attention to the men. Men are more likely to be violent, especially when it comes to preserving their place in society.

Jessica, the matriarch of the family, had married Jameson Overhill. From what I could find out about him, he fell into what most people would call good ole boy. Went to LSU, was a boxer on the collegiate team. Went to LSU law school as well. He and Jessica had married in 1944. He had been born in 1920, so that made him now eighty-five years old, if he was still alive. Probably too old for actual murder, but not too old to hire some thugs, like the ones I had seen, to carry out his orders. Then I found his obit; he had died in 2003.

John was hale and hearty enough to have done it himself, but again, he had money and a position to maintain, so it was likely that he'd hired someone. As was his son, Jared.

Which made sense, as I'd had a run-in with the people he'd hired.

Or that somebody had hired. Much as I'd like rich white men to be the villains, that didn't mean they were.

Maybe Brooke O. saw a career being eaten away by an ugly family scandal. It's hard to be hip and cool if you got there because your family was a bunch of racist cheats.

Any one of the Overhills could have hired the thugs I saw at the house. Oddly, those men had a small-time, amateur feel about them, the kind of goons whose experience was shaking down small corner stores in Chalmette. That might mean that the Overhills weren't used to engaging in criminal acts, or at least not often enough to have them on the payroll.

Brooke O. was doing several concerts in the area to raise money for Katrina recovery. Well, how could she not? There was a big picture of her in a hard hat working on a Habitat for Humanity house. My cynical side was about to wager that the headgear had come off once the cameras were pointed a different direction, but even if it was for the wrong reason, someone was moving into that house, someone would benefit, and maybe the cameras and attention helped. I wasn't that desperate family.

I glanced at the clock. I needed to get ready for my—friendly outing? Sort of date? She's a stranger in town, probably just wants some company, someone it's okay to be lesbian with and I'm the only available candidate. Probably—but the truth was I liked Liz. She was an attractive woman.

I glanced again at the notes I had taken. What was I doing? No one had hired me to find the killer of Alma Groome. Stumbling over her didn't give me ownership rights—or any rights other than to report what I knew to the authorities and be on my way. I started to throw the sheets of paper into the trash, then thought, if it were me I'd want someone to look. Even if they couldn't look for very long or for the right reasons.

Chapter Seventeen

My clothing choices weren't exactly plentiful. I hadn't thought through packing for more than a day or two, assuming that I'd run back to the house for whatever I needed. But with Cordelia there, that didn't seem possible.

Okay, black jeans, a cobalt blue sweater, and a dark gray blazer that lived in the office and had somehow survived the vandals. It was night and, besides, enough people were still struggling with the few clothes they had taken with them that anything short of madras Bermuda shorts and a hot pink Hawaiian shirt should count as dressed up. Parties were already starting up with themes of "wear what you evacuated in."

Elizabeth was within five minutes of being on time—more than respectable for someone new to New Orleans. It was her rental car; she had asked to drive, saying that she paid attention to where she was when she was behind the wheel.

I didn't feel like talking, so I asked her questions. She worked for the CDC as an epidemiologist. She had an MD and a MPH, Master in Public Health. She had traveled the world, mostly for work, so she mostly saw the places that the tourists don't go, locations where there was a cholera outbreak or Ebola.

"Don't worry, I've had all my shots," she joked, then added, "Most diseases follow poverty—people already under stress from malnutrition, lack of clean water."

"So that's why you're here in New Orleans?"

"This is the first time I've been sent someplace this close to home," she said. "Have to admit, at first, I was a little shaken by it."

"Now it's just another third-world country with better music?"

"The good news is that's it's not a third-world country at all. Fragile as tax-cut mania has left some of our public-health systems, they basically held. We haven't seen the outbreaks of things like cholera and typhoid as was first feared. People have been immunized. Not perfect, especially at first, but people had access to clean drinking water, food that wasn't spoiled. Those things can make a big difference when you see what happens to people who live without them."

"Serious point taken."

"If you think it's such a backward place, why did you return?" she asked.

"It's my backward place. Besides, at least here I know how to get around," I said as I pointed for a left turn.

"You're smart enough to learn streets somewhere else. Why come back?" We passed the house where the party was, now looking for a parking place. "I'm always curious about these things."

"Why go to Atlanta? Why do you travel the world looking for nasty bugs?"

"Fair enough. I'm in Atlanta because that's where the CDC is. I've made friends there, have enough connections that I guess it's home now. As for disease-chasing, after Tia died, I just couldn't stay at home and stare at the walls, so I signed up for the farthest-flung assignment that I could. Now I think I've gotten used to the adrenaline rush, the combination of science and adventure. Is this legal?" she asked, referring to a parking spot.

"Legal enough. I don't think many of the meter maids are back at work yet."

"Your turn," she said as she eased into the space. "Why come back to New Orleans?" I noticed her eliding over Tia, presumably her partner, dying.

"I guess…It's home," I mumbled. I couldn't think of a good, company-ready reason.

"What ties you here?" she probed.

Nothing, not one goddamn thing. I didn't say that. "Even if I move on, I had to come back. I'm not sure what my ties are here anymore. Still sorting that out."

She left a silence; I didn't fill it. It's a technique I often use. Silence invites people to talk. But I had no answer, and to risk speaking might let my incoherent, jumbled life spill out.

"Don't we have a party we need to go to?" I finally asked.

"Yes, and one you've been kind enough to navigate me to."

"So how did you get invited to this?" I bantered as we got out.

"Right place, right time. Bumped into an old med-school colleague who's teaching at Tulane now. He had the connection, or rather his partner does."

"Is this a somewhat-gay party?"

"Hard for an outsider like me to know for sure. I assume there's no need to dive back into the closet behind the skis and down coats. Raul—my friend—will be here with his partner. He offered to find me a date, but if he has matchmaking skills, they're better suited to the gay male world than the lesbian world."

The house was a beautiful old Uptown one, part of the "sliver by the river" that had not flooded. It was lit up, paper lanterns hung on the wide porch, light shafting out of the front windows. The house wasn't pretentious, the leafy trees in front obscuring it save from the few who made it to the front-porch steps. As we got closer, I could see that the paint wasn't gleaming new and the steps had a few places where the sun had done its work. The house would need to be painted in a few years. Some of the bushes out front needed cutting. I was relieved to be entering a house that wasn't perfect. It made it seem more like this was a gathering of people who were still here, who wanted to celebrate being here, rather than show off and see and be seen, as too often parties in this part of town were.

"Liz!" a man shouted. "Glad you could make it."

Liz introduced me to her friend Raul and his partner Peter. They were middle-aged gay men, a few pounds over ideal weight, but comfortable with who they were, seemingly more interested in good wine than pursuing a youth that would only leave them farther and farther behind.

The good wine was poured and we were each handed a glass.

"Two's my limit," Liz informed me. "But I'm clearly the designated driver, so you do what you usually do."

I usually didn't drink, so that was little guidance.

It was a mix of people, most of whom I didn't know, but a few I recognized. Liz had called it right; it was a gay enough party that we could have walked around the room holding hands without anyone blinking an eye. It seemed to have a lot of medical people, which I was less than thrilled with as that almost guaranteed that I'd run into someone who knew Cordelia.

Of course, living in New Orleans almost guaranteed I'd run into someone who knew Cordelia. Maybe that was reason enough to start again somewhere else.

I spotted one of those people across the room—a nurse who had made it clear that she deserved a doctor as a partner and had never been especially friendly to me as I was a non-medical person who had the audacity to remove a lesbian doctor from the dating pool. It took me a moment to recall her name. Patty something. Not that Cordelia would have dated her had I not been around, but that thought didn't seem to have ever occurred to Patty. She wasn't bad looking—especially after a few glasses of wine. An amount of alcohol I intended to avoid. Perfectly dyed blond hair, nicely dressed, a slim figure that seemed more due to diet than exercise—she was one of those who would fit into the weight-proportional-to-height category if it killed her. But she'd mistaken the outside package as all that mattered.

I decided it was time to refill my glass and headed to the bar in the opposite direction.

This time I ran into someone I was happy to see.

"Torbin." I greeted my cousin. "When did you start crossing Canal Street?" He and his partner Andy were also at the bar.

He took a quick glance at my wineglass, then pretended he didn't notice it in a manner that was just exaggerated enough to let me know that he knew what it meant.

"If they let you across, they have to let me across," he bantered. "What are you doing here?"

"Same thing you are?"

"Let me get to the point, who's your date?"

That was pointed. Keeping as much as I could to the party-friendly details, I told Torbin about meeting Liz over a dead body ("That's romantic," was his comment), that she wasn't a date, just a friend, someone new in town who wanted someone to show her around. I barely got that part out before Liz joined us.

Torbin and I are the queer cousins, bonded by growing up gay in an extended Cajun family and being the only ones who understood each other and what we were going through. We had just sort of always been there for each other, from lending spices and drills to a shoulder to cry on. Torbin had seen me at my worst, met me at sunrise to extract me from situations my earlier less-than-sober days had occasionally gotten me into.

The bartender refilled my glass. I waved for her to stop when it was half full. I wouldn't be an idiot about it this time. I was too old for Torbin—or anybody—to have to rescue me.

"So other than the dead body tour, has Micky shown you some of the more appealing areas of the city?" Torbin asked Liz.

"I've been here once or twice before. Alas, this is mostly a work trip."

From there Torbin asked about her work and she explained, with a glance at me as if to say, "I'm sorry, you just heard this on the way here." But her work was interesting and I was more than willing to hear about it again, especially as I could tell that Torbin and Andy were both engrossed.

As they were talking, I felt my elbow jostled.

Patty What's-Her-Name had bumped into me.

Intentionally. "You go for the doctors, don't you, Knight?" Her voice was slurred; she was drunk. "Just dumped one and now you've already latched onto another."

How the hell did she know this?

"I wasn't aware you and Liz were acquainted," I said as calmly as I could.

"She gave a presentation yesterday. I was there. Tried to talk to her afterwards, but didn't have a chance. Saw the two of you walk in together."

"I have a lot of friends," I said shortly.

"Everyone knows that Cordelia was in Boston and you weren't there."

"It didn't work out for us to be together." I took a sip of my wine. I was too close to throwing it in her face and, for the sake of our host, wanted the glass as empty as possible. "And don't assume you know more than you think you know."

"Yeah? So why are you here with Elizabeth and not Cordelia? Everyone knows—"

"If everyone knows, why haven't I gotten the Presidential call yet? Or maybe 'everyone' is an exaggeration. I'm here with my friends. Why don't you go find some of your own?"

"Fuck you, Knight. You were never good enough for her. That's why she's here without you," she said as she stalked off, weaving ever so slightly.

I turned away from her, not wanting her to think I was enjoying her drunken stumble as much as I was. Then I glanced back. At the tall woman across the room.

Damn, damn, and damn. This is not the place I wanted to run into Cordelia for the second time.

You're here with a friend. You're hanging out with Torbin and Andy. Fully clothed in a well-lit room.

I watched Patty grab her by the arm and lead her into a different room. I had an urge to rush after them, tell that little twerp to shut up, and dump her headfirst into a plate of humus. And then what? Put my arms around Cordelia and kiss the hell out of her? Or scream at her for leaving me?

I wouldn't do either of those. We'd stay on opposite sides of the room or house, if possible. A few awkwardly polite moments before I could reasonably make my exit. Maybe I would need Torbin to rescue me one last time—to come up with some plausible excuse to get me out of here.

"Micky?" Tobin asked. Clearly something had been addressed to me and I was out of town.

"Too much wine?" he followed up.

"No...no," I said. "Sorry, I let my mind drift."

"My fault." Elizabeth gamely jumped in. "She's already heard my life story on the way here. A bit much to expect Micky to pay rapt attention twice in one evening."

"What was the question?" I asked.

"It's been too long. I've forgotten," Torbin said.

"Too much wine?" I asked sarcastically.

Torbin gave me a look. I had crossed a line. Torbin never had a drinking problem. I did. One that had affected him in ways that would give him a lifetime lease on chiding me about it.

"Sorry," I muttered. What the hell was wrong with me? This was a party; I was with friends. I should be having a good time. Instead I was either out of focus or pissing off the very friends I had no right to piss off. "I guess I'm just not used to the Uptown air," I joked. Not very funny, but they laughed just to relieve the tension.

I flung my arm around Torbin's shoulder. "I am sorry," I said. "Just too…too much shit hitting too many fans."

"Hear that," he said, his arm around my waist. Then very quietly to me, "Try not to fall too far apart."

There was a change in the room. A voice called out, "Brooke!" Even from this distance I could recognize her face. People pivoted in her direction as if desperate to touch her fame.

I watched her as she made her way across the room, stopping at just about every person. Some were clearly a friendly greeting, others seemed to be fans, strangers who craved a word. She was polite, even lingering with one man who gushed on and on about what she meant to him. I could hear half of it and even that was too close to the edge of creepy: "I listen to you every night in bed and when I wake up. I can't imagine any other woman I'd like to sleep with." An older woman with her grabbed her arm and led her away from him.

"You need a drink," I heard her say to Brooke, and they came our way.

Torbin greeted her. "Hello, Brooke."

"Torbin! It's great to see you." She gave him a hug. Then Andy a hug, too. To her companion/chaperone she said, "Torbin and I spent many an evening backstage in smoky bars. Sometimes I miss those days," she added wistfully. For a moment, her face was open and vulnerable, as if she wanted to shuck the burden of being a star and instead be able to crack jokes with drag queens in a bar where no one knew her name.

Up close, she was beautiful in the way women who don't care how they look often are. She wore either no makeup or only the barest touches. Her eyes were a hazel green, large and welcoming. She was tall, almost my height. Her hair was a chestnut brown flowing to her shoulders. She wore jeans, loose enough to be comfortable and not a fashion statement, with a lavender sweater and brown suede vest. It was an outfit I could have worn.

Tobin introduced Liz, she was closest. Brooke seemed genuinely interested, thanking her for coming here to help. Then he introduced me.

"This is my cousin, Michele, but everyone calls her Micky. She's a private investigator."

Brooke O. was shaking my hand, then saying, "Wow. That's impressive."

"It's not like the TV shows," I said.

"Nothing is like the TV shows," she answered. "It's astonishing how many times we have to practice a few dance steps to make them look simple and effortless. Still, it's not an easy job and has to be more interesting than data entry."

"Maybe, but there have been some cold nights when data entry looked mighty good."

She laughed, then said, "You may not look alike, but clearly the sense of humor runs in the family. Hey, Torbin, can we run away and barhop through the Fruit Loop?" She was referring to a section of the French Quarter that had gay bars on almost every corner.

He bowed and said, "Anything for a lady as talented as you are."

The light wasn't quite bright enough for me to be sure, but she looked like she blushed at his compliment.

However, others wanted her attention and she had time only for a hurried, "Catch you later," before being swept off to the next adoring group.

"Can I touch you?" I asked Torbin. "I didn't know you hobnobbed with the rich and famous."

"You can touch, just don't leave any grubby fingerprints." He brushed the alleged dirt marks off my shoulder. "Brooke and I crossed paths when she was playing in some of the local bars. I emceed several shows where she performed and we hung out between acts. She's always kept in touch, mostly a quick e-mail now and then. She's both talented and real. I'm very happy for her."

I trusted Torbin's judgment, but a few hours in a bar couldn't reveal the whole person.

Even more than ten years in a relationship didn't reveal the real person, I thought, glancing around to make sure I didn't accidentally run into Cordelia.

Wanting to avoid just that, I said, "Maybe we should move away from the bar. It's getting crowded here."

Liz stopped to talk to her friend Raul. Torbin, Andy, and I kept moving, heading to the deck and some breathing room. Liz motioned that she would join us shortly.

It was much less crowded outside, still chilly, but after the press of bodies inside, a relief. The deck surrounded a large swimming pool, filled for the occasional warm days that New Orleans could produce even during what the rest of the country called winter.

I was still on my second half-glass of wine, sipping it sparingly, as if to prove something to Torbin. Or maybe myself.

We chatted about who was back, what stores had opened. Who was moving to Houston or Atlanta. Where people went when they evacuated, when they got back. Others joined us, most of them I didn't know. Liz was in and out, sometimes hanging with me, other times with her medical friends, almost as if she didn't want to mix the two worlds.

Someone took my almost-empty wineglass and gave me a full one. I was beginning to feel safe and comfortable out in this little corner of the party. I didn't have to think about all the things I needed to think about. There was nothing I needed to do other than stand here, sip a nice Shiraz, and listen to someone talk about spending a month in Hattiesburg, Mississippi.

Or how many feet of water they had in their home.

I saw Patty What's-Her-Name standing in the doorway. Or rather being supported by it. I edged around Torbin so she couldn't see me. Several other women joined her and they spilled out onto the deck. At least she's no longer with Cordelia. Probably Cordelia had seen me and left.

Then Patty spun around and went back inside, leaving her friends. She wasn't gone long though. She returned with a woman firmly grasped in each hand. The first one out the door I recognized as a very closeted dentist. The second one was Cordelia.

I took a large swig of wine.

We were on the other side of the deck. I moved to the other side of Torbin, so I was next to the pool. That way they couldn't come up behind me, even if I wasn't watching them. Which I was trying not to do.

But somehow I couldn't not look at her. She seemed different, changed. She's tall, usually a head taller than most women. She even has a few inches on me. I knew that her eyes were blazingly blue, her hair a rich, deep auburn. Now it was dusted with gray, at this distance the colors mixed, muting the reds and browns. She looked like she'd lost weight. Getting skinny for the new girlfriend, I surmised. Or maybe she'd lost the weight during the week she'd been trapped in Charity after Katrina.

You don't know, Micky, you just don't know, I bitterly reminded myself. The woman I thought I'd spend the rest of my life with and I didn't know what or how she'd changed, just that something was different from when we were last together.

Our group, at the edge of the light, had thinned out. People were going back inside to get warm.

"Do you want a refill?" Liz asked me.

I looked down at my empty wineglass. "Yeah, thanks," I said, handing it to her.

"I need one, too. I'll give you a hand. Besides, it's getting a little chilly out here," Torbin said. "You coming?" he asked as I didn't move.

Patty and her group were still hogging the door. To go back inside would mean passing Cordelia.

Torbin noticed her. And my hesitation.

"I'll be back," he said, then added needlessly, "Don't do anything stupid."

I wasn't planning to do anything at all.

Safe and comfortable were gone. Not that they'd ever really been here. I couldn't just stand around, but had to calculate angles and directions. A side door on the other side of the pool probably led to the yard. And freedom. But I'd either have to cross around the long way in the dark or go right by the door—and Cordelia—to get to it.

They didn't seem to be moving. Maybe if I didn't move we'd be okay. Or at least far enough away to avoid each other.

The last few people in my group left, seeking either booze or warmth. Or both.

I stepped farther out of the light, trying to be invisible.

But I wasn't.

Cordelia was looking directly at me. I couldn't quite read her expression. Sad. Far away. I took a step toward her. I'd always been the one to hold her when she was sad. Then stopped. She was surrounded by women I barely knew.

Cordelia seemed to notice my movement to her, then hesitation. She broke away from the group and crossed the deck to me. She stopped a few feet away, then noticed the wineglass in my hand.

I looked down at it as well. I half-expected her to turn around and walk away, but she didn't. I quickly pivoted around and wedged my glass between two of the plants on a plant stand a little way back. I had to get it out of my hand. Probably the host would find it there weeks later.

"Never said I was perfect," I said quietly.

"Neither am I. Clearly," she replied. She took a step closer, then looked down at the glass in her hand. A glance back at me, as if to say that she, too, was finding respite in the blur alcohol provided.

"Hey, Cordelia, what are you doing?" Patty. She saw us together. And clearly didn't like what she saw.

Patty stomped over to us, her face bright and flushed with anger and alcohol. "What are you doing?" she asked again.

"Talking to me," I said, enunciating each word slowly as if speaking to someone who needed extra help.

Patty ignored me. "She's drunk—"

"No I'm not."

"Drunk. I've been watching her suck down drinks all night," Patty spewed out, presumably talking about me, although if she was referring to herself she would have been more accurate.

Cordelia took a big gulp of her vodka and tonic. The irony was lost on Patty. But Cordelia had a slight arch to her eyebrow that I knew well, as if acknowledging that no one here could be high and mighty about drinking.

"You have not seen me—"

"I'm not talking to you." Patty overrode me. "Cordelia, you don't need a drug addict for a girlfriend." Patty had been moving closer and closer to Cordelia, and now she was directly between us, making me step back to not have her hair in my face.

"Shut the fuck up." I lost my temper. "The only addict here is you, trying to leech onto a doctor and—"

"You shut up." Patty turned to me. "You shut the fuck up!" She was so drunk and angry that her spittle flew in my face.

Disgusted, I backed away another step, but that was a mistake as she took it as a cue to attack.

"You're a revolting, lazy, drunken asshole. You piece of crap—"

"Hey." Cordelia cut in. "Not here."

"You don't have enough of a brain for her," I shot back. That really pissed her off because it was true.

"You fucking asshole!" Patty took a swing at me, but she was so drunk it was ineffective, a flailing of fists.

I put a hand on her shoulder and pushed her back. I was not going to get into a physical fight. She was an idiot, but she was a drunken, bitter, twisted idiot and not worth it.

She lunged at me, shoving me hard.

I had just enough of an alcoholic buzz that my balance and reflexes weren't as quick as they needed to be.

I stumbled back, trying to right myself. My heel caught on the hose for the plant stand. There was nothing I could do; I was going to fall backward.

I braced for the blow.

Instead I went under. I had fallen into the pool and was going down.

The water was cold and my clothes were heavy. I hit the bottom with a jolt, banging my head on the concrete.

This would be an ugly irony—to survive Katrina only to drown in someone's swimming pool.

You're a bayou rat, swim, I ordered myself. My arms and legs tried to comply, but the cold and the blow had stunned me and my jeans weighed a ton and my jacket was twisted in a way that caught my arms.

First I had to struggle to right myself. I'd gone in backward, hit the back of my head, and was disoriented to be upside down. I flopped around so that I wasn't faceup. Then I pushed off the pool bottom, trying to make it to the surface.

But I couldn't generate enough force as weighed down as I was, so I hit bottom again, this time desperately pushing off, needing to breathe.

This time I broke the surface, managed one half-gasp before a wave created by my thrashing around slapped me in the face and went up my nose.

I need to breathe, my brain shouted.

A desperate dog paddle again got my face out of the water. Another breath.

Get to the shallow end. Get out.

Which way was the shallow end?

Someone shouted, "She's drowning!"

I sloshed in a circle trying to see which end was shallow. Hair and water were dripping in my eyes; my vision was distorted and blurry.

Steps. Handrail. That signaled shallow to me.

The water was chilling me and I felt exhausted.

If I gave up right now I wouldn't have to think about anything, do anything, worry about anything anymore.

There was a splash and I suddenly realized that another shape was coming at me.

Pool sharks?

I cannot be eaten by pool sharks and drown in an Uptown swimming pool when I'm half a foot out of the shallow end. That would be just too undignified, even for me.

But the shape was a rescuer.

"I've got you," she said. Even more mortifying, my savior was Liz.

"I'm okay," I coughed out.

"Relax, let me do the hero thing," she said as she wrapped an arm across my body and firmly pulled me through the water.

It took her only a few strokes to get us to the steps; she helped me as I flopped up them to the edge of the pool.

The chlorinated water burned my throat as I spat up what I'd swallowed.

Somewhere a voice said, "She was drunk and fell in the pool." It sounded like Patty.

"I was pushed," I rasped. Then had to cough out more water.

I started violently shivering from the cold. Liz put her arm about my shoulder. Even though she was wet, the body heat helped. Someone draped towels over us.

"I'm okay," I said, although the chattering of my teeth didn't do much to prove my case.

"You will be. You need to get someplace dry and warm," Liz said.

"You do, too," someone else said. I looked up. Torbin. "Let's get both of you out of here." With that, he gave me a hand up. I was still shivering almost uncontrollably.

Torbin was on one side and Liz on the other, and they half-carried me out the side screen door. We had an unspoken agreement that we were leaving. I was humiliated. I hadn't been drunk—well, not so drunk that I would have just stumbled into the pool without Patty's push—but that would be what most people would think.

As we went through the door, I took one backward glance, but I didn't see Cordelia.

Only Patty, waving her arms and laughing uproariously.

Torbin had sent Andy out to get their car, so he was waiting out front with the heater already blasting. It was a small SUV, since they both, between Torbin's costumes and Andy's computer equipment, hauled a lot of stuff around. From the rear, Torbin produced a blanket. After stuffing both Liz and me in the backseat, he wrapped it around us. Liz snuggled against me, her arm again around my shoulder.

Between her, the blanket, and the blasting heater, my shivering slowly subsided.

Torbin said little. I felt judged.

"I wasn't drunk. I didn't fall in. I was pushed," I threw into the silence. "That is what happened, even if you don't believe it."

"Who pushed you?" Liz asked.

"Patty somebody. I can't remember her name."

"Why'd she push you?" Torbin asked.

"She was drunk and angry." That didn't seem enough of an explanation. "She thinks that if she could just snag a dyke doctor, her life would be happily ever after. She was pissed that…" That I showed up at the party with Liz and had been with Cordelia for so long. Like I was rubbing her face in dating any doctor I wanted when she couldn't get even a one-night stand. But that didn't sound politic to say with Liz sitting here.

But politic wasn't Torbin's style. "Pissed about you showing up with the new doctor in town or that you lived with one for so long?"

"I don't know. You'd have to ask her. Probably both."

"And she just walked up and pushed you in the pool?"

Andy was very sensibly driving and keeping out of this conversation.

"We were arguing."

"About?" Torbin asked.

"Cordelia and I…Cordelia had come over where I was standing…

and we…Well, Patty didn't like that, so she came over screaming that I was drunk, had been drinking all night, was a fucked-up asshole. That kind of crap."

"Then she pushed you?"

I sighed. He'd keep asking until I told him. "I informed her she wasn't smart enough to get a doctor. She took a swing at me. I pushed her away, she pushed back, and I was closer to the pool than I thought." I added, "But I wasn't drunk. Not so drunk that I just fell in."

"Then why are you acting so guilty?" Torbin queried.

"Because everyone thinks I'm guilty."

He reached around to the backseat, found one of my hands with his. "Hey, girl, I'm on your side. You had a couple of glasses of wine. That's stone-cold sober for New Orleans. Post-K, it's sober and a saint. Patty Gander gives you any more trouble, she'll be wishing she'd stayed in Grapevine, Texas. The vicious drag-queen gossip circle will take her down."

He gave my hand an extra squeeze. "Now let's go home and get you warm."

Torbin had rescued me one more time.

Chapter Eighteen

Torbin insisted on taking me to his house. He knew that Cordelia and I were still wallowing in relationship limbo, that I wasn't likely to go to the house in Tremé with heat, and that my office down in Bywater still lacked gas service. He tossed me in one bathroom and Liz in another, with instructions to get ourselves in some hot water.

Halfway through my shower, the door briefly opened. Torbin shouted, "Incoming," and tossed a heap of sweatpants, T-shirts, socks, and just about anything else I might want to wear. I let the water wash over me. After having been so chilled, I felt like the world had possibilities again. A voice whispered in my head that it was okay. I had warm water and Torbin was on my side, still willing to rescue me. And lend me his clothes. I quickly dressed, wanting to keep the warmth from the shower caught in the cloth.

When I emerged, Torbin and Andy were in the kitchen making hot chocolate, the real kind with milk and cocoa.

"We all got a little chilly," he said.

Liz joined us. Torbin and I are close to the same size, so I wasn't quite as lost in the borrowed clothes as she was.

He handed me a steaming cup and I took a sip. "Ah, chocolate and being toasty warm. Life is good." At the moment, it didn't even feel like a lie to say it.

Out of the seeming blue, Torbin asked, "Can you find out what kind of car that woman drives?"

"Patty What's-Her-Name?" I asked. "Why?"

"No one pushes my lavender cousin into a swimming pool in December and gets away with it. It's time to go nuclear. Shrimp in the hubcaps."

Taking her cup of cocoa, Liz asked, "Shrimp in the hubcaps? Why?"

Andy answered. "Revenge is a dish best served cold. Put the shrimp in when the weather is like this and no one will notice for a while. Then have a few hot days and the car will smell like rotting fish."

"And no one ever looks in the hubcaps," Torbin said with glee.

"I am never crossing any of you," Liz said, but there was admiration in her voice.

"Many times merely the plotting was enough," Torbin said, "but this might have to be one of those times when the fantasy just doesn't do it."

"I can probably find out what kind of car she drives," I offered.

"Do so," Torbin said, "and we'll take it from there. We have to make sure it is indeed her car. It's too tacky to shrimp someone else."

"I'm glad you have some morals," Liz said wryly.

"Only the most immoral kind," Torbin clarified.

From our nefarious plotting we moved to sorting out practical details. Liz's rental car was still Uptown where we'd parked it. She was polite enough to offer to get a cab, which Torbin turned down. She seemed relieved, like whatever happened here was a much better adventure than going back to her hotel room alone.

We decided that cars could wait until tomorrow. That left sleeping arrangements. Liz and I could bunk together in the spare bedroom or one of us could sleep there and one on the living-room couch.

"Bunk beds for the nephews and nieces," Torbin explained. His and my cousins could be just as homophobic as anyone, but they seemed willing to suspend that prejudice for a kid-free weekend of leaving the children with their doting gay uncles. I suspected he was pointing out to Liz that he wasn't throwing us together in the same bed.

"I claim the top bunk," Liz said. "I always was stuck in the bottom one as a kid and I think it scarred me for life."

I opted for the bottom one. Torbin and Andy kept this room ready for guests, so the beds were made, which saved them some time and trouble. Plus the couch was lumpy.

Besides, Liz was a smart woman. Just from what she'd observed tonight she had to know that I had a drinking problem I wasn't handling very well and was in the midst of some major cable-TV-worthy dyke drama. Add to that how tired we all were—Andy had been yawning since we got here. I felt like I'd done a marathon. Being cold, soaking wet, and shivering is hard work.

I thanked Torbin for his kindness, showed Liz the guest bathroom, and let her go first while I washed our mugs and the saucepan. Andy was even polite enough to say they could wait until morning, but I felt like I had to do something to make up for the mess I'd caused.

Just as I put the last dish away I heard Liz exit the bathroom.

She was sitting on the bottom bunk when I finished with my bedtime routines.

"Hey, I thought you wanted the top."

"Thought I'd be polite and wait for you. It's not much fun to get on top with no one below you."

Is she flirting or am I just tired, I wondered.

She scooted over to make room beside her.

Flirting.

I was tempted. Liz was smart, attractive. Available. Leaving in a few days. Sex would be another escape from thinking about all the things I needed to think about.

I sat down beside her. The warmth of her leg next to mine felt good.

"It's been a while since…I've been in a situation like this," she said.

"What, stuck with a bunch of insane strangers?"

"That, I'm used to. That's about the definition of jetting into disaster zones. No, being with a woman who reminds me that I have a body attached to my brain."

"But is your brain attached to your body?".

She looked at my quizzically. "I think so. Why?"

"Don't tell me you didn't notice the who's-sleeping-with-who mess I'm involved in? Plus, the comments about drinking…have some justification."

"Tell me what I need to know."

"You planning to be here that long?"

"Let's start with the alcohol. Did you start drinking after Katrina?"

I struggled with the answer, finally saying, "Katrina didn't help… but I started just before."

"Why? Does it have anything to do with the so-called mess you're involved in?"

I liked Liz and felt okay talking to her. Given her life, I doubted I could say much that would shock her. Plus, she didn't live here. If I regretted what I said, at least she would be gone and not around to remind me of my foolishness.

"It has everything to do with it. On the Friday before Katrina hit, I walked in on my partner in the arms of another woman."

"That has to hurt. Live-in, share-chores kind of partner?"

"Had our tenth anniversary not that long ago."

"Was it a 'sorry, I made a mistake' or 'sorry, I'm leaving you' kind of thing?"

"I walked out, went to a place I own—used to own." That was another hole in my heart, the shattered debris left where my childhood home used to be. All the memories were tangled. The last time I would ever see it whole was in the misery of Cordelia's betrayal. "I took a bottle of Scotch with me. Then Katrina hit, and we weren't together… and haven't really had a chance to talk yet."

"Wow. That's kind of a long time to let something this important hang."

"It's a big part of does anything still tie me to this place."

"Have you talked to her at all?"

"Some, but it's been hard. Mostly practical things. And over the phone. We seemed to have an unspoken agreement that we would wait until we're seeing each other face to face to hash things out."

"By any chance was she at the party last night?"

"I was talking to her just before I got pushed into the pool."

"The tall woman? She was about to jump in, but that obnoxious woman was blocking her."

Another mark against Patty. At the moment, she'd be lucky if she got only shrimp in her hubcaps. "That sounds like her," I said.

"I met her. She was part of a group I ended up talking with that Raul knows here."

"You met her? What did she talk about?"

"I don't think she said much. The usual introduction pleasantries. She mostly listened, from what I recall. I asked Raul about her and he told me she had been one of the doctors stranded in Charity after Katrina. If I noticed anything about her, it was that she seemed lost. And that made sense after he told me about her experience."

"We're all lost here," I said quietly. "Every single one of us has lost something—friends, family, a house, a job, a life."

Liz turned my face toward her and gently kissed me. She held it only a moment, then pulled away. "I have a great fondness for women who take in scared kids from the Midwest. Atlanta and New Orleans aren't that far away. But right now you need to find what you've lost, not add complications."

She stood up, then climbed into the top bunk. We said good night.

I was still awake when I heard her fall into the steady breathing of sleep.

It had been a long day. I realized how right Liz was. Cordelia had come over to talk to me, then tried to go into the pool after me. Then had watched as Liz did dive in, drag me out. And sit next to me with her arm around my shoulder. What did Cordelia think? Especially with Patty giving everything the most negative spin possible.

I didn't know. I didn't know what she thought, what she wanted, what was possible. I didn't even know what I wanted. No, that wasn't completely true. I wanted her to want me back, to give me the power to decide. I wanted to not be in this limbo anymore. Except maybe I did, if it saved me from knowing that she was gone, only a live ghost haunting me with what might have been.

Right now all I wanted was to go to sleep and not think about it until tomorrow.

CHAPTER NINETEEN

Eventually my churning brain relaxed into sleep enough for me to wake to the smell of coffee and bright sunlight streaming through the window. I could hear three voices out in the kitchen, informing me that I was the only sluggard still in bed.

I have an excuse, I thought as I tried to get up. My muscles were screaming. In the last few days, I'd dragged a heavy chest out of an attic, jumped off a roof, then been pushed into a swimming pool on a brisk evening. When I was in my twenties all the above would have been a walk in the park. Forties? A day in bed before I was human again.

The promise of caffeine got me up—on the second try—and into the kitchen.

Torbin, Andy, and Liz were there, ringing the kitchen table, with full mugs and plates a hint that once upon a time there had been French toast.

"That's okay, just coffee for me," I said as I poured a mug.

"Woeful, woeful, woeful," Torbin said as he got up and walked to the stove. Without even asking he uncovered what he was saving for me and started making me my very own French toast.

"You are the best cousin ever," I said as I took his seat. It was already warm and I didn't intend to waste any warmth.

"Andy is about to take me to retrieve my car," Liz said. "Much as I'd like to hang around, I'm supposed to be a working girl and weekends mean nothing when you're out in the field."

"We did enlist her in our resistance movement," Torbin said as he dropped a dripping piece of bread into the skillet.

"What are we resisting?" I asked.

"Evil pool-pushing lesbians."

"I agreed to help insert *Penaeus aztecus* into her hubcaps." Torbin translated. "AKA common old brown Gulf shrimp."

"Too many years hanging with scientists," Liz explained.

"So we've already made plans for a seafood boil. We'll mix in shells with actual shrimp. It's just a waste of good shrimp otherwise."

"Shrimp and crawfish only, right?" I asked.

"Maybe oysters," Andy said.

Liz cocked an eyebrow.

"No crabs," Torbin explained. "We all agreed that we will not eat crabs for the next year or so."

Liz nodded. The look on her face made it clear that she understood. Crabs eat carrion, and right now some of what was in the water could well be human.

"Living in New Orleans," I said, "even a seafood boil has echoes of Katrina."

"No crabs," she agreed. With that she got up. Torbin and Andy had clearly done laundry as Liz was wearing what she'd had on last night and her clothes didn't look like they'd been left in a sodden heap. "Time to be a productive member of society." To me she said, "I still need to get in contact with your young friend."

"I'll give her a call."

Liz gave all of us a quick hug, me an extra smile, and then she and Andy were out the door.

Torbin plopped a plate of French toast in front of me.

"She's a nice woman," he said as he refilled his coffee cup.

"Yes, she is. And if I were single…" I started to say.

Torbin finished the obvious for me, "But you're not."

"Goddamn it! I never cheated on her!" Just say it and get it out, I told myself, this anger that had been brimming so close to the surface.

Torbin joined me at the table. "So dump her ass and go after Liz."

Of course I fell for it. "That's easy for you to say. What if it were you and Andy?"

"If it were me and Andy, I'd grab him by the scruff of the neck and sit down and talk and talk and talk until we came to some resolution." He took a sip of coffee. "But as you're not willing to do that—"

"Damn it. I'm not not willing to do that. It's just that—"

"Just that in three months and counting you haven't managed it yet."

"That little old windstorm Katrina has something to do with that."

"True. I'll give you a break there. But Micky, you're tearing yourself up—and you've got a lot of other people involved here as well. You and Cordelia have a lot of friends in common—myself included—and we're also caught up in this."

I started crying. Torbin put his arm around my shoulder, but didn't say anything, just let me cry myself out.

When I'd finished, he handed me a paper towel and simply said, "You need to eat. Let me give that French toast a spin in the microwave."

I didn't have an answer as to what I would do about Cordelia, although Torbin was right. I needed to do something.

I changed the subject. "Do you think I might be able to talk to Brooke Overhill?"

"Why?"

I gave him a brief overview of Alma Groome and her murder.

"You think Brooke might have murdered her?" he asked.

"I think someone in the Overhill family had the most to gain," I said. "What she found out could have destroyed their wealth." Torbin looked skeptical. "Or they could have nothing to do with it, but it's hard to know if I can't talk to some of them."

"As it just so happens, Brooke is supposed to call me in a little bit so we can arrange a time to eat, drink, and be merry and recall the good old days. Hang around, eat a decent breakfast, and I'll see what I can do."

He got three other calls and I finished eating before Brooke called.

I finished another cup of coffee before he and she finally caught up, made plans, gossiped about people I didn't know, and gnashed teeth about our political leadership, or lack thereof, and the recovery efforts in New Orleans.

Torbin finally said, "Oh, my cousin Micky, the private eye, wants to talk to you."

He handed me the phone.

"Hi, Brooke, I know this will sound really flaky—I promise I'm not trying to weasel my way into being a backup singer or anything like that—but I've been working on a case, and in a convoluted way, your family's name is connected to it. You might be interested as it involves another singer. Would it be possible for me to come talk to you about this? Whatever works for you, of course."

Torbin looked relieved that I hadn't blurted out that I suspected her family of foul play.

I was relieved that she didn't immediately blow me off. Instead I listened to her as she ran through her schedule—packed, as one might expect for a celebrity in her hometown.

"Could you do five this evening?" she asked.

"That's great. Tell me where to meet you."

"My house. Well, my parents' house. Is that okay?"

"That's fine." It was more than fine. It'd give me a chance to get a better sense of the family, not just Brooke. She gave me directions and that was it.

"See," I said as I handed the phone back to Torbin, "I don't intend to give her the third degree."

"I'm happy to hear that. Brooke is a friend, even if she lives in another world now."

"People reveal so much more when they think you agree with them."

Torbin shook his head in disapproval.

"Okay, how about this. I won't take advantage of your friendship with her. But I won't help conceal a crime either."

"Fair enough. Now get on with your life and let me get on with mine."

His phone was ringing again, so after changing into my clean clothes, I let myself out. Torbin waved good-bye as he was talking to someone about an upcoming show.

We live fairly close to each other. It would have been a quick walk to my house, but I headed for my office instead. Cordelia would be at the house. I had to face her soon, but wasn't up to it just yet. I was still too humiliated from my tumble into the swimming pool at a posh Uptown party. The distance to my office was about twice as long, but still easy enough, especially as the day was bright and clear.

Alma Groome had been murdered. The goons that I'd run into

during my breaking-and-entering expedition made it seem like someone was interested in the family history and its tainted flow of money.

I owed her a little more poking around. At least to see if I could find something I might be able to turn over to the police. Without incriminating myself.

I also had to follow up with Nathalie and contact her for Liz. That worried me. I didn't want to worry about Nathalie. She needed so many things, mostly to grow up and get away from that family, but I couldn't give her that. There was little I could give her and I didn't want to walk into that failure, even if it was the right thing to do.

When I got to my office, one of the first things I did—besides going to the bathroom and realizing that I would need more toilet paper soon or I was going to regret it—was to create a family tree for the Benoits to show the different family lines. It would be hard to explain without a visual. I would take it with me when I went to talk to Brooke.

I wanted to have as much information as I could before seeing her. Especially to have a better idea of who Alma Groome was, why she shouldn't have been murdered.

First I had to re-establish connections to all the various Web sites I'd used in the past. My new computer didn't have anything bookmarked or set up to connect automatically. That only took twice as long as it should have. Luckily for me one of the things I carried with me on my mad flight was a briefcase of most of my important papers, including the little notebook where I kept the myriad of passwords I needed to access the Internet.

Once those were in place, I started my search for Alma Groome.

She was born on April 23, 1972. That meant she was thirty-three when she died. Far too young. She'd gotten a BA in music from UNO, then a master's in music from the University of Wisconsin in Milwaukee, although she hadn't gone directly into graduate school. Her BA was in 1995 and the MM in 2004. I could just see that New Orleans girl shivering the entire time she was up there. Maybe she could take her coat off in June.

No announcements of weddings or births, so presumably she was not married and had no children.

From what records I could find, she seemed to have grown up in New Orleans, lived in the house where she was found, and stayed there while getting her undergraduate degree. After that it was harder to track her. A few addresses came up, most in New Orleans, but the one that seemed the most current was in Wisconsin. Maybe she'd stayed there? Or only recently come back? If she still lived up north, how had she come down here to be killed? But she had only recently gotten her master's degree, so maybe any new address didn't show up. She might have moved in with someone.

Did she have a lover? Someone who didn't know what had happened to her?

That thought haunted me.

She had been a performer, using her skills to re-create the career of her foremother. I found notices of shows she did and, as I got a better idea of what to look for, was able to create a chronology of her performances. She started while she was getting her graduate degree, only a few performances during that time. Once she had graduated, the pace picked up. She seemed to travel mostly in the Midwest and Northeast, often performing at colleges, but also a number of other venues. Some of them were advertised in the gay papers, but not always.

At first there were gaps of months between shows, but she seemed to have performed pretty steadily during the last six months, with no more than a week or two between dates. The last two dates I could find were a week or so ago, both in Illinois, one at the University at Champaign-Urbana and one in Chicago.

Then she disappeared.

I looked at the timeline. Her last performance was about three days before her body was discovered here.

Had someone reported her missing? I could at least call my law-enforcement friends and have them check that out.

I needed to call Danny anyway. As a lawyer, she'd probably punt this one on to Joanne, but it was way past time to connect with her.

Pointing my cell phone in the right direction, I dialed her number. An unfamiliar voice answered. Then I recognized it. "Elly?" Elly was Danny's partner. "Danny stuck outside?"

"Micky, hi. No, she's in the hospital."

"What?" How the hell had I missed that?

"Pneumonia. You know the courthouse flooded, and she's been helping sort through the muck in the evidence room. I think the mold—and stress and overwork—got to her. She picked up a bacterial infection.

You know how she is. She blew it off as a cold as long as she could. Until the fever hit 102 and I insisted she see a doctor."

"Hell, Elly, I'm sorry. Yeah, I can see Danny being stubborn about being sick. Can I do anything? Is she up to visitors?"

"She should be soon, but we're in Alexandria. The hospitals around New Orleans are overwhelmed. This was the closest place we could find that could keep her for as long as I think she needs to be observed and on IV antibiotics."

Alexandria was about four hours from New Orleans in the center of the state.

Elly sounded tired, like she could use a few days of bed rest as well.

"If you need me, let me know. You know I'd drive to Texas for either you or Danny. Alexandria isn't half that far."

"Save the gas. Maybe come help me get her home. I'll keep you posted."

"Please."

I put the phone down, then just stared at it. Danny in the hospital, Alex falling apart—I needed to call her, too—me drinking again, and falling, if not apart, certainly not holding it together all that well. What had Liz said about Cordelia? That she seemed lost? Elly was exhausted. With so many of us stumbling and falling, could anyone remain standing? Torbin seemed okay, but I knew him well enough to know that he also seemed to be chasing normalcy by going to parties, seeing friends, as if he needed those talismans of the time before to get through. Andy was never a chatterbox, but even he seemed quieter, more introspective.

I called Joanne on her official line, but she wasn't in. I could have left the message with someone else, but Hutch wasn't around either— someone else falling apart—and I didn't want to just let Alma Groome disappear into a bureaucracy. I left a message for her to call me.

Next on my list was Nathalie. Again, all I got was voice mail. I didn't leave a message, worried that Nathan would get it and that would only cause her more problems.

I went back for one final search on Alma Groome, to see if I'd missed anything.

This time I stumbled onto a recent video, filmed within the

last month. It was both a performance and a talk about the historical background of what she was doing.

The video wasn't high quality, but Alma had stage presence, a way of taking over the space that made you want to watch her. She had a rich alto voice and the ability to not just sing, but act her songs.

Between songs, she talked about them, gave the history of the performers who sang them. Annie Hindle, who published love poetry to women in the newspapers and married a woman, not once but twice. As Alma told it, the marriage was quite possibly legal, as marriage at the time was only illegal if falsehood was involved. Because the woman was Annie's dresser, it wasn't possible that she thought she was marrying a biological man. Ella Wesner was part of a family of dancers and she supported many of them with what she earned as a woman performing as a man. She was also part of a scandal, running off to Europe with Josephine Mansfield, who was the mistress of Colonel James Fisk, murdered by his business partner in the Grand Central Hotel—the murder of that century.

Then Alma sang a song that was her ancestor's signature. It was a ballad of love lost, about someone who knew that she would always look back even as she was looking forward. After the song, Alma told her story: "Octavia Alma Despaux was probably raised to be someone's mistress—she was what was called an octoroon at the time. Or a very light-skinned black woman. That wasn't what she wanted to do with her life, however, and once she saw a variety performance, she recognized a way out. It's been hard to reconstruct her life, mostly from playbills and newspapers hidden in archives. She probably started on the black circuit up around Atlanta, or at least disappeared long enough from New Orleans that when she reappeared in a talent show, she could pass herself off as an amateur and, more importantly for the bottom line, as white. She claimed to be from southern France to account for her dark looks and French-sounding name. New Orleans had a special affinity for anything French as long as it spoke English, so Octavia did quite well there. Once she had gained a reputation, she was able to get bookings elsewhere, even doing a European tour. Although over there, she probably billed herself as from New Orleans, as that would be more exotic on that side of the Atlantic—plus explain why she spoke very little actual French. After a scandal—she was caught in a compromising position with her dresser, another woman—she and the woman fled to Europe permanently. Then she disappeared, could be sitting on the beach in the south of France right now smoking cigars and telling wild tales that are true. Family lore has it that she still sent money and that at least one female of every generation has to have one of her names, as her sister Maria-Josephina vowed that she would never forget Octavia's generosity and kindness when she had no one else to turn to.

"It has taken years of digging—and luck—to find out this bare outline of her life. Like many performers of her time, she wasn't considered important enough for anyone to keep records, so what we've found has been by the happenstance of what was saved. The papers that advertised the performances, some newspaper articles, diaries, and letters. No one thought these people were valuable enough to record who they were or what happened to them."

Then Alma sang a final song, one about good-bye and the chance of meeting again.

The applause was long and loud and well-deserved.

Her performance seared me. The forgotten history she had found would be left moldering in archives again; her voice, her knowledge and passion had been stolen from us. The acts, and the women who created them, had been lost to history; now her voice and her reclaiming of them was also lost. I copied the performance on a flash drive. If I got the chance, I would show it to Brooke. It didn't seem fair. The two branches of the family both produced talented performers, but Alma would be as lost to history as Octavia Alma Despaux was. Brooke would have the spotlight.

My phone rang. I grabbed it, then had to jump up from my desk to get it pointed in the right direction so I could actually talk.

"Micky Knight," I answered.

"Joanne. I have some news for you."

"I know about Danny."

"Danny?" Clearly her news wasn't about Danny.

"Pneumonia. In the hospital in Alexandria," I summed up for her. "Elly says she'll be okay, just needs some drugs and some rest."

"Don't we all?" Joanne commented sardonically. "Damn, I hadn't heard that. I'll give her a call later."

"If that wasn't it, what is your news?"

"Bad, I'm afraid. The Jane Doe you reported was murdered.

Looks like she put up a fight—lot of bruises, broken fingernails. She had contusions on her head, but what killed her was being strangled. She'd been dead about two days when you found her. Cold weather slowed decomposition."

"Guess I was expecting something like this. I knew she was dead. I have a name and a possible address."

"You've been busy."

"Yeah, the PI business hasn't exactly been booming post-Katrina. Might have to learn to hang drywall."

"Look, Micky, if you're tight—"

"I'm okay. It's not like I have a flooded house to replace."

"Not a picnic by any stretch, but we had insurance, and flood insurance, so we'll be okay. How the hell do we always end up talking about this?"

"It's always in our lives. What do you go home to every night?"

"Let's talk about something else. Can you give me her name and address?"

I did, then asked, "Do you think someone is looking for her? Missing her?"

"I sure as hell hope so. It's hard for the people left behind, but what kind of life did you have if there's no one to miss you when you're gone?"

Then Joanne was off the phone and I was left wondering who would miss me if I disappeared? Dead, but that was morbid. Who would miss me if I moved away from here and started over again? I could call Shannon Wild—e-mail her in Eastern Europe where she was doing a story on Kosovo—and tell her I was willing to give it a try with her. We had been thrown together by Katrina; she said she was in love with me. Maybe I loved her, maybe I didn't. Maybe I'd just wanted someone to hold me in the night. The truth was that I didn't love her enough to turn away from everything here and go with her. Liz? No, too new, just hints of possibilities. She didn't know me well enough to miss me. Why did it even have to be with someone? I could just go where I wanted to go—no strings, a new beginning.

I wanted to go home, to the home I used to have, to quiet evenings with me chopping vegetables in the kitchen while Cordelia told me about her day. I wanted to be able to walk in the door and have her put her arms around me.

Forgive her and tell her you want her back. You can have that home again.

If it were only that simple. Did she even care if I forgave her? What sins had I committed that I wasn't aware of? Had I taken her for granted over the years? What if what was broken couldn't be mended? If there was no way to have that home again?

I got up and crossed the room to look out the window, chastising myself for this wallow in self-pity. There were bodies in the morgue up in St. Gabrielle that no one would claim, heartbreaking that no one was left to claim them, no one knew to claim there, or no one cared to claim them.

Torbin and Andy, Joanne and Alex, Danny and Elly, my mother, all my friends and family. Maybe Cordelia. I wouldn't be left unclaimed.

I picked up the phone, one more call to make. I dialed Nathalie's cell-phone number.

"Hello?" a male voice answered. Nathan.

I pinched my nose and pitched my voice high and did my best yat accent—from the catch phrase, 'where y'at, dawlin'?' "Hey, I'm callin' for Nat'lie. This her friend Bernice."

"Who?"

"Bernice, 'nother volunteer, down chere. Nats said to give her a call 'bout seeing some 'gators."

"Just a second." He dropped the phone and I heard voices in the background. I couldn't make out the words, but it seemed that a discussion was taking place. It took so long I was beginning to wonder if my subconscious had skimmed a story about Bernice, the serial killer who fed Midwestern volunteers to alligators, and I had inadvertently picked the wrong cover.

Finally the phone was picked up. "Who's calling?" a female voice asked. It wasn't Nathalie. High-pitched, nasal. Carmen?

"Who's askin'?" I stayed in the character of Bernice. "I'm a friend of Nat'lie's, trying to get 'holt of her."

"She's not available right now. Can I take a message?" she said coolly.

I doubted that any message I'd leave would get to Nathalie. Carmen was probably only asking to find out whatever she could.

"Naw, I'll call her later." I quickly hung up. That was weird. Why was Carmen, the bitch, intervening in a phone call to Nathalie?

It sounded like Carmen still had Nathan wound around her fingers and they had teamed up to make Nathalie's life miserable.

Another thing on my to-do list—drive out there and actually talk to her.

I glanced at my watch. Time to be heading out for my meeting with Brooke O. I gathered the family tree, the recording of Alma's performance and the rest of my notes, and was out the door.

The sun was setting; it would be dark before I got there. These were the short days of late fall.

As I turned onto her street, I noticed a large house, ablaze with light as if that could keep the dark and cold out. It was larger than the others on the block, with an imposing wrought-iron fence topped with menacing spears surrounding it. I started to pull up in front, then realized it wasn't the right address. I had just assumed that the Overhills had the most ostentatious house on the block.

Their house was farther down, a rambling Uptown house, but not one that said "The richest people in the neighborhood live here." Only a low brick wall separated the property from the street. The yard was well maintained, but it didn't have the neatness and precision that said a garden service took care of it. The house was off-white with green trim, a scattering of plants in pots on the veranda that surrounded it. A few lights were on, enough to indicate that people were here. One light on the porch was all the welcome offered.

I parked my car, looked at the house for a moment as I gathered my thoughts, then headed up the walkway to the door.

The brass door knocker was shaped like an alligator head. I lifted the jaws then realized that to knock I had to bring the faux teeth down onto a nutria in its mouth. I chuckled as I made it chomp.

Brooke herself opened the door.

"So were you horrified or amused?" she asked with a nod toward the brass alligator.

"Do I get demerits for a sick sense of humor if I said I found it funny?"

"In my nonscientific survey, the ones who are amused fit in here, the horrified ones not so much." She ushered me in.

She was in jeans and a T-shirt, covered by a well-worn navy hooded sweatshirt, and bright purple and gold LSU Tiger socks. Little or no makeup.

"Would you like some tea or coffee?" she asked. "Or it's officially five o'clock, we can move on to the cocktail hour."

"I'll have whatever you're having."

"Wheatgrass and bitterroot tea? Being too polite can get you in trouble."

"Can I do just wheatgrass and hold the bitterroot?"

"All made up. How about cinnamon stick? I'm trying to take care of my throat. I'm doing two benefit concerts in the next few days, so it's mostly tea these days."

"Cinnamon sounds lovely." I followed her to the kitchen.

It was a comfortable room, stained pine cabinets, a cheery yellow color, pots hung on the walls with blackened bottoms that proved they'd cooked a lot of food. There was just enough clutter—a stack of mail, dishes in a drainer—to indicate that people lived in this kitchen. The refrigerator, a stainless-steel one, was the exact same one that Cordelia and I had in our kitchen before the storm.

Brooke put the kettle on to boil.

"Thanks for agreeing to see me. Feel free to kick me out when you need to move on to other things."

"Torbin did me a lot of favors in the past, so lots of debt to repay." She added with a grin, "Have you recovered from last night's swim?"

"I was pushed," I said too quickly.

"Pushed?" she said as she took tea bags from one of the cabinets. "Now it gets intriguing? Who pushed you?"

"A woman whose name I can never remember. Patty something."

"Why'd she push you?"

"She's never forgiven me for my charm, brains, and good looks."

Brooke let out a whoop of laughter.

"The pool called to her with its siren song of revenge," I said.

"You are as crazy as Torbin. Which I love about him."

"Torbin's a good person. So I have to warn you that whatever I do or say here should not in any way reflect on him."

"Oh? Why?" She dropped the tea bags into two pottery mugs.

"Because he was worried I might accuse you of murder."

Brooke turned from the mugs to look at me. "This is a joke?"

"I wish it were." I pulled out a picture of Alma Groome, a still from one of her performances, and showed it to Brooke. "Her body was found in the destroyed house she grew up in. She wasn't killed by the storm. She was murdered—strangled to death and left there. Maybe the killers were hoping she wouldn't be found and if enough time passed, it would be assumed that she was just another victim of Katrina."

"Why would I want to murder her?" Brooke asked. She seemed genuinely puzzled.

"She's your cousin. Long lost, a branch of the forebearers that divided about a century ago." I pulled out the family tree to show her.

Brooke studied it intently, her finger tracing the family lines.

The screech of the tea kettle interrupted her. She quickly snatched it off the stove, hovering indecisively as if torn between making the tea or following the lines. The hot water won; she poured it into the mugs, then came back to the paper.

Finally she looked up and said, "Okay, so we're related. Why would I want to kill her?"

"She's black. It seems that Josiah Benoit crossed the color line and passed as white to marry your great, etc. grandmother."

"You think I care about that?"

"Some people might, but no, I doubt that matters to you. What might matter is that Josiah never divorced his first wife, so his second marriage wasn't valid." It wasn't that cut and dried—there was no record of the divorce, so his second marriage might not be legal—but that would take a team of lawyers to wrangle through."

"Meaning?"

She was beginning to understand, but I got the sense she wanted to hear what I'd say.

"Josiah left the Perdido Street properties to his second wife and her children, with nothing for his first wife and her children."

"And that's the property my family sold to make a lot of money." Brooke finished making the tea as she said, "That's a lot of history."

She handed me a mug and I took a sip to let her mull things over.

"It's poisoned, by the way," she said.

I almost spit it out, but caught the impish quirk of her eyes. She was doing a very good job of not smiling.

"Oh, well, gotta go sometime." I took another sip.

"So what does this all mean? I don't have all the family finances in my head, but I'd bet we could easily part with whatever we sold those properties for back then. If that's what someone wanted."

"It's hard to know without a gaggle of lawyers going through it.

If Josiah was 'legally' white, maybe his first marriage didn't count. I'd guess that lawyers could argue it multiple ways. Probably the bottom line is that Alma and her family could have sued for, and gotten, a pretty significant settlement from your family."

"Would someone really murder another person over that?" Brooke seemed so wide-eyed and innocent when she asked that, either she had nothing to do with this or she was some mean-ass psychopath who could do or say anything and get away with it. My money was on the former, though. I found myself liking her and didn't want her to have anything to do with this.

"People kill for just about any reason—to steal a jacket or because they had too much to drink and weren't thinking. Greed is a big one."

"Look, I don't think I'm part of a family of murderers," Brooke said, as if testing the waters to see if that was really what I was accusing her of.

"I know someone did kill Alma Groome. Who or why, I don't know and may never know. It seems she discovered information about your two families that indicated that your side got all the goods and her side was left with nothing. Did that lead to her death? I don't know. Maybe she was trying blackmail—had some less-than-nice people in on it and it got messy and she was killed."

Brooke nodded as if thinking about this. Then she put down her tea cup and went to a door to an inner hallway. "Hey, Dad," she called. "You might be interested in this."

Well, I had wanted to meet the whole family.

A man in his late fifties or early sixties entered the kitchen. He was tall and had a full head of silver hair that he wore a little long, either flaunting his lack of hair loss or too busy for regular haircuts. He wore a blue striped button-down shirt with the sleeves rolled up and gray chinos. Both the shirt and pants were rumpled, as if he'd been in them all day and finally at the end of the day come home and taken off his tie, loosened his collar, and rolled up his sleeves. Behind him was a woman about his age, I assumed his wife. She was more casual than her husband, a nice pair of jeans and a lavender cotton sweater. Like her daughter, she wore little makeup.

Brooke introduced us. "This is Micky Knight, a friend of my friend Torbin. She's a private investigator and has uncovered some very interesting family history." She paused as if done, then remembered to say, "This is my mom and dad, John and Marilyn Overhill."

I quickly oriented myself. John was the son of Jameson and Jessica Stern. Jessica brought the Perdido Street properties into the family; Jameson sold them for a lot of money.

I decided to leave out the word "murder" other than to say that Alma Groome had been killed. As I had for Brooke, I narrated what I'd uncovered about their family history.

When I was done, John Overhill said, "Wow, fascinating," as if he were a history buff and had been shown something truly interesting. In response to what was probably the look on my face—I try to keep it neutral, but I'm not always perfect—he said, "I can see how it might be a mess for us personally, if someone were to sue. But at this point most of our holdings have been acquired in the last two decades or so. This claim has to predate that by a long time. If we lost half of what we own, we'd still be more than comfortable, so I'm almost more fascinated by how this would play out—what are the laws, how do you decide these things when so much time has passed."

His wife, Marilyn, asked, "Do you think the woman being killed had something to do with this?"

That was the question. I answered carefully. "It's hard to know. She was murdered, that's not in doubt. This could possibly be a motive, but there could be other things in her life that I don't know about that caused her to be killed."

Unlike her husband, she seemed less interested in the history and more concerned about the here and now. She continued. "It's odd because just recently I got a phone call from someone I didn't know, but who seemed to know me. She said something about there being information that we wouldn't want anyone else to discover and if we paid her a million dollars she'd keep quiet. I didn't take it seriously, told her I thought this wasn't a very funny joke. That seemed to make her angry. She said it was no joke, that my family didn't deserve any of the money we had and that if we didn't pay up, we'd lose everything."

"When was this?" John asked. "Why didn't you tell me?"

"Oh, honey, with everything else going on, it seemed so minor. I mentioned it to Jared. He had just come home. He said if she ever called again, we could trace the line."

"She never called back?" I asked.

"Not that I know of. I hung up on her with the first call. It just sounded so outlandish and...we came through Katrina okay. So many of our friends, the people that work for us, have lost everything. It seemed a waste of time to worry about some bizarre threat."

"We've had our share of hangers-on. Long-lost cousins or old college buddies—who can't remember where we went to college," John said. If you have money, people want it. Some with very good reason—a sick child, help for a needy school. But a number of people will try any scam to get it."

Brooke said, "We have the Jessica Stern foundation to try and help those who truly need money. It gives individual grants for things like medical bills and also grants to local organizations for projects like a new school playground."

"It's not possible for us to examine the legitimacy of every request. That's why we set up the foundation and route most requests through that," John said.

"Even then some people worm their way in," Marilyn said. "Remember last summer, just before Katrina? That young man who said his father had been killed while working at one of our hotels."

"Yes," her husband said. "He didn't need anything for himself, but his mother had just been diagnosed with cancer and he needed something immediately to help his sister stay in school."

"You gave him a couple of hundred," Marilyn narrated. "And we saw him in a French Quarter bar about a week later. He claimed that his sister had just been killed in a car wreck and he was drinking away his sorrows." The arch of her eyebrow indicated how much she believed his story. "And that woman who claimed to be related to your Midwestern branch of the family? She showed up, claimed that she'd been raped and robbed. So of course you took her in. She said she didn't want the police, just needed a thousand dollars to get home."

"And I gave it to her," John said. These had the feeling of well-worn stories.

"Once she got the money and discovered where we kept the kitchen money, she left in the middle of the night. I go away for two days—John is just too kind."

"Sad thing is, she really was a cousin, about ten times removed," John said. "I had one of our security guys check her out."

"Did you press charges?" I asked.

"No, it didn't seem worth it. She was young, maybe nineteen or twenty, the age people do foolish things that can cost them forever. I didn't think jail would help her."

"And then there was that time when another young woman came by with a pack of what she claimed were rescued dogs," Marilyn said. "Turns out she'd gone to the animal pound the day before and—"

She was interrupted by the entrance of someone I guessed to be Jared, the oldest son,

I had to repeat the story one more time.

"Hey, I always wanted to be the suspect in a murder," he said. "I am a suspect, right?" He shot me a sardonic grin, as if daring me to say it.

"Where were you on the night on November 22nd?" I asked, deadpan.

"Out wandering the streets of New Orleans. I had no witnesses."

"Jared," his mother admonished him. "This is perhaps not the best time for your sense of humor."

"Damn, and I was looking forward to some interrogation," he said, winking at me in an exaggeratedly flirtatious manner.

"We can arrange that. I leave all the interrogating to my assistant, Guido. He likes making men talk."

"In that case, I was home here in the bosom of my family."

"Then I'm sure you're innocent," I said. I was tired of his banter. He was either trying to hide something or just liked the attention. I turned to his mother. "On the phone call, are you sure it was a woman?"

"I never really thought about it. She just sounded like a woman to me."

"I have a video of Alma performing her act. Could you listen to part of it and see if the voice is familiar?"

"You think she may have tried to blackmail us?"

"If it's her voice that might answer some questions." If Alma had attempted blackmail, she might have skimmed other legal lines, and any of those could have led to her murder.

"Yes, of course."

Brooke ran to her room and retrieved her laptop, a brand-new Mac with a big screen. I gave her the flash drive with Alma's performance saved on it.

It took less than a minute for Marilyn to say, "No, that's not her."

"Close your eyes," I instructed. "Picture yourself holding the phone."

She did so, but after another minute, again shook her head. She opened her eyes and looked at me. "No, definitely not. The voice I heard was not a pretty voice at all, harsh and flat. And…it sounded like a white person. Or I just assumed that it was."

"Could you detect any accent?" I asked.

"I didn't notice one, but I wasn't really paying attention. It wasn't a long conversation."

"If you were to picture this person, what would she look like?" I asked.

"Um, I guess, well, female. Maybe twenties or thirties. Not big, she seemed to have a small voice. And Caucasian. Maybe an accent, but not from the South. Maybe the Northeast. And…and that's all."

"Thanks, that's very helpful. Sometimes we know more than we think we know," I told her.

"Time to go," Jared said.

Marilyn explained. "We're helping with a big red-beans-and-rice cookout for the soldiers and rescue workers who've been helping in the area where a lot of our employees lived."

"We never decided, did you want me to go?" Brooke asked.

"We have decided," her mother said firmly, "that you're doing enough. You need to stay here and not be out talking all night in the cold air. You have a concert tomorrow night and you can't get sick."

"Yes, Mother," Brooke said affectionately. To me she asked, "Can I watch all of this?" referring to Alma's video.

"Yeah, sure. I can come by later and get it."

"If it's not too long, why don't you stay? I could even offer you another cup of tea, since the first one has to be cold by now."

I accepted. The rest of the Overhills quickly bundled up and were out the door with Jared, carrying several huge pots from the kitchen. Brooke finished making the tea, gave me a mug, then sat in front of her computer.

She watched the entire video without a word. When it was done, she turned to me and said, "She was very talented. I could feel the energy and focus in her performance, feel the history in what she was doing, like all those voices were singing through her for us." She took a sip of her tea, then said, "I can't do that. I can't make all those layers resonate. I can sing a song, sing what I write and what I know. But I can't do what she did." The catch in her voice told me she knew something special had been lost.

I thanked her for the tea and for answering my questions. I let her keep the flash drive and Alma's last performance.

Chapter Twenty

It was still early in the evening, barely eight o'clock. I drove back via Magazine Street. It was close to the river and hadn't flooded. I needed the lights and people flashing by as I drove home, a balm to the empty blocks and darkened swaths that I too often had to traverse.

The Overhills seemed like decent people, with a healthy perspective on what money could buy and what it couldn't. Like Brooke, either they were innocent or were great actors. Except for Jared. Maybe he was tired and a bit wired, but he seemed to be hiding something. Maybe he always used humor to distance himself from the messy business of life. I didn't know him well enough to judge. Brooke had her singing career; he was the one whose prestige and worth were invested in the family business and wealth.

Much as I wanted Alma to be a brilliant, selfless performer and not someone who had brought chaos into her life, someone had tried to blackmail the Overhills. It appeared to be a clumsy attempt. Though Marilyn didn't recognize Alma's voice as the one on the phone, it could still be her. She was a performer who could act and possibly even change her voice. Or have an accomplice make the call. That it was another woman also implicated her. It could have been her lover; as a lesbian she was likely to have more women in her life than a man or a straight woman, women that could help her with her blackmail. Lesbians aren't perfect, but we're a little better about gender stereotypes than most. We don't automatically assume that a woman is too girly for a little blackmail.

After I'd turned off Magazine onto Camp, I'd pretty much been driving on autopilot. I realized I was heading for my house—and Cordelia—not my office.

Just do it, just get it over with. Waiting another day and another day won't change anything or make it easier. Tomorrow had become too seductive, always beckoning, "Do it tomorrow." But tomorrow never came; in the night it turned into today. I needed to do it today.

I drove by the house, then made the block, coming back around and parking two houses down. I noticed the changes in the neighborhood. The water had reached this block. When I'd first come back about half the cars parked on the street had muddy black water lines on them. It seemed like those derelict heaps had finally been towed away. A tree near the corner was about half the size it had been before, with all the limbs ripped away by the wind.

Several of the houses were dark, perhaps empty, abandoned or still waiting for those who lived there to return.

The lights were on at our house, although I didn't see a car that I recognized as Cordelia's. Had she flown in? And did that mean she would soon be flying out? Or had she bought a new car? Hers had close to a hundred-thousand miles on it before Katrina. Maybe she had traded it in. I should know all these things and I didn't. I felt a stab at the loss of the daily rhythm of my life, the little things that added up.

What do I want, I again asked myself. I wanted to talk to her and find out what she wanted. And then…that would depend on what she wanted.

A big boxy SUV drove past me and parked right in front of my house.

Patty What's-Her-Name got out. Carrying flowers.

"You fucking bitch," I muttered under my breath, as I slunk down low in my seat so she wouldn't notice me. I wasn't sure if I was referring to Patty or Cordelia or both.

She marched confidently up the stairs and knocked on the door.

She waited for about a minute and knocked again.

I began to suspect that Cordelia was not expecting her.

Patty was about to knock a third time when the door finally opened.

Cordelia was in sweatpants and an old sweatshirt. Definitely not expecting company. Unless she was trying to get rid of her.

Patty presented the flowers with a flourish.

Cordelia hesitantly took them.

I was almost enjoying the show since I knew Cordelia well enough to know she hadn't agreed to this. I could almost picture it. Someone told Patty that she needed to be more assertive and chase the woman she wanted. Either Patty hadn't listened or didn't seem to realize that the other woman had to want to be chased for this to work.

I could almost hear the sigh as Cordelia finally stepped aside and let Patty in.

"You are too nice," I told her, much too quietly for her to hear.

I considered hanging around and waiting to see Patty put out, but she was quite an obtuse person and I wasn't sure Cordelia could manage the level of impoliteness that would probably be required.

"But you, my little pretty," I said to her vehicle, "have walked into my evil clutches." It was a Chevy Tahoe—why does anyone with less than ten kids need something that massive—dried-blood red and ugly. I noted down the license number.

I stayed another fifteen minutes, but it was cold and I was tired and hungry. Only the lights on the first floor were on when I left, the bedroom chastely dark.

"Your hubcaps will be mine oh-so-soon," I told the Tahoe as I drove past it.

Then it was back to my office. By myself. To a sumptuous dinner of peanut butter, strawberry jam on whole-wheat bread.

Why hadn't I banged on the door and told Patty to get the fuck out of my house?

Because it didn't seem quite like the right time for a macho possessive act? Because it gave me an excuse to put everything off once again? Because I wasn't sure how Cordelia would respond? She might just throw us both out.

I decided to focus on an easier task. Catching a murderer.

I went back through my case notes, seeing what Mrs. Frist had said about the family next door. Jordy, the father, was dead and Mae, the mother, wasn't doing too well. One child had overdosed, one was in prison, one killed in a motorcycle accident, one married to a woman fifteen years older than he was with four kids already. They might want to know that their sister was dead.

Time for some more Internet sleuthing.

After an hour or two I found out that the sister, Latisha Mae, had done time for helping her scum-dog boyfriend run drugs. She had gotten out of St. Gabrielle, the women's prison, a week before Katrina. The only address for her was her parents' house. Somehow I didn't think she was living there. She probably had a parole officer and Joanne could find out who that was.

The living son was Calvin. His address was a place in the Lower 9th Ward, so it was a good bet I wouldn't find him there either.

Katrina had spread people all over the country, from the north shore of Lake Pontchartrain to Alaska. I had seen an article about refugees who'd ended up in Milwaukee needing winter coats. Sometimes people just got on buses or planes with no idea where they'd end up. Some of the planes had landed in places like Utah.

Maybe it was less than kind, but I posted on a where-are-you Web site, "Calvin, Latisha Mae, and Mae, your sister/daughter Alma is looking for you," with a nondescript e-mail address I sometimes used for this purpose.

I searched for another few hours, but could find nothing else useful. A few more listings of performances by Alma, a mention of Calvin winning an award for being the lead water boy on the high-school football team. But nothing that would help me find them.

Another thought occurred to me. What if Alma hadn't wanted to use what she had discovered as a way to get money from the Overhills, but someone else had, someone who wanted to get the information from her. To the point that he (or she) murdered Alma to get it. That might explain what I saw at the house, why those thugs were there looking for what I had to assume was the information Alma had uncovered.

But it didn't seem likely that, for example, her just-released-from prison sister would have the wherewithal to hire thugs like the ones I'd seen. Plus they were white. Would a black woman hire two white thugs when presumably she could get any number of her ex-boyfriend's associates to help her? Maybe she didn't want to murder her sister or have anyone she knew do it for her, so she hired someone she didn't know.

You're getting tired and making things up. The sister had just got out of jail, presumably she didn't want to go back, and a quick way to go back to jail was to engage in criminal activity with people who'd be more than willing to sell her out for a shorter prison sentence.

Nothing was making sense. Except for the scenario that I didn't much like, that it probably was the Overhills—maybe only Jared—who had the most to lose and the resources to prevent that loss.

I was tired. It was time to pile on the blankets and go to bed.

I made a list of what I needed to do—contact Joanne about the parole officer and get my butt out to Kenner to find out what was going on with Nathalie and connect her with Liz. Tell Torbin that Operation Shrimp de Jour was afoot.

Talk to Cordelia.

That was enough for one day. I went to bed.

Chapter Twenty-one

It was cold when I woke up, I could see my breath. No hot water and no heat were getting beyond old into ancient and decrepit. I jumped out of bed, threw on clothes, did as abbreviated a tooth-brushing and face-washing as I could get away with and still be seen in public, then hastened downstairs and outside. Mercifully, my car was parked in the sun, so it was far warmer than inside my office.

I needed more clothes. A hot shower would also be nice. Could I impose on Torbin for a second one in less than a week? That wouldn't solve the clothes problem, though. I could—and had—borrowed dresses from him, but they wouldn't be much help in this weather.

I'm clean enough for Kenner, I decided. I'd go out there, find Nathalie, call Liz, and the two of them could talk about whatever Liz needed to talk about.

First stop was a coffee shop to get caffeinated, something resembling breakfast, and someplace warm to sit.

The caffeine got my brain going. And my cell phone. First I called Joanne to pass on what I knew about Alma's family. The next of kin needed to be notified.

"That's proving to be a major challenge," she told me. "People are spread out everywhere. Some, who went to Red Cross shelters, can be tracked if you're persistent. By now most of them have been to three or four locations, moving from the shelters to hotels to another hotel to a temporary apartment. But a number of people just got in their cars and left. They're staying with friends or relatives and aren't on anyone's radar."

She told me she'd see if she could locate a parole officer for

Latisha Mae Groome. Maybe if we could find Latisha Mae we could find Mae and Calvin.

After finishing with Joanne, I started to call Torbin, but it was a bit early for drag-queen hours. I'd catch him later in the afternoon.

Driving to Kenner is truly odious. I'd always felt like I needed a passport to cross the Orleans Parish line, but the contrast was especially harsh now. The floodwalls on the canal dividing the two parishes were some of the ones that failed. The wall that gave way was on our side, so the waters had gushed through with astounding force, sweeping houses from their foundation, washing contents, even cars, blocks away.

Nothing was damaged on the other side of the canal. So now crossing the parish line was going from destruction to unflooded, undamaged. The contrast was stark.

It took me about thirty minutes to get out there and an encounter with every annoying driver in Jefferson Parish. I had to run through my entire repertoire: "It doesn't get any greener," "Your turn signal is broken," "No, of course the stop sign don't apply to you," "Get any closer to my rear and you'd better be wearing a condom," and the general-purpose one, "What, you messed up and took a double dose of stupid pills this morning?" It didn't help that a lot of the license plates were from Texas. "You went to Houston and forgot how to drive?" I asked one egregiously large Hummer making a left turn that was not only illegal, but stupid. He couldn't make the turn, had to back up, holding up two lanes of traffic instead of going around the block.

I finally found the church where Nathalie and her group were staying.

Now I confronted the minor detail of coming up with a plausible reason for driving out here to see her, one that might get me through the Nathan/Carmen gauntlet.

Ah, perfect. Nathalie had mentioned that she was interested in a medical career, like working at CDC, and I'd met a doctor from there who was willing to talk to her about it. I was out in this area anyway, so thought I'd stop by. Well, not perfect, but it would have to do.

As I nosed around for a parking spot, I noticed a large black SUV that had pulled over halfway into a ditch. What I really noticed was the rhythmic rocking of the vehicle; someone's passion was threatening to take it all the way into the culvert. I parked in front with one car between me and the rockin' robins. I had other things to do, but it was hard not to watch. Besides the one-big-orgasm-and-there-she-goes interest was the fact that someone was going at it in the bright daylight in the heart of a nice middle-class neighborhood. This was a mixed commercial/ residential area and they were parked in front of a high metal fence, so it wasn't like any kids would be tripping out the front door and getting an eyeful, but it was still pretty blatant.

I was using my rearview window to keep an eye on the action. In almost a cliché, the truck stopped its motion, a window went down an inch, and cigarette smoke curled out.

To get to the church I'd have to walk by the SUV, so I gave it another minute, hoping they'd get dressed and I wouldn't be at risk for seeing something I didn't want to see.

Talk about plot thickening—the door opened and Carmen got out.

Then it went from thick to gooey. Her paramour rolled down the window for one last kiss. He looked like the older thug I'd seen while at the house.

No, it can't be, that would be just too strange. Maybe I was getting to the jaded point in my career when all straight white male thugs of a certain age looked alike. Same greasy hair, day-old stubble on the chin, sloping forehead, thick neck. I was wrong, conflating one ugly black SUV and even uglier thug with Carmen and her boyfriend of the moment. She was no better than other eighteen-year-olds, impressed with a man because he had a car and a place to live, so much more sophisticated than the high-school boys she was around. He didn't seem as tall and big-shouldered as the one I'd seen.

It was only a brief glance, distorted through my rearview mirror, a quick sloppy kiss, then he was again hidden behind tinted windows. His engine roared to life, accompanied by a throbbing bass beat, and he squealed away.

I tried for one more look as he drove by me, but he was already going faster than he should have, plus if by a coincidence so bizarre that it would be worthy of a world record, it was the same guy, I couldn't be sure he wouldn't recognize me.

Maybe I'd get the chance to ask Carmen a few questions after I found Nathalie. If Carmen was here, the rest of the kids were probably around as well. She couldn't very well send them off alone with Coach Bob still unable to do more than hobble a few feet.

As it turned out, Carmen could.

When I went to the hall where they'd set up sleeping quarters for the kids, no one was there, only the older woman that I'd seen when I dropped Nathalie off.

She was kindly and nice and clueless. I asked her where the kids were. She said that they were somewhere in New Orleans, specifically in one of the flooded areas. Eighty percent of the city had flooded. She thought they'd be back this evening, she wasn't sure about the time, somewhere around when it got dark. Except maybe this was the evening that they were going to a service with another group from the same area. She couldn't remember. She wasn't quite sure which one Nathalie was, but she was sure I could give a message to Carmen and Carmen would get it to her. Carmen was such a nice girl, always polite and neat. Oh, yes, Carmen was here, she had really wanted to go out with them, this work is so important to her, such a nice pious girl, but she had—in a whisper, although no one else was around—girl problems, and it just wouldn't do for her to be out there in the land of dirty toilets until "it" was over.

I thanked her and asked if she could direct me to where Carmen was. No, I wouldn't disturb her, just leave a brief message for Nathalie.

Because Carmen wasn't feeling well, she'd been given a room upstairs instead of having to bunk with the other girls.

Yeah, right, I thought as I trotted up the stairs in the direction the woman had pointed me. Carmen was a con woman. No one dying of cramps would have been going at it like she was, unless her boyfriend wanted a bloody mess in the van. A week of putative cramps would keep her out of the hot, dirty work and here with no one to notice her comings and goings. And comings.

I tapped briefly on her door, then opened it.

"Hey, you're supposed to knock," she yelled.

"I did, but I'm in a hurry."

"You!" she said, actually paying attention now. "What do you want? A perv breaking into young girls' rooms?"

"Save it for your naïve church folk. I caught your performance out on the road. Girls who do it with guys in cars in the middle of the day disgust me."

"What do you want?" she demanded again. I noticed a small baggie of white power on her bed.

"Who's your boyfriend? Besides Coach Bob and the pathetic Nathan."

"None of your business."

"He looked familiar. Think I've seen him around some cop shops. In handcuffs."

"What's it to you?"

I doubted that Carmen was the eighteen she claimed, but she couldn't be more than her early twenties. Just young enough and foolish enough and filled with the feeling that nothing bad could really happen to her, she was oh-so strong and smart. I knew that life rarely protected the foolish and that it would all come crashing down around her; her boyfriend would cheat, turn her in to the cops if it would help him.

"You're playing a dangerous game. It's going to bite you in the butt and bite you hard. You want to be stupid, go right ahead, but you're dragging in other people. Jail or worse. You might want to think about it."

"I don't know what you're talking about. I'm here with a church group trying to help people."

"With cocaine laying on your bed? Using Nathan as a mule to keep your hands clean and let him take all the risk? And screwing your dealer boyfriend in broad daylight. Not everyone will be as gullible as your chaperone."

"You've got it all wrong," she said, trying for a sexy pout. It probably worked on horny and not-too-bright males—the type she seemed to surround herself with. Me? Not so much.

I strode into the room and snatched the baggie away from her.

She tried to grab it back.

"This, young lady, is cocaine. Your level of con might work in the land of rural pastures, cows, and cheese, but it's big city, bright lights in this part of the world. Here, you're a nun, this is a whorehouse. Don't think we're stupid just because you want us to be?"

A sly look came into her eyes. "You want a cut?"

"A cut?" I didn't want a cut of anything she was involved with, but playing her might get me some more info. "A cut of what?"

"Nuh-uh, you gotta agree to it before I tell you anything."

"You want me to agree to something I know nothing about?"

"And even then you just gotta do what I tell you. You can't know everything."

"Running small-time cocaine deals for your boyfriend?"

"It's not his thing, it's mine. I'm the real brains in this."

Right. And I am Marie of Romania. I didn't say that. No way would this child get a reference to a Dorothy Parker poem. "No, I'm not interested in a cut. All I'm interested in is your leaving Nathan and Nathalie and everyone else out of whatever sordid mess you're involved in."

"What are you going to do about it?" she spat at me.

"Stop you anyway and every way I can." I turned around and walked away as quickly as I could.

She was a perfect little juvenile delinquent who'd made it to adulthood still thinking she could get away with whatever she wanted to. She was wrong, deluded enough, but nothing I could say to her would get through. Even a hard crash into reality might not make a difference. She'd just find someone else to blame.

As I got back to my car I wished I'd been quick enough to have noted the license tag of her boyfriend's SUV. Carmen should have been warned when Joanne and I broke up the drug deal she involved Nathan in. We'd essentially given her the chance to be young and foolish and avoid the worse consequences of her actions. Maybe it would have been better to have really busted them—Nathan would been arrested, possibly Nathalie as well, but we would probably have been able to argue them out with only a slap on the wrist. What was the cliché about hindsight? Some messes can't be cleaned up, no matter what route you take. I was hoping this wasn't one of them.

I drove slowly around the block that encompassed the church and its buildings, but the SUV was gone and no one else showed themselves. I'd have to come back later and see if I could find Nathalie.

Then I decided to take advantage of being in the 'burbs with the box stores and do another real grocery run. The toilet-paper situation was getting dire.

Plus, I had to admit, the sliced turkey was gone and my office wasn't well stocked in much beyond peanut butter and jelly. I'd lived there a long time ago, but hadn't used it as a place to cook or live for years now. The big refrigerator had died and I'd replaced it with a smaller one since I mostly used it for water and drinks.

As I stood in the grocery, I realized that without gas, I couldn't do much cooking. So I had to strategically shop for food that didn't need more than a microwave or could be eaten cold. I grabbed a few frozen meals, a small enough number to fit in the tiny freezer, plus some canned pasta and soup. Bread and some cold cuts. And a big bundle of toilet paper.

Then back to my office to put everything away.

Once that was done, I pulled out my cell phone to call Torbin and plan the shrimp caper. But before dialing him, I noticed that I'd missed a call.

I didn't recognize the number. It was local. Maybe Nathalie had managed to get a phone and call me. I cursed the spotty cell service and hit redial.

"Hi, Micky, you called back. Thanks." The woman's voice that greeted me was naggingly familiar.

"Yeah, sorry I missed you."

"My mother got another phone call."

That placed the voice. I have to admit, I was just a little thrilled that Brooke O. had called me. "Same woman?" But not so thrilled I couldn't do my job.

"No, this time it was a male voice. Or a woman with a low voice. According to my mother the voices weren't the same. I was home and managed to pick up another line and hear part of it."

"What did he say?"

"Pretty much like the first call. He said he had damning information on us and if we paid them—it was plural—a million dollars he'd keep it quiet."

"How did you respond?"

"I didn't say anything, didn't want him to know I was listening in. My mother told him no, that we wouldn't pay a million dollars, that there was no information that needed to be hidden. Then it sounded like he was talking to someone else, like he'd covered the phone. It was silent for over a minute. Then when he came back he was nasty, said something like 'You think you're so fucking nice and perfect, but pretty soon everyone will know what pieces of shit you are.' Not the kind of language my mother is used to hearing."

"It was probably meant to shock her, or at least make it as vile as possible. The purpose is to intimidate you enough to make you pay."

"Not my mother. Whoever this is, he'd do better talking to my dad. He might give them some money just because he'd think if they're desperate enough to resort to blackmail, they must be hard up. My mother blew him off, saying, 'You mean that stuff from a hundred years ago? We already know and we don't care.'"

"How did the caller react to that?"

"It was hard to tell. If he was taken aback, he didn't show it. Again there was the silence, then he recovered quickly, said he had lots of stuff from now and in the past. So my mother asked him what he had. He said for half a million he'd let us know and the other half would keep it secret."

"Are you considering doing it?"

"My mother? Hell, no. She told the man that we would not be blackmailed, that we had an investigator looking into it and that he should crawl back under the rock he crawled out of and stay there."

"Your mother really said that?"

"I think by that point she was more angry than worried. My mother is a strong woman."

"Good for her, although to catch him or them it might have been better to string him along."

"I was wondering about that. We've never been blackmailed before, so I'm not sure how to handle it. My mother is all for just forgetting about it. She says it seems so minor in post-Katrina New Orleans."

"But you're not so sure."

"He roundly cursed us out after my mother told him to go to hell, nasty, threatening. I have to admit I'm worried. I don't want anything bad to happen to anyone in my family."

"What if he really does know something?"

"Like what?"

"This might be hard to think about, but what if your father is having an affair? Or your brother likes boys below the age of consent? Even people we think we're close to can hide things."

"I did consider this. He didn't say anything or hint that 'Daddy's been stepping out,' just left it very vague. It made me wonder if there wasn't something going on. That's the ugly part of this. It puts those thoughts in your head. My mother and I talked about it even. Her answer is no. My father is where he's supposed to be. She goes with him on a lot of his trips, and he goes with her on hers."

"What about your brother?"

"He's not married, so it's not like he could have an affair."

"He seemed evasive when I was there, making jokes about everything."

"Oh, that. Jared's a nerd. I mean, he's a handsome man now, but he was a science geek growing up. He's always a bit of a jerk when a good-looking woman is around. Give him a little time to get used to you and you'd see a different side to him."

"You're his sister. You know him much better than I do." She was his sister and she might also have a sisterly blind spot.

"I noticed you don't have a wedding ring. Are you single?"

"No, I'm not." That seemed like the least complicated answer.

"Too bad. Jared really is a catch."

"Spoken like a true sister."

"So what do we do?"

"About the caller?"

"Yeah. Should we just forget it, like my mother said?"

"What do you think?"

She considered for a moment, then answered. "I'm not sure. A woman's been murdered. It could be connected to the blackmail. That worries me a little too much to just forget it."

"What about the investigator looking into it? What does he—or she—think?"

"Ah, well, that would be you. My mother just said it. I know you're not working for us and may not be able to comment. Or you may get in trouble with the person who is paying you for this."

I debated whether to tell her no one was paying me, that this was my own particular obsession. What I did say was, "This is blackmail, you could go to the police."

"Normally that might be a good idea, but now? Like everything else here, the police force is struggling to just get to the most essential. It seems foolish to burden them with this when they're trying to protect people's flooded homes from being looted."

She had a point.

"And, well, we have the resources to hire people to look into this.

It seems only fair to do that and let the police assist other people. You're already investigating this."

"Are you requesting my help?" I asked.

"Can you? Or is there some ethical rule that says you can't work for two people?"

I decided to be honest with Brooke. "I'm not working for anyone. I got hired to retrieve some keepsakes from a flooded home, and while I was out there a church group renovating the house next door discovered Alma's body. This is my own curiosity. As you said, the police are overwhelmed and I felt someone should try to find out how she ended up there."

"Would you work for me?"

"What if I find out something you don't want to know?"

"So everyone would find out?"

"No, I'm not a blackmailer. If I work for you, one of the things you pay for is confidentiality. But you'd know. Also, I won't cover up crimes. Major ones. A little illegal gambling or pot smoking is one thing, but if I find any evidence that someone in your family had something to do with Alma's murder, I will turn that over to the police."

"We're not above the law. I can't imagine that anyone in my family would harm someone, especially just for money, but, God forbid, if they did, then they need to answer for it."

"Okay, if you're sure."

"I'm sure. So what do we do now?"

"Boring paperwork. You sign a contract, we discuss what you want me to try to accomplish. I make sure you understand that I can't work miracles."

"Sounds good to me. Would it be too much of an imposition to ask you to come up here? I have a concert tonight and have to get ready. Or we can do it tomorrow."

Other than calling Torbin and planning an illegal adventure—it was a good thing that I ignored minor infractions of the law—I had no major plans for the day. I agreed to come Uptown and said I could be there in an hour.

As I hung up, I wondered if they were trying to co-opt me, although again, if Brooke was acting, she'd easily clean up every award.

I made it to her place in about forty-five minutes. When I arrived, her mother was puttering in the yard, repotting several plants.

WATER MARK

"I should have done this a few months back. Everything just grows if you don't watch it."

"Your plants are gorgeous," I said.

"As long as I don't kill them I'm happy. Brooke told me she's hiring you to look into this blackmail thing."

"Yes, how are you with that? She said you thought it better to just ignore your caller." I wondered how she'd react; the mother might know secrets that the daughter didn't.

Marilyn Overhill thought for a moment, then said, "I guess I'd like to ignore the blackmailer, but he or she doesn't seem to be giving us that option. What do you think you can do?"

"Not make promises. I might be able to find out who they are, I might not. I don't have the resources the police do."

"You have time, which is a resource the police are very short of now."

"I'll have to ask a lot of questions. This might be someone you know, perhaps a disgruntled employee or someone with some connection to your family."

She nodded. "Ask what you need to, I'll do my best to answer."

"Could it have been the same person, disguising his or her voice?"

"Maybe, but I don't think so. The voice was different, but so were the speech patterns. Slower, more deliberate."

"How would you describe this person from his voice?"

"Still young, but other than that it's hard to say. He spoke slowly, but indistinctly. I had a hard time understanding some of what he said, especially when he was cursing us. Hard to place the voice. It could have been local, could have been any color. Not much help, I know."

"Did either of the voices sound familiar in any way?"

"No, I'm pretty sure I've never heard them before outside the phone calls."

"Did you get any impression that it was distorted or disguised?"

"No, I heard a bird in the background and it sounded normal. Although I guess it could have been. Brooke would probably know more about that."

Brooke worked in recording studios, so she would be more familiar with that kind of equipment.

"Do you have caller ID?"

• 189 •

"Yes, but the number was blocked."

"They asked for a million dollars. Is that a reasonable—well, doable might be a better word—sum?"

"Are we worth that much?"

"Some of my questions might seem intrusive. How much do they know about you? If the number is wild, then they don't know much. If it's realistic, they might know more. That could give me a clue as to where to look for them."

"A million is realistic. It's a sum we could, with some scrambling, come up with."

"This is the hard question. Do you know of anything they could use as leverage?"

Marilyn looked at me, as if weighing the question.

"This is all confidential. I know it's a hard question. I only asked because it will help me know how to stop them. If they know something that only a few people should, then they're likely to be someone in that range of people."

Marilyn sighed. "There is only one family scandal that I know of. My youngest son, Harold, was developmentally delayed, what used to be called mental retardation. I can't say it wasn't a hardship, taking care of him. He had a lot of stomach problems and was very limited in speech, so he couldn't tell us where he hurt. As hard as that was, it also pulled us together as a family. Brooke and Jared both helped care for him. John managed his schedule so he could be home as often as possible.

"Just over ten years ago, when Brooke was seventeen, Jared twenty-two. Harold was dropped off from his special school. I meant to be home by then, but my car broke down. Jared was making him a sandwich, and he noticed that Harold had left the kitchen. We had hamsters and he could stare at them for hours on their wheels. So that's where Jared thought he would be. He went upstairs to look for him there, but he wasn't there. Then Jared asked Brooke if she'd seen him and they both looked for him."

She paused, quickly wiping her eyes.

"He climbed over the fence next door and got into their swimming pool. He didn't know that one end is deep…" She turned from me and wiped her eyes with both hands.

"He drowned," I said for her.

She turned back to me, the tears clearly in her eyes. "Yes, Brooke and Jared found him. When I got home an ambulance was in front."

"I'm very sorry," I said. I *was* sorry, it was a heartbreaking story, but I was also hired to do a job. "How could anyone use this against you?"

"I don't know. Brooke and Jared felt horribly guilty. Both John and I as well. If only I'd been home sooner, I could have—"

"Was there any cover-up, changing the facts?"

"No, oh, no, nothing like that. What happened happened. There was a notice in the paper, the police came and asked questions. They were kind, both the police and the news people, treating it as a private misfortune. It's just…still very painful for us. He was such a large part of our life. He could be amazingly happy, just laughing and smiling, and when he was like that we all had to laugh and smile with him."

"I'm very sorry to have asked these kinds of questions. This isn't a scandal, it's a tragedy. There seems little the blackmailer could use against you," I said gently. Marilyn Overhill had been honest with me and I needed to honor her trust.

She wiped her face again and said, "Oh, you mean like me having three gigolos in a pied-a-terre in the French Quarter?"

"In New Orleans, three is hardly a scandal, especially in the French Quarter."

"So, I'd have to throw in a German shepherd to make it a scandal?"

"Probably, especially if the German shepherd was underage."

She smiled at me, sadness still in her eyes, but Brooke was right. Marilyn Overhill was a strong woman. "Then I guess we're boringly scandal-free."

"Thank you for answering my questions. It probably doesn't feel like it right now, but you've been very helpful."

"The plants soothe me," she said as she went back to repotting them. "Although at times I think I might need another yard to have enough." Again a sad smile. "Just let yourself in. Brooke is expecting you."

I nodded and headed up the brick path.

Brooke was indeed expecting me, opening the door as I approached.

She ushered me into a comfortable den. "You have to excuse me. I'm trying not to talk much. To save the voice for tonight."

I hadn't really thought about that, but if I had to talk, give a lecture or presentation of some sort, my voice often felt worn out when I was done, tired and raspy. A night of singing probably took the same toll even on a well-trained voice.

"I talked to your mother out in the yard. She was able to answer a lot of my questions." I pulled a standard contract out of my briefcase and handed it to her. "Look this over, see what you think."

She studied it for a couple of minutes, then mimed writing. I pointed out where she should sign her name. I signed the second copy, then handed it to her as I did the same on the first copy.

"I plan to do research on the people around you, especially people like fired employees. Can I talk to Jared about that?"

She nodded yes.

"I need all of you—your mother, brother, and father—to try and think of anyone who might want to retaliate against your family. Even if it's crazy by our standards—the kid you beat in the third-grade singing contest—let me know. I'll be discreet, but that might be the most likely pool. Also, anyone with knowledge of your finances, even a bank teller. It might not be that person, but they might be the link. They tell the wife something, the wife mentions it to a brother-in-law, and he gets an idea and gets his girlfriend to call you.

"I'll come out tomorrow with a device for your phone. If either of them calls again, record it if you can. This time play along with the caller, let him or her think you're scared. The best way to catch the blackmailers is to reel them in. If we can get them to agree to a drop location, we call the police, have the cops meet them, and they go to jail and out of your life."

Brooke nodded.

"Call me the minute they phone again. If they give you a time for another call or anything like that, let me know and I'll be here. Don't agree to meet until you talk with me. Tell them you need to discuss getting the money together and you don't know how long that will take. Try to get them to call back at a specific time."

She again nodded.

"Any questions?"

This time she shook her head.

"See if you can get that list of names in the next day or two. Even a few will be helpful. Is tomorrow around this time good for me to come back?"

She smiled her thanks that I was asking questions in a way that she could answer without talking, and nodded.

"That's it for starters," I said as I stood up.

She waved her checkbook at me, then wrote out the check and handed it to me.

I looked at it. "If it takes less time, I'll refund the difference."

"Don't worry about a refund. We have the resources," she said with a smile. Then she said, "Hey, do you want tickets?"

"Tickets?"

"The show tonight." She answered shyly, as if not assuming I'd want to attend.

"Wow. Yeah, I'd love to go." Because in truth I *would* love to.

"How many? Torbin already has some."

"Would three be pushing it?"

"Three it is. I'll leave backstage passes as well, if you want to come by after the show." She smiled as if happy that I did seem to really want to see her perform. "I'll have them at the door for you."

"Thanks," I said as I turned to go. "I really mean that. I have two friends who are in great need of getting out and having some fun."

As I was at the door, she said, "Oh, Micky, I want you to stop the blackmailer, but if you can find out who killed Alma, bill me. Her voice shouldn't have been silenced."

I thanked her and left.

I waited until I was in my car to grab my phone and dial.

"Hey, Alex, we're going to the Brooke O. concert tonight."

"Micky? We are? I'm not feeling great—"

"You have to get out of the house, okay? If you fall apart, I fall apart, so you can't fall apart. You have to go to the concert with me. And Joanne, too. Unless you have some other girlfriend you want to bring."

Alex laughed. "No, it'll be Joanne. Damn, I haven't even taken a shower yet."

"You have hot water?"

"Yeah, I—"

"No excuse. If I can shower without it, you can shower with it. And I have backstage passes for after the show."

"To meet Brooke O.? Wow, how'd you manage that?"

"All in good time, dear Alex. I'll pick you guys up around seven."

"I'm calling Joanne now. See you then."

I started the car and headed home. I wanted to take a little more of a shower than I'd started the day out with, and that meant heating some water.

CHAPTER TWENTY-TWO

Alex, Joanne, and I had a great time at the concert, especially as we were one row in front of Torbin and his friends. I gave Alex and Joanne a bare-bones version of how I knew Brooke O.—that she was a friend of Torbin from way back and through him had hired me to do some private investigating. One of the things she was paying me for was confidentiality, after all.

We did get to go backstage, although it was pretty chaotic there. We had time for a quick hello and all got our photos taken with her, then she was consumed by other friends and well-wishers. I didn't want to abuse her generosity.

Besides, I'd see her tomorrow.

After the show we went out to the French Quarter where the bars were busy, but it was different than before Katrina. Still we had a good time; it's hard not to have a good time with Torbin. It was good to see Alex throw back her head and laugh. At one point in the evening, Joanne had smiled at me as if to say thank you for getting Alex out.

I didn't get to bed until after two a.m.

My cell phone woke me a little after nine.

It was Liz. "Did you get in touch with Nathalie?"

"No." Then to prove I wasn't a total sluggard I ran down what I'd done to try to contact her—the phone call, going out there, and how unhelpful the supposed adult guardian was being.

"Drugs?" Liz said about Carmen's little activities. "That's a mess."

"I think she's already sucked Nathan, Nathalie's twin brother, into her spiderweb, and I'm worried that Nathalie might get mixed up in it, or that the two of them dump on her."

"If you want to go out this evening, I can go with you."

"You found something on the blood test?"

Instead of answering my question, she said, "What do you know about her home life? Did she talk to you much?"

"Some. Lives on a farm in the middle of nowhere Wisconsin. Pretty conservative, religious family. The sole phone is in the barn because it's only supposed to be used for business. The kids did get a cell phone for this trip, but Nathan has custody because he's the boy even though he's less responsible than Nathalie."

"Boys often lag behind girls in maturity at that age," Liz said, then asked, "Do you think she's sexually active?"

"Not unless you count sex as milking cows. Why?"

Again Liz didn't answer my question. "Can you be positive about that?"

"She's not just fifteen, but a sheltered fifteen. She seemed very embarrassed about things that most kids wouldn't blink an eye about."

"Like what?"

"Like a blow job. Seems that Carmen and Coach Bob did that. Nathalie saw a head go below desk level. She was bright red when she told me. Plus, I suspect she's a dykling—maybe not even aware of it yet, but I'd bet money that she's coming out some day."

"Interesting."

"She's pregnant. Or she has a sexually transmitted disease." I stated it as fact to see if she would confirm what I already seemed to know.

Liz was silent for a long time. Finally she said, "This is a mess. She's a minor, but is old enough to make some decisions. I really need to talk to her."

"We'll go out this evening and find her. You can yell 'health department' and scare the crap out of that church kitchen."

We agreed to meet around five at my office.

Lovely, another trip out to Kenner scheduled as a start to my morning.

I got up. After the bars and the concert, I needed a bath, which meant heating water on the hot plate. I got a few inches in the tub of water that was warm enough to put my naked body into and did a quick sponge job.

As I hurriedly toweled dry I vowed that on the day I had hot water I would take a long bath that lasted for hours, just soaking in the luxury of that enveloping warmth.

Once I was dry, I put on the most professional of the few clothes I had—black jeans, a blue sweater, and a blazer. I would really have to make a run by the house today and get more clothes. I'd let fate decide for me. If Cordelia was there...she would be there. If she wasn't, I'd just grab my stuff and come back another time to talk to her.

Now that I had an actual case—plus the Nathalie problem—my schedule was filling up. Of course, I should have met with Cordelia right after she came back. Of course, I should have been better than I was, stayed away from booze, not let life just dribble past me.

Maybe this evening, after I'm done with Liz and the trip to Kenner. We should be back before too late.

Right now I wanted to meet with Jared, ostensibly to get his input on any disgruntled employees, but also to have more time with him and see if Brooke was indeed right, that there was another side to him. Or if there was a side to him that she hadn't seen.

As befitted a multi-faceted corporation, their offices were in the CBD. This gleaming swath of modern office buildings is situated between the French Quarter on the downtown side and the Warehouse District on the uptown side.

Their office was on the edge between the CDB and the Warehouse District, in an older building. The actual company name was La Petite Crescent, Inc. I took a creaky old elevator up to the fifth, and top, floor.

I hadn't called ahead; I might not find Jared here or be able to see him, but I wanted to discover what he was like without any time for preparation. Brooke had hired me to investigate not only the blackmail, but Alma's death. Neither of us might like where that took us.

The office area was welcoming without being ostentatious, with a leather couch and several comfortable chairs in the reception area. Marilyn's love of plants obviously carried over here, as the area was filled with greenery.

I gave my name and asked to see Jared. The receptionist didn't question me, just said she'd let him know I was here.

After about five minutes Jared came out. He had on a blazer, tie, and jeans, professional and comfortable.

He approached me with his hand out. "Hey, that's service. I didn't expect you to get here this soon."

I returned his handshake, a little macho, a little hearty. He seemed surprised by my visit, but was putting a game face on.

"A lot of what I do is cull through heaps of information, so the sooner I have the information, the sooner I can look at it."

"Follow me." Jared led me down a hallway to a corner office also with a number of plants, an old wooden desk in one corner, and a table with chairs opposite it. It was a nice office, but hardly one that shouted, "I'm the boss's son and this will be mine someday." The furniture was good quality, but had seen years, if not decades, of use.

He motioned to the table and I sat.

"Can I get you anything? Coffee? Tea? Water? Juice?" He remained standing.

"Only if you're having something." That was my standard answer.

"I am," he said. "I have a bad sparkling-water habit. Could that be blackmail material?" He crossed the office to a small refrigerator behind the desk. "Lemon or lime?"

"Raspberry might be blackmail material, but lemon or lime is too tame."

He snorted a laugh. "No raspberry. I guess I'm boringly normal. Would you like lemon or lime?"

I opted for lime and he took lemon. Then Jared joined me at the table.

"So what can I do for you?" he asked.

I decided to ask the intrusive questions first to see how he reacted. "Anything in your life that could be used against you? We're not talking sparkling water here."

He looked at me, then took a sip of his water. "Why don't you tell me what you really want to know and not beat around the bush?"

"Liaisons with men, underage women, married men or women, drug addiction, S&M, DUI's—anything a blackmailer might use against you?"

"That's a pretty long list. I thought you were here for possible names of people who might want to get us."

"That, too. But it's hard to investigate when I'm missing big pieces of information. If the blackmailer knows something that I don't, then he or she has a major advantage."

"What if the blackmailer doesn't know it and we tell you our business?"

"I keep it quiet. Everything I find out is confidential. A way to look at it is information resides in boxes. Knowing the information and who has access to it can be very helpful in determining who might be doing this."

"You keep it quiet, but what if you're subpoenaed? Or stumble over something illegal?"

"I've never been subpoenaed and would try like hell to avoid it. As to discovering something illegal, that depends on what it is. I'm not the police. It's not my job to enforce the law. However, there are some things I wouldn't overlook."

"Like what?"

"Murder. If you diddled little girls."

"Ugh. If I did that you should turn me in." He took another sip of his water and avoided eye contact.

"You can try and hide things, but it's hard to do when a trained investigator is looking into your life. You might weigh whether it's better to tell me up front or have me find out anyway." I looked at him directly. He was still drinking his water and avoiding me. Was his sparkling-water addiction really an excuse to have something to do with his hands and his eyes?

"Okay, I'll confess. I forgot to send my mother flowers on her last birthday. Guilty, guilty, guilty." He gave me a shy-boy grin.

"I'll put you down as the choirboy who never misses a chance to help old ladies across the street. Since that covers you, what about ex-employees or anyone who might have it in for your family?"

"I honestly can't think of anyone."

"You're one of the richest families in the area and you've never pissed anyone off?"

"Well, I'm sure we've pissed people off, but it's all been things like a business deal, nothing that anyone would murder or blackmail over."

"Really? You screw someone out of a deal that they need to keep going and you don't think they might not be happy?"

"We don't operate that way. Maybe Jameson did back in the day, but my dad and I are truly committed to being ethical and aboveboard. Most people are happy to do business with us."

"What kind of business do you engage in?"

"Mostly investment banking and venture capital. We provide a lot of seed money for local businesses and development. We own or co-own a number of enterprises, especially hotels and restaurants. With most we have long-term relationships. It's good for them and good for us."

"Can you give me a list of any of those long-term relationships that ended in divorce? What about employees? Any fired who weren't happy about it?"

"You can't please everyone. But we try to work with employees who aren't performing up to standard. Usually by the time they're let go, it's clear to both sides that this wasn't a good fit."

"In a rational world, yes. But we're not looking for a rational person. We're looking for a criminal. This person could be stewing over the janitor's job he lost ten years ago."

"My mother said it was a woman's voice. So shouldn't we be looking for women?"

"The first call was. The second was a man. No transsexuals yet. A fair number of women are involved with men, and a fair number of them do foolish things for those men. He had her call first as women tend to be more verbal, then for whatever reason, he called the second time. It could be a couple, but it's also possible that it's more than two people. Men are criminals at a much higher rate than women."

"What about the woman that uncovered this stuff? Are you looking into her?"

"I am, but she's the one person I can eliminate."

"Why?"

"She was already dead when the second phone call came. If she was involved, she's been cut out of the deal."

His assistant buzzed and reminded him of a meeting that was about to start.

As he saw me out, Jared agreed to get me a list, although it was clear that he thought this was a waste of time.

I was again in the creaky elevator. Jared had given me very little information; he even seemed to be trying to misdirect me. He had done a good job of controlling the interview and keeping the walls up. It was hard to tell why—if he was socially awkward, as his sister seemed to think, or if he was trying to hide something.

As I left the building, I mused that just as crime is more likely to have a man involved than a woman, men with power are often the ones who will do anything to maintain that power. Jared hit every mark: a straight white male with lots and lots of money. Those with power often did the most damage. The destroyed levees, the neglect of those in authority to a drowning city destroyed much more than even a dozen petty thieves.

Driving back to my office, I had to admit that Jared was right about looking into Alma. Obviously she was out of the picture, but she had a sister who'd gone to jail and a brother who was married to a white woman. Could Marilyn have heard one of them on the phone? Both had been hit hard by Katrina, the brother losing his house and the sister losing the one home she could go back to and be taken in. How close was the family and how likely was it that Alma had shared what she had uncovered about their twisted and unfair family history?

If power was a motivator, so was desperation.

Chapter Twenty-three

Back at my office, I had a hot lunch for the first time in more days than I cared to think about. Admittedly it was a frozen dinner thrown into the microware and not a home-cooked meal, but a definite step up from peanut butter.

I glanced at my watch. I didn't want to delay too long in getting a recording device hooked up to the Overhills' phone, but it had also probably been a late night for the entire family, especially Brooke. By now though it should be reasonably late enough that even the latest of night partiers would be through half a cup of coffee.

There are a plethora of gizmos that come in handy in private-eye work, phone-recording devices being one of the basics. I specialized in missing persons and security, so I didn't do a lot of phone taping, but I did have a couple of the devices hanging around. Not using them much had probably saved them, as they were in a box on the top shelf of the closet, and the vandals hadn't bothered to rip that apart.

I ferreted out the newer one, a digital recorder. Amazing what technology can do these days. Because it was digital, I could save its recordings as a computer file. That made it easy to make multiple copies, which could be sent as e-mail attachments, if, for example, I needed to let the police hear the conversation.

Then back Uptown. I called on my cell phone when I was a few blocks away.

Marilyn answered.

"It's Micky Knight. I'd like to swing by and attach a recording device to your phone."

Marilyn said she would be there.

When I arrived, she told me that Brooke had left a few hours ago, to help rebuild houses in the Lower 9ᵗʰ Ward.

"That's a busy schedule," I commented, as Marilyn showed me the main line for the phone. "She did a high-energy show last night and now she's out hammering nails."

"She's young, with that glorious energy that comes in the mid-twenties. And this is important to her. New Orleans taught her music, from what she learned in school to what she learned walking the streets. And…I think she feels guilty. We weren't flooded. Most of our holdings came through okay. Compared to most, we've been lightly touched."

"That was the luck of the wind and the water, not anything you should be responsible for. Or feel guilty about."

"I wish it were that easy." Her look told me she knew I carried the same guilt. "Brooke told me you were investigating Alma's murder even though no one was paying you."

I nodded, realizing how right she was. The loss was enormous. We all had to do what we could to recompense for what had been taken, then maybe, just maybe, New Orleans and our lives in it could come back.

I showed Marilyn how to use the recording device and talked to her about what to say if anyone called again.

"I'll do it," she said to my suggestion she lead the blackmailer on, with a grim set to her mouth, "but if anyone else is home, I'll let them talk, especially if it's the woman. She's a vile person. The extortion, yes, but just the way she talked, sly and slimy and as if the world owed her anything she wants."

It only took me about twenty minutes to set up the recording machine, then I was back heading downtown. I wanted to do some more digging into Alma's family. Until I had a list of names from the Overhills I couldn't do much on that end.

Stop by and get some clothes. I needed my heavy jacket and a few more layers, especially as the weather was getting colder and the gas wasn't getting fixed.

Okay, I was being a coward. Cordelia probably had a lot to cram in, given how long she'd been gone. Her clinic had been damaged, she'd have to deal with insurance, all the decisions about whether to rebuild. She probably wasn't home in the middle of the day. I could run in, pick up some clothes, and get out.

And what, wait until you're dead to talk to her?

No, tonight after I meet with Liz and Nathalie. I'll call first, make sure Patty What's-Her-Name isn't around, ask if I can come over, then stay all night if need be.

Several work trucks were parked on the street, one roofer and one plumber. A few other cars scattered about, but none in front of our house.

It was quiet, desolate even. I was guessing that she'd left our cats with her sister in Boston. I hoped they were okay. No. I caught myself. Cordelia would tell me if anything happened to either of them. She folded socks, made sure the lights were turned out, still sent out Christmas cards. I remembered last year around this time, coming up behind her as she was diligently addressing envelopes, leaning over and putting my hand down her shirt. She complained that my hand was cold, but I could tell she wasn't truly upset. I said something about needing to get my hands warmed. And she'd offered to really warm them up. The envelopes didn't get finished until the next day.

I paused at the door, overcome by the memory. I desperately wanted to be able to put my arms around her again. I wondered if I ever would.

As if not wanting to disturb any further memories, I quietly let myself in. This was to be a quick, pragmatic mission. I would save the emotions for another day.

No lights were on and I left them off, with enough daylight seeping in even to the inner hallway and the stairs. We had put carpet runners on the steps, tired of the thumping of the cats as they chased each other up and down. And their befuddled skidding when we polished the wood.

Stay away from the memories, I admonished myself. I wanted to be sitting on the couch with a cat on my lap and Cordelia's arm around my shoulder.

Sunlight came through the window at the top of the stairs, a shaft of light falling on a photograph of us together. It was taken about five years ago; we were outside, a brilliant day, blue sky. She was sitting on a log, looking up at me, our hands touching. I don't remember the picture being taken we were focused on each other—I think it was Danny who snapped the shot—but I remembered the blue of her eyes that day, the way she smiled at me. Holding hands in the warmth of the sun.

I turned from the picture and walked into the bedroom. Cordelia was there.

We were both surprised. She was changing clothes, a suit jacket on the chair and her shirt half unbuttoned.

For a moment, neither of us moved or said anything.

Finally, I spoke. "I just needed some warmer clothes. I was coming by to get them."

She managed a half-smile and answered. "It's your house, too. You can come whenever you want." To fill the silence, she continued. "I have to meet an adjuster about the clinic and it's going to be messy. Had a meeting with some people at Tulane, so that required dressing decently. Now I have to slog in the mold." She shrugged. Then, as if making a decision, she resumed undressing.

We'd done this hundreds of times, been together in our bedroom, one of us changing clothes. It should have felt normal. But everything had changed.

I crossed to the chest of drawers where my sweaters were, but turned my head enough to watch her. She was altered. Not much, only to someone who knew her as well as I did. She seemed to have lost weight, but also toning and muscle, less definition. Lost. Liz had called it well. More gray in her hair.

She took her shirt off, tossing it onto the chair with the jacket.

At times, gestures, a look, a shift of the head can say more than words. She could have turned her back to me, even gone into the bathroom. But she remained, still facing me, still as open as she had been those hundreds of times before.

Cordelia shimmied out of her pants, folding them neatly over the chair.

I pulled out a couple of sweaters, not even knowing which ones I was getting.

She reached around behind her back to unhook her bra.

She'd always had nice breasts, voluptuous and full. That hadn't changed.

She was struggling with the hook. That hadn't changed, either.

It was almost instinctual, not a conscious decision. As I had so many times in the past, I stepped in to help her.

Maybe some inchoate desire to touch her one more time.

I did what I usually did, stood in front of her and reached around. I heard an intake of breath at our closeness. Save for her breathing, she didn't move, not pushing me away, not pulling me in. I heard her shallow breathing as if she was unsure whether to let our breasts touch.

I wanted to make her want me. I wanted to banish the other woman, to cover the places she had touched, so that my hands and body were the last ones there.

As if I needed the extra room to fumble with the clasp, I edged in closer and eased my body into hers so we touched—breasts, hips, thighs. She didn't move back. Her breath caught again.

Unhooking her bra I slid it over her shoulders, my fingers brushing her skin, skimming her breasts, over her nipples before sliding the straps down her arms. As if all the other times I'd done this gave me the right to do it again.

Throwing the bra aside, I wrapped my arms around her. I took a step, backing her against the bed, then using my weight against her, pushing her down, toppling us onto the bed.

I was kissing her, hard, as if a fire had flared and couldn't be put out. My hands roamed wildly over her body, embracing her fiercely, cupping her breasts, my fingers on her thighs, opening her legs.

She responded, kissing me back, letting me touch her in every way I wanted to.

I let go of her long enough to throw off my clothes, then pressed the heat of my skin against hers, pushed into her, grabbed her panties, hurriedly pulled them off.

She was naked and I was on top of her.

I wanted so many things. I wanted to touch her, to own her, to make her regret what she had done, to make her want me, to blot out the past and the future, to feel everything I could possibly feel. To make love long enough for my anger to go away. To make love long enough to heal us both. But the merely physical could make no such promises.

I was over her, my body thrusting against hers, her legs open, letting me in. It remained unspoken, her atonement for breaking trust, what she would offer, what I would take. She would let me do whatever I wanted to her, whether kind or cruel.

I ran my hand down her side, over her thigh, then plunged my fingers inside her, not even checking to see if she was wet enough for them to easily slip in. She was. Even if she didn't want this, her body did.

She gasped as I took her, maybe pleasure, maybe on the edge of pain. I pushed in again, this time harder. She wrapped her arms around my shoulders, buried her head against my neck, her breathing hot and harsh. She didn't say anything.

I relented, becoming gentler, my fingers gliding in and out, finding the places I knew would make her feel good. She cried out, relief and pleasure, a sound that I knew meant she was getting close. I slowed, not hurrying her, some oblique apology for my earlier roughness. Much as part of me wanted to hurt her, to have her feel pain the way I had, I couldn't do it. She had been kind and loving and generous for over ten years, and that couldn't just go away as if it had never been.

I was slow and gentle, making it last.

Her breathing came fast, small moans escaping her lips. I'd made love to this woman over and over again. I knew her, knew how to please her, and now I was doing everything I could to once again give her as much physical ecstasy as I could.

Her back arched, liquid gushing down my fingers. I let her ride me, come over and over again until finally she stilled, closing her legs, holding my hand inside her. She wrapped her arms around me, kissing me, my lips, my cheeks and neck, then back to my lips.

Then she slid under me, letting me stay on top, taking me in her mouth, working to please me, doing what she knew I liked, taking her time, as if she didn't want it to end either.

But my body desperately needed the passion, had been primed by touching her. I couldn't stop the orgasm that coursed through me, couldn't hold out longer and keep this moment from passing.

Trembling and spent, I rolled beside her. For a moment we lay together.

Then I couldn't stop myself from saying, "So who was better, me or Lauren?" My rage came out. I shouldn't have said it and I had to know.

Cordelia stiffened. I propped myself on one elbow to look at her. Her eyes were shut as if she couldn't bear to see me. Her face contorted in misery, jaw tense, her lips turning downward.

"I'm sorry…" she said, her voice strangled. "I'm so sorry…"

Then she broke down, turning away from me, crying, heaving sobs that wracked her body.

If I wanted to hurt her, I had. The truth, as much of it as I could divine, was that I didn't want to hurt her; I just wanted to stop my own pain. Maybe that was true for her as well; she hadn't wanted or intended to hurt me. She was merely human and love isn't perfect.

Cordelia didn't shed tears often. I was the emotional one who raged and cried, and she would hold me until the storm passed. I had only rarely seen her break like this, once when her mother died. And in the immediate aftermath of Katrina, right after her week of hell in Charity Hospital.

I clasped her to me. She was rigid in my arms, as if I could offer her no comfort. I didn't let go, gently tugging on her shoulder and turning her to me. I held her close, quietly rocking her, alternating a tight embrace with gently wiping the tears off her cheek.

Finally I said, "I'm sorry. I didn't mean it."

We both knew that wasn't quite true. What I really meant is that it wasn't the time or the place and I was wrong. I realized that if we were to find our way back to each other, it would take time and the slow rebuilding of trust. And remembering all the ways the water of Katrina had marked us. That one day in August had changed us irrevocably.

I felt her start to let me hold her, the unyielding way she held her body letting go, molding into me. Maybe she was too tired to fight anymore; maybe she needed to be held. Or maybe some place in her wanted me to hold her as much as I wanted to be the one whose arms she sought for comfort.

I took an edge of the sheet and helped her dry her eyes.

A car door slammed outside.

"Oh, shit," she said. "The adjuster is supposed to meet me here." She started to sit up. "Shit," she said again. Then she barked out a laugh as she wiped the tears off her face.

This was an absurd situation. Even at twisted moments like this, Cordelia was able to recognize how bizarre this was. That was one of the things I loved about her, her sense of perspective.

"I'll throw on clothes and stall him. You get dressed and wash your face."

We both hauled ass out of bed. I jerked on my clothes, hoping they weren't too wrinkled. But what did I care. I wasn't trying to get money from this guy.

By the second time he knocked I was at the door and told him that Cordelia was running late. She was upstairs searching for her mud boots and would be down shortly.

Which she was. Looking like hell, but since he'd never seen her, he might not know that.

She didn't glance at me as she passed. Then she paused, briefly touched my hand before abruptly pulling away, and said, "I'm sorry. I'm…so sorry. It's broken, it can't be…" With a quick glance back, she said, "Good-bye, Micky."

That was all. She was out the door and gone.

Her good-bye was final.

I started to chase her. But what would I do? What could I say? With the insurance adjuster, the workmen in the street? Even if they weren't there, what would I do?

I ran up the stairs, racing to the front window, but she was gone, only taillights of a car turning the corner.

"Why the fuck didn't you just keep your mouth shut for another day? Or week? Or forever?" I raged at myself. Then turned on her. "Why the fuck do you think you can just leave me? You make a mistake, I'm supposed to forgive you, but I make a mistake and you just walk out? Fuck you! Goddamn you, fuck you!"

I fell onto the bed and started crying, wiping my tears with the sheet I'd used to wipe hers.

She can't handle my anger and I can't let go of it. It's broken and it can't be fixed.

I finally ran out of tears. Got up, went to the bathroom, scrubbed my face. Even the brokenhearted have to go to the bathroom.

I wasn't supposed to be here when she came back. That was clear. Grabbing a laundry bag, I hurriedly stuffed it with clothes, barely paying attention to what I was taking. I had three pairs of shorts in it before I realized I wouldn't be needing those for a while. I looked wildly around. Was there anything else I wanted, needed? I didn't know when or even if I would come back here. I left the bed disheveled. She could clean one of the messes she'd made in our lives. Then I fled the house as if a banshee was chasing me.

How the hell do I get through the rest of the day, I thought as I pulled up to my office. No, my home. I needed to start thinking of it that way.

You get through the day the way the people who have lost their houses do, the way people whose grandparents died in the attic get through the day.

I pounded up the stairs, but no one else was in the building to hear the noise. Sara Clavish, who shared the top floor and had occasionally done work for me, had tried to talk her sister and her husband into leaving until it was too late. He was the only one who made it into the boat.

I'd get through the day the same way as those who lost everything. The minutes would tick by because nothing would stop them. A day would pass, a year would pass. I'd get through.

Somehow.

Without even thinking, I walked into the kitchen, pulled the Scotch from the cabinet, and took a long pull straight from the bottle.

Then another.

Alcohol or the Bible. Defensive walls or nonstop partying. Therapy or drugs. Somehow we all would get through the day.

I smashed the bottle against the sink, the glass shattering, the golden liquid spilling onto the floor. I'd clean it up later.

I ran back down the stairs. If I stayed in the office, I would start throwing things, and I'd already replaced everything once in the last month. As upset as I was, I couldn't afford to do that again.

I ran for a block, then slowed to a rapid walk, the houses I was passing just a blur. I turned a corner, then another corner, and another. Finally I slowed, the energy expended, leaving me empty and hollow. But I had to get through the day.

The sun was getting low. I was meeting Liz at five so we could find Nathalie. That was important; I had to do it.

I needed to be a sane, normal person. I glanced at the street signs and turned to head…home.

It was around four-thirty when I got there, enough time to wash my face and thoroughly brush my teeth. I even had time to hastily sweep up the glass and wipe away the worst of the spilled Scotch.

Liz was on time. I didn't let her come upstairs—the Scotch smell lingered—but hurried down to meet her on the street.

"I'm probably not going to be good company," I mumbled. "Couldn't sleep last night and I'm pretty tired."

"That's okay. This isn't a bright and witty mission."

We'd agreed to take my car, since it was dark and we were going to a completely different part of the city. I turned on the radio. I just wasn't up to talking.

Liz seemed to understand that something was going on and let me have my silence.

As we cruised down the interstate, I glanced at her. She was smart, a tempting woman. Maybe this afternoon was what I needed to move on. The final good-bye.

Then I quietly shook my head. Not tonight, not until I could find a place with actual hot water so I could rid myself of the smell of Cordelia. I wondered if Liz could tell that I'd had sex. Nasty, messy break-up sex.

Atlanta and New Orleans weren't far apart.

I would get through today and the next day. Time wouldn't stop. Maybe in days or weeks. Or months. I could move on.

"We're close to the airport?" Liz asked, seeing a plane flying in low.

"Yep, one exit before it. Almost to the swamp." Maybe I couldn't be perky and bright, but I could at least be a decent human being to both Liz and Nathalie. Neither of them had done anything to me.

To prove my point, I turned at that exit.

"Thought you were going to dump me off there," Liz said jokingly.

"Why, you need to get out of town?"

"Not just yet." Then she put the joking aside. "You sure we'll find your friend this evening?"

"She's not really my friend. Just hit the same place at the same time." But that sounded callous, so I said, "They should be back. They can't work in the dark, and adolescents are known for being insistently hungry."

"Especially after gutting messy houses all day."

"Are you ever going to tell me what this is about?"

"That may be up to Nathalie. I'm gathering that the adults around her aren't the most appropriate for the situation," Liz said drily.

"Nut-cake religious family? And supposedly adult chaperones, one who is out of control in the big bad city and the other who is just out of it? That what you mean?"

"That would be about it, yes."

Matching her seriousness, I said, "This kid's going to have a rough time. I get major mojo baby-dyke vibes from her, and she's growing up in a place where one of the worst things she could be is queer. But she's stuck there until she's eighteen." I knew the way to the church so well I didn't even need to glance at street signs. I did keep a lookout for big, ugly black SUVs, however. This seemed to be the land of bloated vehicles, at least three were massive and black, but they all seemed empty, perhaps used more for PTA meetings than romantic trysts.

"I realize that. Well, we'll just have to take things as they come."

Another turn and we were in front of the auxiliary buildings, where the kids were camped out. Lights were on, people seemed to be home.

"How do you want to do this?"

"I was about to ask you for advice," Liz said with a smile. "Let's find Nathalie, see if we can arrange for me to talk to her alone. If not now, if we can set up a time for it. That do for over-planning?" She put her hand on my forearm.

"Way too many details. Let's see if we can find the kid."

She took her hand away and we got out.

Some of the young people were outside enjoying the night air. Amazingly enough, no one seemed to be sneaking a smoke, but these were corn-fed, hell and brimstone-raised Midwesterners. Nathalie wasn't among them.

They watched us as we entered the front door; clearly Liz and I were strangers here.

"Can I help you?" a girl who looked no more than just-turned-fourteen asked.

Yep, we'd been noticed. "We're looking for one of the volunteers, Nathalie"—what was her last name?—"Hummle."

"Just a minute. Please wait here," the girl said.

Clearly even a fourteen-year-old knew better than to let two secular humanists like us wander around loose.

Waiting didn't bring Nathalie, instead the older clueless woman. Now she seemed both agitated and oblivious.

"What can I do for you?" Ms. Clueless asked in a high-pitched tone, wringing her hands.

"We'd like to see Nathalie Hummle."

"What about?"

Liz stepped in, pulling out a very official-looking ID badge. "I'm Dr. Elizabeth Ward with the CDC. What we need to talk to Nathalie about is confidential."

Ms. Clueless looked from me to Liz to Liz's badge then to the floor then back to her badge. Finally she said, "Just a minute. Please wait here."

They must have rehearsed that line for anyone who got through the door.

Waiting still didn't bring Nathalie. Instead we got Coach Bob hobbling on crutches with Ms. Clueless trailing behind.

"What's this about?" he demanded.

"As we've already explained, this is confidential," Liz said.

Ms. Clueless interjected, "Carmen said to not let this woman back in." Presumably she meant me, as Carmen and Liz hadn't set eyes on each other.

"I'm in charge here," Coach Bob grumbled. Then he said, "You're not supposed to be here," like it was a decision he thought up all on his own. "Besides, you can't talk to Nathalie without a parent or guardian around."

"Sorry, this is Louisiana," I said. "Over the age of thirteen, we can talk to her without parents or guardian."

"Huh?" Coach Bob said.

"This state, in its infinite wisdom, allows minors over thirteen to give consent to certain activities, medical tests, procedures, etc. You're in Louisiana. Louisiana laws apply." I knew from Cordelia and her practice that she could test kids that age and above for things like HIV. Since I didn't know exactly what this was about, I might be bluffing. But since I didn't know, I wasn't lying either.

"I really need to speak to her," Liz said in an assertive, professional voice. "If you cannot or will not allow that, I will contact the authorities and have them assist me. But it would be easier for you, me, and Nathalie to avoid that."

"Who the hel-heck are you anyway?" Coach Bob now thought to ask.

"Dr. Elizabeth Ward, CDC." Liz again showed her badge.

"Michele Knight, private investigator. I'm Dr. Ward's security."

Coach Bob looked at the badge, at me, at Liz, then at Ms. Clueless, who was staring at something in the far corner where there seemed to be nothing to stare at. Then back at the badge. I could almost hear wheels slowly grinding.

At last he said, "Just a minute."

"Wait right here," I said, sotto voce.

"Wait right here," he—as expected—said. He clomped back across the room, Ms. Clueless following him.

After about ten of those just-a-minute minutes, Nathalie finally appeared.

She seemed pale and tentative at first, until she spotted me, then she started to smile, then clearly thought better of it with Coach Bob and Ms. Clueless on either side of her.

"Here she is," Coach Bob said. "Now say what you have to say."

"In private," Liz said.

"You can talk right here," he argued.

A slight flare of her nostrils was the only annoyance Liz showed. "Come on, Nathalie. Let's go outside where we can talk in private." She motioned for Nathalie to join us.

Coach Bob started to follow.

"No," Liz told him. "This has to be private and I will enforce that." She reached for Nathalie and pulled her away from him. She stared at him as if daring him to challenge her.

Coach Bob was a lover—of skanky blow jobs from twenty-year-old girls—not a fighter. He looked almost relieved at his defeat. He'd done his duty. Now he could go back to watching TV.

Liz led Nathalie outside. She kept going until they reached the street, then crossed to the other side to give them plenty of distance from anyone else. I followed only as far as the near side of the street.

There Nathalie looked at me, then said to Liz, "Is it okay for Micky to be here?" She was clearly scared and I didn't blame her. As much as I didn't want to be her support, I understood why she asked for me. She didn't know Liz very well, and clearly the adults in the church were more concerned with following procedure than being there for the kids. Especially a very young woman who was questioning some of the beliefs they didn't want her to question.

"If it's okay with you," Liz said. She pulled her aside, out of my hearing, to make sure that Nathalie really wanted me there and wasn't being coerced by my presence.

When they were done, Liz motioned me to join them.

Once I was beside Nathalie, Liz said to her, "Let me get right to the point. The blood test found evidence of infection with syphilis."

I was slightly behind Nathalie and she was looking at Liz; otherwise, she would have seen a look of absolute shock on my face. Fifteen-year-old kids like Nathalie don't get syphilis. Maybe chlamydia or even gonorrhea, if they fooled around with one of those older boys. But Nathalie wasn't the kind of girl to fool around with older boys, probably not with boys at all. Now I understood why Liz was worried.

Liz said, "It's fairly easy to treat. Antibiotics, usually penicillin, get rid of it."

She paused, giving Nathalie time to take it in.

Nathalie looked bewildered. "But what is it? How do you get it?"

Liz cast a quick glance at me. These would be hard questions to answer. I was relieved that this was Liz's department and not mine.

"It's a bacterial infection. It causes a chancre or sore, which is usually painless. If someone comes into contact with that sore they can get infected." In the same neutral tone Liz said, "It's usually passed on via sexual contact."

"Sex?" Nathalie looked as dumbstruck as I had been. "I've...never had sex. With anyone. Could it come from barnyard animals? Cows? I've shoveled a lot of manure. Or...or I had to wade in the flood waters last year, there was a dead cow there. That could have done it."

Liz was gentle when she said, "Humans don't catch syphilis from farm animals, or any animals. It's a disease passed only between humans. Someone has to come into direct contact with the sore on another person."

Nathalie turned to me. "You believe me, don't you? That I never did anything like that?"

Denial needs something to deny. Nathalie's voice was about an octave above normal.

"Dr. Ward isn't accusing you of having sex," I said. "You have a disease that can only be passed directly from human to human. I believe you—we both believe you—when you say you didn't have sex."

Liz was clearly aware that Nathalie was getting upset. "It's not so important how you got it. What is important is that you get treated and that we cure you."

"Okay." Nathalie's voice was still a little shaky. "How do we do that?"

"It takes antibiotics, usually a shot. Have you noticed any symptoms?" Liz asked.

"No, nothing."

"There is usually a small sore, but it's often painless."

"No, I didn't notice anything like that."

"Fever, chills?"

"No."

"A rash on your hands or palms?"

Nathalie hesitated. "No…not that I remember." She wasn't a good liar.

"It's okay," I said. "You can tell us. It might be important."

She looked at me, then down at the ground. I had to lean in to hear. "Maybe a year or two ago. But it didn't hurt and we prayed it away. It really went away after we prayed."

Liz looked like she wanted to say something, but thought better of it. "When was the last time you saw a doctor?"

"We don't believe in doctors. Nathan said he didn't let them do anything to his ankle and it's okay now."

"You've never seen a doctor?" Liz asked.

"No, doctors are just men. Prayer speaks directly to God," she said, clearly repeating something she'd heard.

Nathalie was still staring at the ground. Liz shot me a look over her head as if to say that this was a big mess.

But she was smart enough to know that right now was not the time to blast the religious beliefs that Nathalie had been raised on with the cold facts of science. "Prayer does speak directly to God, but God also helps those who help themselves. He brought you into contact with me and Micky, so maybe he wants us to cure you, let him answer someone else's prayer instead."

Nathalie looked up at me.

I nodded agreement with Liz. "You're here in New Orleans, a whole new world has opened up to you. If God"—I almost said 'your god'—"meant you to stay on the farm he would have kept you there."

"Okay," she said softly, as if still unsure. "So what do I do now?"

"Let's get this taken care of as soon as possible," Liz said. "Can you get away tomorrow?"

"I...I guess. What do I tell them?"

"Tell them you have rabies," I said, then added, "sometimes it's better to hold things back for a little while. This might be one of them." Sometimes it's better to lie through your teeth and this did, indeed, qualify.

"Okay. I guess I can do that."

"I'll make some calls in the morning and figure out where to send you," Liz said.

"I'll come get you tomorrow. About one or two?" I glanced at Liz to see if that would be enough time. She nodded.

To Nathalie, she said, "Tell them that you've been exposed to something, call it rabies if that works. Tell them it's a reportable disease, that you have to show up tomorrow for more tests and treatment. If you don't, people from the health department will come here looking for you."

The story appeared to give Nathalie the cover she needed to answer the questions she would get.

"You'll be okay," I said. "We just have to take care of you."

"Thanks," she said. "I guess I've been a lot of trouble, haven't I?"

"No, you haven't, you—" But the booming bass of an approaching vehicle drowned me out. A big black SUV with tinted windows.

It screeched to a halt just past us. Carmen jumped out and stormed over. She barely got her door shut before it screeched off again.

"You!" she shouted at me. "What the hell are you doing here?"

"Such language for a nice, pious churchwoman," I said.

She started to say something then quickly glanced around. Evidently too many ears were within hearing distance, as she hissed at me, "You have no right to be here, molesting us. You need to get out of here now and not come back."

"This is public property. I have as much right to be here as you do," I informed her.

"You stay away from us and her," a nod of her head at Nathalie, "or I'll make you regret it."

Carmen was aggravating and imperious. Never mind that Liz and I each had a good twenty years on her, she could tell us what to do and threaten us with impunity.

"Regret it?" I shot back "You don't—"

"We're here on a medical matter," Liz said.

"Yeah? So? One of the volunteers here is a nurse. She takes care of everything. So the two of you need to leave." Then Carmen added, "Now!" as we weren't moving fast enough for her.

"It's not that simple," Liz replied. I knew her well enough to realize that the cool way she said it meant she didn't like being ordered around by a woman barely old enough to drink. Carmen started to say something, but Liz overrode her. "It's possible that Nathalie has been exposed to a reportable disease, one that requires far greater treatment than a nurse outside of a medical setting can provide."

"You can't just barge in here and order us around." Carmen stamped her foot. Yes, indeed, she actually stamped her foot.

"On the contrary, I can," Liz answered. "I'm a lieutenant commander in the Public Health Service, attached to the Centers for Disease Control and Prevention, and in certain medical matters such as this one, I can order you around."

"I'm supposed to be impressed, right?" Carmen replied.

"I don't much care," Liz said. "This is the law and you will obey it. We will be getting Nathalie tomorrow and taking her in for proper treatment. Whether you're impressed or not."

"We'll see about that. C'mon, Nats, time for you to go beddy-bye. And get away from these perverts." Carmen grabbed Nathalie by the arm and propelled her across the road.

"We'll be back tomorrow," I told her.

"You need to stop fucking interfering in what we're doing. You got that?"

"Oh, please, you little gutter snipe—" Liz put her hand on my arm. There was no point in arguing with Carmen, it would only keep us standing here. "Let's go, we have better things to do," I said as I turned and started to walk away.

Carmen had to have the last word. "You won't win this one."

Nathalie, sensibly, had kept walking and was halfway back across the lawn. She held up a finger for "one," then did a quick motion with her hands as if running. She'd find a way to meet me at one.

Liz and I walked in silence back to my car. We could hear Carmen; she was probably deliberately being loud enough for us to be unwillingly included in the conversation. "God's work is hard work. We need to be careful about what strangers we let in here. They don't understand us and what we do. There are dangerous people out there…"

I slammed my door on the rest of it.

"Let's get out of here," Liz said.

She waited until I was almost to the interstate before speaking again. "I'd put money on that woman—girl, not really mature enough to be a woman—being a sociopath. Or worse."

"The rules don't apply to her. She believes in the gospel of riches and greed. But she's not really our problem."

"Agreed. Only if she makes it difficult to get to Nathalie."

"She can huff and puff all she wants. At the end of the day, she's a twenty-something claiming to be eighteen so she can be the leader of a young group for a small religious sect. Not exactly the zenith of power." I pulled onto I-10. Traffic was heavy, as usual, but more outbound than the inbound direction we were going.

"True. Our real problem is Nathalie."

"Wait, I thought you said it could be treated by antibiotics."

"It can. But you don't get syphilis from mucking up manure in a barn or wading in water when the crick overflows."

"It pretty much has to be sex."

"Yes. I could be wrong, but I'm seeing a young, naïve girl from an isolated area and part of a non-mainstream religion. She says she didn't have sex, but I think what she really means is that she didn't have what she defines as sex," Liz said.

"She was getting agitated when we asked her about it."

"Was she agitated because she's lying? She did a quickie with one of the boys here behind the altar and now she's guilty and sure God is punishing her? Or is she covering up for someone?"

"Or realizing that what she and Daddy have been doing in the barn will come to light and be very messy?" I speculated.

"Or has she been assaulted and just found out she got an STI from it?"

"That might explain why she's so adamant about not having sex," I said angrily. "It's not sex if it's rape."

"Something happened to that child that shouldn't have, and that's a major problem. Also, she may need a course of antibiotics, not just one shot. The longer the infection, the longer the treatment."

"What do we do now?"

"I make calls in the morning, arrange for her to start treatment in the afternoon. One of the calls will be to child-protective services. I'd like to keep her long enough for her to get treated and us to sort this out. If someone in her family is responsible, we don't want to just send her back there. She trusts you more than anyone. When you pick her up tomorrow, see if you can get her to talk."

"I'll do my best, but in a not-so-long drive, it might be hard to get her to open up."

"Just do what you can. We need to find out what happened to her to be able to prevent it from happening again."

That was a dismal thought to take us back over the parish line. It was odd to drive on the interstate with swaths of darkness beside it, the only light from car beams and distant glimmers from the areas that had power restored.

Liz and I said little, each of us preoccupied with our thoughts or just tired.

I dropped her off where she was staying and we briefly reviewed the plans for tomorrow again, made sure we had each other's cell-phone number. She kissed me on the cheek for good-bye. I pressed her hand.

The touch felt good, I thought as I drove away. It can mean so much, the affirmation that contact gives, the message of "I like you well enough to lay a hand on you."

Then I thought of the disastrous afternoon with Cordelia. If I hadn't said what I had, maybe I could be going there now instead of back to my unheated office. But I wouldn't have said what I said if I didn't feel what I feel, and I wouldn't feel what I feel if she hadn't done what she'd done. I wasn't denying that I could have been a lot more sensitive, but I'd had little choice in creating the situation.

It was still early, just past eight. For a moment I debated going there, demanding we talk. But I kept driving to my office. I didn't really want to talk. What I really wanted was for her to apologize to me, to say that she was wrong and that she wanted to be with me. She could also add that I was the best thing that ever happened to her and she couldn't imagine how she'd live without me, but I'd consider those two optional at the moment.

However, I wasn't sure what she wanted. Even if she'd been open to the idea of working things out when she came down here, the events of the past few days might have changed her mind. Finding me chugging straight vodka by myself. Falling into a swimming pool—you were pushed, I reminded myself—at an Uptown party. Being rescued by another woman, the one I'd arrived at the party with. More or less forcing her to have sex with me. Ambushing her with my anger when she was naked and vulnerable.

I wasn't sure I wanted me back after that.

We did have to talk, if only to hash out the house and how I'd get my cat back.

Call her when you get back to the office, I decided. Apologize. I did owe her one for my behavior this afternoon. Set up a time and place when we both could talk. Make time before that to run a marathon so I would be as exhausted as possible. That might tamp the anger down a little.

But I didn't need to call her. Of course, when I got back to my office I didn't rush to the phone, instead found other things that demanded my attention or at least were excuses for me to delay just a little longer. Like checking e-mail.

She'd sent one. I was almost reluctant to open it.

Finally I reminded myself that I was a total and complete jerk this afternoon, and if she was going to call me on it, I deserved it. And that was why I'd come here instead of going to the house, to avoid hearing in person what she might say.

It was long and rambling. Cordelia doesn't do long and rambling.

Micky,

I'm very sorry for everything. There is no apology that will make up for what happened—what I did—so I won't waste your time by trying. A haunting line from Shakespeare, "Bid time return, call back yesterday," has become my refrain. So many things I'd call back and erase, change if I could. But I can't.

I know what I did was wrong. I can't explain. It's easy to say no when no one is asking. Anyone can be perfect if they never have a chance to sin. Maybe life was trying to teach me a lesson about my hubris—except it was a messy lesson and I made choices and have no one to blame but myself.

I wish I could do better than this, but I can't. There haven't been that many days, but it feels so long ago. So much has happened. Maybe I could fix us, but I have to fix me first and I don't know how to do that. That week in Charity—no, just five days, could it be just five days?—broke me. I still wake at night with the stench in my nostrils, a nightmare that I'm there again. I cry over little things or nothing at all. I thought a little rest, some time away, I'd be okay, but I'm not. I should have returned weeks ago, but couldn't face being back here. I finally just bought the airline ticket and didn't let myself think about it until I was up in the air and it was too late to turn back. I was the last person off the plane, my memory of the airport was as a triage center. I had this bizarre picture of passengers disembarking through gurneys and IV poles. I was afraid that I would see it all over again if I came through the airport—real or in my mind.

The clinic had seven feet of water. The second floor was okay before it was looted. Copper wiring stripped from the walls, toilets ripped out. It'll take about a year to get it fixed and workable again. But I have no way of knowing whether there will even be patients if we reopen it. Will people come back? Can they? Will anyone return to that ruined neighborhood? Can I bet a year of my life on that?

Right now the answer is no. If I can't even sleep at night how do I find the energy and the patience to slog through all the insurance and rebuilding mess for something that might not even matter?

I've had some job offers here, but New Orleans is haunted for me now. Maybe I should face my ghosts, but I'm not sure I can. Or that there is any point in doing so. Right now everyone is taking in Katrina refugees, helping them find jobs and places to live.

I've spent the last few months just sitting at my sister's, watching television (yeah, me, watching TV) or walking, long walks to nowhere until it got too cold to be outside. That's not a life. I need to move on. Work seems like a good way to heal. Maybe if I spend enough time in a hospital where the lights always stay on, medicine is available, the worst smell is ammonia from cleaning—and no one is dying because all *the king's horses and all the king's men couldn't get boats through a thousand feet of water for days and days and days. Maybe if I do that the memories will recede and I'll be okay.*

I could stay in Boston, but the only person I really know there is my sister and her family. As you know, her husband and I aren't best friends. He was never happy about having a lesbian for a sister-in-law, and my living in their spare bedroom hasn't improved our relationship. Plus it's too cold there for me. Guess the South is in my bones.

It was just one phone call, but it took me forever to call a headhunter. She's been lining up interviews for me. It's almost like I need these little "grab bars" to haul myself along—an interview, I have to be there, be ready for it, but without that motivation, I'm floundering through the days. I've never been like this. I keep hoping that a little more time, a little more structure, maybe work to go to every day and it'll all be okay. That something will make it okay.

Alex and I don't talk much anymore. It seems such a distant past when we'd call each other every few days and feel like we'd just started talking when an hour or two was gone. But I don't seem to be helping her and we just get on the phone and then neither of us says anything. I know she's struggling with losing her house and her job and the baby—who wouldn't be struggling with all that. Maybe if we could see each other instead of having to endure a bad cell connection, we could struggle together instead of apart. I don't know.

I don't know if there is a place for me in New Orleans anymore.

I had to come back to take care of things, start the arrangements to have the clinic building gutted. I'll come back when that's being done, if possible. Insurance, FEMA, it's all a mess. There is so much crap and paperwork to deal with.

You can stay in the house; you didn't need to leave just because I'm here. We don't need to sell or divide it or anything like that. I'm okay. Granddad's money will keep me going for a while even if I don't work. But I have to work to have something to define my days. I'm scared that if I keep falling, I'll fall so far there'll be no way back up.

The cats are still at my sister's. I was flying and didn't want to have to put them in a carrier. Once I have a better idea of where I'll end up I'll go get them and bring them back here. Before Christmas, at any rate. I've told myself I have to make some decisions in the next week or so and get on with my life. I know that Hepplewhite is officially yours and Rook mine, but they've been together so long now it's not right to separate them. If you don't want to take them, of course, I will, but New Orleans is their home and I think they'd like to be back in the house they're used to. They miss you.

I don't know if this is making any sense. I miss you. You've been my best friend for so long. I don't know how to get along in the world without a best friend anymore. But that's all my fault. I'm sorry I broke it; I'm sorry I can't fix it.

You have a right to be angry. To be angry at me. But I just can't face your anger now. I'm sorry.

I'm flying to Dallas tomorrow for two interviews there, last plane out. I'm leaving late, have things to do in the morning here, more insurance crap. I'll probably be back at the house around three or four and leaving for the airport around six.

That sounds rushed and demanding, doesn't it? I guess it is. I've been scared to leave too much time unstructured, so I crammed everything—maybe too much—into a few days. If you want to talk, we can. About the house. Or how much you hate me. Or anything in between. I hope that someday I come through this and find some way to keep you in my life.
Love, Cordelia.

My heart broke. For both of us. The screen was blurry because I'd been crying. A part of me was angry that she could just do this hit-and-run back into my life. But that part of me kept screaming, "What about me, what about me?" and I couldn't very well condemn her for thinking about herself first when I was thinking about myself first.

I started to write back, but no words came. I stared at the screen for a long time trying to find terms that could say everything that I wanted to say, words that would build and help and heal us both. But no mere expressions were equal to such a task. Or none that I could come up with. Tomorrow. I could talk to her tomorrow.

I didn't want what I said to her today to be the last thing I said. To at least give myself the chance to be a better person than that for both our sakes. That if I was angry, that I kept it leashed and caged so I didn't just rage and destroy.

There were other tragedies, I reminded myself. A young woman murdered and her remarkable voice forever silent; a young girl with burdens of shame and silence and a disease no child her age should have.

I poured myself a generous serving of Scotch. Maybe I should be better than this, needing it to dull the sharp edges of life. But I just couldn't bear all the thoughts raging through my head tonight; I needed to quiet them to be able to sleep. Things were falling apart; the center was not holding.

CHAPTER TWENTY-FOUR

I awoke early, again the mocking sunshine, perfect days of clear skies as if nature thought she could make up for her furies of the late summer.

What if Katrina hadn't happened, I wondered as I lay in bed. Or even if the storm had come, the levees and floodwalls had held?

If wishes were horses, we all would ride. Something my mother would say to me when I was little. Where did that come from? Oh, yeah, that pesky subconscious. I swung my legs out of bed, trying to figure out what my sub-brain was up to as I wiped the sleep from my eyes. It seemed pretty obvious—Katrina had happened. I couldn't wish it away. Or maybe I just wanted that mythical perfect moment of childhood, when I was cared for and loved and the adults around me could make all the problems disappear.

If Katrina hadn't happened, I wouldn't be here right now. I wouldn't be sleeping in my unheated office; Cordelia wouldn't have spent a week in hell and be struggling to get over it. We'd be back together. I didn't know how I could know that, but I did. Then I realized that I did know how I knew that. I'd forgive her. Duh. Why hadn't I thought of that before? I headed to the bathroom and a shower.

Lauren Caulder was a compelling and attractive woman. What if she had thrown herself at me? What if I'd worked with her everyday as Cordelia had? A hand on the arm, a shoulder rub, a lingering hug. Return to the same place the next day.

So instead of buying a little red sports car as a mid-life crisis, Cordelia had a fling. It was just sex. Well, not that anything is just sex, but sometimes it really is just wanting that brief flash of flesh, and sometimes it's an expression of love forever.

The one place she hadn't mentioned interviewing for jobs was New York City, where Lauren Caulder lived. I turned on the water, waiting for it to get hot. Then remembered that it wasn't going to get hot until the gas lines were repaired and they weren't likely to be fixed in the next ten minutes. I filled the sink half full. Today would be another chilly sponge-bath day.

If Katrina hadn't happened, I'd still have walked in on them, then run out, fled to the shipyard in the bayous. But instead of having to suddenly evacuate from the storm, I'd have stayed there. Probably long enough for Cordelia to have come out to find me. I would have had my well-deserved blowup. She would acknowledge that I had a reason to be enraged and apologize. Probably several times. Reality is that I'd have required at least three before responding. She would have given me three. She would have fixed it.

That was our pattern, perhaps a part of why we worked. Cordelia was calm and stable. Me, not so much. I'd fly off—sometimes with good reason, other times not—and she'd be there, calm, waiting, talking me down. Giving me time, space, what I needed to work things out. She was the rock; I was the wind.

Katrina had broken my rock. After ten years together, it was my turn. I'd have to take over her role, be calm and stable and look for ways to find a way back to each other instead of being the one who railed and fumed.

Could I do it? Could I do it ever? Can I do it now?

I plunged my face into the cold water, quickly scrubbing it, then just as quickly drying myself. For the rest of my body, I dipped a washcloth in the water, but was just as hasty with the washing.

Let her go—it's broken and it can't be fixed. Or be different—and better—than I've ever been before. That was my choice.

I wrapped myself in a big towel, trying to get warm and dry.

Could I do it? It scared me to think about trying. I could go there when she got home around four. If I couldn't at least be a decent person, I might do better to skip seeing her again. Dallas wasn't that far away. In six months to a year, we could probably be friends again. Or avoid ever seeing each other again.

I dithered for a moment, trying to decide whether to put the coffee on before I got dressed or after. Clothes won. I was too cold to be naked a second longer than necessary even if it meant delaying the caffeine.

I couldn't think about Cordelia anymore. I had a lot to do today, a lot of things to worry about. I'd delegate worrying about her to my sub-brain. Maybe by four o'clock it would tell me whether to go see her.

A couple of granola bars and a banana would do for breakfast. Plus a big mug of coffee.

I sat in front of my computer. It was time to work on the one case someone was paying me for.

I didn't have a lot to go on. No one wants to think that someone is deliberately trying to do them harm. The Overhills were no different. Even if they didn't lose any money, crime eats at your soul. Makes you suspicious of those around you. Makes you wonder, is it punishment for sins or just a brutal randomness that could strike again? I could understand their reluctance to suspect those around them.

Jared had sent me a list of employees fired in the last six months. It had three names on it. Two were in prison on drug-related charges that didn't seem to have much to do with the day job. One had moved to Hawaii. None of them seemed likely, especially as they were in positions—night maintenance, custodian—that wouldn't require much contact with the Overhills.

It had to be someone who intersected with the Overhills and Alma. The records she had uncovered were public, so in theory someone else could find them as well, but that seemed unlikely. Blackmailers weren't usually archive hounds.

I went to the company Web site, not that I expected to find out much. I'd looked it over before, but this time I was culling through all the names listed. It was a stretch, to go through names of the top managers to see if I could discover anything like a gambling problem that might make someone resort to extortion.

It was tedious going. All I could find was apple pie and rosy cheeks. The top dirt was a speeding ticket from three years ago.

After about two hours I broke off and started looking at photographs of various events. No, I wasn't expecting to see someone sharpening a knife in the background, but body language can be telling and it at least might give me a way to winnow the list.

The truth was we might never know who the blackmailer was.

Culling through these names was like looking for a needle in a haystack when I had no idea if this was even the right haystack. The most likely way to catch them—I assumed more people were involved beyond the two on the telephone—was to set up a fake payoff and apprehend whoever tried to pick up the money. Then hope that person would snitch on the higher-ups.

Company picnic. New hotel opening. Employee of the month. Blah blah. Helping construct a new playground. Company softball tournament. Visitors from the West Coast. Visitors from the East Coast. Visitors from Europe. Visitors from outer space. No, that was our congressional delegation. Decorating the office for Christmas. Decorating the office for Mardi Gras. It seemed that any picture that didn't have radiantly smiling people wasn't posted.

Wait. Decorating for Mardi Gras. Third from the left, second row. Mildred Groome. Alma Groome. Not a common name, although it was possibly just a coincidence. I hurriedly looked through my notes. Alma's brother Calvin had married a white woman over a decade older than he was.

I stared intently at the woman. She tried to look younger than she was, dyed blond hair, eye makeup obscuring the lines around her eyes. What was it that Mrs. Frist had said? Teased blond kind of woman? This one could fit the bill. I printed the picture.

I needed to ask Jared about her. Just as I was about to pick up the phone, it rang.

It was Marilyn Overhill. "She called again."

"When?"

"Just now. I literally hung up the phone with her to call you."

"You talked to her?"

"Yes, unfortunately. I was the only one home."

"What did she want?"

"The money. She said we have to have it this evening by ten o'clock. She was very insistent about that."

"Where are you supposed to meet her?"

"She wouldn't tell me. Said she'd call later and let us know."

"Were you able to get her to call back at a specific time?"

"No. I tried. I informed her that we had to go out and she told me that was too bad, that someone had better be hanging around the phone or we'd regret it."

"Same person? Or at least the same voice?"

"Yes. The woman who first called. She didn't talk long, like she was in a hurry. Just that we had to have the money by tonight or all our, quote, shit would be smeared over everything, unquote."

"This might be the time to call in the police. Probably the best way to capture her and whoever she is working with will be when they attempt to get the money. That's my advice, but it's your choice. Some people have paid blackmailers off to avoid the publicity and having the authorities involved."

"And just let this woman and her cohorts walk away with it? I think not. Should I call law enforcement?"

"I have contacts there. I can if you want me to. Again, your choice."

"Would you do it? This is out of my comfort zone by a few thousand miles."

I agreed and, glancing at my watch, asked if it was okay for me to drop by and get a copy of the phone call.

"It's not like I can go anywhere. I have to wait around for an important phone call." Her words were etched in acid.

I called Joanne, waiting on hold for about ten minutes before finally speaking to her. I updated her on everything. Before she could ask I told her I'd send her a copy of the latest phone call and e-mail the company photo, and the cherry on top, anything that Jared told me about Mildred Groome, I'd immediately pass on to her.

"You'd better," she admonished me. "You get a ringside seat, but it's our show now. Call for anything and everything."

Then it was a call to Jared to ask about Mildred Groome. The best he could do was tell me the name sounded vaguely familiar, but he couldn't place her. I gave him Joanne's fax number and e-mail and told him to send anything he could find to both of us.

I looked at my watch. I needed to get moving if I wanted to get uptown, retrieve the recording of the phone call, and make it out to Kenner at one to fetch Nathalie.

As I was gathering what I needed to take with me, I called Liz.

"Where do I go from Kenner?" I said in greeting. She had caller ID, she'd know it was me.

"Still working on it. Trying to get all the players in the same location. A doctor and a social worker, who'd have thought it would be so hard. Probably around Touro, exact location TBA."

"That's close enough for now. I'll make sure to bring the car charger for the cell phone. I'll give you a call once I have her on board."

"Thanks. You're a great partner. Drinks and dinner after this is all over?"

I must have hesitated, as she said, "As a thank-you for helping me do my job."

"If we can find a decent restaurant that's reopened, you're on the hook."

Then it was time to make my appointed rounds. I had my laptop, cell phone, phone charger. Pens, paper, tampons. What else did I need? Gun.

Cordelia hated for me to carry the gun, but if I went by to see her, I'd leave it in the car. Unless I wanted to have sex with her one more time. Ouch, the humor was too black even for me.

One advantage of so few working stoplights was speed, no waiting for the light to change. Rarely was more than one car at any given intersection. I was in front of the Overhills in twenty minutes.

Marilyn greeted me at the door with, "No phone calls yet. Guess I'll be waiting a little longer."

Technology is wonderful. I could capture the phone call on a jump drive, leaving the recording device in place. Once I had saved it, I could download it to my computer and e-mail it to Joanne.

As I was doing this, I explained what was going on to Marilyn. Someone from NOPD would be here shortly. They might well ask her the same questions that I did. She was stoic enough to reply only that at least my questions had given her time to think about the answers. I wasn't quite sure how NOPD would handle this, but they knew what they were doing. If she or any of her family had questions or concerns, I'd be around to help and advocate for them. NOPD wanted to catch the crooks. My job was to look after Brooke and her family. Those were mostly the same goals, but not always.

She let me have the security code to their wireless system so I could send Joanne the audio file. I made sure she had my cell-phone number and also Joanne's. I trusted Marilyn Overhill to use them only if needed.

I did a quick calculation. I just needed to pick up Nathalie. I was assuming that I could drop her off, or at least decline to be the designated driver. I'd be done with her by about two, three at the latest. Cordelia was leaving for the airport around six. That meant that, no matter what happened, I could easily be back here by seven to be with them during the most crucial time. I quickly sketched out my schedule to Marilyn—being rather vague—"an important errand for another client and a meeting"—assuring her that I would be back this evening and that she should call if anything happened, or even if she had any questions.

Then I was out of her house and heading for the interstate to go pick up Nathalie.

CHAPTER TWENTY-FIVE

It was the middle of the day so traffic wasn't too bad heading out to get Nathalie, save for one slow section for rubbernecking a fender bender on the other side.

As I exited, I looked at my watch. I'd made good time; it was about a quarter to one. I took advantage of being early to drive the block around the church, looking for the tell-tale black SUV. I could deal with Carmen if I had to, but I'd prefer to avoid her. Actually I'd really prefer to upend her smart mouth into a garbage can. Maybe Nathalie had even learned some Devious 101 from her and claim female maladies to be left alone long enough to sneak out.

I didn't park in front, but a little farther down the street, close to an intersection. Three ways to go might give me some extra options.

I stayed in my car, hoping Nathalie would pop her head out around one and look for me. That would be far easier than me running the gauntlet of "Just a minute. Wait right here" I was bound to encounter if I knocked on the door.

At one-fifteen, there was still no sign of Nathalie. I sighed; it was time to do it the hard way. I got out of my car and headed across the lawn. The place felt oddly empty, as if no one was here. True, the kids were supposed to be out gutting houses, but surely by this point at least one or two of them had had more mud and mold than their sinuses could handle.

I tried opening the door, but it was locked. Another sigh and I knocked.

And knocked again.

I was about to knock a third time, when I heard the lock turn.

Ms. Clueless opened the door.

"I need to take Nathalie for medical treatment," I announced without any preamble.

"She's not here."

"Not here? Why isn't she here?"

"I don't know. I just know she's not here."

I started to argue that Nathalie should be here, but that was pointless. "Where is she?"

"I don't know."

"So, we have a child who has contracted an infectious disease, she needs treatment by the end of today, and you have no clue where she is?"

"Oh." Even Ms. Clueless couldn't miss the disdain. Her brow wrinkled, then her lips downturned in distaste. "Well, if she needed a doctor so much why didn't you take her last night?"

Why hadn't we? Other than being unrelated adults with no real authority. I took a step closer to her. She backed up. I explained. "This is New Orleans. A nasty hurricane came through here a few months ago. It flooded a large number of hospitals in the area, totally disrupted medical services. We have to make special arrangements for treatment and that would have been difficult last night. We thought it would be okay to leave her with you, that it wasn't possible any competent adult would withhold medical treatment from a child."

I had taken a step closer to her with each sentence and had now moved her halfway across the room until she was backed up against a Ping-Pong table.

"Oh."

"Who did she go with? Do you have cell-phone numbers for any of them?"

"Um…she went with the rest of the group. I don't have a cell phone."

"Their cell-phone numbers. How do you contact them?" I said very slowly and deliberately, miming dialing a phone.

"I talk to them in the morning before they leave or after they come back."

"You have no way to get ahold of anyone once they've left here?"

"No. There seemed no reason for that."

"When are they supposed to be back?"

She was trying to edge around the Ping-Pong table so she could skitter across the rest of the room. I stepped in at an angle to cut off that escape. She started working her way to the other end of the table, somehow thinking that for some reason I wouldn't do the same thing at the other end. "I don't know."

"What city do you live in?"

"What city? Why do you ask?"

"Just checking to see if there is anything you do know." I moved to her other side again, cutting off her escape.

"I don't live in a city. I live out in LaPlace."

The only question she could answer was one I didn't give a damn about.

"What area of the city are they working in?" Yes, I had asked that before, but after listening to them talk about what they were doing she might have gotten a clue.

But I was calling her Ms. Clueless for a reason. "Somewhere in New Orleans. I don't know the city at all. It's too dangerous to go there."

I pulled out my phone. "I'm calling the police and the Office of Public Health. They'll be out here to question you shortly. We need to find Nathalie as soon as possible."

Did that scare her? Yes. Did it get me any more information? No. She clearly worked very hard at knowing as little as possible about things she should know.

I let her off the hook and told her the police probably wouldn't be able to come by. That they were all working a gruesome serial-killer case out in LaPlace.

I was back out on the street. It was close to two o'clock. I called Liz.

"You on your way?" she answered. Caller ID.

"No, she's not here." I gave her a quick rundown of my conversation with Ms. Clueless.

"Give me strength. What planet are these people on? Do you think she's avoiding us?"

"I guess it's possible." We had rocked Nathalie's world, which can be very scary. Maybe she had decided to retreat into what she knew.

"But…it doesn't seem like her to sneak away. My money would be on her calling me to tell me not to come out here." I looked at my watch. Two hours between now and when Cordelia would be home. "I'm going to look for her. I'd like to talk to her directly before assuming that she's not willing to cooperate."

"How will you find her?"

"They wear lime-green T-shirts. It's hard to miss a swarm of lime green. I'll prowl the neighborhood where I first met them."

"Okay, I need to make some phone calls and tell my friends to put the big penicillin needles away."

"Will she be okay? If she doesn't get treated soon?"

"The sooner the better. It may depend on how long she's been infected. Syphilis can attack just about any part of the body once it gets established. It can still be eradicated, but once the damage is done, it can't be fixed. A day or two might not make much difference. But if she disappears and doesn't get medical attention for a long time, it's not good."

"It can kill her?"

"Worse. It can eat her brain and leave her an empty shell."

I roared out of the neighborhood. The minutes were ticking away. The fender bender on the inbound route had been cleared, and with a little weaving and a little speeding, I was in Gentilly in under half an hour.

No lime green in the area where I'd first encountered them. There were sporadic signs of activity, every block or so a car that hadn't been left here by the flood, or even people working. But for the most part, desolate, brilliant sunshine on houses that had once been white or cream brick or bright yellow, now all dusty gray with black lines of water covering everything—houses, cars, trees. Lives. The water marked us all.

It was three-thirty. I needed to be heading back to Tremé soon to talk to Cordelia. If I wanted to see her before she left.

I had one more idea. I drove back to Elysian Fields and found a cell signal. Channeling pimply-faced adolescent boy, I dialed what I hoped was the right number from those left on my cell phone.

"Hello?" someone vaguely male answered. Close enough.

"Hey, I lost your location. The folks sponsoring y'all are sending some pizzas to the work site. Can you tell me where you are?"

"Oh, uh…yeah, sure. Let me figure it out." The phone was moved about a quarter of an inch from his mouth as he shouted, "Hey, where are we? Someone needs to know."

At least the cell service wasn't great, so his yelling didn't destroy my hearing like a good connection would have.

I had guessed right, dialing the number that Nathalie had given me and getting Nathan. Like a good, trusting Midwesterner, he had fallen for my ploy. Given that he was fooled by drug dealers that Catholic schoolgirls could spot, my deception wasn't masterful.

I hadn't been that far away, just far enough that I never would have found them. They were about ten more blocks away from the lake and five blocks downtown.

"'Kay, be there soon," I promised, and hung up before he realized he wasn't talking to a teenage pizza-delivery boy.

Maybe they had coerced Nathalie to go with them, I thought as I hung a U-turn. At that age peer pressure can be powerful. Or maybe she didn't want to go, but didn't have any choice.

Or maybe she did, maybe Liz was right, she wanted to retreat into the world where all your troubles could be prayed away. I'd know soon enough, I thought, as I swerved to avoid a muddy tire in the middle of the road.

A turn and another turn and then I spotted the gaggle of lime green. I couldn't see Nathalie, but she had to be here somewhere. I felt bad about making them think they were getting pizza, but gobs of cheese and pepperoni aren't really good for growing kids.

I drove by, taking a closer scan for Nathalie, but still didn't see her. I wasn't trying to be discreet. Mine was probably the first car that had come by in the last hour, so there was no way to escape notice. I parked a little down the street in the clearest spot I could find.

As I walked back to them I could see that this was clearly a tired group. They'd been here about a week, most of them weren't used to this kind of labor, it was the end of the day, and it was showing.

No sign of Carmen or Coach Bob. I wondered who was supervising them. Still no sign of Nathalie, but I did see Nathan.

No surprise, he looked surprised to see me.

"Where's Nathalie?" I asked him.

He blinked, looked confused, then asked, "I was about to ask you that. She went with you for whatever it was she needed."

"No, she was supposed to meet me at one out in Kenner, but she wasn't there."

"Yeah, she came with us this morning—Carmen said it wouldn't hurt her to work, we're behind. Then around noon, Carmen came back and got Nathalie to take her to meet you."

"I waited until almost two. No one showed up."

"You weren't meeting out there, somewhere not too far from here."

"What? We told Nathalie that I would pick her up at around one out there. We didn't change plans."

"Carmen said she talked to you and that you said Nathalie should go with her."

What fucking game was Carmen playing? I didn't use that language in front of Nathan. As far as I could tell, he was actually answering my questions, and at the moment, he was my only lead.

"I never talked to Carmen. I never asked her to take Nathalie anywhere."

"But that's what she said."

"If I talked to Carmen, why would I be here?" I asked in as calm and reasonable a voice as I could.

"I don't know. Maybe you're stupid and you forgot."

Nathan was getting truculent. His love for Carmen wasn't going to waver. Even if it meant his sister didn't get taken care of.

Again, being calm and reasonable, I said, "I didn't forget. I never talked to Carmen. She wasn't taking Nathalie to meet me. Maybe Carmen doesn't understand the importance of the situation. Maybe she didn't believe that Nathalie really needs medical treatment. Clearly Carmen and I had a misunderstanding. You have to help me find Nathalie. It could save her life." Clearly Carmen and I had no understanding, even "mis," of any sort, but trashing his beloved as thoroughly as she needed to be trashed wouldn't get him to cooperate.

Nathan chewed his lip, then looked down, away from me. "I don't know. I should wait for Carmen to come back and see what she wants to do."

I noticed that several other kids were listening to our conversation. One of them, a girl about Nathalie's age, rolled her eyes at Nathan's comment. She was behind him and he couldn't see.

"Carmen is playing games with your sister's life." Nice and

reasonable weren't getting through to him. I might as well try a harsh dose of reality. "She is using you, she's clever." No, she's not, he was stupid, but even as angry as I was, I knew better than to point that out. "She likes to control things, and right now her insistence on keeping Nathalie from me and the doctors is a far bigger problem than either she or you realize."

"I'll wait to talk to her."

"Call her on your cell phone." Then I remembered that there was no cell coverage here. Then I remembered that I had just called him on it. A cell tower must have been restored.

"It doesn't work here," he said petulantly.

"Only for pizza orders?"

That made him look up at me.

"That was you?" Emotions rolled across his face—disbelief, then outrage. "You lied to me? How could you?" He ended on a fifteen-year-old's note. "That wasn't fair."

The girl shook her head as if in disgust and caught my eye as she did it.

I almost felt sorry for him; he was so upset by my subterfuge. How would he feel when he finally found out that Carmen was using him in a far worse manner? If he ended up in jail because of her, he'd have a lot of time to think it over.

"Not fair? Carmen keeping your sister away from needed medical treatment is fine and dandy, but me misleading you isn't kosher?"

The look on his face told me he didn't know what kosher meant.

"She's nice to me. You're mean." He pouted.

He was useless. As much as I wanted to tell him exactly what kind of self-absorbed petulant little boy he was, it wouldn't help me find Nathalie. I'd call Liz and we'd figure out what the next step was. Or get Joanne involved. Carmen's interference with medical treatment for Nathalie had to be breaking some laws.

I turned and walked away.

I'd done what I could to find Nathalie.

The girl ran after me and called, "Hey, you dropped your wallet."

I patted my front pocket. It was still there.

I started to shake my head, but she mouthed something I couldn't make out. Just as she reached me, she hastily looked over her shoulder as if making sure no one had followed.

"It's Nathalie's," she said. "Carmen isn't nice. Nathan is an idiot."

I didn't disagree with any of that.

She spoke in a rush, as if needing to get everything out as quickly as she could. "We all put our purses and wallets in one place. When Carmen took Nathalie she wouldn't let her get it, said she wouldn't need it where she was going. She hurried Nathalie into that big black truck. She says it belongs to a pastor from a local church and that he's counseling her. But what pastor needs tinted windows and plays music real loud?"

I nodded. Her intent was clear; she couldn't be seen talking to me any longer than it should take to give a wallet back.

"Carmen did tell her she was taking her to you, which was the only reason Nats went. But when she shut the door so Nats couldn't hear her, she got on that stupid cell phone and said 'she fell for it. That stupid cow won't spy on us again. Now you do your part and we celebrate at ten-fifteen tonight. I remember it 'cause it was so weird."

"Hey," Nathan called, "is it her wallet or not?"

"Who made him king?" she groused.

"It is my wallet," I answered loudly. "I'm trying to give her a reward and she won't take it." I pulled two twenties out of my real wallet and handed it to her. More quietly I said, "Buy pizza for you and your friends. Any idea where they went?"

"Carmen had her keys, phone, purse, and she's kind of a klutz. She had a piece of paper and she dropped it. Acting helpful, I grabbed it up. It was a map, with a street named Flood and another one circled. She snatched it before I could read more."

"Thanks, that's helpful." Seeing Nathan heading our way, I said, "No, no, I insist. I'd be in big trouble if you hadn't found my wallet."

"You need to get back to work." He was taking lessons from Carmen in how to be an obnoxious prig.

"I'm leaving," I said, marching toward my car. Over my shoulder I had to tell the girl, "Don't work too hard, you know he won't." I managed to shut the door on whatever he replied.

I looked at my watch. A little before four o'clock. Between four and six. If I got there at five, it would be okay.

I hoped.

I was worried about Nathalie. Flood Street was in the Lower 9th

Ward. It had been flooded from just about everyplace water could come and was so destroyed that only recently had they allowed people to come back in and look at what was left. Even now there was a strict curfew; everyone was supposed to be out by nightfall.

Carmen was enough of a sociopath that she could have dropped Nathalie off in some vile place, abandoning her on a desolate, destroyed street. Or worse, in the name of their god, punishing her. Given that she was already infected with syphilis, I didn't like what her church and Carmen's sick mind could come up with.

I got in my car and once again went in search of Nathalie.

The Lower 9th isn't a large area, and the all-too-aptly-named Flood Street ran from the river to an inner levee where the land turned into marsh and the gulf outlet.

I shot down Elysian Fields. As I was driving, I wondered about what Nathalie's friend had overheard. "Won't spy on us again" was probably about Nathalie telling me about the drug deal. "She fell for it" was obvious, the ruse to get her away so I couldn't pick her up. But that made no real sense. Could Carmen really think we wouldn't be back tomorrow? "We celebrate at ten-fifteen tonight." Celebrate what? Keeping Nathalie away from medical help for a day? Why ten-fifteen? Carmen didn't strike me as a precise person, why not just ten?

Because they're getting the money at ten.

But that was the Overhills and their blackmailer. That had nothing to do with this.

There was very little traffic in this destroyed neighborhood, which was a good thing as I veered across two lanes turning on my laptop. I kept my eyes on the road and stuck the jump drive in using touch and then only a quick glance down to hit Play.

The tinny speaker of the laptop blared, "You'd better get us the money by ten or you'll regret it." I hastily turned down the volume.

Marilyn Overhill said, "But it will be hard—"

"I don't care how fucking hard it is. You'd better do it or I'll smear your shit all over. You want hard? I've had hard. No more hard for me. You get us the money by ten tonight or you will regret it."

I hit Stop. Carmen liked people to regret things. Driving frantically while trying to listen to cheap laptop speakers isn't the best way to compare voices, but her annoying nasal tone was distinctive.

It just made no sense. What could Carmen—what was her name?—

Gecklebacher from Wisconsin have to do with the Overhills and Alma
Groome from New Orleans? If that was her real name.

My next stupid driving maneuver was to get out my cell phone
and make a call, while zooming through the stop sign at Elysian Fields
and Gentilly Boulevard—six lanes meeting four lanes.

Joanne's cell phone went to voice mail. I was about to hang up
and call her back later, but it was so close to as late as it could be, that
a message seemed in order.

"Joanne, this is Micky—weird twist. I listened to the tape. It sounds
like the psycho from Nathalie's church group, Carmen Gecklebacher,
which may not be her real name. Anyway, she's sending me on a wild-
goose chase to find Nathalie, who needs medical treatment for a disease
she shouldn't have. Long story. I'm heading down to the Lower 9th.
They're supposed to be somewhere on Flood. If you don't hear from
me in an hour, come looking."

Could this be true? It only made it more imperative that I find
Nathalie and see if I could glean some idea of what was going on.

I was working for the Overhills, but there shouldn't be any way
that Carmen could know that. As far as she was aware, I was just the
pesky PI trying to get Nathalie in for her shots.

Then it was back to driving, to the Claiborne Avenue Bridge over
the Industrial Canal. That's why it was named the Lower 9th. When the
canal was built, it divided the voting district and the side on the lower
end became, of course, the Lower 9th Ward.

A national guard checkpoint at the bridge stopped me. I pulled out
my private investigator's license and driver's license and used what
was turning into my standard story.

"Some friends who are now in Houston asked me to run by their
property and see if anything is left." I'm a middle-aged woman in a
sensible car, plus I had paperwork to back up my story.

"Not much light left," one of them told me. "Be out by dark."

"Just a quick look, maybe a few pictures. Too depressing to stay
after dark."

I drove over the bridge.

This was where the water came through, rushing in from the ruined
levee on this side of the canal. A huge, heavy, destructive force, washing
aside houses and car, throwing them in the air like a child's game. As bad

as the haunted houses in the other area were, with their staring, empty windows and harsh waterlines, this was far worse. Nothing was intact; the bones of the houses had been broken and scattered, roofs upside down on a pile of lumber that had once been a house. Cars in trees or rammed into the shattered remains of a living room. Half houses, walls gone, pitched partway across a street. These were drunken, wavering, broken houses, tumbled on top of trucks and trees, reeling, blocks from their foundation.

A horrific place to take a young girl.

Flood is only about ten blocks beyond the bridge, so I found it easily enough. A path through the debris on the road had been cleared, but it was still slow going, with wrecked cars and houses pushing into the street.

I first headed down to the river levee, but saw only one family in a silver minivan. I was looking for that big black SUV.

What if they had just dropped her off and left her? Nathalie wasn't stupid, I reminded myself. She'd stick to the road. Or even walk until she found someone.

Or what if they had been turned back at the checkpoint and weren't even here? I needed to call Joanne in an hour. No, forty-five minutes from now. If I hadn't found Nathalie by that point, I'd let the police and Liz take over.

I turned around and headed the other way, trying not to look at the houses, what was left of them. Each one hurt. Someone had lived there and I couldn't let that pain in when I had to find a lost girl.

I again crossed Claiborne.

In the next block, I had to crawl by a house that slopped over almost two-thirds of the road. I'd already gone through two tires from all the crap on roads around here, from glass to nails to potholes. I wondered if I'd add another two after today?

Then I saw it. Another four blocks or so on. Parked in the middle of the road as if no one needed to get by, a big black SUV.

"What fucking game are you playing?" I muttered. I kept one hand on the wheel—at least now I wasn't going very fast—and tucked my gun into the back waistband of my pants. My jacket would cover it. I put my cell phone in a front pocket.

I parked far enough behind the SUV to have room to turn around.

My plan was to get Nathalie, even if it meant throwing her over my shoulder and zooming out of here. It would be dark soon and I didn't want to be in a place as haunted as this after the sun went down.

I got out of my car, just barely closing the door, to be quiet, although if anyone was paying the remotest bit of attention, they had to have heard my car. However, maybe I would be lucky and Carmen and her boyfriend de jour would be lustily going at it, and Nathalie and I would be able to scamper away.

I could see the light at the end of tunnel and it wasn't a train.

It was an eighteen-wheeler. The distinctive snick of a gun being cocked sounded off to my side.

I stopped midstep and raised my hands in the standard surrender position. It could be a rabid home owner desperate to preserve what might be salvaged.

"I'm looking for a friend, that's all," I called.

"Micky! I'm—" It was Nathalie, but the sound of a slap cut her off.

"Shut up, you whining bitch." Carmen.

I hurled myself in the direction of the voices.

A shot whizzed by my head. That slowed me down. If I was dead I wouldn't be much help to anyone. "I just need to take Nathalie to the doctor. Whatever else is going on, I don't care about. I'm not the police."

"Keep your hands up," a male voice called.

As I passed the SUV, I saw them. They were in what was left of a side yard that had a few patches of clear space left by the whims of the water. It was hidden from the street by a sagging wooden fence. In that space stood Carmen, one of the men I'd seen at Alma Groome's house—the stoop-shouldered one. And Nathalie. She was chained to a badly listing telephone pole.

Carmen and the older man both had guns.

"Well, well, Ms. Private Dick." Carmen mocked me. "Frisk her," she ordered one of the men.

The younger one, Mr. Stoop Shoulders, stepped up. I cooperated, leaning against the SUV. Carmen had hit Nathalie, so I knew they'd knock me around if they had to. He ran his hands down my arms, then around front over my breasts—presumably because he could, not because he thought that was where I hid my gun—then down my sides, down the legs, up the inside of the legs, and one last hand over my groin—again probably because he could. I kept my face impassive. The groping was annoying, but my earlier call was right; these crooks were total amateurs. He'd missed my gun. I was wearing a bulky jacket and had slightly arched my back so it wouldn't stick out, but I didn't expect that to really work.

That knowledge made it both easier and harder. Pros would know when to fade into the shadows and cut their losses. They also kept their focus. If they wanted money, they would be smart enough not to throw in an unnecessary murder rap. Carmen and her boys had gotten as far as they had by luck and the reality that destruction and deception are easy in the short run. It was about to come crashing down on them. Joanne had her name and some idea of my location. The Overhills were cooperating.

Desperate and stupid is a very dangerous combination.

"Get her cell phone," Carmen ordered. She wasn't totally stupid.

To avoid another grope, I used two fingers to take it out of my front pocket and throw it to them. No one moved to catch it and it fell to the ground. Mr. Stoop Shoulders glanced at it, but it evidently was too boring to bother to pick up.

"Car keys," she demanded. I did the same thing. Carefully took them out of my pocket and threw them to her.

Mr. Stoop Shoulders picked them up, looked at my decade-old Honda, and threw them back on the ground. I didn't know whether to be relieved or insulted that neither my car nor my cell phone rated being stolen.

"Little Nats here claims she hasn't told you anything," Carmen said sneeringly. "So far we haven't been able to persuade her to tell the truth. So why don't you spill the beans?"

"About what?" I looked closely at Nathalie. Her lip was split and a nasty bruise was starting to show on her cheek.

"Don't fuck with me! How'd you get to work for those snotty Overhills? How'd you happen to just be there when the body showed up?"

I had to think how to play this. Carmen was a schemer and it seemed unlikely that she'd believe the truth—clearly she didn't when Nathalie told her. And if she didn't believe earnest, naïve Nathalie she sure wouldn't believe me.

"That's pretty smart of you. How did you figure it out?"

"It was easy," Carmen replied. "You just happened to be there when those kids stumble over poor Alma. I don't believe in those kinds of coincidences. If you guys hadn't screwed up so badly, it would have been funny. Especially Tiny Coach Bobby breaking his leg." She made a motion that indicated what Tiny referred to.

"Hey," the older one said. "We were lost. It was late. You should've written things down better. We confused the addresses."

"That wasn't planned?" I asked as gullibly as I could realistically pull off.

"No, her body was supposed to be dumped in a place no one would touch for a year. They mixed that up with the place to look for the stuff she found."

"So how'd you find out about the family history?"

"It's my history, too. The stupid bitch just talked openly about it. I was with the boring cousins in some college town in Illinois and they dragged me to see the show. I was bored until she started talking about the history stuff she'd found out. Everyone else thought it was kind of interesting, didn't see how it affected them. Idiots. I could see it was the ticket to getting what we deserved."

"Deserved? How?" I acted genuinely interested, as if she was telling the most fascinating story. I was marginally curious as to how and why she was doing this, but my real concern was getting myself and Nathalie out of here. Keeping her talking would tick the minutes down until I could reasonably hope the cavalry would rescue us.

"My great-grandmother was Florence Stern. Her sister Jessica married into the Overhills. They took the money and made a lot of money with it. Grannie Flo married a poor dirt farmer and they got swindled out of their share. Aunt Jessie wouldn't give them a dime more. So we stayed poor and they got rich. Now I'm just getting what we should had gotten back then."

"Why kill Alma?" I asked.

Carmen shook her head in disgust. "She didn't get it! I caught her after she finished her last show, had to sit through the whole fucking thing again. I explained everything to her, how those fucking Overhills had cheated both her and me. She just laughed me off. I gave her a chance, I really did. Then she had to say if I did anything with what she'd found out, she'd report me. Real snotty, like I was some stupid kid. So I showed her. We were in a back alley behind the theater and there was a piece of pipe just sitting there. Bang, then my scarf around her neck and she wasn't so smart anymore."

She recounted the murder with a chilling pride in her voice.

"We had to get rid of the body and were coming to New Orleans anyway. So I came up with the brilliant idea to leave it in one of those houses. Would've worked if you hadn't got lost," she said, with an annoyed glance at the two men.

The older one rolled his eyes. Carmen seemed to have that effect on a lot of people.

"Hey, babe," he said, as if needing to counter the eye rolling, "it's all worked out and we're gonna be rich soon."

"Yeah, lucky for you."

The blow jobs would have to be very, very good for him to put up with that for much longer.

Mr. Stoop Shoulders hadn't said much, but clearly both Carmen and the older man had accents that were probably Midwestern, hers Wisconsin, his maybe Chicago. Which meant that neither of them was from here. Another point in my favor. And I needed every point I could get. If it was just me, I'd chance a run. They didn't know their way around, and given how sloppy everything else was I'd put money on them not spending enough time on a shooting range to have a chance in hell of hitting a furiously dodging and weaving runner.

But I couldn't leave Nathalie.

"So you killed Alma?" I asked.

"Yeah," Carmen said. "It was easy. It's all been way easier than I thought it would be."

"Why hook up with the church group?"

"Oh, I was with them for real. Got into a mess and the judge told me it was jail or church. So I learned to praise Jesus with the best of them. If you pray it's amazing what you can get away with. Besides, what was I supposed to do? Flip burgers? I can dump those pious farts after tonight anyway."

Mr. Stoop Shoulders finally spoke. "Are we going to get on with this?" Definitely not a New Orleans accent. "It's getting dark and I don't want to be here much longer."

"What, worried about the ghosts?" Carmen cackled out a laugh.

He shuffled his feet. "Naw, just it's getting dark and I'm getting hungry."

Beating up girls must be hard work, I thought, and had to bite my lip not to say it. Nathalie was sagging against the pole. Instead I asked, "What are you going to do? Leave us here?"

"I had a great plan. This time we're going to make it work." Carmen said it as if discussing getting rid of roaches.

I understood her intent. We were to be murdered and dumped in a destroyed house, left to rot until it was assumed that we were killed by the storm.

"Bang, bang, then we throw you under some of this junk," she explained.

Nathalie jerked up straight, a look of fear on her face.

I kept my voice calm. "That might work, except for a few things."

"Yeah, like what?"

"My partner is expecting me in half an hour to take her to the airport. A half an hour after that, she'll call in a missing person."

"Yeah, so?" Carmen said. "Guess she'll have to get a taxi. They ain't gonna find you before we get the money."

"But they will," I said. "I have GPS on my cell phone. The cops will follow it right here."

The three of them exchanged looks. Clearly they didn't have an answer for this.

I could only hope they didn't know enough about cell phones to know that I was lying. Joanne would eventually get my message and come looking for us, but I didn't want her to find our dead bodies—both for her sake and ours.

I needed to get them to unchain Nathalie. They'd have to do that to move us somewhere else.

"Shit," Carmen finally said. "This is pissing me off. I shouldn't have to muck with this right now." She looked at her two henchmen. "I gotta call them rich fuckers soon, give them the drop-off. Shep, you march these two somewhere else. Petey and I'll go make the call."

"You're leaving me here with them?" Shep, aka Mr. Stoop Shoulder, said. "What am I supposed to do with 'em?"

"It's simple," Carmen told him. "Move them somewhere and kill them."

Shep, bless his heart, didn't look like someone for whom killing was easy. It might have been the approaching evening light, but he even looked a little green.

I was hoping that she overrode him. Being left alone with Shep was about as close as we would get to being handed a get-out-of-jail-free card.

"Jesus fuckin' Christ, I gotta do everything," Carmen muttered. "If this gets screwed up, it's your fault."

"Look, you don't need to kill us. Why add another murder rap?" To Shep I said, "Right now, you're just an accessory. Kill us, and you could be looking at the death penalty. Chain us up someplace where no one finds us until tomorrow. You get your money, you're gone. You'll get away whether you kill us or not. But at least if you ever get caught, you won't—"

"Shut up," Carmen said. "I can't think with you yammering."

I pointedly looked at my watch. It was just before five. If Joanne had gotten my message and took me at my word, they should be looking for me soon. I just had to hope that it was soon enough. "She's probably already called my cell phone at least three times," I said. I'd picked the wrong lie; it made me think about Cordelia going to the airport and out of my life. No chance to say good-bye. Or…anything else.

"I told you to shut up," Carmen barked.

The sun was close to setting. Soon it would be the dim blush of twilight before final darkness. This area would be especially dark. Street lights, porch lights, the glow from windows, neon signs; we've become accustomed to a dim light in even the darkest night. None of those existed here anymore. No power, no light, only the faintest of starlight would remain.

"We need to get them out of here," Carmen said. "Unlock that little cunt."

This would be my only chance. They wouldn't keep us alive here long enough for Joanne to arrive. We'd have to get away. Somehow. My gun and darkness were our only allies.

"Uh, you have the key," Shep told Carmen.

"I do have to do everything, don't I?" She handed him her gun. He gingerly took it, first by the barrel, then awkwardly turned it around, so the grip was finally in his palm. He didn't seem very used to handling guns. She dug in her purse and, after a good full sixty seconds of fumbling, finally found the key. She stalked over to Nathalie, shoved her roughly aside, and after another minute of trying the key three different ways finally opened the lock. She pushed Nathalie toward the truck, but she was still caught in the chains. Carmen took out her frustration by slapping the child. Nathalie whimpered at the blow.

"If you want to hit someone, hit me," I yelled at her. Ignoring common sense—they might well just shoot me—I strode to Nathalie, helping her get untangled and, more importantly, putting me between her and Carmen.

"Get in the fuckin' truck," Carmen told us.

The older guy didn't say anything. He shoved his gun into his waistband—I hoped the safely was on or his days of getting blow jobs might soon come to an end—and just climbed into the driver's seat.

"In the backseat," she instructed.

Just as we got to the back door, she said, "Since you asked," then slugged me in the face. I reeled against the truck. It wasn't a hard punch, but I wasn't prepared to take it.

"That was fun. Remind me to do that a few more times before I kill you." She was gloating now.

If we survived more than the next ten minutes, it would be for Carmen to explore her sadistic side. Only Shep had a gun pointed vaguely in our direction.

I helped Nathalie into the backseat. "You'll be okay," I said very softly to her.

Then I went around the SUV to get in the other side. Carmen was heading for the front passenger seat.

Ah, I did appreciate the human tendency to believe that because something hasn't happened, it wouldn't happen. Nathalie and I hadn't tried to escape. They seemed to think we wouldn't.

Carmen opened the front door and got in. Shep had followed her around.

"What do I do?" he asked her, blocking her from closing the door.

She thought for a moment, then said, "You gotta jam in back with them. It won't be long."

I opened the back door, put one foot in, grabbed Nathalie by the arm, and pulled her across the seat and out the door. The open car door was between me and Shep. He didn't have a clear shot. Even if he could shoot.

"Run!" I yelled at Nathalie. As I said it, I pulled my gun out and clicked off the safety. Unlike this gang, I spend about an hour a week at the rifle range.

Unfortunately Shep was the one person with a gun. I fired around the truck door, aiming at his knees before I took off running. His scream of pain told me I'd hit something. I glanced back to see him go down and to fire a couple of shots at the tires.

"Weave," I yelled at Nathalie. She heard me, zigging and zagging across the road.

"Corner, right," I called. The more debris between us and their guns the better.

I heard the SUV start behind us.

Nathalie hit the corner and careened around it. I closely followed her.

Halfway down the block, I caught up with her. I was rapidly scanning the sides of the street. Even with blown tires, we couldn't outrun them in a vehicle. We'd have to cleave our way through the destroyed houses.

"This way," I said, grabbing her arm. I led her down a driveway, jumping boards and bicycles. We clambered over half a wall. It was still light enough to see our way. We needed to be well hidden before it got too dark.

These damaged houses were a danger; many of them would need only a footstep in the wrong place to collapse. Add to that, glass, nails, all manner of sharp and nasty things on the ground.

I heard the truck turn the corner.

"Down," I whispered to Nathalie. We crouched behind a pile of boards.

The SUV slowly drove by. It stopped at the next corner. Then I heard it slowly back up.

"Come on," I told Nathalie, picking our way into what had once been someone's yard.

A board cracked under my foot. It sounded far too loud in the dense silence of this ghost town.

But I heard a bass beat from the street. Those idiots hadn't turned off their radio.

I took Nathalie's hand and led her behind a downed tree. Our combined breathing was raspy and labored. Fear and exertion.

The SUV stopped, the bass beat fixing its position.

"I think that's a footprint," Petey said.

A bright beam cut through the dim light of the setting sun. They had flashlights. We weren't hidden well enough here.

I motioned to Nathalie that we needed to keep moving. Fear was in her eyes. I hoped my eyes didn't reflect back her alarm.

It was treacherous going with haphazard piles of junk to clamber over, barely visible holes in the ground. We had to be quiet and we had to be fast. And not kill ourselves by pulling a derelict house down on us.

"I heard something," Carmen shouted.

The beam shot just above us. I put my hand on Nathalie's head to keep her crouched low. Lucky her, she had young knees; mine creaked as I squatted.

An overturned car blocked our way. It was jammed between two houses that had floated off their slabs, only the car keeping them from ramming.

"Over," I whispered to her. I put my hand on her shoulder to keep her still and looked back at the flashlight beam. When it swept the other way I tapped her, cradling my hands for her to step in. She wasted no time—up, and then her feet disappeared.

I followed quickly.

"Back there!" Carmen yelled.

The light found me, bright white against the muddy underside of the car. I flung myself over just as the gun went off. The bullet clanged against the car. I tumbled down onto a pile of boards that clacked loudly from my weight. Something cut my elbow.

I'd had my tetanus shot; a scrape I could handle. A bullet, not so much.

Nathalie had my arm and was pulling me to my feet. The car gave us a temporary barrier against bullets. But we had to be long gone before they got here. Nathalie indicated an opening between the houses. It was tight, under part of a listing roof that had slid halfway down the side of the house, caught partly on a still-standing tree, although it wasn't possible to tell if the tree was holding up the roof or the roof the tree. I let Nathalie shimmy through first; she was smaller than I was, so if it came down, I'd be the more likely person to cause it. Plus, I wanted to keep myself between her and our pursuers.

I could see swatches of light as they moved toward us. They weren't going very fast, but neither were we, and they had the advantage of being able to see where they were stepping.

It was a bizarre, almost apocalyptic scene, destruction and chaos outlined in the bare rim of the setting sun, punctured by the glare of a jerking flashlight. And the report of a gun going off. I was hoping that the sound of guns would bring some bigger guns running, but it might be hard to pinpoint the sound. If anyone was close enough to hear.

Nathalie was through, now it was my turn. Sucking in my stomach, I started to inch through the gap. An ominous creak sounded just above my head.

"I'm not climbing over that." Carmen's voice carried. "You get on top and shoot. That should take care of them."

Push through, I told myself. Better a house than a bullet. And Nathalie had made it.

I hastily took off my jacket and threw it to her, then thrust my body into the gap. Something cracked, then broke. A board slid down my shoulder, a nail raking my forearm. Maybe I'd need another tetanus shot.

The light shot over the car, searching for us.

Another shove and I was on the other side, the listing roof wobbling unsteadily. I grabbed the corner and pulled, then threw myself away from it.

"Let's go," I told Nathalie over the crash and roar of cracking timber. I thought I heard a gunshot, but the noise masked it. We used the racket to thrash our way through the mess in what was once a backyard, a brick barbeque pit with an easy chair upended in it, a swing set impaled in a house. We weaved our way around the obstacles, clambering over a fence listing at a forty-five degree angle. It was slow and laborious going, even relieved as we were for the moment of being quiet.

I looked back. It was hard to tell in the dark, but it appeared I had blocked the way for them to follow us. And by now there were probably enough walls, trees, and cars that even a bullet couldn't get through. The flashlight was no longer visible.

"What's that smell?" Nathalie whispered.

Something rancid and decaying was close to us.

"Refrigerator," I said quickly. That was the most likely explanation. A freezer in the garage stocked full of shrimp and fish would be disgusting after three months. "Animals knocked it over." I didn't want to think about what else it could be.

I put my hand on her shoulder to stop her. We couldn't be faster, so we had to be smarter than they were. I needed to know where they were.

Silence. They were listening for us. I gently pulled Nathalie into a cul-de-sac made by a concrete back stairs. The house was brick and seemed less hazardous than the wooden ones. I put my finger to my lips to indicate quiet, betting that we had more patience than they did. I took a long look around. The sun was gone, only a wan gray light remained. It would be dark in a few minutes and I needed to imprint on my brain the barriers we'd face in getting out of here.

Their lights gave us one advantage; we could easily see them if they were close. My plan, such as it was, was to keep this deadly game of hide-and-seek going long enough for Joanne to come looking for me. If she saw my car unlocked and abandoned, she'd know something was wrong. I looked at my watch. It was almost five-thirty.

Cordelia was packed; she'd be leaving soon. By now she'd given up on me coming by.

Why hadn't I been a better person? My anger had so slammed and shut the door that she couldn't reach me, come back to me. Katrina had changed everything. It had changed her; it had changed me. If I was a better person I would have recognized that. She'd kissed another woman. Maybe had sex with her. It had been overwhelming on August 27. But by September 1 it shouldn't have mattered. What should have mattered was that she was trapped in Charity Hospital for a week. What should have mattered was that New Orleans was beaten and battered and it would take all of us who came back being better than we had been before to pull her from the muck and mud. We'd need higher ground, of the earth and our souls.

Why hadn't I written her back, something as simple as a reply to an e-mail?

What if it came to this? What if I didn't make it this time? One bullet and she'd never know that I wanted her back, wanted one more chance. Wanted to tell her once more that I loved her.

I heard the sound of an engine and the faint throb of a bass beat. I let out the breath I didn't know I'd been holding.

Then the bass beat got louder. It started moving away quickly.

Had they given up? Were they leaving?

I saw a quick flash of light, probably on the street, but not where the SUV had pulled out. The light disappeared, like someone briefly turning on a flashlight, then flicking it off. Maybe only Carmen had left and they were setting a trap for us.

It was cold. I took my jacket off and put it around Nathalie. She was dressed for the middle of the day, not the cooling night.

The bass beat suddenly disappeared. It hadn't faded like it would have if they had driven off.

I was right. They were amateurs and didn't know when to give up.

Or how to properly do a stakeout.

There was a flash of orange out on the street. I angled my head, peering through cracks until I saw the glowing tip of a cigarette. Carmen didn't smoke, so it had to be Petey or possibly Shep. Either they were content to let him bleed to death or my shot hadn't done much damage. He might have gone down just from seeing the gun and hearing the shot. Most people aren't prepared to be fired at and it can be quite surprising.

Nathalie shivered. We couldn't stay here all night. Well, we could if it meant avoiding a bullet. As long as they were content with this standoff, we could stay here. Maybe if we were quiet enough they'd think we'd slipped by them. I put my arms around Nathalie to keep her warm. And give her the illusion I could keep her safe.

A breeze was picking up, rustling the bare branches. The houses groaned under a gust. In the silence I could hear the skittering of animals. This was probably rat heaven—few people, and rotting food spilled everywhere.

The glow of the cigarette was moving away. Carmen had probably ordered him to walk the perimeter.

"How are you doing?" I askcd very quietly.

"Scared," she admitted. "Are they going to kill us?"

"I won't let them hurt you," I said, a fierce whisper.

"I need to see a doctor soon, right?"

"Yeah, but you'll be okay for a while. It's not a quick disease." That wasn't quite what Liz had said, but it was dark and Nathalie needed reassurance.

"How did I get it?"

Cordelia was good at this.

Cordelia was getting on a plane, leaving my life forever.

"Someone touched you. Someone who has the disease." I struggled for the words. "Not like this, like we're touching now. Someone—"

"It hurt," she said so quietly I could barely hear her. "Down there. We marry the church. All girls age thirteen. It's dark. They blindfold us. Then the elders pray over us. If we're accepted, the spirit enters us. But…" She started crying softly.

"Shhh," I said, smoothing her hair back.

"But spirits don't smell like chewing tobacco or aftershave. And that's what I smelled when it hurt. They touched me down there, didn't they? That's how I got this?"

"Probably."

"How could the spirit give me syphilis?" she asked, a question she knew the answer to.

"I won't let them hurt you either" was all I could say. I didn't know how I'd keep that promise, but somehow I would. "Tell someone, tell Liz, Dr. Ward. Or my friend Joanne Ranson, she's a police officer. Promise me you'll tell someone."

She nodded her head against my chest.

I heard the sound of a vehicle coming back. No bass beat this time. Maybe a patrol? Or had Carmen finally been smart enough to turn off the radio?

I got my answer as two flashlights swept the area where they had last seen us.

"We have to find them." In the silence it was easy to hear Carmen's voice. "Rip this fucking place apart." She was way too close for safety. I never wanted to hear her obnoxious whiny voice again.

Desperate and stupid was a deadly combination.

"If we get separated, you keep going, you understand?" I told Nathalie. "If…if something happens to me, keep going. I know how to fight them and I can beat them. Your only job is to escape and tell someone."

"Okay."

"Promise me."

"Okay…I promise."

She'd somehow gotten reinforcements. I could count four lights.

Joanne, where the hell are you? It'd been over an hour.

I felt around on the ground, gathering pieces of brick, bolts, anything heavy enough to throw. Save for one, I stuffed them in my pockets. The piece of concrete in my hand I flung as far away as I could. It clattered noisily against something metal.

"Let's get out of here," I whispered to Nathalie.

The flashlights were heading toward the sound. Nathalie and I felt our way in the opposite direction. I led the way. It was now full dark. There was a little light from a waning moon, but shapes were dark and dense, all of them treacherous.

I had two plans. I was hoping we could weave our way to Claiborne without them noticing, then hightail it to the bridge and the checkpoint there. But if Carmen wasn't quite as stupid as I wanted her to be, she'd make sure she cut off our most viable route of escape. Plan, well not even B, but something like X, was to work our way back to my car, somehow find the keys in the dark, and drive out of here. Obvious why that one was in the X range of the alphabet.

Of course, I was also hoping that planning on my part would be rendered moot at any minute by the flashing lights of New Orleans' finest.

But the only sounds were our quiet shuffling and the thrashing of Carmen and her boys as they waded to where I'd thrown the concrete.

Suddenly they were quiet. "No one can be here." It sounded like Shep. Damn, I'd wanted him hurt enough to be out of action for a day at least. No such luck.

"Want me to fire a few shots and make sure?" Petey, it sounded like.

"Fire shots? You might hurt someone."

Nathalie abruptly stopped. The voice was Nathan's.

Carmen had recruited her lovesick puppy to hunt down his sister. And left out a few details, I'd bet, like her plan to kill Nathalie.

"Keep going," I said quietly.

"She'll hurt him."

"She'll kill you. She has no reason to kill him. Unless he sees her kill you. And we want to avoid that."

I took her hand and led her for a few steps until I needed both hands to scramble over a bathtub.

Carmen said something I couldn't hear.

But her instructions were clear. Nathan called, "Hey, Nats, stop playing around. It's cold and nasty out here. We all want to go home. Come out."

Nathalie again stopped to listen to him. "Maybe she changed her mind," she whispered to me.

And gold-plated pigs will fly us out of here. "We can't take that chance. And she might change her mind again if she finds us." I gently touched the bruise on her cheek, the one Carmen had left.

Nathalie took my hand and again started walking away from them.

I felt a fierce protectiveness for this child—to keep her from getting hit, from being always second to the boys in her family, from a so-called religion that raped thirteen-year-olds. She was smart and resilient and all she needed was a chance.

The flashlights were fanning out again, widening the search for us. We were feeling our way along the side of a house. It was hard to be sure of the direction. Some of the houses were so canted that they were faced away from the street that had once addressed them.

I backed away from the wall to give myself throwing room and heaved a heavy bolt.

There was an odd thunk, then Shep shouted, "Shit, I just got hit in the head."

Damn, my aim was a little too good.

Petey replied, "Crap is about to fall down around our heads. This is crazy."

Perhaps a little rebellion in the ranks?

One more bad aim and they'd figure out it was me. I'd have to lay off the throwing trick for a while.

I could see open space beyond the house. I was guessing that it was the next street over. If we could scurry across without anyone seeing us, we could continue our slow and quiet crawl out of this. We had to get far enough away that they would be looking where we no longer were.

I put my hand on Nathalie's shoulder, signaling her to let me lead. I wanted it to be my head that first poked out into the open.

Cautiously I peeked around the half-fallen side of the house. But a car was upturned in front; I could see little beyond that. I signaled Nathalie to stay put and eased around the hood.

I didn't see anyone. I took another step out. The flashlights were moving closer. We needed to be across the street. I motioned Nathalie to hurry after me. I let her pass me and run across. I quickly followed, jumping over an upturned sofa.

"What was that?" Carmen yelled.

Damn, young women have better hearing than men. I threw another piece of concrete back on the other side of the street, and it clattered down a canted wall. The flashlights came running in this direction but were pointed the opposite way. Nathalie and I had to make our way into the heart of the debris to be safely hidden. They could easily see us if they turned around.

But it was dark and we had to feel our way around a listing wall and over a pile that had once been a shed. The pile was only about waist high, so even behind it we were still partly visible. Before the storm this had been a cleared area, backyards touching each other. It didn't give us great cover, but it was easier going than before. A couple of times we had to crouch to avoid stray arcs of light. They seemed to still be looking in the previous block.

Then my foot went into a hole, a place where a pipe was ripped out of the ground. I barely stifled a groan.

"You okay?" Nathalie whispered.

I glanced behind us as I gingerly pulled my foot out. It was the same ankle I'd landed hard on when I'd fallen/jumped off the roof of Alma's house.

I nodded yes. I had to be okay. No time for a sprained ankle. I put my weight on it and grimaced, but it was too dark for Nathalie to see my pain.

At least I'd been quiet and not brought the flashlights our way.

Two steps later I blew that by kicking a glass bottle invisible in the dark.

Carmen yelled, "What the hell? That way!"

"Damn." I breathed out. I grabbed Nathalie's hand and we started running as best we could. How the fuck could I have been that careless? A light raked near our feet.

"This way." I pulled her to the left. We had to get where the light couldn't find us. I plunged us back into the debris of a house, but its shattered and leaning walls blocked us from the light.

I made a quick calculation. Between someone hearing the gunshots or seeing the flashlights in a place where nobody was supposed to be and my message to Joanne, the police should be here soon. I had to keep Nathalie safe long enough for that to happen.

The only way I could do that was to lead them away from her. They wouldn't expect us to split up.

"I have a plan," I told her quietly. "When we get to the road, you go right. Run, just run as fast as you can. When you get to Claiborne—it'll be the first wide street you come to—go right again and don't stop until you get to the checkpoint on the bridge."

"What about you?" She was panting.

"I'm going to lead them on a chase they'll never forget. But I need to do it alone. You'll slow me down too much. We'll both be okay. Just trust me. Please."

She was young enough that she did. Maybe she even believed that she'd slow me down instead of me slowing her down. I knew that on my ankle I'd never make the twenty blocks between here and the bridge. But if I could delay Carmen and her cohorts for five minutes, Nathalie would have enough of a lead to get there.

We climbed over a porch that was no longer attached to the house and then were back on Flood Street. I gave her a quick hug. As I let her go I said, "One more thing. Tell…someone to tell Cordelia fifty years wouldn't be enough." Then I gave her a push on the shoulder to send her running.

I turned in the opposite direction, going back the way we came.

Cordelia had once said she wanted fifty years with me and I told her fifty years wouldn't be enough. It had stuck, one of those things we said to each other that only we knew the meaning of.

I ran as far as I could, every step an agony. Several times I glanced back to where I'd left Nathalie. When I could no longer see her I slowed down enough to take another rock from my pocket and fling it in the direction of the flashlights. It didn't make enough noise. I had to stop and scrabble on the edge of the road to find more rubble to heave.

I threw a rock and then another. Then I kicked a can down the road and muttered, "Damn," in what I hoped was just loud enough for them to think I didn't want them to hear. In a harsh stage whisper I added, "Can't you be more careful? They'll hear us."

It worked. The flashlights paused, then angled in my direction.

I glanced at my watch. A good five to ten minutes of cat and mouse, with me the very much outnumbered mouse, and Nathalie would be safe. I trotted down the road a bit farther, then cut into the destruction on the other side of the street. I was back to Plan X—work my way back to my car, hope I could find my keys, and hightail it out of here. In the meantime I had to stay hidden enough that no one could take a clear shot at me, yet make enough noise that they kept following me.

A plane flew overhead.

Cordelia was on her way to the airport by now.

I made a silent plea to whatever fate or god was listening. If I survived this, I would be a better person—the kind of person she had been for ten years with me, listening to my rails and rants, my demons, helping me though my mess of a family. Tired and human, of course, but mostly kind and patient and loving. I could always count on her opening her arms to me.

As she had when I last saw her. She wouldn't have done that, made love, let me embrace her if she knew that she'd moved on. She understood how cruel giving me hope was when there was none. She would have turned from me, made it clear how final her decision was. But with the clarity that comes when someone is trying to kill you, I realized that she wouldn't have let me touch her, or even come back to New Orleans, if she hadn't wanted to see me, to give us one more chance.

Whatever it took I would find her and tell her I loved her. It might be too late—some hurts remain too long, cut too deep to be atoned for—but I had to try.

A flashlight raked over the wreckage close to me. Then it paused and slowly made its way back. I slithered under the raised foundation of the house I was next to. But the dried mud crackled under me. I crawled a little farther along, then skittered back out around another foundation pillar.

"Hey, hey, I think I found them." Nathan.

Damn. I'd be tempted to shoot any of the rest of them. I was relieved to hear him refer to us as them. That meant they thought Nathalie and I were still together.

"She's trying to kill us, Nathan," I said, then thought, oh, why bother. He might believe me if his sister lay bleeding on the ground with Carmen gloating over her body.

"Carmen is right, you're crazy paranoid." How refreshing that I was right about him.

I quickly glanced behind him; the rest of the flashlights were spread out.

Betting that he didn't have a gun, I charged him, using the flashlight as a target. My gun bet was right; my other assumption, that he was a naïve Midwestern chauvinist who wouldn't expect that kind of aggression from a woman, was also right.

I was twisting the flashlight out of his hand while his jaw was still dropping. This was no time to be nice. I snatched his glasses and flung them into a pile of something vile. Then I hooked a foot behind his heel and jerked his feet out from under him. He went down hard. Finally a kick in the groin. Oh, I was tempted to kick a lot harder, but I pulled it, just enough so he wouldn't be jumping up real soon.

Then I jerked the flashlight, pointed it in the opposite direction, and, in the lowest voice I could muster, shouted, "That way!"

My ploy might not have fooled them, but it confused them. I snapped off the flashlight I was now holding and took off running away from them as fast as my ankle would let me. Seconds could make a difference now.

My reprieve didn't last long. After a couple of fish-like gasps, Nathan found his voice, if not his glasses or his brain. "Help me. She hurt me. Help me." It came out pathetically high. "I think she might have shot me."

Crybaby.

I kept running, reaching the next cross street. My car should be one block up and over.

Nathan's mewling helped cover the noise I was making.

Could I risk it, running in the street instead of bushwhacking through the jungle of destruction?

I got my answer; headlights appeared at the other end of the block. Someone was smart enough to patrol with the SUV.

I plunged into a thicket of boards, tumbling and rolling over the top, just as a shot rang out.

Nathan cried out, "See, I told you, she's shooting us."

The top timbers tumbled after me, rolling onto my back. The headlights out in the street got closer as I attempted to get out. Just as I shoved them off me and rolled into a kneeling position, the truck stopped. The driver jumped out.

"I got her! I got her!" Shep crowed as he fixed his light on me. I guess he hadn't forgiven me for trying to shoot him.

An hour older, but no wiser. He had a gun, but wasn't pointing it in any direction that would do any good, instead keeping the light on me and motioning with the gun hand for his comrades to join him.

Oh, Shep, you shouldn't give me a second chance to shoot you in the knees.

"Guess Nathan was right after all," I said.

Shep swiveled his head back to me, not understanding what I'd said. Show, don't tell. I pulled the trigger. He fell hard and heavy, blood pouring from his right knee.

"Sorry, track star next lifetime."

Time for me to fade back into the destruction.

Shep added his wails to Nathan's. Nathan escalated his as if this was a competition.

I carefully picked my way into the dark, weaving around piles of trash, stepping into some that I couldn't see in the dark. A look back told me that the closest light was still the headlights from the SUV. The flashlights didn't seem to be following me anymore. With Nathan and Shep down, that probably left Petey and Carmen. If she was dragging Mr. Puppy Love into this, it seemed that her gang had little depth. Carmen seemed to be good at leaving the crawling through the muck to others, and Petey was smart enough to follow her lead. Shep, presumably winged earlier, had been given the keys to the SUV. I briefly debated going back and grabbing it. But Shep still had a gun and I'd been kind enough to leave him alive to use it.

I was starting to develop an expertise at crawling around ruined houses in the dark. Or maybe it was easier knowing that Nathalie was safe by now and that I'd disabled half of the posse chasing me.

From out in the street, I heard Carmen shout, "Goddamn it! You've got to find them. What kind of idiots are you anyway?" Desperate and stupid times two.

I edged between two houses, a path that seemed barely passable but would take me to the street where my car was.

The SUV started up. Shep yelled. His voice stayed where it was as the vehicle moved on. Carmen, I guessed. The ship was sinking and her rat nature was asserting itself.

First the sound was moving away, then coming in my direction. She had turned the corner. I pressed flat against the side of the house. The SUV passed me, going back to where I'd first seen them. Curious, I picked up the pace. Shep and Nathan were still yowling and I could again hear a faint bass beat. Carmen, it seemed, had stopped looking for me and Nathalie.

I peered about an upended refrigerator. It had been knocked open so whatever was in it had spread its rot down the block.

Flat tire. The SUV wobbled badly. I might have missed Shep's knee the first go-round, but I got those rubber suckers.

Carmen intended to steal my car. That bitch.

She walked from where she parked to where they'd had Nathalie chained. I quickly crossed the street to her side, then slowly slipped through the shadows of the ruined houses until I got to my car. There was a ruined truck just off the road. I hunkered down on the other side of it.

She was frantically looking around for the keys, her flashlight twitching back and forth over the ground. I might as well let her do the work. Suddenly she bent down, snatched something off the ground, and strode back to my Honda. She tried to open the door, not realizing I hadn't locked it.

I crept up behind her and put the barrel of my gun against the back of her head.

"Ill met by moonlight, proud Carmen," I said. Not that she would recognize a paraphrase of the line from *A Midsummer Night's Dream*.

"There is no moon." Nope, not a Shakespeare scholar.

Now there were sirens in the background.

"Give me the keys," I told her. I didn't wait for her to comply, but grabbed them out of her hand. "We're going for a stroll." I yanked her by her ponytail, marching her back to the small clearing. I wanted to find my cell phone, too.

"Look, we can work this out. It was just business. The Overhills are still going to turn the money over to me at ten tonight. How about I give you ten percent? That's a cool hundred grand."

Still desperate and still stupid. I didn't reply.

After a moment of silence, she said, "Okay, how about twenty percent?" Silence. "My last offer. Twenty-five percent."

"It's over, Carmen. You're going to jail," I finally told her. She'd murdered Alma Groome and discovered a taste for blood and sadism. Behind bars was the only place for her.

"You'll regret this!" she spat at me.

I had a gun at her head. I could spare the state the cost of trying and incarcerating her. I was tempted—for beating Nathalie, for stilling Alma's voice.

But, even if Cordelia never knew it, I had promised her I would be a better person, and that argued that I not become a cold-blooded killer.

Not moving the gun from her temple, I grasped the shackles that had been used to hold Nathalie. I didn't have the key, but the padlock had been left open.

"You're going to lock me with those? I can slip out of them," Carmen told me.

"I'm not cuffing you." I hefted the chains over my shoulder, the gun still at her head, then kicked over a large garbage can, letting water run out of it. Once it had mostly emptied, I told her, "Pick it up."

"What are you gonna do?"

"Stand it upright." I pressed the gun barrel against her ear menacingly.

She did as she was told, using only two fingers to grasp the lip and right the garbage can.

Again, show, don't tell. In a quick motion, I put my gun into my waistband—she didn't need to know the safety had been on the entire time—gripped the waistband of her pants, and jerked her hair, bending her into the can. Then a sharp yank on the pants got her most of the way in. I was angry and she wasn't a big girl in any sense of the word.

I used the lid to shield myself from her kicks and to stuff her feet in. Then I looped the chain through the handles so the lid was securely fixed in place.

Ignoring her outraged screams, I turned on the flashlight and found where I'd tossed my cell phone.

The sirens were closer now; I could even see the flashing blue light of the police cars.

They'd find Carmen, between her yelling, the conspicuous chains over the can, and the parked SUV. Just in case those clues weren't enough I'd call when I had the chance, but I had more important things to do.

Joanne was going to be pissed at me. I was leaving the scene of a lot of crimes.

CHAPTER TWENTY-SIX

I sped up Flood, using the Florida Avenue Bridge to avoid what was surely a major commotion around Claiborne crossing.

My harrowing journey in the dark seemed like it should have taken all night, all the fear should have been forever, but it was just past seven-thirty. Cordelia's plane hadn't taken off yet. If I drove as fast as I sanely could, I might catch her at the airport.

That was my intent, why I was blowing off Joanne after she'd done me an incredible favor. I couldn't have Cordelia leave thinking I'd deliberately avoided her today, that I wanted our last encounter to be how we ended. I had been bitter and angry for too long, letting those toxic emotions overshadow what was really important: that she was my best friend, knew things about me no one else did, that we'd laughed and loved for days and years, that she'd opened herself to me in a way no other woman had. And probably no one woman would. Fifty years wasn't enough and it was about all I had left now.

I desperately wanted to say "I love you" one more time, hold her one more time, even if it was in good-bye.

From Florida Avenue it was a short trip up Franklin to the interstate. There were no lights, only sporadic car beams. This, too, had flooded, all the houses, all the lives watermarked. It was dark for miles, all flooded, all wrecked, past City Park, only the dark shapes changed, from ruined hulks of homes to downed trees.

Then suddenly, a bright glow, closer as I sped to the dividing line, the 17th Street Canal, one wall held, one failed. I had to go to the light, to where power flowed and the houses and the people were still there.

There was little traffic on I-10. So many people hadn't returned that its normal slow crawl was suspended.

I sped around slow trucks and taxis, pushing the speed limit as much as I dared. I couldn't risk getting pulled over.

Exit after exit whizzed by. The airport was about as far as you could go before falling off into the swamp that surrounded and defined this city.

"Let her plane be delayed," I begged as I passed a slow minivan.

Another exit.

Another.

Then the one for the airport.

After leaving the interstate, I had to slow down. The airport access road was much slower. It swooped around the length of the airfield.

I impatiently drummed my fingers as I waited at the stoplight that regulated traffic into the actual airport loop road. I glanced at my watch. It had taken me under twenty minutes to get here. A record. New Orleans isn't a huge area, so getting to the airport wasn't the slog that it was in other cities.

The light changed and I shot past a dawdling Cadillac. I'd have to park my car and that would take some time. Entering the garage, I didn't bother to look for a parking spot, just headed straight for the roof, where there were usually plenty of spaces.

Once parked, I ran to the elevators, my ankle hurting with every step. Waiting for the elevator, I again looked at my watch. Eight-oh-five. She'd already be past the security gate by now.

Buy a ticket. See if you can get on the same plane. I'd talk to her if I had to fly to Dallas to do so.

As the elevator slowly descended, I wondered what I was doing. I could call her in Dallas and explain what had kept me away. That was a lot cheaper than buying a last-minute airfare.

But it wasn't enough, it was too small and paltry a gesture to make up for the months of my anger and distance. I had to prove to her—and me—that I'd changed, that I would do whatever it took for us. On that scale a plane ticket to Dallas didn't seem like much.

Exiting the elevator, I hurriedly scanned the flights. There was an eight-thirty to Dallas on Southwest.

On the first bit of luck of the night, my friend Larry was working the counter.

"Whoa, what happened to you?" he asked as I approached.

"Long story, no time. I need a ticket for the Dallas flight."

He looked me up and down as if wondering if I was crazy. Either he decided I wasn't or that even if I was, a trip to Dallas was a mild bout of insanity.

"Let me see what I can do. I think the flight's booked."

"Even standby, if nothing else."

It was agonizingly slow as he took my information and punched it into the computer. I knew he was going as fast as he could, but every second was one less that I could spare.

Finally he handed me a boarding pass. "Good luck," he said. "You may not be able to get on. It's pretty booked. Come back if you can't. I'll set you up for first thing tomorrow."

I didn't have time to tell him it was now or never. I threw a hurried thank you over my shoulder and sprinted for the gate.

The security guard there gave me a long, hard look as she examined my ticket and driver's license. I had to look like hell, dirty and bruised, certainly not like someone who should be traveling.

"Family emergency," I said. "Was gutting the house when I got the call. No time to change."

She nodded sympathetically and waved me on.

I kicked off my shoes only to be slowed by a couple who seemed not to have gone through airport security in about twenty years. They had to be told to take off their shoes. Then his belt, then her keys.

Finally they were through and I was right behind them. They were still futzing as I reached between them to grab my shoes. I took time only to shove them on and stick the laces inside so I wouldn't trip on them.

I was hurting as I dashed past the gates. My ankle, but also all the other places I'd fallen, been cut and bruised. And hit. I wondered how big a bruise Carmen had left. I hoped that it took the cops a while to find her.

It was eight-twenty when I got to the gate. The passengers had all boarded, only the gate agent was there.

My chest was heaving; I could barely talk from the exertion of running. I placed my ticket on the counter.

She gave me a sad smile. "I'm sorry, it's already full."

"I was," I gasped, "supposed to meet someone, travel together."

"I'm sorry," she said again. "I can get you on the next plane, I promise."

Damn and damn. She wasn't being a jerk; she seemed genuinely to want to be helpful. But the plane was full. I was too late.

"Can I get a message to…my friend?"

"Cell phone?" she suggested. "They're probably about ready to close the boarding doors."

I nodded. My luck had run out.

Turning away from her I flipped open my cell phone, then quickly punched in Cordelia's number.

It rang.

And rang.

And went to voice mail.

Of course, she had turned it off. You can't use cell phones on the plane, so she was always a good girl, turned it off and put it away.

If the gate agent hadn't been watching, I would have crumpled to the floor and started crying.

It was too painful to just give up. I could at least leave her a text message to let her know I'd come to the airport in search of her. Maybe that would be enough.

I typed in, "I'm here. Tried to see you. Long story. I love you. Fifty years isn't enough." Then punched Send.

That was it; that was all I could do.

I trudged back down the terminal, each step hurting more.

Halfway back I found an empty gate area and sat down. I faced the glass wall, not wanting to see the people walking by. It was a shimmering darkness, glimpses of the planes overlaid with the glare of the terminal fluorescents.

I'd saved Nathalie.

I'd lost Cordelia.

I tried to console myself that even if I'd talked to Cordelia it might not have made a difference. And if I'd abandoned Nathalie, she'd be decaying in a ruined house by now.

Off to the side I noticed someone. I wanted to be alone. It was a janitor changing out the trash bag. I ignored her. I couldn't do small talk right now. If someone so much as commented on the weather to me, I'd bite her head off.

The janitor hastily finished her task and moved off.

I must have looked scary. Dirty, clothes ripped, face bruised.

I wanted to cry. I wanted to scream. I wanted to be in enough control that I could get up, walk by strangers, and get in my car and drive home. All I managed was to finally tie my shoes.

Which home would I go to?

"Fuck, the one with hot water," I muttered out loud, looking at the dirt under my fingernails.

But I couldn't move.

I needed to call Joanne. I looked at my cell phone, but couldn't even bring myself to dial her. She had called three times. I hadn't checked it to see how many calls I'd missed while it was left on the ground.

A shape again intruded in my peripheral vision. I ignored it, looking resolutely at the floor.

I heard footsteps. Damn it, I thought, this whole empty airport and someone has to do their wandering near me.

Suddenly the seat next to me was occupied.

I looked up just as she said, "Oh, honey, what happened to you?"

Cordelia. She gently touched the bruise on my face.

"Long story," I got out. I could barely speak. "I called. You didn't answer. How did you…?"

"I was talking to Alex. She was trying to convince me to stay longer, when you called. I couldn't answer, then saw your message. I got off the plane."

We looked at each other. She brushed dirt out of my hair. She's here; we were finally together. I wished we could just blot out the last few months, pretend they didn't exist. But they did.

"You could have talked to me. At least told me you wanted to leave rather than…what happened," I finally said.

"I didn't know…that I wanted to leave. I…but it shouldn't have happened the way it did." She was silent, but I knew her well enough to know she had more to say. "I was…I guess I was stupid and naïve. I…as you know, I didn't have all that much experience before we got together. With…sex. I could stand outside and think that there are rules and you just follow them." She gave a sad smile. "Easy to do when… when nothing is tempting you to break them."

"So why did you break your rules?"

"I guess…I thought, of course, Lauren and I can work together, flirt a bit. She has a partner, I have a partner, nothing can happen. I was flattered at her attention. It was easy to let her tell me I had beautiful eyes, or how smart I was. Or a hug that we held for a long time. I kept telling myself, we can't really go any further. And I guess I thought she had the same boundaries that I did.

"One day, when we were alone in the office, she turned to me and said, 'I'm sorry, I can't help it,' and she kissed me. And…suddenly, we were over the boundary and I didn't know how to get back." She looked at me for a moment, then continued. "Not then. I pulled away and said we can't do this. She said okay, she would respect my wishes. And we went home. But the next day she told me she couldn't stop thinking about kissing me and how much she wanted to do it again."

"She seduced you."

Cordelia looked away from me. "Maybe. But…I let myself be seduced. I could have…I should have said we had to stop, not to talk about it, not to bring it up, not to even consider it. But I didn't."

"She left the burden of stopping what was happening on you."

"I…guess." Cordelia stammered. "Her attention was beguiling and…I didn't say no."

"It went beyond kissing? You slept with her?"

For a moment, she didn't answer, her head down, staring at the floor. Finally, very softly she said, "Yes." Then, "I'm sorry." And then, "She said that she thought you and Shannon were sleeping together."

"We weren't." Then I had to add, "At least not then."

She understood the impact of my words, but her only reply was, "I'm sorry. This is all my fault."

"This isn't all your fault. Oh, it's a lot your fault. But in my past I've been Lauren, pushing for sex because I wanted it, knowing how powerful it can be to touch someone that way. I don't think you've ever done anything like that."

"Until now."

"Why did you believe her? Why didn't you ask me if I was sleeping with Shannon?"

"I guess…part of me wanted to believe her. And I didn't think you'd tell me if you were. I…I've assumed that there have been other times."

"You thought that I've…Goddamn it, Cordelia, no! All these years and you still don't trust me?" I stood up and paced down the row of chairs, then back to her. I put my hand under her chin, lifting her face so she was looking at me. "You want to know the goddamn truth? I've never had sex with another woman in all the time we were together!"

"It's not...not you. It's me. I've seen the looks we get, like why are you with someone who looks like me? I'm too tall, what they politely call big boned, my nose is—"

"Cordelia, you are beautiful. This isn't even the issue. I'm not with you because I want some goddamned model. How can you not trust me?"

"I trust you, Micky. I trust you in just about every way there is to trust someone. I just never thought...I'd be enough. I guess I thought I was lucky that you only went away for an occasional night, and you always came home to me."

"So you thought I'd fooled around all these years we've been together, and that made it okay for you to, is that it?"

"I...it wasn't okay. But I guess...I did think that."

"I'm the bayou rat from the broken family. I thought I was goddamn lucky to get someone like you—kind, smart, decent in a way few people are. Beautiful, if not in the model way, in every way that counted."

She was crying.

That was the fault line, that neither of us trusted that the other wouldn't someday find someone better. I thought about it, all those nights when I worked late, at times all night, only coming home after dawn. Some of the clients I'd had, alluring and powerful woman. With regret, I realized that at times I'd been consumed with work, my cases demanding all my time. If a client described some of my behaviors, I'd assume that divorce papers would soon be filed. And most stupidly of all, it never occurred to me that Cordelia needed some reassurance behind "I can't really talk about my cases" to explain those long nights. I sat back down beside her.

"I learned my lesson," she said. "When I got out of Charity, I called Lauren. But...I was distressed, babbling about people dying. She was polite, told me she was sorry if things had gotten out of hand and if she'd accidentally created the impression that we were more than just a fling."

"That bitch," I said. Then we both looked at each other, catching at the same time the absurdity of me being angry at Lauren for dumping

Cordelia in a callous way. "Well, at any rate, I'm glad she showed her true colors before you did something like move up there."

"I was too much of a coward to call you."

"So you went through hell by yourself?"

"I deserved it."

"You deserved about a day of me being vile and angry. And I'd say…I'm over the limit. You didn't deserve being left to rot in Charity. You didn't deserve me building a big, angry wall between us that probably was only partly about you and a lot about Katrina and the levees failing and people being left to die on the streets I've lived most of my life. Can you forgive me?"

"Micky. Yes, of course. How can I not forgive you? If you're willing to absolve me?" She put her hand on my neck, under my collar. "Yes, yes, and yes."

"Prove it."

"Anything."

"Wild sex. And doing the dishes for the next month."

She rubbed my neck, then burst into laughter.

"Oh, and cat litter," I added.

"You are the only person who can make me laugh at times like this." She shook her head. An announcement about not accepting packages from strangers blared over the loudspeakers.

"You've missed your plane," I said.

"I can get one first thing in the morning," she said, then paused as if thinking and said, "Or not go at all."

I took her hand, my dirty, scratched fingers over hers. "Stay. Please stay."

She didn't answer.

I looked at her; she was crying. I tightened my grasp. "Please." My voice broke.

She lifted my hand, held it against her cheek as she nodded yes.

I wrapped my arms around her. All the other passengers be damned. They could deal with two women holding each other. But it was New Orleans and no one seemed to care.

We held each other for a long time, alternating who got to cry, until my cell phone finally interrupted us.

"I need to answer that," I said, digging in my jacket pocket.

"Where the hell are you?" Joanne, as I expected, demanded. There were voices in the background; otherwise the "hell" might have been something more appropriate.

"At the airport."

"Leaving? Don't you fucking dare."

"No, picking someone up."

She was quiet for a beat before asking, "Cordelia?"

"Yes."

"Okay," she said, taking a breath. "The sooner you can get here, the better."

"On my way." I hung up. "Want to go to the police station with me?" I asked Cordelia.

"Does that have anything to do with your bruises and long story?"

"Everything to do with it."

She kept her arm around me; I needed her support to limp out of the airport.

As we got to the car, I said, "Oh, Cordelia, I love you." No, the parking garage at the airport wasn't the most romantic of places. "I… spent a lot of time tonight wanting another chance to say that."

"You're okay?" she asked as she helped me into the car, wisely easing me into the passenger seat. She looked at me with concern. From Joanne's call to my limp, she was obviously beginning to suspect that I'd had a bit more of an adventure than I was letting on.

"Yeah, I'm fine, no blows to the head."

She didn't answer immediately, just went around to the driver's side and got in.

"You could have been killed, right?" she finally asked.

I hedged. "Um…driving in New Orleans can get you killed." She left a silence, telling me I needed to answer her question. "Yeah, there were some not-nice people. And…a young girl from the Midwest got tangled with them."

"You saved her instead of coming to see me?" Cordelia asked.

The only answer was the honest one. "Yes. She might have been hurt. Maybe killed." Definitely killed, but Cordelia was smart enough to know that would have included me as well. "I had…to. I'm sorry."

She took my face between her hands and looked me directly in the eyes. "I love you. At times like this more than I can say. Don't apologize for doing the right thing." Her kiss was soft and gentle, more than words could say.

And then we left the not-so-romantic parking lot for the even less romantic police station.

CHAPTER TWENTY-SEVEN

Joanne only forgave me because I'd gone to the airport after Cordelia. And, as she said, "We're all crazy now. This was yours."

The police found Carmen a good hour after I'd chained her in the garbage can, in the company of a very dead pigeon. She'd screamed and yelled and claimed just about any and everything she thought might work. Still stupid, still desperate. But Nathalie and I had bruises and she didn't, so her claim that we'd kidnapped her was given the attention it deserved—a derisive guffaw. Shep and Petey turned into choirboys— singing all day long. Carmen had killed Alma Groome; they weren't going down for that, so they were more than willing to testify against her.

Her name really was Carmen Gecklebacher. She really did grow up in some small farming town in Wisconsin and was really related to the Overhills. But the money that had been split up a few generations back had disappeared into gambling and get-rich-quick schemes long before the sperm and egg met to create her. Carmen had been an only child, treated as if she could do no wrong to the point she believed it. She'd passed herself off as eighteen to get taken in by the church group, but she was really twenty-five. She'd become quite adept at church scams—pretending to be a holy woman, telling congregations that a very religious man was ill; he collected cars and wanted them sold only to other true believers at very discounted prices, like a two-year-old, loaded Lincoln for a thousand dollars. Carmen got half up front and claimed that she'd get the other half when she delivered the cars. Which, of course, never happened. There were no cars, no ill rich man, just a greedy woman who would do anything to get what she thought she deserved.

Nathan got busted, too, and spent about a day being the gallant man who would stand by his woman, until the cops played him the tape of Carmen trying to blame him for as much of everything as she could. Of course, by that point she'd tried to blame me, blame Shep and Petey, blame her parents, blame the church, so the police gave little credence to anything she said other than her claiming he was stupid and immature. Poor Nathan got a walloping dose of reality between jail and seeing his lady love lie and lie again to protect herself, even if it meant leaving him to rot in prison. Shep's brother was the dope dealer Joanne and I had encountered out in Kenner. He managed to stay out of jail—this time. It was an all-in-the-family affair. Petey's older brother, Paul, was the man I'd seen with Carmen in the SUV and at Alma's house with Shep during my roof sojourn. He was smart enough to avoid the dirty work, telling Carmen he'd meet them later, in time to collect the money. He was rounded up, and it seemed there were limits to brotherly love, as Petey sang a song about how his brother and Carmen were the ringleaders; he didn't know half of what they did.

Nathalie had made it to the bridge with no one chasing her; my ruse had worked. But she needed more than that to keep her safe. The Wisconsin public-health workers got an answer to something that had been troubling them—a woman in Nathalie's church with a pregnancy complicated by syphilis. They couldn't figure out how a woman like her could have contracted an STI, until Nathalie let them in on the secret of how girls were married into the church. Not that they got much cooperation from the church elders, but it seemed that one of them had fallen into sin and temptation in the wicked city of Milwaukee, had sex with a prostitute who'd been infected, and he took it back and passed it on to at least five other girls, including Nathalie. Of course all the elders claimed that she was a delusional girl, making things up, but no insanity can create a microbe, especially something like a syphilis infection. Her father was one of the church elders. She told me she really believed that he hadn't done anything with her. I wanted to believe it, too. That sounded too horrible to contemplate. But he sided with the church that gave him power, not the daughter who was trying to take it away. His wife stayed with him. Nathan went back to Wisconsin.

I talked to Marilyn Overhill. They looked perfect on paper to take in a young girl. And more importantly, they were perfect in real life. When I told Marilyn I thought Nathalie might be a budding lesbian, her only comment was, "That saves worrying about her getting pregnant." They took her in, ostensibly until something could be decided, but Brooke confided that it would probably be until they could argue that Nathalie had been with them long enough that she should stay.

The Overhills were pretty happy with me—I'd caught the blackmailer and the killer. Brooke was right about Jared. Once he realized that I was gay and had a partner, he relaxed around me and dropped the jerk shtick. We got along quite well, so well that he hired me to do a lot of work for them. They wanted me to track down the people who had worked for them, find out what had happened to them, to see if they wanted to come back to New Orleans.

I hired Alex to help. She was smart, learned quickly, and was good on computers. Joanne didn't want her working on their house alone, which was understandable, and Alex needed something to do besides sit alone in their temporary apartment. She was doing better. It helped her to have something to do every day, something that was important, helping reconnect the scattered people. I think it also helped that Cordelia had returned. She and Alex had known each other since high school, had been maybe ten minutes' drive away from seeing each other for decades.

On the last evening Liz was in town, Torbin and Andy had a big shrimp boil for Liz. (No crabs). We were all there, even Hutch, although he still mostly sat in the corner and nuzzled a beer. Late in the party, Torbin told Joanne, Danny, and Hutch that they needed to go watch TV while the rest of us went on a beer run, and that as we might have to go to the suburbs, it could take us a while. It just wouldn't do to have law enforcement along on this ride.

Elly elected to stay with Danny, but the rest of us piled into one car. Andy grabbed a pound of bait shrimp from their new freezer and we somehow managed to put shrimp in all four of Patty What's-Her-Name's hubcaps without being caught or even causing a light to come on. We even drove about five blocks away before we started hooting and laughing so hard we started crying.

Danny was recovering nicely, especially after Joanne and I

dragged her to a mega-hardware store and forced her to buy the ultra-super mask and filter, plus just about every piece of protective gear they sold. Elly was making sure she used it.

Cordelia and I spent most weekends helping either Joanne and Alex or Hutch and Millie or other friends as they cleaned and gutted their houses, trying to reclaim a part of their lives that had been washed away.

Cordelia found work. A number of the hospitals had been destroyed and few would come back any time soon, but many doctors had also left. As she said, "I need something to give me routine and pull me through the days."

The nights were harder. She had nightmares, waking in a sweat as if she was still sweltering in Charity. I held her, told her she was safe, repeated it until she finally fell into a fitful sleep again.

I had my own nightmares. The days weren't easy and I wasn't perfect, and at times I wondered if all my promises to be a better person were made only in darkness and desperation and wouldn't hold in the day after day after day. I didn't have to castigate Cordelia; she did it to herself. All it took on my part was to hint that she'd hurt me, or held me to standards she didn't hold herself to. Until the day I looked in the mirror and understood that just because I wasn't screaming at her didn't make me the better person I promised I would be.

That night I looked at her face after she finally fell asleep, the lines that life had given her, gray in her auburn hair. As fragile as she was, it would have been easy for her to let my anger drive her away. That anger was a fury I'd conflated with my inchoate rage at the horrors of Katrina, building it to a conflagration far beyond anything Cordelia deserved. She'd been the one who picked up the phone and called me. Called again when I didn't answer and didn't call back. Come back to New Orleans when she was scared and desperate and didn't want to, one last attempt to see and talk to me. We both had our sins. We both needed forgiveness. I curled around her, holding her as she slept.

The better person cleaned the cat box without saying anything. The better person cooked and then helped clean up as well, also without pointing out what a nice person I was for doing so. The better person didn't complain about losing sleep to her nightmares. A shoulder rub without her having to ask for it. Taking her hand as we walked in the evening.

The better person I wanted to be remembered that she might not have survived Katrina, that Carmen might have killed me and Nathalie. That it was a profound kindness and grace that I could hold her hand as we walked in the twilight, lie beside her at night.

The change was slow, like the rebuilding of New Orleans. Another working stoplight. The reappearance of a smile I hadn't seen since before the storm. A grocery store opened. Cordelia standing behind me, her arms loosely around my waist as I cooked and we talked of the mundane details of our day. A night, then another when she didn't wake from nightmares.

We stayed in New Orleans over Christmas and New Year, despite invitations to go other places where even a short trip didn't require driving by black lines, the mark of water on houses where people used to live, buildings where they worked. Where you had to look and let your heart break or look away because you could no longer bear to see it. People outside New Orleans didn't understand. We stayed to be with the ones who had been through what we'd been through.

All our different stories, those who stayed and witnessed, and those who left and watched from afar. We all wondered, would New Orleans survive, would we? Ultimately for all of us, it was the same story: the levees failed and our lives changed. The water marked us.

AUTHOR'S NOTE

While this is a book of fiction, I have tried to be as close to facts as I can be. I need to acknowledge a few places where I've taken some liberties. In the fall after Katrina, there were no murders in New Orleans. It was a brief respite, as if the storm had taken enough lives and for a few months no more would be claimed. Also, the Lower Ninth Ward was more closely guarded than the end of this book indicates—no one attempted the events I made up, so whether they might really have been possible or not can't be ascertained.

The family histories I've made up are fictional, but the fact that women of the nineteenth century performed on stage in male dress is historically accurate. Annie Hindle and Ella Wessner are real people and the information included about them is true. Their histories are quite remarkable and should be more widely known.

About the Author

J.M. Redmann has written six novels, all featuring New Orleans private detective Michele "Micky" Knight. The fourth, *Lost Daughters*, was originally published by W.W. Norton. Her third book, *The Intersection Of Law & Desire*, won a Lambda Literary Award, as well as being an Editor's Choice of the *San Francisco Chronicle* and featured on NPR's *Fresh Air*. *Lost Daughters* and *Deaths Of Jocasta* were also nominated for Lambda Literary Awards. Her books have been translated into German, Spanish, Dutch, and Norwegian. She currently lives in New Orleans, just at the edge of the flooded area.

Books Available From Bold Strokes Books

The Long Way Home by Rachel Spangler. They say you can't go home again, but Raine St. James doesn't know why anyone would want to. When she is forced to accept a job in the town she's been publicly bashing for the last decade, she has to face down old hurts and the woman she left behind. (978-1-60282-178-1)

Water Mark by J.M. Redmann. PI Micky Knight's professional and personal lives are torn asunder by Katrina and its aftermath. She needs to solve a murder and recapture the woman she lost—while struggling to simply survive in a world gone mad. (978-1-60282-179-8)

Picture Imperfect by Lea Santos. Young love doesn't always stand the test of time, but Deanne is determined to get her marriage to childhood sweetheart Paloma back on the road to happily ever after, by way of Memory Lane-and Lover's Lane. (978-1-60282-180-4)

The Perfect Family by Kathryn Shay. A mother and her gay son stand hand in hand as the storms of change engulf their perfect family and the life they knew. (978-1-60282-181-1)

Raven Mask by Winter Pennington. Preternatural Private Investigator (and closeted werewolf) Kassandra Lyall needs to solve a murder and protect her Vampire lover Lenorre, Countess Vampire of Oklahoma—all while fending off the advances of the local werewolf alpha female. (978-1-60282-182-8)

The Devil be Damned by Ali Vali. The fourth book in the best-selling Cain Casey Devil series. (978-1-60282-159-0)

Descent by Julie Cannon. Shannon Roberts and Caroline Davis compete in the world of world-class bike racing and pretend that the fire between them is just professional rivalry, not desire. (978-1-60282-160-6)

Kiss of Noir by Clara Nipper. Nora Delany is a hard-living, sweet-talking woman who can't say no to a beautiful babe or a friend in danger—a darkly humorous homage to a bygone era of tough broads and murder in steamy New Orleans. (978-1-60282-161-3)

Under Her Skin by Lea Santos Supermodel Lilly Lujan hasn't a care in the world, except life is lonely in the spotlight—until Mexican gardener Torien Pacias sees through Lilly's facade and offers gentle understanding and friendship when Lilly most needs it. (978-1-60282-162-0)

Fierce Overture by Gun Brooke. Helena Forsythe is a hard-hitting CEO who gets what she wants by taking no prisoners when negotiating—until she meets a woman who convinces her that charm may be the way to win a battle, and a heart. (978-1-60282-156-9)

Trauma Alert by Radclyffe. Dr. Ali Torveau has no trouble saying no to romance until the day firefighter Beau Cross shows up in her ER and sets her carefully ordered world aflame. (978-1-60282-157-6)

Wolfsbane Winter by Jane Fletcher. Iron Wolf mercenary Deryn faces down demon magic and otherworldly foes with a smile, but she's defenseless when healer Alana wages war on her heart. (978-1-60282-158-3)

Little White Lie by Lea Santos. Emie Jaramillo knows relationships are for other people, and beautiful women like Gia Mendez don't belong anywhere near her boring world of academia—until Gia sets out to convince Emie she has not only brains, but beauty...and that she's the only woman Gia wants in her life. (978-1-60282-163-7)

Witch Wolf by Winter Pennington. In a world where vampires have charmed their way into modern society, where werewolves walk the streets with their beasts disguised by human skin, Investigator Kassandra Lyall has a secret of her own to protect. She's one of them. (978-1-60282-177-4)

Do Not Disturb by Carsen Taite. Ainsley Faraday, a high-powered executive, and rock music celebrity Greer Davis couldn't be less well suited for one another, and yet they soon discover passion has a way of designing its own future. (978-1-60282-153-8)

From This Moment On by PJ Trebelhorn. Devon Conway and Katherine Hunter both lost love and neither believes they will ever find it again—until the moment they meet and everything changes. (978-1-60282-154-5)